Maxim Jakubowski was born in
He began his career in business and then moved on to publishing, where he has worked for twelve years. He has written or edited over twenty-five books, covering a variety of subjects, including crime, science fiction and music. His yearly anthology of *New Crimes*, collections of new stories by prominent US and UK authors, is now in its fourth year. Maxim Jakubowski is currently the owner of the Murder One Bookshop, and runs the Blue Murder Imprint.

His last book was *100 Great Detectives* (1991).

MURDERS
FOR THE
FIRESIDE

MURDERS
FOR THE
FIRESIDE

The Best of *Winter's Crimes*

EDITED AND INTRODUCED
BY
MAXIM JAKUBOWSKI

PAN BOOKS
LONDON, SYDNEY AND AUCKLAND

First published 1992 by Pan Books Ltd,
Cavaye Place, London SW10 9PG

3 5 7 9 8 6 4 2

ISBN 0 330 32149 8

Designed by Fraser Hogg
Printed and bound in Great Britain by
Cox & Wyman Ltd, Reading, Berkshire

CONTENTS

CONTENTS

INTRODUCTION

Why do we read crime and mystery stories?

Is it because we are all, to a certain extent, fascinated by the spectacle of death and suffering? If so, wouldn't the unfolding of human misery that we witness on our television screens and in our newspapers be sufficient for our vicarious thrills?

Is it because we identify with the murderers and solvers of the genre? Maybe. There is that delicious sensation of fear that sometimes grips us while reading a particularly frightening book or story, the feel of 'could it have been me with the knife in my gut or the bullet between the shoulders?' There is that wondrous feeling of bravery by proxy when we follow sharp-witted private investigators down dark and wet mean streets or clever policemen unravelling mysteries clue by clue, like a spider's cobweb, in search of the ultimate truth.

Is it because we recognize a mirror image of the world we know and love and dread? Sometimes, but not always necessarily so. Surely the genteel groupings in country houses of yore when the amateur sleuth reunites all the guests and suspects before fiendishly exposing the dastardly culprit belong to a world that no longer exists (if it ever did).

In a way, we enjoy crime and mystery fiction for all the above, often ambivalent, reasons. But, foremost, it's a form of literature that endures so well because at its heart lies entertainment of the highest order, whether it be reflected in the pace and suspense of the chase and the investigation, in the tortuous psychology of the deviant, murderous characters and flawed sleuths or in the compelling intellectual reasoning through which so many of the genre's problem solvers, from old

Sherlock Holmes onwards, exhibit to our utter amazement and revelation.

Even though, today, the field of crime and mystery fiction is so fragmented, with talented exponents of the Golden Age's elegant traditions, hardboiled veterans, gallant lady private investigators, psycho and medical chillers, and many other categories all jousting for attention in the bookshops, there is more good, entertaining crime fiction than ever before, and I, for one, see no reason for the field not to keep on thriving well into the twenty-first century.

As long as there are flaws in human nature, envy, lust, jealousy, greed . . . there will be wonderful authors out there to scrutinize our failings under the most ingenious of microscopes (where do you buy, or steal, this mythical contraption, I wonder?), who will highlight the deviant psychology, the fiendishness of the crimes, the fires of passion, the twists of morality on the skids and other manifestations of the continuous battle between good and evil. Some of these writers will see this as a purely intellectual form of entertainment, others will get to grips with the darkness within like demented wrestlers of the psyche, while yet more others, in differing ways, will extrapolate meaningful, lasting insights into matters fleshly, divine or colloquial from the exciting proceedings.

But all these crime writers with different backgrounds, methods and ambitions will keep on making us want to turn that page, and then another, until the night is dark and the solution/outcome is revealed.

Entertainers all.

For twenty-three years already, the *Winter's Crimes* series of anthologies has offered a platform for leading crime and mystery writers to practise with their usual consummate elegance the art of writing mystery short stories. And it is an invitation that few have refused. All the great names in British crime writing have featured in past volumes, under a series of different and creative editors.

For commercial reasons, these anthologies have somehow

been geared towards the library market, and it's been a most pleasurable duty to collect a selection of the best stories from almost a quarter-century of the series for the larger paperback market. These are the wonderful tales that those of you who haven't been able to afford hardcover books have been missing. Naturally, this is perforce only a limited selection, but I have tried to include most of the more popular crime writers who have contributed to the series (with the exception of the grandest dame of all, Agatha Christie, whose 1971 *Winter's Crimes* story, 'The Harlequin Tea-set', was not available for reprint for contractual reasons).

Still, there are so many stories that I would have liked to include, authors you would also have enjoyed. But maybe there will be another time. Enjoy the originality and diversity of today's writers of crime and mystery fiction as it is practised today in Britain.

Maxim Jakubowski

MURDERS
FOR THE
FIRESIDE

TED ALLBEURY

The Party of the Second Part

BREWSTER had been managing clerk for the chambers ever since he came back from the war. He knew the skills and vagaries of his principals like a farmer knows his dairy herd. When he knocked on the door marked Mathew Porter he stepped into the QC's office with the brief held firmly in his hand. The lawyer was scribbling notes on his pad, one hand keeping open one of the bound Law Reports for 1938. He glanced up at Brewster and pointed to a space on his desk with his gold pencil.

'Stick it down there, Brewster, please.'

'I thought I'd better have a word with you about it, sir. It's from Mr Maclean.'

'What is it?'

'Defence of a divorce petition.'

Porter shook his head. 'You know I never do Family Court cases. Give it to Mr Henry.'

'Mr Maclean insisted it should be you, sir.'

'He ought to know better, he's been dealing with us for long enough.'

'Quite, sir. He gives the chambers a lot of work. That's why I hesitated to refuse the brief. But he says you'd understand when you'd perused it.'

Porter leaned back in his chair looking at Brewster. 'Don't use words like peruse to me, Brewster. You sound like a City of London copper first time in court. I don't peruse the bloody things. I read 'em.'

'It was Mr Maclean's word, sir.'

Porter laughed. 'OK, I'll have a look at it, but you'll have to pass it over to our Henry.' He paused and reached for a pack of Gauloise. 'Why does he want me to take it?'

'The party was in Special Operations Executive during the war. That was your mob wasn't it, sir?'

Porter raised his eyebrows. 'Leave it with me. I'll talk to Maclean myself when I've read it.'

'Right you are, sir.'

'What's the defendant's name by the way?' He leaned forward and looked at the brief. It said Pryke *v.* Pryke. 'Pryke. I don't recognize the name. Was he in the French Section?'

'No idea, sir. It's not a chap, it's a woman.'

'OK. Leave it with me.'

Mathew Porter read through the brief and agreed to have lunch with Maclean at the Law Society. They were neither of them great social chatterers and Porter got down to business as soon as they had ordered.

'I wanted to have a word with you about that Pryke brief. It's not my kind of thing you know, Jamie. I never do divorces. Why not let Henry take it over? He's the expert.'

Maclean smiled. 'Have you read the brief?'

'Of course.'

'What did you think of it?'

'Not a cat in hell's chance. Can't see why she's defending it. If her husband can substantiate half what he alleges she's wasting her time and ours. And her money too.'

'She's got a fantastic war record, Mathew. OBE and Legion of Honour from the French. I thought you might have a fellow feeling. Comrades in arms and all that.'

'I say, this soup is terribly salty . . . comrades in arms you say.' He paused with the spoon raised to his lips. 'You know SOE wasn't like a regiment. Too dispersed. Loyalties were very local and personal.' He sighed. 'Apart from all that they were a very mixed bunch. Couldn't say that there were more than half a dozen I'd like to see again. Who's been briefed for the other side?'

'Lowther. Sir Geoffrey himself.'

'Why the big guns? I'd have thought the plaintiff would sail through this. Why the hell does she want to defend anyway?'

'Two reasons, I think. First she doesn't believe in divorce and secondly she was staggered at the stuff they were using against her.'

'What's she like?'

'A nice woman. Quiet, but plenty of guts. Intelligent and well educated. And quite attractive.'

'I'd have advised her to cut her losses. Call it a day.' He smiled. 'Plenty of other fish in the sea and all that.'

'I feel she's being put upon, Mathew. Blackmailed almost.'

'How do you make that out?'

'I think I could have persuaded her to let it go through, until she saw the other side's accusations. That really put her hackles up. And the husband's a poor specimen anyway.'

'Why do you say that?'

'No decent chap would want to throw this sort of muck at a woman like her. She doesn't deserve it, believe me.'

Porter smiled. 'Sounds like you've got a soft spot for her, Jamie.'

'I have. She was a heroine and she's being abused for it.'

'Was the husband in the services during the war?'

'No. He was some minor civil servant at the War Office. That's how he met her. He was her escort to the Palace when she was presented with her medal. Fell madly in love with her. Swept her off her feet, and now he turns on her.' He dabbed his lips with a paper napkin. 'I thought I might persuade you to put up a bit of a fight on her behalf. As things are she'll lose but she deserves a helping hand.'

'All anybody can do is make the other side look as unpleasant as they really are. Henry could do that better than I can. I'm not much of an advocate. Industrial courts don't like advocates. Just precedents.'

'Would you have a word with her? Just a quick conference. For me, Mathew.'

Porter smiled. 'Of course I will, Jamie. How about you send her over to me tomorrow about three?'

Maclean smiled. 'I won't forget it. Thanks.'

'You said just now, as things stand she'll lose. What did you mean?'

'Did I say that? Well, I shouldn't have. Talking out of turn.'

'Come on. Out with it.'

'You won't mention this to her will you?'

'Not if you say I shouldn't.'

'She knows something about him that could knock his whole case down. The real reason why he wants the marriage finished. She won't let me use it. Made me promise.'

'Do you know what it is?'

'Yes.'

'Tell me.'

'I can't. I promised. I did a bit of rooting around on this fellow Pryke and came across this . . . fact . . . let's call it. I told her about it but she already knew. Flew off the handle at me for being a busybody. Said that using it would make her no better than him. She's right of course, but by God *I'd* have used it.'

'Give me a clue.'

'Don't tempt me, Mathew.'

Porter laughed. 'An indirect clue.'

For a few moments Maclean sat silent and then he opened his mouth to speak, hesitated, and then closed his mouth. Porter waited. Then Maclean said, 'Think of the reasons why he might not have been called up in the war.'

Porter shrugged. 'I'll think about it. Tomorrow at three.'

She wasn't at all what Porter had expected. She was prettier. Forty-ish, but with one of those faces whose bone-structure would always make her look younger than her years. She wore a summer dress that gave her an almost schoolgirlish air of innocence. The grey-blue eyes looked at him calmly, but the tension showed in her tight-clasped hands.

He didn't refer to her husband's statement, but talked about what she hoped for by defending the action.

She shrugged. 'I'd just like somebody who believes in me to

make me seem less of a . . . harridan . . . than they're trying to make me out.'

'I could call people from SOE or their records to establish that you were very brave and operated in enemy-occupied territory.'

'I wouldn't want them dragged in. The publicity will be bad enough whatever I say. And I don't want to pose as a heroine.'

'But you were.'

She laughed softly. 'You were in SOE, so you know better than that. The heroines were burnt in the ovens at Mauthausen and Ravensbruck.'

'You didn't get an OBE for sitting around in the Dordogne.'

She shook her head. 'The things I did were done in desperation. I'm a natural born coward, not a heroine.'

'Mr Maclean asked me to take the brief, but I must point out that I'm not a divorce lawyer and that could be to your disadvantage.'

'I'd still be grateful if you took it on.'

'Why?'

'Because you were in SOE and I'll know that there's one other person in court who knows what it was all about.' She smiled. 'Somebody to wear my lace hankie on his lance.'

Porter smiled and stood up. 'All right. On your head be it. I'll phone Jamie Maclean and tell him I'll act for you.'

She was trembling as he walked her to the outer office and he went back to his own office and picked up the phone.

'Get me Colonel Ramage, please. His number's in our book. It might be under War Office Records or the Military Secretary's office . . . thank you.'

Standing in the court corridors always lowered clients' morale and he took her down to the canteen until they were called.

She was wearing a pale blue two-piece suit and a frilly blouse. No attempt to impress the court with a sombre appearance.

'What can we talk about?' she said as she stirred her coffee.

'What's your favourite piece of music?'

She laughed. 'Either Josephine Baker singing *J'ai deux amours* or the Mendelssohn fiddle concerto.'

'Favourite flower?'

'Daisies in a field. Marguerites.'

'Favourite food?'

'Chocolate eclairs.' She laughed.

'And favourite book?'

'Elizabeth Smart's *By Grand Central Station I Sat Down and Wept*.'

And then Maclean came for them and the grimness of the corridors set her trembling again.

Porter sat listening, watching her face as the questions were put to her. Sir Geoffrey was silky and polite but he was there to do a job. A demolition job.

'You admit that you abused your husband on occasions, using foul language.'

'No, I don't admit anything of the sort.'

Sir Geoffrey raised his ginger eyebrows in surprise as he looked at his notes. 'But you have already agreed that you said: "You lying sod get out of my sight", wouldn't you say that was foul language?'

'I was angry at something he'd done. He'd . . .'

'Thank you, Mrs Pryke. Now let me come to the question of violence.' Sir Geoffrey looked up quickly at her. 'Are you a violent woman, Mrs Pryke? Do you have a violent temper?'

'I can be tormented into being angry if that's what you call violence.'

'Have you ever struck your husband, Mrs Pryke?'

'I slapped his face once. Nothing more than that.'

'Did he ever strike you?'

'No.'

'I see. But when you – as you put it – slapped his face, it was with sufficient force to injure his eye. Yes?'

'It cracked his contact lens. That's all.'

'Causing damage enough to keep him from his office for ten days.'

'That was the time it took to replace the lens. Nothing more.'

'Of course not.' Sir Geoffrey smiled at the jury. 'Just a wifely love tap.' Then Sir Geoffrey's voice was very soft as he looked at her. 'I must ask you one last question, Mrs Pryke. I want you to listen very carefully.' Sir Geoffrey glanced at the jury and then back at the witness box. 'Mrs Pryke. Have you ever killed a man?'

Porter saw the blood drain from her face and her knuckles were white as they grasped the edge of the box. Then she said quietly, 'Yes. But that was . . .'

'Mrs Pryke, how many men have you killed in your lifetime?'

She took a deep breath. 'Two, and in both cases . . .'

'Thank you, Mrs Pryke. And one last question to you. In the case of one of the men you killed you used a pistol. What did you use in the other case?'

'I used a knife.'

'You stabbed him several times? Three or four times perhaps.'

'I don't remember.'

'I see.' Sir Geoffrey raised his eyebrows in the general direction of the Press benches. 'That will be all, thank you, Mrs Pryke.'

Mathew Porter stood up slowly. 'My Lord, I know we are already running late but after my learned colleague's last few questions I should like a few moments more so that this matter does not hang over the night.'

His Lordship nodded. 'Don't be too long, Mr Porter, but carry on.'

Porter turned to his client. 'Mrs Pryke, would you tell the court who the two men were who you killed.'

'I don't remember their names.'

'Their ranks perhaps. Or the circumstances.'

'One was a Gestapo officer and one was a sergeant in the Sicherheitsdienst. The Nazi Security Service.'

'Tell us very briefly what happened.'

'They had arrested the seven leading people in my SOE network. I killed the two men to set my colleagues free.'

'This was in wartime? In German-occupied France?'

'Yes.'

'And for this you were awarded the Order of the British Empire. You received it from King George the Sixth himself at Buckingham Palace.'

'Yes.'

'And was the plaintiff, your husband, aware of these facts even before he married you?'

'Yes. He accompanied me to the medal presentation.'

'Thank you, Mrs Pryke.' Porter turned to look at the judge. 'My Lord, tomorrow I should like to suggest to the court that this application is dismissed on the grounds that the evidence put forward to denigrate my client's character has been done with deliberate malice and was to a large part intended to create both a totally false impression of the real facts and an attempt to deceive the court . . .'

'Mr Porter. Can we leave the rest of it until tomorrow at ten?'

'As Your Lordship pleases.'

Porter and Maclean had walked over to the Wig and Pen with their client and taken a table at the far end. She seemed to have recovered from her nervousness.

'Thanks for what you said. About the SOE business.'

'I ought not to have needed to say it. It was a scurrilous attack on their part and I'm surprised that Sir Geoffrey would wear it. The rest was pretty thin but to my mind that last bit went too far. I don't think His Lordship liked it too much. What do you think, Jamie?'

Maclean grinned. 'I'd say there's a good chance of them throwing it out tomorrow.'

Jill Pryke looked at Maclean. 'Does that mean he might not get a divorce?'

'It's quite possible, my dear, and I'd think you might even be able to consider bringing a cross-petition citing today as your reasons.'

As they chatted Porter was aware of his client's silence and eventually he said, 'What's the problem?'

She took a deep breath. 'I want to withdraw. Let it be undefended.'

'But why?'

'I don't want to be married to him any more.'

'You can cross-petition like I said.'

'That would take time. I'd like to be free of him tomorrow.'

Porter looked at Maclean who said, 'Think about it overnight. Don't rush into it.'

She shook her head as she looked at Porter. 'Don't think I'm not grateful. I am. Terribly grateful. But hearing you sticking up for me in court was enough. I felt hounded, but not any more. I just want to be free of it. All of it.'

Maclean said, 'If you're sure that's what you want.'

'It is,' she said as she stood up. 'I'd like to leave while I feel happy, if you don't mind.'

She shook hands with Porter, and Maclean walked her into the Strand, waved down a taxi for her, and walked back to Porter at the table.

'My God. Human beings. What a turmoil we're always in.'

Porter smiled. 'She's right you know. She should have gone this way right at the start. She's only doing what we both counselled her to do. But she's had her bite back in court. And why shouldn't she?' He paused and looked at Maclean. 'I didn't realize until this afternoon what her little secret was that you wouldn't let me know.'

'OK. Why this afternoon?'

Porter smiled. 'Watching Sir Geoffrey. He was loving every minute of it. Hounding her. Hating her. They're two of a kind aren't they? Him and Pryke. Brothers in sex.'

Maclean nodded. 'He made a declaration when he was called up, about his . . . er . . . predilections. That's why he wasn't in the services. The marriage must have been hopeless from the start.'

'Ah well. All's well that ends well.'

The small boy was looking at the things on the table.

'What's the music, Daddy?'

'It's a violin concerto by a chap named Mendelssohn.'

'What a funny name.'

'It isn't really, it's just a foreign name.'

'And you always give her these things as well as a proper present. Why eclairs and a bunch of daisies and always this same book?'

'A long time ago we sat in a rather gloomy tea place and I asked her about her favourite things. These were the things she chose.'

'Were you two married then?'

'No. It was a long time ago.'

'Did you like her when you had tea with her?'

'I admired her. I got to like her later.'

'Why?'

'Oh, lots of reasons. I'll tell you some day when I've worked out what they are. She's coming in from the garden now. Thinks we've forgotten her birthday.'

The small boy smiled. 'Women are funny aren't they?'

ERIC AMBLER

The Blood Bargain

EX-PRESIDENT Fuentes enjoys a peculiar distinction. More people would like to kill him now that he is in retirement than wanted to kill him when he was in power.

He is a puzzled and indignant man.

What he fails to understand is that, while men like General Perez may in time forgive you for robbing them, they will never forgive you for making them look foolish.

The *coup d'état* which overthrew Fuentes' Social Action Party government was well organized and relatively bloodless.

The leaders of the *coup* were mostly Army officers, but they had understandings with fellow-dissidents in the Air Force and Navy as well as the discreet blessing of the Church. A price for the collaboration of the Chief of Police had been agreed upon well in advance, and the lists of certain left-wing deputies, militant trade union officials, pro-government newspaper editors, Castro-trained subversives, and other undesirables whose prompt arrest would be advisable, had been compiled with his help. Similar arrangements had been made in the larger provincial towns. Although the conspirators were by no means all of the same political complexion, they had for once found themselves able to sink their differences in the pursuit of a common goal. Whatever might come afterwards, they were all agreed upon one thing; if the country were to be saved from corruption, Communist subversion, anarchy, bankruptcy, civil war, and, ultimately, foreign military intervention, President Fuentes had to go.

One evening in September he went.

The tactics employed by the Liberation Front conspirators followed the pattern which has become more or less traditional when a *coup* is backed by organized military forces and opposed, if it is opposed at all, only by civilian mobs and confused, lightly armed garrison units.

As darkness fell, the tanks of two armoured brigades together with trucks containing a parachute regiment, signals units, and a company of combat engineers rolled into the capital. Within little more than an hour, they had secured their major objectives. Meanwhile, the Air Force had taken over the international airport, grounded all planes, and established a headquarters in the customs and immigration building. An infantry division now began to move into the city and take up positions which would enable it to deal with the civil disturbances which were expected to develop as news of the *coup*, and of the mass arrests which were accompanying it, reached the densely populated slum areas with their high concentrations of Fuentes supporters.

A little after eight-thirty a squadron of tanks and a special task force of paratroopers reached the Presidential Palace. The Palace guard resisted for a quarter of an hour and suffered casualties of eight wounded. The order to surrender was given personally to the guard commander by President Fuentes 'in order to avoid further bloodshed'.

When this was reported to General Perez, the leader of the *coup*, he drove to the Palace. He was accompanied by five senior members of the Liberation Front council, including the Chief of Police, and no less than three representatives of the foreign press. The latter had been flushed out of the Jockey Club bar by an aide earlier in the evening and hastily briefed on the aims and ideals of the Liberation Front. General Perez wished to lose no time in establishing himself abroad as a magnanimous, reasonable, and responsible man, and his regime as worthy of prompt diplomatic recognition.

The newsmen's accounts of the interview between President Fuentes and General Perez, and of the now-notorious 'blood bargain' which emerged from it, were all in substantial agreement. At the time the bargain seemed to them just another of those civilized, oddly chivalrous agreements to live and let live which, by testifying to the continued presence of compassion and good sense even at moments of turmoil and destruction, have so often lightened the long, dark history of Latin American revolution. The reporters, all experienced men, can scarcely be blamed for misunderstanding it. They knew, as everyone else knew, that President Fuentes was a devious and deeply dishonest man. The only mistake they made was in assuming that the other parties to the bargain had made due allowance for that deviousness and dishonesty and knew exactly what they were doing. What the reporters had not realized was that these normally wary and hard-headed officers had become so intoxicated by the speed and extent of their initial success, that by the time they reached the Presidential Palace they were no longer capable of thinking clearly.

President Fuentes received General Perez and the other Liberation Front leaders in the ornate Cabinet Room of the Palace to which he had been taken by the paratroopers who had arrested him. With him were the other male occupants of the Presidential air raid shelter at the time of his arrest. These included the Palace guard commander, the President's valet, the Palace majordomo, two footmen, and the man who looked after the Palace plumbing system, in addition to the Minister of Public Welfare, the Minister of Agrarian Education, the Minister of Justice, and the elderly Controller of the Presidential Secretariat. The Minister of Public Welfare had brought a bottle of brandy with him from the shelter and smiled glassily throughout the subsequent confrontation. Agrarian Education and Justice maintained expressions of bewilderment and indignation, but confined their oral protests to circumspect murmurs. The thin-lipped young captain in charge of the paratroopers handled his machine pistol as if he would have been glad of an excuse to use it.

Only the President seemed at ease. There was even a touch of impatience in the shrug with which he rose to face General Perez and his party as they strode in from the anteroom; it was as if he had been interrupted by some importunate visitor during a game of bridge.

His calm was only partly assumed. He knew all about General Perez' sensitivity to foreign opinion, and he had immediately recognized the newsmen in the rear of the procession. They would not have been brought there if any immediate violence to his person had been contemplated.

The impatience he displayed was certainly genuine; it was impatience with himself. He had known for weeks that a *coup* was in preparation, and had taken the precaution a month earlier of sending his wife and children and his mistress out of the country. They were all now in Washington, and he had planned, using as a pretext his announced wish to address personally a meeting of the Organization of American States, to join them there the following week. His private spies had reported that the *coup* would undoubtedly be timed to take advantage of his absence abroad. Since the *coup* by means of which he himself had come to power five years earlier had been timed in that way, he had been disposed to believe the report.

Now, he knew better. Whether or not his spies had deliberately deceived him did not matter at the moment. A mistake had been made which was, he knew, likely to cost him more than temporary inconvenience. Unless he could retrieve it immediately, by getting out of the country within the next few hours, that mistake would certainly cost him his liberty, and most probably his life, too.

He had risked death before, was familiar with the physical and mental sensations that accompanied the experience, and with a small effort was able to ignore them. As General Perez came up to him, the President displayed no emotion of any kind. He merely nodded politely and waited for the General to speak.

For a moment the General seemed tongue-tied. He was sweating too. As this was the first time he had overthrown a government he was undoubtedly suffering from stage fright. He took refuge finally in military punctilio. With a click of the heels he came to attention and fixed his eyes on the President's left ear.

'We are here . . .' he began harshly, then cleared his throat and corrected himself. 'I and my fellow members of the Council of the Liberation Front are here to inform you that a state of national emergency now exists.'

The President nodded politely. 'I am glad to have that information, General. Since telephone communication has been cut off I have naturally been curious as to what was happening. These gentlemen' – he motioned to the paratroopers – 'seemed unwilling to enlighten me.'

The General ignored this and went on as if he were reading a proclamation. In fact, he was quoting from the press release which had already been handed to the newsmen. 'Directed by the Council and under its orders,' he said, 'the armed forces have assumed control of all functions of civil government in the state, and, as provided in the Constitution, formally demand your resignation.'

The President looked astounded. 'You have the effrontery to claim constitutional justification for this mutiny?'

For the first time since he had entered the room the General relaxed slightly. 'We have a precedent, sir. Nobody should know that better than you. You yourself set it when you legalized your own seizure of power from your predecessor. Need I remind you of the wording of the amendment? "If for any reason, including the inability to fulfil the duties of his office by reason of ill-health, mental or physical, or absence, an elected president is unable to exercise the authority vested in him under the constitution, a committee representative of the nation and those responsible to it for the maintenance of law and order may request his resignation and be entitled . . ."'

For several seconds the President had been waving his hands for silence. Now he broke in angrily. 'Yes, yes, I know all about that. But my predecessor was absent. I am not. Neither am I ill, physically or mentally. There are no legal grounds on which you are entitled to ask for my resignation.'

'No legal grounds, sir?' General Perez could smile now. He

pointed to the paratroopers. 'Are you able to exercise the authority of a president? *Are* you? If you think so, try.'

The President pretended to think over the challenge. The interview was so far going more or less as he had expected; but the next moves would be the critical ones for him. He walked over to a window and back in order to give himself time to collect himself.

Everyone there was watching him. The tension in the room was mounting. He could feel it. It was odd, he thought. Here he was, a prisoner, wholly at their mercy; and yet they were waiting for him to come to a decision, to make a choice where no choice existed. It was absurd. All they wanted from him was relief from a small and quite irrational sense of guilt. They had the Church's blessing; now the poor fools yearned for the blessing of the law, too. Very well. They should have it. But it would be expensive.

He turned and faced General Perez again.

'A resignation exacted from me under duress would have no force in law,' he said.

The General glanced at the Chief of Police. 'You are a lawyer, Raymundo. Who represents the law here?'

'The Council of the Liberation Front, General.'

Perez looked at the President again. 'You see, sir, there are no technical difficulties. We even have the necessary document already prepared.'

His aide held up a black leather portfolio.

The President hesitated, looking from one face to another as if hoping against hope that he might find a friendly one. Finally he shrugged. 'I will read the document,' he said coldly and walked towards the cabinet table. As he did so he seemed to become aware again of his fellow prisoners in the room. He stopped suddenly.

'Must my humiliation be witnessed by my colleagues and my servants as well as the foreign press?' he demanded bitterly.

General Perez motioned to the paratrooper captain. 'Take those men into another room. Leave guards outside the doors of this one.'

The President waited until the group from the air raid shelter had been herded out, then sat down at the table. The General's aide opened the portfolio, took out a legal document laced with green ribbon and placed it in front of the President.

He made a show of studying the document very carefully. In fact, he was indifferent to its contents. His intention was simply to let the tension mount a little further and to allow the other men there to feel that they were on the point of getting what they wanted.

For three minutes there was dead silence in the room. It was broken only by the sound of distant machine-gun fire. It seemed to be coming from the south side of the city. The President heard a slight stir from the group of men behind him and one of them cleared his throat nervously. There was another burst of firing. The President took no notice of it. He read the document through a third time then put it down and sat back in his chair.

The aide offered him a pen with which to sign. The President ignored it and turned his head so that he could see General Perez.

'You spoke of a resignation, General,' he said. 'You did not mention that it was to be a confession also.'

'Hardly a confession, sir,' the General replied drily. 'We would not expect you voluntarily to incriminate yourself. The admission is only of incompetence. That is not yet a criminal offence in a head of state.'

The President smiled faintly. 'And if I were to sign this paper, what kind of personal treatment might I expect to receive afterwards? A prison cell perhaps, with a carefully staged treason trial to follow? Or merely a bullet in the head and an unmarked grave?'

The General reddened. 'We are here to correct abuses of power, sir, not to imitate them. When you have signed you will be conducted to your former home in Alazan province. You will be expected to remain there for the present and the Governor of the province will be instructed to see that you do so. Apart from that restriction you will be free to do as you please. Your family will naturally be permitted to join you.'

'You mention the house in Alazan province. What about my other personal property?'

'You will be permitted to retain everything you owned when you took office.'

'I see.' The President stood up and moved away from the table. 'I will think about it. I will let you have my decision tomorrow,' he added casually.

The silence that followed this announcement did not last long, but one of the newsmen reported later that it was one of the loudest he had ever heard. Another remembered that during it he suddenly became conscious of the presence and smell of a large bowl of tropical flowers on a side table by the anteroom door.

The President had walked towards the windows again. General Perez took two steps towards him, then stopped.

'You must decide at once! You must sign now!' he snapped.

The President turned on him. 'Why? Why now?'

It was the Chief of Police who answered him. 'Son of a whore, because we tell you to!' he shouted.

Suddenly they were all shouting at him. One officer was so enraged that he drew his pistol. The General had difficulty in restoring order.

The President took no notice of them. He kept his eyes on General Perez, but it was really the newsmen he was addressing now. As the din subsided he raised his voice.

'I asked a question, General. Why now? Why the haste? It is a reasonable question. If, as you say, you already control the country, what have you to fear from me? Or is it, perhaps, that your control is not in fact as complete and effective as you would have us believe?'

The General had to quell another angry outburst from his colleagues before he could answer, but he preserved his own temper admirably. His reply was calm and deliberate.

'I will tell you exactly what we control so that you may judge for yourself,' he said. 'To begin with all provincial army garrisons, air force establishments, and police posts have declared for the Liberation Front, as have five out of eight of the provincial governors. The three objectors – I am sure you will have guessed who they are – have been rendered harmless and replaced by military governors. None of this can come as a great surprise to you I imagine. You never had much support outside the capital and the mining areas.'

The President nodded. 'Stupidity can sometimes be charted geographically,' he remarked.

'Now as to the capital. We control the airfields, both military and civil, the naval base, all communications including telephone and radio and television broadcast facilities, the power stations, all fuel-oil storage facilities, all main traffic arteries, all government offices and city police posts together with the offices and printing presses of *El Correo* and *La Gaceta*.' He glanced at his watch. 'In connection with the broadcast facilities, I may mention that while the television station is temporarily off the air the radio station will shortly begin broadcasting an announcement of the establishment of the New Liberation Front regime, which I recorded two days ago. As I told you before, everything is now under our control.'

The President smiled and glanced significantly at the newsmen. 'Are the *sumideri* under control, General?'

Sumideri, meaning sinks or drains, was the popular slang term used to describe the slum areas on the south side of the capital.

The General hesitated only an instant. 'The southern area is effectively contained,' he replied stiffly. 'The first infantry division reinforced by the third tank brigade has that responsibility.'

'I see.' The President looked again at the newsmen. 'So the civil war may be expected to begin at any moment.'

With a quick motion of his hands the General silenced the chorus of objections from his colleagues. 'We are fully prepared to deal firmly with any mob violence which may occur,' he said. 'Of that you may be sure.'

'Yes,' said the President bitterly, 'perhaps civil war is not the phrase to use for the planned massacre of unarmed civilians.' He swung around suddenly to face the newsmen and his voice hardened. 'You have been witnesses to this farce, gentlemen. I ask you to remember it well and let the civilized world know of it. These men come to ask for my resignation as head of state. That is all they want! Why? Because outside in the streets of the city their tanks and guns are waiting to begin the slaughter of the thousands of men and women who will protest their loyalty to me. And the way to bring them out for the slaughter is to fling my resignation like so much filth in their faces!'

General Perez could stand it no longer. 'That is a lie!' he shouted.

The President turned on him savagely. 'Do you think they will *not* come out? Why else are they "contained" as you call it? Why else? Because they are my people and because they will listen only to me.'

A glow of triumph suffused General Perez' angry face. 'Then their blood will be on *your* hands!' he roared. He stabbed a forefinger at the newsmen. 'You heard what he said, gentlemen. *They do what he tells them!* It is his responsibility, then, not ours, if they oppose us. *He* will be the murderer of women and children! Let him deny it.'

This time the President made no reply. He just stood there looking about him in bewilderment, like a boxer who has staggered to his feet after a count of ten and can't quite realize that the fight is over. At last he walked slowly back to the cabinet table, sat down heavily and buried his head in his hands.

Nobody else moved. When the President raised his head and looked at them again his eyes were haggard. He spoke very quietly.

'You are right,' he said; 'they are my people and they will do as I tell them. It is my responsibility. I accept it. There must be no senseless bloodshed. I think it is my duty to tell them not to protest.'

For a moment they all stared at him incredulously. The Chief of Police started to say something, then stopped as he caught General Perez' eye. If the man were serious this was too good an opportunity to miss.

General Perez went over and addressed the President. 'I

cannot believe that even you would speak lightly on such a matter, but I must ask if you seriously mean what you say.'

The President nodded absently. 'I will need about an hour to draft my statement. There is a direct line to the radio station here in the Palace and the necessary equipment. The station can record me on tape.' He managed a rueful smile. 'In the circumstances, I imagine that you would prefer a recording to a live broadcast.'

'Yes.' But the General was still reluctant to believe in his triumph. 'How can you be sure that they will obey you?' he asked.

The President thought before he answered. 'There will be some, of course, who will be too distressed, too angry perhaps, to do as I ask,' he said. 'But if the officers commanding troops are ordered to use restraint, casualties can be kept to a minimum.' He glanced at the Chief of Police. 'There should be moderation, too, in respect of arrests. But the majority will listen to me, I think.' He paused. 'The important thing is that they must believe that I am speaking as a free man, and not out of fear because there is a pistol at my head.'

'I myself can give them that assurance,' said the General. The fact that he could make such an ingenuous suggestion is an indication of his mental confusion at that point.

The President raised his eyebrows. 'With all respect, General, I don't think we could expect them at this time to believe you of all people. I also think that the news that I am to be kept under what amounts to house arrest in Alazan province will not help to convince them either.'

'Then what do you propose? You can scarcely remain here in the capital.'

'Naturally not.' The President sat back in his chair. He had assumed a statesmanlike air now. 'It is quite clear,' he said, 'that we must achieve an orderly and responsible transfer of power. I shall, of course, resign in order to make way for the Liberation Front. However, in your place, I must say that I would regard my continued presence anywhere in this country as undesirable. These people to whom I am to appeal tonight will only respond with restraint because of their loyalty to me. That loyalty will continue as long as they are able to give expression to it. You would do better really to get rid of me. As soon as I have spoken to my people you should get me out of the country as quickly as you can.'

'Exile?' It was the Chief of Police who spoke up now. 'But if we exile you that looks no better than house arrest in Alazan. Worse, possibly.'

'Exactly.' The President nodded approvingly. 'The solution I suggest is that I am permitted to announce to my people that I will continue to serve them, the nation, and the Liberation Front, but in a different capacity and abroad. Our embassy in Nicaragua is without an ambassador at present. That would be a suitable appointment. I suggest that after I have recorded my broadcast I leave the country immediately in order to take up my post.'

The council discussion that ensued lacked the vehemence of the earlier exchanges. The strain of the past twenty-four hours was beginning to tell on General Perez and his colleagues; they were getting tired; and the sounds of firing from the south side were becoming more insistent. Time was running out. It was one of the newsmen who drew their attention to the fact.

'General,' he said to Perez, 'has it occurred to you that if the President doesn't talk to these people of his pretty soon they're all going to be out on the streets anyway?'

The President recognized the urgency, too, but refused to be hurried. As he pointed out, there were matters of protocol to be dealt with before he could make his appeal to the people. For one thing, his resignation would have to be redrafted. Since, he argued, he was now to be appointed his country's ambassador to Nicaragua, references in the present draft to his incompetence would obviously have to be deleted. And there were other clauses which might be interpreted as reflections on his personal integrity.

In the end, the President wrote his own act of resignation. It was a simple document but composed with great care. His radio speech, on the other hand, he scribbled out on a cabinet desk pad while technicians, hastily summoned by jeep from the central radio building, were setting up a recording circuit in the anteroom.

Meanwhile, telephone communication had been restored to the Palace, and the Controller of the Presidential Secretariat had been released from arrest and put to work in his office.

His first task had been to contact the Nicaraguan Ambassador, give him a discreetly censored account of the current situation and request him to ascertain immediately, in accordance with Article 8 of the Pan-American Convention, if his government would be prepared to accept ex-President Fuentes as *persona grata* in the capacity of ambassador to their country. The Nicaraguan Ambassador had undertaken to telephone personally to the Minister of Foreign Relations in Managua and report back. His unofficial opinion was that there would be no opposition to the proposed appointment.

With the help of the air force council member present the Controller next spoke to the officer in charge at the International Airport. He learned that of the two civil airliners grounded earlier that evening, one had been southbound to Caracas, the other, a Colombian Avianca jet, had been northbound to Mexico City. Fortunately a Vice-Consul from the Colombian Consulate-General was already at the airport, having been summoned there by the Avianca captain to protest the grounding. The Controller spoke with the Vice-Consul who said that Avianca would be willing to carry ex-President Fuentes as a passenger to Mexico City if the Mexican Government would permit him to land. A call to the Mexican Embassy explaining that ex-President Fuentes would be in transit through Mexican territory on his way to his post as an accredited diplomatic representative to the Republic of Nicaragua secured the necessary permission.

The President already had a diplomatic passport which needed only minor amendments to fit it for its new role. All that was needed now to facilitate his departure was confirmation from the Nicaraguan Ambassador that he would be accorded diplomatic status in Managua. Within an hour, the Nicaraguan

Government, acting promptly in the belief that they were helping both parties to the arrangement, had replied favourably.

The escape route was open.

President Fuentes made two tape-recordings of the appeal to his supporters, one for the radio, the second for use by a loudspeaker van in the streets of the *sumideri*. Then he signed his resignation and was driven to the airport. General Perez provided an escort of armoured cars.

The plane, with ex-President Fuentes on board, took off a little after midnight. Five hours later it landed in Mexico City.

News of the Liberation Front *coup* and of the President's voluntary resignation and ambassadorial appointment had been carried by all the international wire services, and there were reporters waiting for him. There was also, despite the early hour, a protocol official from the Department of External Relations to meet him. Fuentes made a brief statement to the reporters, confirming the fact of his resignation. On the subject of his appointment as Ambassador to Nicaragua he was vague. He then drove to a hotel in the city. On the way there he asked the protocol official if it would be convenient for him to call upon the Minister of External Affairs later that day.

The official was mildly surprised. As Ambassador Fuentes was merely passing through Mexico, a brief note of thanks to the Minister would normally be the only courtesy expected of him. On the other hand, the circumstances of Fuentes' sudden translation from President to Ambassador were unusual and it was possible that the Minister might be glad of the opportunity of hearing what Fuentes himself had to say on the subject. He promised that he would consult the Minister's personal assistant at the earliest possible moment.

The Minister received Ambassador Fuentes at five o'clock that afternoon.

The two men had met before, at conferences of the Organization of American States and on the occasion of a state visit to Mexico paid by Fuentes soon after he became President. It was a tribute to the Minister's natural courtesy as well as his self-discipline that Fuentes believed that the Minister liked him. In fact the Minister viewed him with dislike and disapproval and had not been in the least surprised or distressed by the news of the Liberation Front *coup*. However, he had been amused by Fuentes' ability to emerge from the situation not only alive and free but also invested with diplomatic immunity; and it modified his distaste for the man. He was, one had to admit, an engaging scoundrel.

After the preliminary politeness had been disposed of the Minister enquired courteously whether he could be of any service to the Ambassador during his stay in Mexico.

Fuentes inclined his head: 'That is most kind of you, Mr Minister,' he said graciously. 'Yes, there is one thing.'

'You only have to ask.'

'Thank you.' Ambassador Fuentes straightened up a little in his chair. 'I wish,' he said, 'to make formal application to be considered here as a refugee, and formally to request political asylum in the United States of Mexico.'

The Minister stared for a moment, then smiled.

'Surely you must be joking, Mr Ambassador.'

'Not in the least.'

The Minister was puzzled, and because he was puzzled he put into words the first obvious objection that came into his head.

'But in the United States of Mexico, even though you are not accredited to the Federal Government, you already, by virtue of the Pan-American Convention, enjoy diplomatic status and privileges here,' he said.

It was a statement which he was later to regret.

Ambassador Fuentes never took up his post in Nicaragua.

One of the first official acts of General Perez' Council of the Liberation Front was to set up a committee, headed by the Professor of Political Economy at Bolivar University, to report on the financial state of the Republic.

It took the committee only a few days to discover that during the past three years ex-President Fuentes had authorized printings of five-hundred-peseta banknotes to a total value of one hundred million dollars and that twenty of those hundred millions could not be accounted for.

The Governor of the National Bank was immediately arrested. He was an old man who had spent most of his life in the National Archives gathering material for a scholarly study of colonial Spanish land grants. He had been appointed to the bank by Fuentes. He knew nothing about banking. He had merely carried out the orders of the Minister of Finance.

Fuentes had been his own Minister of Finance.

Interviewed on the subject by the press in Mexico City, ex-President Fuentes stated that the committee's revelations had shocked, horrified, and amazed him. He also said that he had no idea where the missing twenty millions might be. Regrettably, he was unable quite to refrain from smiling as he said it.

Ex-President Fuentes' retirement has not been peaceful.

During the five years he held office as President there was only one serious attempt on his life. Since he resigned the Presidency, ceased to concern himself with politics, and went to live abroad, no less than three such attempts have been made. There will doubtless be others. Meanwhile, he has had to fight off two lots of extradition proceedings and a number of civil actions directed against his European bank accounts.

He is wealthy, of course, and can afford to pay for the protection, both physical and legal, that he needs; but he is by no means resigned to the situation. As he is fond of pointing out, other men in his position have accumulated larger fortunes. Moreover, his regime was never unacceptably oppressive. He was no Trujillo, no Batista, no Porfirio Diaz. Why then should he be hounded and harassed as if he were?

Ex-President Fuentes remains a puzzled and indignant man.

ROBERT BARNARD

Little Terror

IT WAS Albert Wimpole's first holiday on his own for – oh, he didn't know how long: since he was in his late teens it must have been. Because after Mum died, Dad always liked to tag along with him, and though Dad was quite lively, and certainly no trouble at all, still, it was not quite the same, because Albert was a considerate person, conscientious, and naturally he adapted a lot to Dad's ways. Now Dad had decided, regretfully, that he couldn't quite manage it this year, his arthritis being what it was. So Albert was going to enjoy Portugal on his own. A small thrill of anticipation coursed through his slightly old-maidish veins. Who knew what adventures he might meet with? What encounters he might have? On the first day, though, he decided not to go down to the Carcavelos beach, because the breeze was rather high. At the hotel pool it was nice and sheltered.

'Hello.'

The voice came from behind his ear. Albert's heart sank, but he was a courteous man, and he turned round on his sunbed in order to respond. He saw, without joy, a pink, ginger-haired boy, with evilly curious eyes.

'Hello,' said Albert, and began to turn back.

'How old are you?'

'How old? Let me see now . . . I'm forty-two.'

The carroty boy thought.

'That's not three score years and ten, is it?'

'No, it's not, I'm glad to say. In fact, it's not much more than half-way there.'

'*I've* not even used up the ten,' said the child.

'I can see that. You've got an awful lot left.'

'Yes. Still, I wouldn't say you were *old*, yet,' said the boy.

'Thank you very much,' said Albert, and turned over thankfully as the boy left, but not before he had caught sight of the boy's parents, waving in his direction in a friendly fashion. They were heavy, unattractive people of about his own age, or older. Perhaps the Menace was a late blessing, the result of some virulent fertility drug, and spoilt accordingly.

When Albert had been by the pool a couple of hours, he got ready to leave. No sense in overdoing the sunshine on the first day of your holiday. You pay for that if you do, Dad always said, and he was right. As he was just preparing to make his move, the ginger-haired head appeared once more close to his.

'What's your name?'

'My name's Wimpole. What's yours?'

'Terry.'

'Ah – short for "Terror", I suppose.'

'No, it isn't, silly. It's short for Terence. Everybody knows that. And I think Wimpole is a jolly funny name. Do you know what happens to you when you die?'

The abrupt change in the topic caught Albert on the hop, and he paused a moment before replying.

'That's something people have been discussing for quite a long time.'

'No, it's not, stupid. You lie there still, and you don't breathe, and you don't even twitch, and you don't have dreams, because you're dead.'

'I see. Yes, I did know that.'

'Then they put you in a box, and either they put you in the ground and throw earth all over you, or they cre-mate you. That means they burn you up, like Guy Fawkes' Night.'

'I must be getting along,' said Albert, and indeed he did begin to feel a burning sensation on his shoulders.

'You know, you don't *necessarily* die at three score years and ten.'

'That's a comfort.'

'My Gran was seventy-four, and that's more, isn't it? My friend Wayne Catherick said she was past it.'

'Well, it's nice to think I might stagger on a bit longer than seventy,' said Albert, who had gathered together his things and now began to make his way out.

'Terry's taken quite a fancy to you,' said Little Terror's parents as he walked past them. Albert smiled politely.

The next morning Albert ventured on the beach. He walked half a mile towards the fortress, then laid out his towel and settled down. At first the breeze worried him a little, because he knew people often sunburned badly in a breeze, but by half past ten it had died down, and things had become quite idyllic.

'There's Wimpole!' came the well-known voice. Against his wiser instincts Albert looked up. Terry was standing over him, and pointing, as if he were some unusual sea creature.

'We won't intrude,' said Terry's parents, settling themselves down two or three yards away, and beginning to remove clothes from their remarkably ill-proportioned bodies. Terry, however, intruded.

While his parents just lay there tanning those fleshy bodies of theirs (Albert prided himself on keeping in good trim), Terry confined himself to questions like 'What's that?' and to giving information about his friend Wayne Catherick. When his parents went down to dabble their toes in the freezing Atlantic, Terry's conversation reverted to the topics of yesterday.

'When you're cre-mated,' he said, 'they shoot your body into a great big oven. Then when you're all burnt up, they put the ashes into a bottle, and you can put flowers in front of it if you want to.'

'I think I'll be buried.'

'Or they can scatter the ashes somewhere. Like over Scotland, or into the sea. Do you know what Wayne says, Wimpole?'

'No. What does Wayne say?'

'He says my gran's ashes ought to have been scattered over Tesco's supermarket, because she ate so much.'

'That's a very nasty thing for Wayne to say.'

'No, it's not. It's true, Wimpole. She was eating us out of

house and home. Wayne says she took the food from out of our mouths. She just sat up there in her bedroom, eating. Sometimes I had to go up and get her tray, and she hadn't finished, and it was disgusting. She used to spray me with bits. I could have had chocolate cream sponge every day if she hadn't taken the food from out of my mouth.'

'I don't think chocolate cream sponge every day would have been very good for you.'

'Yes, it would. *And* I had to keep quiet, *every* morning and *every* night because she was *asleep*. It wasn't fair.'

'You *have* made a hit,' said Terry's mother, coming back. 'It's nice for you, seeing as you're on your own, isn't it?'

The next day Albert waited in his room until he saw them trailing down to the beach. Then he made his way to the pool, and gratefully sank down on a lilo. Though his sunbathing had been in shorter doses than he had intended, the red was beginning to turn to a respectable brown. Half an hour later Terry was sitting beside him, telling him about Wayne.

'It was awfully breezy on the beach,' Terry's dad called out, in a friendly way. 'You were wise to come here.'

'Wayne's dad has a sports shop,' said Terry. 'I got my costume there. Wayne's got an auntie Margaret and two grannies. His grannies aren't dead!' he ended, emphatically, as if he had scored a definite point there.

'That's nice,' said Albert. 'Grannies are always nice to little boys, aren't they?'

'Ha!' said Little Terror, latching back on to his grievance with the tenacity of a politician. 'Mine wasn't, Wimpole. I had to be as quiet as quiet, all the time. And her up there stuffing food into her mouth and dribbling, and spitting out crumbs. I don't call that nice. It was disgusting. I was glad when she died and they put her in the oven.'

'I'm sure that your mummy and daddy would be very upset if they heard you say that.'

'That's why I don't say it when they're there,' said Terry, simply. 'I expect they quite wanted her to live.'

The next day Albert went to the beach at Estoril, then caught the bus to Sintra in the afternoon. When he got back to the hotel the dinner hour was almost over, and Terry and his parents were tucking into enormous slices of caramel cake.

'We missed you today,' said Terry's mum, reproachfully, as he passed their table.

When Terry's parents got up to go, they came over and introduced themselves properly. They were the Mumfords, they said. And they had something to ask Albert.

'One doesn't like *putting* on people, but Terry's so fond of you, and it is a *bit* difficult shopping with him tagging along, and we wondered if you *could* keep an eye on him one afternoon so we could go into Lisbon. After all, it's not much fun for a child, watching his parents trying on shoes, is it?'

Albert thought the request an outrageous one. All his instincts cried out against agreeing. Why should he ruin a day of his holidays looking after someone else's repellent (and tedious) child? All his natural instincts told him to say no. All his middle-class instincts told him he had to say yes. He said yes.

'Let me see – I have places I'm planning to go to, and some friends I have to see . . .' he improvised, untruthfully.

'Oh – friends in Portugal,' said Mrs Mumford, in a tone of voice which seemed to be expressing either scepticism or disapproval.

'Shall we say Monday?'

Monday was five days away, and the Mumfords would obviously have preferred some earlier day, but *their* middle-class instincts forced them not to quibble, but to accept and to thank him gratefully.

The next day was a day of rest for Albert: the Mumfords went on one of the tours – to Nazaré and Fatima. When he went past their table at dinner time, Mrs Mumford enthused to him about the shrine of Fatima.

'It was a real religious experience,' she said. 'I expect Terry will want to tell you about it.'

Albert repressed a shudder, out of consideration for any Portuguese waiter who might be listening. He merely smiled and went on to his table.

The next day he took the train to Queluz, and the day after he spent exploring the little back streets of Lisbon, then in the afternoon walking up the broad avenue to the park. But all the time Monday was approaching inexorably, and short of going down with beri-beri, Albert could see no way of avoiding his stewardship of the repulsive and necrophilic Terry.

On Monday morning (it turned out, without explanation, to be a whole day's shopping Terry's parents were planning), after the Mumfords had trailed off towards the train for Lisbon, Albert took Terry into Carcavelos and filled him unimaginably full of ice-cream. He hoped it would make him ill or sleepy, but it did neither. When Albert suggested a very light lunch, Terry demanded roast pork at one of the town's little restaurants. Portions were substantial, and he ate with gusto. All this eating at least kept him quiet. Far from responding to suggestions that he have an afternoon's nap, Terry demanded to be taken to the hotel swimming pool. Terry's parents had impressed upon Albert most forcefully that Terry was not allowed to use the diving board, but while Albert was still fussing around removing his own clothes, he saw that Terry was already up there, and preparing to throw himself into the water.

'This is a suicide dive!' yelled the child. 'I want to be cremated!'

'You've got to be drowned first,' muttered Albert. Ten seconds later he was in the pool, fishing out the sobbing, gasping boy. Respect for the susceptibilities of parents prevented Albert giving him a good belting, but he was able to pummel him pretty satisfyingly on the pretext of getting water out of his lungs. He commanded him to lie still for at least ten minutes.

'Would I be in heaven now, if I had drowned, Wimpole?' Terry asked, after five.

Albert did not think it wise to go into alternative destinations for his soul. His parents might be namby-pamby as theologians.

'I believe there is some period of waiting.'

'Like on the platform, before the train comes in?' asked Terry. 'I bet once I started I'd have gone fast. Like a spaceshot.

Whoosh! You wouldn't have been able to see me, I'd have gone so fast.'

'I expect you're right,' said Albert, reading his P. D. James.

'I bet Grandma didn't go fast like that. I can't see it. She was enormous. Wayne's mum called her unwiel . . .'

'Unwieldy.'

'That's right. It means enormous. Colossal. Like a great, fat pig.'

'You know your mother wouldn't like hearing you say that.'

'She isn't,' said Terry, dismissively. 'Anyway, you can't expect to go to heaven like a spaceshot if you eat enough for three elephants. *And* if you're bad-tempered and make everyone's life a misery.'

Terry lay quiet for a bit, watching other children in the pool, children with whom he habitually refused to play. Then, out of the corner of his eye, Albert was aware that he was being watched, slyly, out of the corner of Terry's eye.

'My grandma died of an overdose,' Terry said.

'An overdose of you?' asked Albert, though he knew it was useless to venture humour on this horrible child.

'No, stupid. An overdose of medicine. She had it in a glass by the side of her bed, so she could take it while Mummy was out at work. Mummy does half days at the librerry. And Gran's medicine was left in the glass by her bed. So she didn't have to get up and go to any trouble to get it. Fat old pig!'

'Terry – if I hear any more words like that about your gran I'm going to take you and lock you in your room. In fact, I don't wish to hear any more about your gran at all.'

'All right,' said Terry, equably. 'Only it's funny the medicine was in the cupboard, and she'd have to get up and get it to give herself an overdose, isn't it? 'Cos it was left by her bed like that every day.'

'I expect she felt bad, and thought she needed more,' suggested Albert.

'Maybe,' said Terry.

Then he took himself off once more to the pool, and began showing off in front of the smaller children. Before very long he was on the diving board again, and Albert was in the pool rescuing him. It was during the third time this happened that the Mumfords arrived back at the hotel.

'I do hope he hasn't been any trouble,' said Mrs Mumford. 'Now say thank you to Mr Wimpole, Terry.'

For the remainder of the holiday the sun shone with a terrible brightness. Albert grew inventive about where he spent his days. He took the bus and ferry out to Sesimbra, he found little beaches on the Estoril coast where fishermen still mended their nets and tourists were never seen. He took the train up to Coimbra, and only rejected Oporto because he calculated that he would only have two hours to spend there before he would have to travel back. He had none of the spicy or sad romantic adventures he had hoped for – what lonely, middle-aged person does on holiday, unless he pays for them? – but he arrived back at the hotel for dinner tired and not dissatisfied with his days.

'My, you *have* got a lot of friends in Portugal,' said the Mumfords, who were now spending all their days by the pool. 'We've made good friends with Manuel, the waiter there,' explained Dad Mumford. 'He's introduced us to this lovely restaurant run by his uncle. They're wonderful to Terry there, and they really do us proud at lunchtime.'

So the Mumfords had found they could do without him.

Eventually it was time to go home. On the bus to the airport Albert hung back, and selected a seat well away from Terry. At the airport there was a slight delay, while the plane was refuelled and cleaned, and restocked with plastic food. In any case, Albert knew that there he would not be able to escape the Mumfords entirely.

'Do you think you could just keep an eye on Terry for one *minute* while we go to the duty free shop?' his mum asked. There was something in the tone of voice as she asked it, as if she knew he had considered their earlier request an encroachment, and she regretted having to ask again so obviously selfish a person.

'Of course,' said Albert.

'I'll tell you how she died,' said Terry, as their heavy footsteps faded away across the marble halls.

'I don't wish to know.'

'Yes, you do. She was lying up there, and Wayne and I were playing in my bedroom – *quietly*. How can you play quietly? And we were pretty fed up. And she called out, and called, and called. And when we went in, she said she'd got stuck on one side, and couldn't get over, and her leg had gone to sleep. She hadn't had her afternoon medicine yet. And while Wayne pretended to push her, I got the bottle from the cupboard, and I emptied some of it into her glass, and then I put it back in the cupboard. Then I went and pushed with Wayne, and finally we got her over. She said she was ever so grateful. She said, "Now I can go off." We laughed and laughed when we got back to my room. She went off all right!'

'I'm not believing any of this, Terry.'

'Believe it or not, I don't care,' said Terry. 'It's true. That's how the old pig died.'

'It's an awful swindle in there,' said the Mumfords, coming back from the duty free shop. 'Hardly any cheaper than in England. I shouldn't bother to go.'

'I'll just take a look,' said Albert, escaping.

Albert did not enjoy his flight home at all, though he bought no less than three of the little bottles of white wine they sell with the meal. He was examining the story and re-examining it with the brain of one who was accustomed to weighing up stories likely and unlikely (for Albert worked in a tax office). On the face of it, it was incredible – that a small boy (or was it two small boys?) should kill someone in this simple, almost foolproof way. Yet there had been in the last few years murder cases – now and again, yet often enough – involving children horribly young. And in England too, not in America, where people like Albert imagined such things might be common occurrences.

Albert shook his head over the stewed fish that turned out to be braised chicken. How was he to tell? And if he said nothing, how terrible might be the consequences that might ensue! If adult murderers are inclined to kill a second time, how much more likely must a child be – one who has got away with it, and rejoices in his cleverness. Even the boy's own parents would not be safe, in the unlikely event of their ever crossing his will. What sort of figure would Albert make if he went to the police *then* with his story. Reluctantly, for he foresaw little but embarrassment and ridicule, Albert decided he would have to go to them and tell his tale. In his own mind he could not tell whether Little Horror's story was true or not. It would have to be left to trained minds to come to a conclusion.

At Gatwick Albert was first out of the plane, through Passport Control and Customs in no time, and out to his car, which was miraculously unscathed by the attentions of vandals or thieves. As he drove off towards Hull and home, Albert suddenly realized, with a little *moue* of distaste, that his holiday had had its little spice of adventure after all.

'Well!' said Terry's dad, when the police had finally left. 'We know who we have to thank for *that*!'

'There wasn't much point in keeping it secret, was there? He was the only one Terry talked to at all. And he seemed such a nice man!'

'I'm going to write him a stiff letter,' fumed Terry's dad. 'I know he works in the tax office in Hull. Interfering, trouble-making little twerp!'

'It could have been serious, you know. I hope you make him realize that. It could have been very embarrassing. If we hadn't been able to give him the names and addresses of *both* Terry's grannies . . . Oh, Good Lord! What *are* they going to say?'

'The police are going to be very tactful. The inspector told me so at the door. I think they'll probably just make enquiries of neighbours. Or pretend to be council workers, and get them talking. Just so's they make sure they are who we say they are.'

'*My* mother will find out,' said Mrs Mumford, with conviction and foreboding. 'She's got a nose! . . . And how am I going to explain it to her? I'll never forgive that Wimpole!'

Later that night, as they were undressing for bed, Terry's mum, who had been thinking, said to Terry's dad, 'Walter: you don't think we ought to have told them about Wayne Catherick's gran, do you?'

'What about her?'

'Old Mrs Corfitt, who lived next door. Should we have told them that she died of an overdose?'

'No. Course not. What's it to do with Terry? They said the old lady got confused and gave herself an extra lot.'

'I suppose it would just have caused more trouble,' agreed Mrs Mumford. 'And as you say, it was nothing to do with Terry, was it?'

She turned out the light.

'Well,' she said, as she prepared for sleep, 'I hope next time we go on holiday Terry finds someone nicer than *that* to make friends with!'

SIMON BRETT

Double Glazing

THE fireplace was rather splendid, a carved marble arch housing a black metal grate. The curves of the marble supports echoed the elaborate sweep of the coving and the outward spread of petals from the central ceiling rose. The white emulsion enthusiastically splashed over the room by the Housing Trust volunteers could not disguise its fine Victorian proportions. The old flooring had been replaced by concrete when the damp course was put in and the whole area was now snugly carpeted. This was one of the better conversions, making a compact residence for a single occupant, Jean Collinson thought as she sat before the empty grate opposite Mr Morton. A door led off the living-room to the tiny kitchen and bathroom. Quite sufficient for a retired working man.

She commented on the fireplace.

'Oh yes, it's very attractive,' Harry Morton agreed. His voice still bore traces of his Northern upbringing. 'Nice workmanship in those days. Draughty, mind, if you don't have it lit.'

'Yes, but there's no reason why you shouldn't use it in the winter. When they did the conversion, the builders checked that the chimney wasn't blocked. Even had it swept, I think.'

'Oh yes. Well, I'll have to see about that when the winter comes. See how far the old pension stretches.'

'Of course. Do you find it hard to make ends meet?'

'Oh no. I'm not given to extravagance. I have no vices, so far as I know.' The old man chuckled. He was an amiable soul; Jean found him quite restful after most of the others. Mrs Walker with her constant moans about how her daughter and grandchildren never came to visit, Mr Kitson with his incontinence and unwillingness to do anything about it. Mrs Grüber with her conviction that Jean was part of an international conspiracy of social workers devoted to the cause of separating her from a revoltingly smelly little Yorkshire terrier called Nimrod. It was a relief to meet an old person who seemed to be coping.

Mr Morton had already made his mark on the flat although he had only moved in the week before. It was all very clean and tidy, no dust on any of the surfaces. (He had refused the Trust's offer of help with the cleaning, so he must have done it himself.) His few possessions were laid out neatly, the rack of pipes spotless on the mantelpiece, the pile of Do-It-Yourself magazines aligned on the coffee table, the bed squared off with hospital corners.

Mr Morton had taken the same care with his own appearance. His chin was shaved smooth, without the cuts and random tufts of white hair which Jean saw on so many of the old men she dealt with. His shirt was clean, tie tight in a little knot, jacket brushed, trousers creased properly and brown shoes buffed to a fine shine. And there didn't linger about him the sour smell which she now almost took for granted would emanate from all old people. If there was any smell in the room, it was an antiseptic hint of carbolic soap. Thank God, Jean thought, her new charge wasn't going to add too much to her already excessive workload. Just the occasional visit to check he was all right, but, even from this first meeting, she knew he would be. Harry Morton could obviously manage. He'd lived alone all his life and had the neatness of an organized bachelor. But without that obsessive independence which so many of them developed. He didn't seem to resent her visit, nor to have complicated feelings of pride about accepting the Housing Trust's charity. He was just a working man who had done his bit for society and was now ready to accept society's thanks in the reduced circumstances of retirement. Jean was already convinced that the complaints which had led to his departure from his previous flat were just the ramblings of a paranoid neighbour.

She stifled a yawn. It was not that she was bored by Harry Morton's plans for little improvements to the flat. She had learned as a social worker to appear interested in much duller and less coherent narratives. But it was stuffy. Like a lot of old people, Harry Morton seemed unwilling to open the windows. Still, it was his flat and his right to have as much or as little ventilation as he wanted.

Anyway, Jean knew that the lack of air was not the real reason for her doziness. Guiltily, she allowed herself to think for a moment about the night before. She felt a little glow of fragile pleasure and knew she mustn't think about it too much, mustn't threaten it by inflating it in her mind beyond its proper proportions.

But, without inflation, it was still the best thing that had happened to her for some years, and something that she had thought, at thirty-two, might well never happen again. It had all been so straightforward, making nonsense of the agonizing and worry about being an emotional cripple which had seemed an inescapable part of her life ever since she'd broken up with Roger five years earlier.

It had not been a promising party. Given by a schoolfriend who had become a teacher, married a teacher and developed a lot of friends who were also teachers. Jean had anticipated an evening of cheap Spanish plonk, sharp French bread, and predictable cheese, with conversation about how little teachers were paid, how much more everyone's contemporaries were earning, how teaching wasn't really what any of them had wanted to do anyway, all spiced with staff-room gossip about personalities she didn't know, wasn't likely to meet, and, after half an hour of listening, didn't want to meet.

And that's how it had been, until she had met Mick. From that point on, the evening had just made sense. Talking to him, dancing with him (for some reason, though they were all well into their thirties, the party was still conducted on the lines of a college hop), then effortlessly leaving with him and going back to his flat.

And there it had made sense too. All the inhibitions she had carried with her so long, the knowledge that her face was strong rather than beautiful, that her hips were too broad and her breasts too small, had not seemed important. It had all been so different from the one-sided fumblings, the humourless groping and silent embarrassments which had seemed for some years all that sex had to offer. It had worked.

And Mick was coming straight round to her place after school. She was going to cook him a meal. He had to go to some Debating Society meeting and would be round about seven. Some days she couldn't guarantee to be back by then, the demands of her charges were unpredictable, but this time even that would be all right. Harry Morton was the last on her round and he clearly wasn't going to be any trouble. Covertly, with the skill born of long practice, she looked at her watch. A quarter to five. Good, start to leave in about five minutes, catch the shops on the way home, buy something special, maybe a bottle of wine. Cook a good dinner and then . . .

She felt herself blushing and guiltily pulled her mind back to listen to what Harry Morton was saying. Fantasizing never helped, she knew, it only distanced reality. Anyway, she had a job to do.

'I've got a bit of money saved,' Harry was saying, 'some I put aside in the Post Office book while I was still working and I've even managed to save a bit on the pension, and I reckon I'm going to buy some really good tools. I want to get a ratchet screwdriver. They're very good, save a lot of effort. Just the job for putting up shelves, that sort of thing. I thought I'd put a couple of shelves up over there, you know, for magazines and that.'

'Yes, that's a very good idea.' Jean compensated for her lapse into reverie by being bright and helpful. 'Of course, if you need a hand with any of the heavy stuff, the Trust's got a lot of volunteers who'd be only too glad to—'

'Oh no, no, thank you. I won't need help. I'm pretty good with my hands. And, you know, if you've worked with your hands all your life, you stay pretty strong. Don't worry, I'll be up to building a few shelves. And any other little jobs around the flat.'

'What did you do before you retired, Mr Morton?'

'Now please call me Harry. I was a warehouse porter.'

'Oh.'

'Working up at Granger's, don't know if you know them?'

'Up on the main road?'

'Yes. We loaded the lorries. Had trolleys, you know. Had to go along the racks getting the lines to put in the lorries. Yes, I did that for nearly twenty years. They wanted me to be a checker, you know, checking off on the invoices as the goods were loaded on to the lorries, but I didn't fancy the responsibility. I was happy with my trolley.'

Suddenly Jean smiled at the old man, not her professional smile of concern, but a huge, genuine smile of pleasure that broke the sternness of her face into a rare beauty. Somehow she respected his simplicity, his content. It seemed to fit that the day after she met Mick, she would also meet this happy old man. She rose from her chair. 'Well, if you're sure there's nothing I can do for you . . .'

'No, I'll be fine, thank you, love.'

'I'll drop round again in a week or two to see how you're getting on.'

'Oh, that'll be very nice. I'll be fine, though. Don't you worry about me.'

'Good.' Jean lingered for a moment. She felt something missing, there was something else she had meant to mention, now what on earth was it?

Oh yes. His sister. She had meant to talk to him about his sister, sympathize about her death the previous year. Jean had had the information from a social worker in Bradford where the sister had lived. They tried to liaise between different areas as much as possible. The sister had been found dead in her flat. She had died of hypothermia, but her body had not been discovered for eleven days, because of the Christmas break.

Jean thought she should mention it. There was always the danger of being thought to intrude on his privacy, but Harry Morton seemed a sensible enough old bloke, who would recognize her sympathy for what it was. And, in a strange way, Jean felt she ought to raise the matter as a penance for letting her mind wander while Harry had been talking.

'Incidentally, I heard about your sister's death. I'm very sorry.'

'Oh, thank you.' Harry Morton didn't seem unduly perturbed by the reference. 'I didn't see a lot of her these last few years.'

'But it must have been a shock.'

'A bit, maybe. Typical, though. She always was daft, never took care of herself. Died of the cold, she did. Hyper . . . hyper-something they called it.'

'Hypothermia.'

'That's it. Silly fool. I didn't see her when I went up for the funeral. Just saw the coffin. Closed coffin. Could have been anyone. Didn't feel nothing, really.'

'Anyway, as I say, I'm sorry.'

'Oh, don't think about it. I don't. And don't you worry about me going the same way. For one thing, I always had twice as much sense as she did – from a child on. And then I can look after myself.'

Jean Collinson left, feeling glad she had mentioned the sister. Now there was nothing nagging at her mind, nothing she felt she should be doing. Except looking forward to the evening. She wondered what she should cook for Mick.

Harry Morton closed the door after her. It was summer, but the corridor outside felt chilly. He shivered slightly, then went to his notebook and started to make a list.

He had always made lists. At the warehouse he had soon realized that he couldn't remember all the lines the checker gave him unless he wrote them down. The younger porters could remember up to twenty different items for their loads, but Harry recognized his limitations and always wrote everything down. It made him a little slower than the others, but at least he never got anything wrong. And the Head Checker had said, when you took off the time the others wasted taking back lines they had got wrong, Harry was quite as fast as any of them.

He headed the list 'Things to do'. First he wrote 'Ratchet screwdriver'. Then he wrote 'Library'.

*

Harry knew his own pace and he never tried to go any faster. When he was younger he had occasionally tried to push himself along a bit, but that had only resulted in mistakes. Now he did everything steadily, methodically. And now there was no one to push him. The only really miserable time of his life had been when a new checker had been appointed who had tried to increase Harry's work-rate. The old man still woke up sometimes in the night in the sweat of panic and confusion that the pressure had put on him. Unwillingly he'd remember the afternoon when he'd thrown a catering-size tin of diced carrots at his tormentor's head. But then he'd calm down, get up and make himself a cup of tea. That was all over. It hadn't lasted very long. The checker had been ambitious and soon moved on to an office job.

And now he wasn't at work, Harry had all the time in the world anyway. Time to do a good job. The only pressure on him was to get it done before the winter set in. And the winter was a long way off.

He read through all the Do-It-Yourself books he had got from the library, slowly, not skipping a word. After each one he would make a list, a little digest of the pros and cons of the methods discussed. Then he sent off for brochures from all the companies that advertised in his Do-It-Yourself magazines and subjected them to the same punctilious scrutiny. Finally he made a tour of the local home-care shops, looked at samples and discussed the various systems with the proprietors. After six weeks he reckoned he knew everything there was to know about double glazing.

And by then he had ruled out quite a few of the systems on the market. The best method he realized was to replace the existing windows with new factory-sealed units, but, even if the Housing Trust would allow him to do this, it would be far too expensive and also too big a job for him to do on his own.

The next possible solution was the addition of secondary sashes, fixing a new pane over the existing window, leaving the original glass undisturbed. There were a good many proprietary sub-frame systems on the market, but again these would be far too expensive for his modest savings. He did some sums in his notebook, working out how long it would take him to afford secondary sashes by saving on his pension, but he wouldn't have enough till the spring. And he had to get the double glazing installed before the winter set in. He began to regret the generous proportions on which the Victorians had designed their windows.

He didn't worry about it, though. It was still only September. There was going to be a way that he could afford and that he could do on his own. That social worker was always full of offers of help from her network of volunteers, but he wasn't reduced to that yet.

Then he had the idea of going through the back numbers of his Do-It-Yourself magazines. He knew it was a good idea as soon as he thought about it. He sat in his armchair in front of the fireplace, which was now hidden by a low screen, and, with notebook and pencil by his side, started to thumb through the magazines. He did them in strict chronological order, just as he kept them stacked on their new shelf. He had a full set for seven and a half years, an unbroken sequence from the first time he had become interested in Do-It-Yourself. That had been while he was being harassed by the new checker. He chuckled to remember that he'd bought the first magazine because it had an article in it about changing locks and he'd wanted to keep the checker out of his flat. Of course, the checker had never come to his flat.

He started on the first magazine, and worked through, reading everything, articles and advertisements, in case he should miss what he was looking for. Occasionally he made a note in his notebook.

It was on the afternoon of the third day that he found it. The article was headed, 'Cut the Costs of Double Glazing'. His heart quickened with excitement, but he still read through the text at his regular, unvarying pace. Then he read it a second time, even more slowly, making copious notes.

The system described was a simple one, which involved sticking transparent film on the inside of the windows and thus creating the required insulation gap between the panes and the film. There were, the writer observed slyly, kits for this system available on the market, but the shrewd Do-It-Yourself practitioner would simply go to his local supermarket and buy the requisite number of rolls of kitchen clingfilm and then go to his hardware store to buy a roll of double-sided Sellotape for fixing the film, and thus save himself a lot of money. Harry Morton chuckled out loud, as this cunning plot was confided to him. Then he wrote on his list 'Kitchen Clingfilm' and 'Double-sided Sellotape'.

As always, in everything he did, he followed the instructions to the letter. At first, it was more difficult than it sounded. The kitchen film tended to shrivel up on itself and stretch out of true when he tried to extend it over the window frames. And it caught on the stickiness of the Sellotape before it was properly aligned. He had to sacrifice nearly a whole roll of clingfilm before he got the method right. But he pressed on, working with steady care, perched on the folding ladder he had bought specially for the purpose, and soon was rewarded by the sight of two strips stretched parallel and taut over the window frame.

He was lining up the third when the doorbell rang. He was annoyed by the interruption to his schedule and opened the door grudgingly to admit Jean Collinson. Then he almost turned his back on her while he got on with the tricky task of winding the prepared film back on to its cardboard roll. He would have to start lining the next piece up again after she had gone.

Still, he did his best to be pleasant and offered the social worker a cup of tea. It seemed to take a very long time for the kettle to boil and the girl seemed to take a very long time to drink her tea. He kept looking over her shoulder to the window, estimating how many more strips it would take and whether he'd have to go back to the supermarket for another roll to make up for the one he'd ruined.

Had he taken any notice of Jean, he would have seen that she looked tired, fatigue stretching the skin of her face to show her features at their sharpest and sternest. Work was getting busy. She had ahead of her a difficult interview with Mrs Grüber, whose Yorkshire terrier Nimrod had developed a growth between his back legs. It hung there, obscene and shiny, dangling from the silky fur. The animal needed to go to the vet, but Mrs Grüber refused to allow this, convinced that it would have to be put down. Jean feared this suspicion was correct, but knew that the animal had to make the trip to find out one way or the other. It was obviously in pain and kept up a thin keening whine all the time while Mrs Grüber hugged it piteously to her cardigan. And Jean knew that she was going to have to be the one who got the animal to the vet.

Which meant she'd be late again. Which would mean another scene with Mick. He'd become so childish recently, so demanding, jealous of the time she spent with her old people. He had become moody and hopeless. Instead of the support in her life which he had been at first, he was now almost another case on her books. She had discovered how much he feared his job, how he couldn't keep order in class, and, though she gave him all the sympathy she could, it never seemed to be enough.

And then there were the logistics of living in two separate establishments an awkward bus-ride apart. Life seemed to have degenerated into a sequence of late-night and early-morning rushes from one flat to the other because one of them had left something vital in the wrong place. Jean had once suggested that they should move in together, but Mick's violent reaction of fear against such a commitment had kept her from raising the matter again. So their relationship had become a pattern of rows and making up, abject self-recrimination from Mick, complaints that she didn't really care about him and late-night reconciliations of desperate, clinging sex. Always too late. She had forgotten what a good night's sleep was by the time one end had been curtailed by arguments and coupling and the other by leaving at half past six to get back to her place to pick up some case-notes. Everything seemed threatened.

But it was restful in Harry's flat. He seemed to have his life organized. She found it an oasis of calm, of passionless simplicity, where she could recharge her batteries before going back to the difficulties of the rest of her life.

She was unaware of how he was itching for her to go. She saw the evidence of the double glazing and asked him about it, but he was reticent. He didn't want to discuss it until it was finished. Anyway, it wasn't for other people's benefit. It was for him.

Eventually Jean felt sufficiently steeled for her encounter with Mrs Grüber and brought their desultory conversation to an end. She did not notice the alacrity with which Harry Morton rose to show her out, nor the speed with which he closed the door after her.

Again he felt the chill of the corridor when the door was open. And even after it was closed there seemed to be a current of air from somewhere. He went across to his notebook and wrote down 'Draught Excluder'.

It was late October when she next went round to see the old man. She was surprised that he didn't immediately open the door after she'd rung the bell. Instead she heard his voice hiss out, 'Who is it?'

She was used to this sort of reception from some of her old ladies, who lived in the conviction that every caller was a rapist at the very least, but she hadn't expected it from such a sensible old boy as Harry Morton.

She identified herself and, after a certain amount of persuasion, he let her in. He held the door open as little as possible and closed it almost before she was inside. 'What do you want?' he asked aggressively.

'I just called to see how you are.'

'Well, I'm fine.' He spoke as if that ended the conversation and edged back towards the door.

'Are you sure? You look a bit pale.'

He did look pale. His skin had taken on a greyish colour.

'You look as if you haven't been out much recently. Have you been ill? If you're unwell, all you have to do is—'

'I haven't been ill. I go out, do my shopping, get the things I need.' He couldn't keep a note of mystery out of the last three words.

She noticed he was thinner too. His appearance hadn't

suffered; he still dressed with almost obsessive neatness; but he had definitely lost weight. She wasn't to know that he was cutting down on food so that his pension would buy the 'things he needed'.

The room looked different too. She only took it in once she was inside. There was evidence of recent carpentry. No mess – all the sawdust was neatly contained on newspaper and offcuts of wood were leant against the kitchen table which Harry had used as a sawing bench – but he had obviously been busy. The ratchet screwdriver was prominent on the table top. The artifact which all this effort had produced was plain to see. The fine marble fireplace had been neatly boxed in. It had been a careful job. Pencil marks on the wood showed the accuracy of measurement and all of the screws were tidily countersunk into their regularly spaced holes.

Jean commented on the workmanship.

'When I do a job, I like to do it properly,' Harry Morton said defensively.

'Of course. Didn't you . . . like the fireplace?'

'Nothing wrong with it. But it was very draughty.'

'Yes.' She wondered for a moment if Harry Morton were about to change from being one of her easy charges to one of her problems. He was her last call that day and she'd reckoned on just a quick visit. She'd recently made various promises to Mick about spending less time with her work. He'd suddenly got very aggressively male, demanding that she should have a meal ready for him when he got home. He also kept calling her 'woman', as if he were some character out of the blues songs he was always listening to. He didn't manage this new male chauvinism with complete conviction; it seemed only to accentuate his basic insecurity; but Jean was prepared to play along with it for a bit. She felt there was something in the relationship worth salvaging. Maybe when he relaxed a bit, things would be better. If only they could spend a little time on their own, just the two of them, away from outside pressures . . .

She stole a look at her watch. She could spend half an hour with Harry and still be back at what Mick would regard as a respectable hour. Anyway, there wasn't anything really wrong with the old boy. Just needed a bit of love, a feeling that someone cared. That's what most of them needed when it came down to it.

'Harry, it looks to me like you may have been overdoing it with all this heavy carpentry. You must remember, you're not as young as you were and you do have to take things a bit slower.'

'I take things at the right pace,' he insisted stubbornly. 'There's nothing wrong with me.'

But Jean wasn't going to have her solicitude swept aside so easily. 'No, of course there isn't. But look, I'd like you just to sit down for a moment in front of the . . . by the fireplace, and I'll make you a cup of tea.'

Grumbling, he sat down.

'And why don't you put the television on? I'm sure there's some nice relaxing programme for you to see.'

'There's not much I enjoy on the television.'

'Nonsense, I'm sure there are lots of things to interest you.' Having started in this bulldozing vein, Jean was going to continue. She switched on the television and went into the kitchen.

It was some children's quiz show, which Harry would have switched off under normal circumstances. But he didn't want to make the girl suspicious. If he just did as she said, she would go quicker. So he sat and watched without reaction.

It was only when the commercials came that he took notice. There was a commercial for double glazing. A jovial man was demonstrating the efficacy of one particular system. A wind machine was set in motion the other side of an open window. Then the double-glazed window was closed and, to show how airtight the seal was, the man dropped a feather by the joint in the panes. It fluttered straight downwards, its course unaffected by any draughts.

From that moment Harry Morton was desperate for Jean to leave. He had seen the perfect way of testing his workmanship. She offered to stay and watch the programme with him, she asked lots of irrelevant questions about whether he needed anything or whether there was anything her blessed volunteers could do, but eventually she was persuaded to go. In fact she was relieved to be away. Harry had seemed a lot perkier than when she had arrived and now she would be back in time to conform to Mick's desired image of her.

Harry almost slammed the door. As he turned, he felt a shiver of cold down his back. Right, feathers, feathers. It only took a moment to work out where to get them from.

He picked up his ratchet screwdriver and went over to the bed. He drew back the candlewick and stabbed the screwdriver deeply into his pillow. And again, twisting and tearing at the fabric. From the rents he made a little storm of feathers flurried.

It was cold as she walked along towards Harry's flat and the air stung the rawness of her black eye. But Jean felt good. At least they'd got something sorted out. After the terrible fight of the night before, in the sobbing reconciliation, after Mick had apologized for hitting her, he had suggested that they go away together for Christmas. He hated all the fuss that surrounded the festival and always went off to stay in a cottage in Wales, alone, until it all died down. And he had said, in his ungracious way, 'You can come with me, woman.'

She knew it was a risk. The relationship might not stand the proximity. She was even slightly afraid of being alone with Mick for so long, now that his behaviour towards her had taken such a violent turn. But at bottom she thought it would work. Anyway, she had to try. They had to try. Ten days alone together would sort out the relationship one way or the other. And Christmas was only three weeks off.

As so often happened, her new mood of confidence was reflected in her work. She had just been to see Mrs Grüber. Nimrod had made a complete recovery after the removal of his growth and the old lady had actually thanked Jean for insisting on the visit to the vet. That meant Mrs Grüber could be left over the Christmas break without anxiety. And most of the others could manage. As Mick so often said, thinking you're indispensable is one of the first signs of madness. Of course they'd be all right if she went away. And, as Mick also said, then you'll be able to concentrate on me for a change, woman. Yes, it was going to work.

Again her ring at the doorbell was met by a whispered 'Who is it?' from Harry Morton. It was Jean – could she come in? 'No,' he said.

'Why not, Harry? Remember, I do have a duplicate key. The Housing Trust insists that I have that, so that I can let myself in if—'

'No, it's not that, Jean love,' his old Northern voice wheedled. 'It's just that I've got a really streaming cold. I don't want to breathe germs all over you.'

'Oh, don't worry about that.'

'No, no, really. I'm in bed. I'm just going to sleep it off.'

Jean wavered. Now she came to think of it, she didn't fancy breathing in germs in Harry's stuffy little flat. 'Have you seen the doctor?'

'No, I tell you it's just a cold. Be gone in a day or two, if I just stay in bed. No need to worry the doctor.'

The more she thought about it, the less she wanted to develop a cold just before she and Mick went away together. But it was her job to help. 'Are you sure there isn't anything I can do for you? Shopping or anything?'

'Oh. Well . . .' Harry paused. 'Yes, I would be grateful, actually, if you wouldn't mind getting me a few things.'

'Of course.'

'If you just wait a moment, I'll write out a list.'

Jean waited. After a couple of minutes a page from his notebook was pushed under the door. Its passage was impeded by the draught-excluding strip on the inside, but it got through.

Jean looked at the list. 'Bottle of milk. Small tin of baked beans. Six packets of Polyfilla.'

'Is that Polyfilla?' she asked, bewildered.

'Yes. It's a sort of powder you mix with water to fill in cracks and that.'

'I know what it is. You just seem to want rather a lot of it.'

'Yes, I do. Just for a little job needs doing.'

'And you're quite sure you don't need any more food?'

'Sure. I've got plenty,' Harry Morton lied.

'Well, I'll probably be back in about twenty minutes.'

'Thank you very much. Here's the money.' A few crumpled notes forced their way under the door. 'If there's no reply when you get back, I'll be asleep. Just leave the stuff outside. It'll be safe.'

'OK. If you're sure there's nothing else I can do.'

'No, really. Thanks very much.'

Harry Morton heard her footsteps recede down the passage and chuckled aloud with delight at his own cunning. Yes, she could help him. First useful thing she'd ever done for him.

And she hadn't noticed the windows from the outside. Just thought the curtains were drawn. Yes, it had been a good idea to board them up over the curtains. He looked with satisfaction at the wooden covers, with their rows of screws, each one driven securely home with his ratchet screwdriver. Then he looked at the pile of new wood leaning against the door. Yes, with proper padding that would be all right. Mentally he earmarked his bedspread for the padding and made a note of the idea on the 'Jobs to Do' list in his notebook.

Suddenly he felt the chill of a draught on his neck. He leapt up to find its source. He had long given up using the feather method. Apart from anything else, he had used his pillows as insulation in the fireplace. Now he used a lighted candle. Holding it firmly in front of him, he began to make a slow, methodical circuit of the room.

It was two days before Christmas, two o'clock in the afternoon. Jean and Mick were leaving at five. 'Five sharp, woman,' he had said. 'If you ain't here then, woman, I'll know you don't give a damn about me. You'd rather spend your life with incontinent old men.' Jean had smiled when he said it. Oh yes, she'd be there. Given all that time together, she knew they could work something out.

And, when it came to it, it was all going to be remarkably

easy. All of her charges seemed to be sorted out over the holiday. Now Nimrod was all right, Mrs Grüber was in a state of ecstasy, full of plans for the huge Christmas dinner she was going to cook for herself and the dog. Mrs Walker was going to stay with her daughter, which meant that she would see the grandchildren, so she couldn't complain for once. Even smelly old Mr Kitson had been driven off to spend the holiday with his married sister. Rather appropriately, in Bath. The rest of her cases had sorted themselves out one way or the other. And, after all, she was only going to be away for ten days. She felt she needed the break. Her Senior Social Worker had wished her luck and told her to have a good rest, and this made Jean realize how long it was since she had been away from work for any length of time.

She just had to check that Mr Morton was all right, and then she was free.

Harry was steeping his trousers in mixed-up Polyfilla when he heard the doorbell. It was difficult, what he was doing. Really, the mixture should have been runnier, but he had not got out enough water before he boarded up the door to the kitchen and bathroom. Never mind, though, the stuff would still work and soon he'd be able to produce more urine to mix it with. He was going to use the Polyfilla-covered trousers to block the crevice along the bottom of the front door. His pyjamas and pullover were already caulking the cracks on the other one.

He congratulated himself on judging the amount of Polyfilla right. He was nearly at the end of the last packet. By the time he'd blocked in the plug sockets and the ventilation grille he'd found hidden behind the television, it would all be used up. Just the right amount.

He froze when he heard the doorbell. Lie doggo. Pretend there's no one there. They'll go away.

The bell rang again. Still he didn't move. There was a long pause, so long he thought the challenge had gone. But then he heard an ominous sound, which at once identified his caller and also raised a new threat.

It was the sound of a key in his lock. That bloody busybody of a social worker had come round to see him.

There was nothing for it. He would have to let her in. 'Just a minute. Coming,' he called.

'Hurry up,' the girl's voice said. She had told him to hurry up. Like the new checker, she had told him to hurry up.

He picked up his ratchet screwdriver and started to withdraw the first of the screws that held the large sheet of chipboard and its padding of bedclothes against the front door. At least, he thought, thank God I hadn't put the sealing strips along there.

Jean's voice sounded quite agitated by the time he removed the last screw. 'What's going on? Can't you hurry up?'

She had said it again. He opened the door narrowly and she pushed in, shouting, 'Now what the hell do you think you're—'

Whether she stopped speaking because she was taken aback by the sight of the room and her half-naked host, or because the ratchet screwdriver driven into her back near the spine had punctured her heart, it is difficult to assess. Certainly it is true that the first blow killed her; the subsequent eleven were unnecessary insurance.

Harry Morton left the body on the floor and continued methodically with his tasks. He replaced the chipboard and padding over the door and sealed round it with his trousers, sports jacket, shirt, and socks, all soaked in Polyfilla. Then he blocked up the plugs and ventilator grille.

He looked round with satisfaction. Now that was real insulation. No one could die of cold in a place like that. Always had been daft, his sister. But he didn't relax. One more final check-round with the candle, then he could put his feet up.

He went slowly round the room, very slowly so that the candle wouldn't flicker from his movement, only from genuine draughts.

Damn. It had moved. He retraced a couple of steps. Yes, it fluttered again. There was a draught.

By the fireplace. That fireplace had always been more trouble than it was worth.

It needed more insulating padding. And more Polyfilla to seal it.

But he'd used everything in the room and there was no water left to mix the Polyfilla with. He felt too dehydrated to urinate. Never mind, there was a solution to everything. He sat down with his notebook and pencil to work it out.

Well, there was his underwear, for a start. That was more insulation. He took it off.

Then he looked down at Jean Collinson's body and saw the solution. To both his problems. Her body could be crammed into the chimney to block out the draughts and her blood (of which there was quite a lot) could mix with the Polyfilla.

He worked at his own pace, unscrewing the boxwork he had put around the marble fireplace with his ratchet screwdriver. Then he pulled out the inadequate insulation of pillows and Do-It-Yourself magazines and started to stuff the body up the chimney.

It was hard work. He pushed the corpse up head first and the broad hips stuck well in the flue, forming a good seal. But he had to break the legs to fit them behind his boxwork when he replaced it. He crammed the crevices with the pillows and magazines and sealed round the edges with brownish Polyfilla.

Only then did he feel that he could sit back with the satisfaction of a job well done.

They found his naked body when they broke into the flat after the Christmas break.

He would have died from starvation in time, but in fact, so good was his insulation, he was asphyxiated first.

COLIN DEXTER

A Case of Mis-identity

LONG as had been my acquaintance with Sherlock Holmes, I had seldom heard him refer to his early life; and the only knowledge I ever gleaned of his family history sprang from the rare visits of his famous brother, Mycroft. On such occasions, our visitor invariably addressed me with courtesy, but also (let me be honest!) with some little condescension. He was – this much I knew – by some seven years the senior in age to my great friend, and was a founder member of the Diogenes Club, that peculiar institution whose members are ever forbidden to converse with one another. Physically, Mycroft was stouter than his brother (I put the matter in as kindly a manner as possible); but the single most striking feature about him was the piercing intelligence of his eyes – greyish eyes which appeared to see beyond the range of normal mortals. Holmes himself had commented upon this last point: 'My dear Watson, you have recorded – and I am flattered by it – something of my own powers of observation and deduction. Know, however, that Mycroft has a degree of observation somewhat the equal of my own; and as for deduction, he has a brain that is unrivalled – *virtually* unrivalled – in the northern hemisphere. You may be relieved, however, to learn that he is a trifle lazy, and quite decidedly somnolent – and that his executant ability on the violin is immeasurably inferior to my own.'

(Was there, I occasionally wondered, just the hint of competitive envy between those two unprecedented intellects?)

I had just called at 221B Baker Street on a fog-laden November afternoon in 188–, after taking part in some research at St Thomas's Hospital into suppurative tonsillitis (I had earlier acquainted Holmes with the particulars). Mycroft was staying with Holmes for a few days, and as I entered that well-known sitting-room I caught the tail end of the brothers' conversation.

'Possibly, Sherlock – possibly. But it is the *detail*, is it not? Give me all the evidence and it is just possible that I could match your own analyses from my corner armchair. But to be required to rush hither and thither, to find and examine witnesses, to lie along the carpet with a lens held firmly to my failing sight . . . No! It is not my *métier*!'

During this time Holmes himself had been standing before the window, gazing down into the neutral-tinted London street. And looking over his shoulder, I could see that on the pavement opposite there stood an attractive young woman draped in a heavy fur coat. She had clearly just arrived, and every few seconds was looking up to Holmes's window in hesitant fashion, her fingers fidgeting with the buttons of her gloves. On a sudden she crossed the street, and Mrs Hudson was soon ushering in our latest client.

After handing her coat to Holmes, the young lady sat nervously on the edge of the nearest armchair, and announced herself as Miss Charlotte van Allen. Mycroft nodded briefly at the newcomer, before reverting to a monograph on polyphonic plainchant; whilst Holmes himself made observation of the lady in that abstracted yet intense manner which was wholly peculiar to him,

'Do you not find,' began Holmes, 'that with your short sight it is a little difficult to engage in so much typewriting?'

Surprise, apprehension, appreciation, showed by turns upon her face, succeeded in all by a winsome smile as she appeared to acknowledge Holmes's quite extraordinary powers.

'Perhaps you will also tell me,' continued he, 'why it is that you came from home in such a great hurry?'

For a few seconds, Miss van Allen sat shaking her head with incredulity; then, as Holmes sat staring towards the ceiling, she began her remarkable narrative.

'Yes, I did bang out of the house, because it made me very angry to see the way my father, Mr Wyndham, took the whole business – refusing even to countenance the idea of going to the police, and quite certainly ruling out any recourse to yourself, Mr Holmes! He just kept repeating – and I *do* see his point – that no real harm has been done . . . although he can have no idea of the misery I have had to endure.'

'Your father?' queried Holmes quietly. 'Perhaps you refer to your stepfather, since the names are different?'

'Yes,' she confessed, 'my stepfather. I don't know why I keep referring to him as "father" – especially since he is but five years older than myself.'

'Your mother – she is still living?'

'Oh, yes! Though I will not pretend I was over-pleased when she remarried so soon after my father's death – and then to a man almost seventeen years younger than herself. Father – my real father, that is – had a plumbing business in the Tottenham Court Road, and Mother carried on the company after he died, until she married Mr Wyndham. I think he considered such things a little beneath his new wife, especially with his being in a rather superior position as a traveller in French wines. Whatever the case, though, he made Mother sell out.'

'Did you yourself derive any income from the sale of your father's business?'

'No. But I do have one hundred pounds annual income in my own right; as well as the extra I make from my typing. If I may say so, Mr Holmes, you might be surprised how many of the local businesses – including Cook and Marchant – ask me to work for them a few hours each week. You see' (she looked at us with a shy, endearing diffidence), 'I'm quite good at *that* in life, if nothing else.'

'You must then have some profitable government stock—?' began Holmes.

She smiled again: 'New Zealand, at four and a half per cent.'

'Please forgive me, Miss van Allen, but could not a single lady get by very nicely these days on – let us say, fifty pounds per annum?'

'Oh, certainly! And I myself live comfortably on but ten shillings per week, which is only half of that amount. You see, I never touch a single penny of my inheritance. Since I live at home, I cannot bear the thought of being a burden to my parents, and we have reached an arrangement whereby Mr Wyndham himself is empowered to draw my interest each quarter for as long as I remain in that household.'

Holmes nodded. 'Why have you come to see me?' he asked bluntly.

A flush stole over Miss van Allen's face and she plucked nervously at a small handkerchief drawn from her bag as she stated her errand with earnest simplicity. 'I would give everything I have to know what has become of Mr Horatio Darvill. There! Now you have it.'

'Please, could you perhaps begin at the beginning?' encouraged Holmes gently.

'Whilst my father was alive, sir, we always received tickets for the gas-fitters' ball. And after he died, the tickets were sent to my mother. But neither Mother nor I ever thought of going, because it was made plain to us that Mr Wyndham did not approve. He believed that the class of folk invited to such gatherings was inferior; and furthermore he asserted that neither of us – without considerable extra expenditure – had anything fit to wear. But believe me, Mr Holmes, I myself had the purple plush that I had never so much as taken from the drawer!'

It was after a decent interval that Holmes observed quietly: 'But you *did* go to the ball?'

'Yes. In the finish, we both went – Mother and I – when my stepfather had been called away to France.'

'And it was there that you met Mr Horatio Darvill?'

'Yes! And – do you know? – he called the very next morning. And several times after that, whilst my stepfather was in France, we walked out together.'

'Mr Wyndham must have been annoyed once he learnt what had occurred?'

Miss van Allen hung her pretty head. 'Most annoyed, I'm afraid, for it became immediately clear that he did not approve of Mr Darvill.'

'Why do you think that was so?'

'I am fairly sure he thought Mr Darvill was interested only in my inheritance.'

'Did Mr Darvill not attempt to keep seeing you – in spite of these difficulties?'

'Oh yes! I thought, though, it would be wiser for us to stop seeing each other for a while. But he did write – every single day. And always, in the mornings, I used to receive the letters myself so that no one else should know.'

'Were you engaged to this gentleman?'

'Yes! For there was no problem about his supporting me. He was a cashier in a firm in Leadenhall Street—'

'Ah! Which office was that?' I interposed, for that particular area is known to me well, and I hoped that I might perhaps be of some assistance in the current investigation. Yet the look on Holmes's face was one of some annoyance, and I sank further into my chair as the interview progressed.

'I never did know exactly which firm it was,' admitted Miss van Allen.

'But where did he live?' persisted Holmes.

'He told me that he usually slept in a flat on the firm's premises.'

'You must yourself have written to this man, to whom you had agreed to become engaged?'

She nodded. 'To the Leadenhall Street Post Office, where I left my letters *poste restante*. Horatio – Mr Darvill – said that if I wrote to him at his work address, he'd never get to see my envelopes first, and the young clerks there would be sure to tease him about things.'

It was at this point that I was suddenly conscious of certain stertorous noises from Mycroft's corner – a wholly reprehensible lapse into poor manners, as it appeared to me.

'What else can you tell me about Mr Darvill?' asked Holmes quickly.

'He was very shy. He always preferred to walk out with me in the evening than in the daylight. "Retiring", perhaps, is the best word to describe him – even his voice. He'd had the quinsy as a young man, and was still having treatment for it. But the disability had left him with a weak larynx, and a sort of whispering fashion of speaking. His eyesight, too, was rather feeble – just as mine is – and he always wore tinted spectacles to protect his eyes against the glare of any bright light.'

Holmes nodded his understanding; and I began to sense a note of suppressed excitement in his voice.

'What next?'

'He called at the house the very evening on which Mr Wyndham next departed for France, and he proposed that we should marry before my stepfather returned. He was convinced that this would be our only chance; and he was so dreadfully in earnest that he made me swear, with my hand upon both Testaments, that whatever happened I would always be true and faithful to him.'

'Your mother was aware of what was taking place?'

'Oh, *yes*! And she approved so much. In a strange way, she was even fonder of my fiancé than I was myself, and she agreed that our only chance was to arrange a secret marriage.'

'The wedding was to be in church?'

'Last Friday, at St Saviour's, near King's Cross; and we were to go on to a wedding breakfast afterwards at the St Pancras Hotel. Horatio called a hansom for us, and put Mother and me into it before stepping himself into a four-wheeler which happened to be in the street. Mother and I got to St Saviour's first – it was only a few minutes' distance away. But when the four-wheeler drove up and we waited for him to step out – he never did, Mr Holmes! And when the cabman got down from the box and looked inside the carriage – *it was empty*.'

'You have neither seen nor heard of Mr Darvill since?'

'Nothing,' she whispered.

'You had planned a honeymoon, I suppose?'

'We had planned,' said Miss van Allen, biting her lip and scarce managing her reply, 'a fortnight's stay at the Royal Gleneagles in Inverness, and we were to have caught the lunchtime express from King's Cross.'

'It seems to me,' said Holmes, with some feeling, 'that you have been most shamefully treated, dear lady.'

But Miss van Allen would hear nothing against her loved one, and protested spiritedly: 'Oh, no, sir! He was far too good and kind to treat me so.'

'You own opinion, then,' said Holmes, 'is that some unforeseen accident or catastrophe has occurred?'

She nodded her agreement. 'And I think he must have had some premonition that very morning of possible danger, because he begged me then, once again, to remain true to him – whatever happened.'

'You have no idea what that danger may have been?'

'None.'

'How did your mother take this sudden disappearance?'

'She was naturally awfully worried at first. But then she became more and more angry; and she made me promise never to speak to her of the matter again.'

'And your stepfather?'

'He seemed – it was strange, really – rather more sympathetic than Mother. At least he was willing to discuss it.'

'And what was his opinion?'

'He agreed that some accident must have happened. As he said, Mr Darvill could have no possible interest in bringing me to the doors of St Saviour's – and then in deserting me there. If he had borrowed money – or if some of my money had already been settled on him – then there might have been some reason behind such a cruel action. But he was absolutely independent about money, and he would never even look at a sixpence of mine if we went on a visit. Oh, Mr Holmes! It is driving me half-mad to think of—' But the rest of the sentence was lost as the young lady sobbed quietly into her handkerchief.

When she had recovered her composure, Holmes rose from his chair, promising that he would consider the baffling facts she had put before him. 'But if I could offer you one piece of advice,' he added, as he held the lady's coat for her, 'it is that you allow Mr Horatio Darvill to vanish as completely from your memory as he vanished from his wedding-carriage.'

'Then you think that I shall not see him again?'

'I fear not. But please leave things in my hands. Now! I wish you to send me a most accurate physical description of Mr Darvill, as well as any of his letters which you feel you can spare.'

'We can at least expedite things a little in those two respects,' replied she in business-like fashion, 'for I advertised for him in last Monday's *Chronicle*.' And promptly reaching into her handbag, she produced a newspaper cutting which she gave to Holmes, together with some other sheets. 'And here, too, are four of his letters which I happen to have with me. Will they be sufficient?'

Holmes looked quickly at the letters, and nodded. 'You say you never had Mr Darvill's address?'

'Never.'

'Your stepfather's place of business, please?'

'He travels for Cook and Marchant, the great Burgundy importers, of Fenchurch Street.'

'Thank you.'

After she had left Holmes sat brooding for several minutes, his fingertips still pressed together. 'An interesting case,' he observed finally. 'Did you not find it so, Watson?'

'You appeared to read a good deal which was quite invisible to me,' I confessed.

'Not invisible, Watson. Rather, let us say – unnoticed. And that in spite of my repeated attempts to impress upon you the importance of sleeves, of thumb-nails, of boot-laces, and the rest. Now, tell me, what did you immediately gather from the young woman's appearance? Describe it to me.'

Conscious of Mycroft's presence, I sought to recall my closest impressions of our recent visitor.

'Well, she had, beneath her fur, a dress of rich brown, somewhat darker than the coffee colour, with a little black plush at the neck and at the sleeves – you mentioned sleeves, Holmes? Her gloves were dove-grey in colour, and were worn through at the right forefinger. Her black boots, I was not able, from where I sat, to observe in any detail, yet I would suggest that she takes either the size four and a half or five. She wore small pendant earrings, almost certainly of imitation gold, and the small handkerchief into which the poor lady sobbed so charmingly had a neat darn in the monogrammed corner. In general, she had the air of a reasonably well-to-do young woman who has not quite escaped from the slightly vulgar inheritance of a father who was – let us be honest about it, Holmes! – a plumber.'

A snort from the chair beside which Holmes had so casually thrown Miss van Allen's fur coat served to remind us that the recumbent Mycroft had now reawakened, and that perhaps my own description had, in some respect, occasioned his disapproval. But he made no spoken comment, and soon resumed his former posture.

''Pon my word, Watson,' said Holmes, 'you are coming along splendidly – is he not, Mycroft? It is true, of course, that your description misses almost everything of real importance. But the method! You have hit upon the *method*, Watson. Let us take, for example, the plush you mention on the sleeves. Now, plush is a most wonderfully helpful material for showing traces; and the double line above the wrist, where the typewritist presses against the table, was beautifully defined. As for the short-sightedness, that was mere child's play. The dent-marks of a *pince-nez* at either side of the lady's nostrils – you did not observe it? Elementary, my dear Watson! And then the boots. You really *must* practise the art of being positioned where all the evidence is clearly visible. If you wish to observe nothing at all, like brother Mycroft, then you will seek out the furthest corner of a room where even the vaguest examination of the client will be obscured by the furniture, by a fur coat, by whatever. But reverting to the lady's boots, I observed that although they were very like each other in colour and style, they were in fact *odd* boots; the one on the right foot having a slightly decorated toe-cap, and the one on the left being of a comparatively plain design. Furthermore, the right one was fastened only at the three lower buttons out of the five; the left one only at the first, third, and fifth. Now the deduction we may reasonably draw from such evidence is that the young lady left home in an unconscionable hurry. You agree?'

'Amazing, Holmes!'

'As for the glove worn at the forefinger—'

'You would be better advised,' suddenly interposed the deeper voice of Mycroft, 'to concentrate upon the missing person!'

May it have been a flash of annoyance that showed itself in Holmes's eye? If so, it was gone immediately. 'You are quite right, Mycroft! Come now, Watson, read to us the paragraph from *The Chronicle*.'

I held the printed slip to the light and began: 'Missing on the 14th November 188–. A gentleman named Mr Horatio Darvill: about 5′ 8″ in height; fairly firmly built; sallow complexion; black hair, just a little bald in the centre; bushy black side-whiskers and moustache; tinted spectacles; slight infirmity of speech. When last seen, was dressed in—'

'But I think,' interrupted Holmes, 'he may by now have changed his wedding vestments, Watson?'

'Oh, certainly, Holmes.'

There being nothing, it seemed, of further value in the newspaper description, Holmes turned his attention to the letters, passing them to me after studying them himself with minute concentration.

'Well?' he asked.

Apart from the fact that the letters had been typed, I could find in them nothing of interest, and I laid them down on the coffee-table in front of the somnolent Mycroft.

'Well?' persisted Holmes.

'I assume you refer to the fact that the letters are typewritten.'

'Already you are neglecting your newly acquired knowledge of the *method*, Watson. Quite apart from the point you mention, there are three further points of immediate interest and importance. First, the letters are very short; second, apart from the vague "Leadenhall Street" superscription, there is no precise address stated at any point; third, it is not only the body of the letter which has been typed, but the signature, too. Observe here, Watson – and here! – that neat little "Horatio Darvill" typed at the bottom of each of our four exhibits. And it will not have escaped you, I think, how conclusive that last point might be?'

'Conclusive, Holmes? In what way?'

'My dear fellow, is it possible for you not to see how strongly it bears upon our present investigations?'

'*Homo circumbendibus* – that's what you are, Sherlock!' (It was Mycroft once more.) 'Do you not appreciate that your client would prefer some positive action to any further proofs of your cerebral superiority?'

It is pleasing to report here that this attempt of Mycroft to provoke the most distinguished criminologist of the century proved largely ineffectual, and Holmes permitted himself a fraternal smile as his brother slowly bestirred his frame.

'You are right, Mycroft,' he rejoined lightly. 'And I shall immediately compose two letters: one to Messrs Cook and Marchant; the other to Mr Wyndham, asking that gentleman to meet us here at six o'clock tomorrow evening.'

Already I was aware of the easy and confident demeanour with which Holmes was tackling the singular mystery which confronted us all. But for the moment my attention was diverted by a small but most curious incident.

'It is just as well, Sherlock,' said Mycroft (who appeared now to be almost fully awakened), 'that you do not propose to write three letters.'

Seldom (let me admit it) have I seen my friend so perplexed: 'A *third* letter?'

'Indeed. But such a letter could have no certain destination, since it apparently slipped your memory to ask the young lady her present address, and the letters she entrusted to you appear, as I survey them, to be lacking their outer envelopes.'

Momentarily Holmes looked less than amused by this light-hearted intervention. 'You are more observant today than I thought, Mycroft, for the evidence of eye and ear had led me to entertain the suspicion that you were sleeping soundly during my recent conversation with Miss van Allen. But as regards her address, you are right.' And even as he spoke I noted the twinkle of mischievous intelligence in his eyes. 'Yet it would not be too difficult perhaps to *deduce* the young lady's address, Mycroft? On such a foul day as this it is dangerous and ill-advised for a lady to travel the streets if she has a perfectly acceptable and comfortable alternative such as the Underground; and since it was precisely 3.14 p.m. when Miss van Allen first appeared beneath my window, I would hazard the guess that she had caught the Metropolitan-line train which passes through Baker Street at 3.12 p.m. on its journey to Hammersmith. We may consider two further clues, also. The lady's boots, ill-assorted as they were, bore little evidence of the mud and mire of our London streets; and we may infer from this that her own home is perhaps as adjacent to an Underground station as is our own. More significant, however, is the fact, as we all observed, that Miss van Allen wore a dress of linen – a fabric which, though it is long-lasting and pleasing to wear, is one which has the disadvantage of creasing most easily. Now the skirt of the dress had been most recently ironed, and the slight creases in it must have resulted from her journey – to see me. And – I put this forward as conjecture, Mycroft – probably no more than three or four stops on the Underground had been involved. If we remember, too, the "few minutes" her wedding-carriage took from her home to St Saviour's, I think, perhaps . . . perhaps . . .' Holmes drew a street-map towards him, and surveyed his chosen area with his magnification-glass.

'I shall plump,' he said directly, 'for Cowcross Street myself – that shabbily genteel little thoroughfare which links Farringdon Road with St John Street.'

'Very impressive!' said Mycroft, anticipating my own admiration. 'And would you place her on the north, or the south side, of that thoroughfare, Sherlock?'

But before Holmes could reply to this small pleasantry, Mrs Hudson entered with a slip of paper which she handed to Holmes. 'The young lady says she forgot to give you her address, sir, and she's written it down for you.'

Holmes glanced quickly at the address and a glint of pride gleamed in his eyes. 'The answer to your question, Mycroft, is the south side – for it is an even-numbered house, and if I remember correctly the numbering of houses in that part of London invariably begins at the east end of the street with the odd numbers on the right-hand side walking westwards.'

'And the number is perhaps in the middle or late thirties?' suggested Mycroft. 'Thirty-six, perhaps? Or more likely thirty-eight?'

Holmes himself handed over the paper to us and we read:

Miss Charlotte van Allen
38, Cowcross Street

I was daily accustomed to exhibitions of the most extraordinary deductive logic employed by Sherlock Holmes, but I had begun at this point to suspect, in his brother Mycroft, the existence of some quite paranormal mental processes. It was only some half an hour later, when Holmes himself had strolled out for tobacco, that Mycroft, observing my continued astonishment, spoke quietly in my ear.

'If you keep your lips sealed, Dr Watson, I will tell you a small secret – albeit a very simple one. The good lady's coat was thrown rather carelessly, as you noticed, over the back of a chair; and on the inside of the lining was sewn a tape with her name and address clearly printed on it. Alas, however, my eyes are now not so keen as they were in my youth, and sixes and eights, as you know, are readily susceptible of confusion.'

I have never been accused, I trust, of undue levity, but I could not help laughing heartily at this coup on Mycroft's part, and I assured him that his brother should never hear the truth of it from me.

'Sherlock?' said Mycroft, raising his mighty eyebrows. 'He saw through my little joke immediately.'

It was not until past six o'clock the following evening that I returned to Baker Street after (it is not an irrelevant matter) a day of deep interest at St Thomas's Hospital.

'Well, have you solved the mystery yet?' I asked, as I entered the sitting-room.

Holmes I found curled up in his armchair, smoking his oily clay pipe, and discussing medieval madrigals with Mycroft.

'Yes, Watson, I believe—'

But hardly were the words from his mouth when we heard a heavy footfall in the passage and a sharp rap on the door.

'This will be the girl's stepfather,' said Holmes. 'He has written to say he would be here at a quarter after six. Come in!'

The man who entered was a sturdy, middle-sized fellow, about thirty years of age, clean-shaven, sallow-skinned, with a pair of most penetrating eyes. He placed his shiny top-hat on the sideboard, and with an insinuating bow sidled down into the nearest chair.

'I am assuming,' said Holmes, 'that you are Mr James Wyndham and' (holding up a typewritten sheet) 'that this is the letter you wrote to me?'

'I am that person, sir, and the letter is mine. It was against my expressed wish, as you may know, that Miss van Allen contacted you in this matter. But she is an excitable young lady, and my wife and I will be happy to forgive her for such an impulsive action. Yet I must ask you to have nothing more to do with what is, unfortunately, a not uncommon misfortune. It is clear what took place, and I think it highly unlikely, sir, that even you will find so much as a single trace of Mr Darvill.'

'On the contrary,' replied Holmes quietly, 'I have reason to believe that I have already discovered the whereabouts of that gentleman.'

Mr Wyndham gave a violent start, and dropped his gloves. 'I am delighted to hear it,' he said in a strained voice.

'It is a most curious fact,' continued Holmes, 'that a typewriter has just as much individuality as does handwriting. Even when completely new, no two machines are exactly alike; and as they get older, some characters wear on this side and some on that. Now in this letter of yours, Mr Wyndham, you will note that in every instance there is some slight slurring in the eye of the "e"; and a most easily detectable defect in the tail of the "t".'

'All our office correspondence,' interrupted our visitor, 'is typed on the same machine, and I can fully understand why it has become a little worn.'

'But I have four other letters here,' resumed Holmes, in a slow and menacing tone, 'which purport to come from Mr Horatio Darvill. And in each of these, also, the "e"s are slurred, and the "t"s un-tailed.'

Mr Wyndham was out of his chair instantly and had snatched up his hat: 'I can waste no more of my valuable time with such trivialities, Mr Holmes. If you can catch the man who so shamefully treated Miss van Allen, then catch him! I wish you well – and ask you to let me know the outcome. But I have no interest whatsoever in your fantastical notions.'

Already, however, Holmes had stepped across the room and turned the key in the door. 'Certainly I will tell you how I caught Mr Darvill, if you will but resume your chair.'

'What?' shouted Wyndham, his face white, his small eyes darting about him like those of a rat in a trap. Yet finally he sat down and glared aggressively around, as Holmes continued his analysis.

'It was as selfish and as heartless a trick as ever I encountered. The man married a woman much older than himself, largely for her money. In addition, he enjoyed the interest on the not inconsiderable sum of the stepdaughter's money, for as long as that daughter lived with them. The loss of such extra monies would have made a significant difference to the life-style adopted by the newly married pair. Now the daughter herself was an amiable, warm-hearted girl, and was possessed of considerable physical attractions; and with the added advantage of a personal income, it became clear that under normal circumstances she would not remain single for very long. So he – the man of whom I speak – decided to deny her the company and friendship of her contemporaries by keeping her at home. But she – and who shall blame her? – grew restive under such an unnatural regimen, and firmly announced her intention to attend a local ball. So what did her stepfather do? With the connivance of his wife, he conceived a cowardly plan. He disguised himself cleverly: he covered those sharp eyes with dully tinted spectacles; he masked that clean-shaven face with bushy side-whiskers; he sank that clear voice of his into the strained whisper of one suffering from the quinsy. And then, feeling himself doubly secure because of the young lady's short sight, he appeared *himself* at the ball, in the guise of one Horatio Darvill, and there he wooed the fair Miss van Allen for his own – thereafter taking further precautions of always arranging his assignations by candlelight.'

(I heard a deep groan which at the time I assumed to have come from our visitor, but which, upon reflection, I am inclined to think originated from Mycroft's corner.)

'Miss van Allen had fallen for her new beau; and no suspicion of deception ever entered her pretty head. She was flattered by the attention she was receiving, and the effect was heightened by the admiration of her mother for the man. An "engagement" was agreed, and the deception perpetuated. But the pretended journeys abroad were becoming more difficult to sustain, and things had to be brought to a head quickly, although in such a *dramatic* way as to leave a permanent impression upon the young girl's mind. Hence the vows of fidelity sworn on the Testaments; hence the dark hints repeated on the very morning of the proposed marriage that something sinister might be afoot. James Wyndham, you see, wished his stepdaughter to be so morally bound to her fictitious suitor that for a decade, at least, she would sit and wilt in Cowcross Street, and continue paying her regular interest directly into the account of her guardian: the same blackguard of a guardian who had brought her to the doors of St Saviour's and then, himself, conveniently disappeared by the age-old ruse of stepping in at one side of a four-wheeler – and out at the other.'

Rising to his feet, Wyndham fought hard to control his outrage. 'I wish you to know that it is you, sir, who is violating the law of this land – and not me! As long as you keep that door locked, and thereby hold me in this room against my will, you lay yourself open—'

'The law,' interrupted Holmes, suddenly unlocking and throwing open the door, 'may not for the moment be empowered to touch you. Yet never, surely, was there a man who deserved punishment more. In fact . . . since my hunting-crop is close at hand—' Holmes took two swift strides across the room; but it was too late. We heard a wild clatter of steps down the stairs as Wyndham departed, and then had the satisfaction of watching him flee pell-mell down Baker Street.

'That cold-blooded scoundrel will end on the gallows, mark my words!' growled Holmes.

'Even now, though, I cannot follow all the steps in your reasoning, Holmes,' I remarked.

'It is this way,' replied Holmes. 'The only person who profited financially from the vanishing-trick – was the stepfather. Then, the fact that the two men, Wyndham and Darvill, were never actually seen *together*, was most suggestive. As were the tinted spectacles, the husky voice, the bushy whiskers – all of these latter, Watson, hinting strongly at disguise. Again, the typewritten signature betokened one thing only – that the man's handwriting was so familiar to Miss van Allen that she might easily recognize even a small sample of it. Isolated facts? Yes! But all of them leading to the same inevitable conclusion – as even my slumbering sibling might agree?'

But there was no sound from the Mycroft corner.

'You were able to verify your conclusion?' I asked.

Holmes nodded briskly. 'We know the firm for which Wyndham worked, and we had a full description of Darvill. I therefore eliminated from that description everything which could be the result of deliberate disguise—'

'Which means that you have *not* verified your conclusion!' Mycroft's sudden interjection caused us both to turn sharply towards him.

'There will always,' rejoined Holmes, 'be a need and a place for informed conjecture—'

'*Inspired* conjecture, Holmes,' I interposed.

'Phooey!' snorted Mycroft. 'You are talking of nothing but wild *guesswork*, Sherlock. And it is my opinion that in this case your guesswork is grotesquely askew.'

I can only report that never have I seen Holmes so taken

aback; and he sat in silence as Mycroft raised his bulk from the chair and now stood beside the fireplace.

'Your deductive logic needs no plaudits from me, Sherlock, and like Dr Watson I admire your desperate hypothesis. But unless there is some firm evidence which you have thus far concealed from us . . ?'

Holmes did not break his silence.

'Well,' stated Mycroft, 'I will indulge in a little guesswork of my own, and tell you that the gentleman who just stormed out of this room is as innocent as Watson here!'

'He certainly did not *act* like an innocent man,' I protested, looking in vain to Holmes for some support, as Mycroft continued.

'The reasons you adduce for your suspicions are perfectly sound in most respects, and yet – I must speak with honesty, Sherlock! – I found myself sorely disappointed with your reading – or rather complete misreading – of the case. You are, I believe, wholly correct in your central thesis that there is no such person as Horatio Darvill.' (How the blood was tingling in my veins as Mycroft spoke these words!) 'But when the unfortunate Mr Wyndham who has just rushed one way up Baker Street rushes back down it the other with a writ for defamation of character – as I fear he will! – then you will be compelled to think, to analyse, and to act, with a little more care and circumspection.'

Holmes leaned forward, the sensitive nostrils of that aquiline nose a little distended. But still he made no comment.

'For example, Sherlock, two specific pieces of information vouchsafed to us by the attractive Miss van Allen herself have been strongly discounted, if not wholly ignored, in your analysis.' (I noticed Holmes' eyebrows rising quizzically.) 'First, the fact that Mr Wyndham was older than Miss van Allen *only by some five years*. Second, the fact that Miss van Allen is so competent and speedy a performer on the typewriter that she works, on a free-lance basis, for several firms in the vicinity of her home, including Messrs Cook and Marchant. Furthermore, you make the astonishing claim that Miss van Allen was totally deceived by the disguise of Mr Darvill. Indeed, you would have her not only blind, but semi-senile into the bargain! Now it is perfectly true that the lady's eyesight is far from perfect – *glaucopia Athenica*, would you not diagnose, Dr Watson? – but it is quite ludicrous to believe that she would fail to recognize the person with whom she was living. And it is wholly dishonest of you to assert that the assignations were always held by candlelight, since on at least two occasions, the morning after the first meeting – the *morning*, Sherlock! – and the morning of the planned wedding ceremony, Miss van Allen had ample opportunity of studying the physical features of Darvill in the broadest of daylight.'

'You seem to me to be taking an unconscionably long time in putting forward your own hypothesis,' snapped Holmes, somewhat testily.

'You are right,' admitted the other. 'Let me beat about the bush no longer! You have never felt emotion akin to love for any woman, Sherlock – not even for the Adler woman – and you are therefore deprived of the advantages of those who like myself are able to understand both the workings of the male and also the female mind. Five years her superior in age – her stepfather; *only five years*. Now one of the sadnesses of womankind is their tendency to age more quickly and less gracefully than men; and one of the truths about mankind in general is that if you put one of each sex, of roughly similar age, in reasonable proximity . . . and if one of them is the fair Miss van Allen – then you are inviting a packet of trouble. Yet such is what took place in the Wyndham ménage. Mrs Wyndham was seventeen years older than her young husband; and perhaps as time went by some signs and tokens of this disproportionate difference in their ages began to manifest themselves. At the same time, it may be assumed that Wyndham himself could not help being attracted – however much at first he sought to resist the temptation – by the very winsome and vivacious young girl who was his stepdaughter. It would almost certainly have been Wyndham himself who introduced Miss van Allen to the part-time duties she undertook for Cook and Marchant – where the two of them were frequently thrown together, away from the restraints of wife and home, and with a result which it is not at all difficult to guess. Certain it is, in my own view, that Wyndham sought to transfer his affections from the mother to the daughter; and in due course it was the daughter who decided that whatever her own affections might be in the matter she must in all honour leave her mother and stepfather. Hence the great anxiety to get out to dances and parties and the like – activities which Wyndham objected to for the obvious reason that he wished to have Miss van Allen as close by himself for as long as he possibly could. Now you, Sherlock, assume that this objection arose as a result of the interest accruing from the New Zealand securities – and you are *guessing*, are you not? Is it not just possible that Wyndham has money of his own – find out, Brother! – and that what he craves for is not some petty addition to his wealth, but the love of a young woman with whom he has fallen rather hopelessly in love? You see, she took *him* in, just as she took *you* in, Sherlock – for you swallowed everything that calculating little soul reported.'

'Really, this is outrageous!' I objected – but Holmes held up his hand, and bid me hear his brother out.

'What is clear, is that at some point when Wyndham was in France – and why did you not verify those dates spent abroad? I am sure Cook and Marchant would have provided them just as quickly as it furnished the wretched man's description – as I was saying, with Wyndham in France, mother and daughter found themselves in a little tête-à-tête one evening, during the course of which a whole basketful of dirty linen was laid bare, with the daughter bitterly disillusioned about the behaviour of her step-father, and the mother hurt and angry about her husband's infidelity. So, together, the pair of them devised a plan. Now, we both agree on one thing at least, Sherlock! There appears to be no evidence whatsoever for the independent existence of Horatio Darvill except for what we have heard from Miss van Allen's lips. Rightly, you drew our attention to the fact that the two men were never seen together. But, alas, having appreciated the *importance* of that clue, you completely misconceived its *significance. You* decided that there is no Darvill – because he is Wyndham. *I* have to tell you that there is no Darvill – *because he is the pure fabrication of the minds of Mrs Wyndham and her daughter.*'

Holmes was staring with some consternation at a pattern in the carpet, as Mycroft rounded off his extravagant and completely baseless conjectures.

'Letters were written – and incidentally I myself would have been far more cautious about those "e"s and "t"s: twin faults, as it happens, of my very own machine! But, as I say, letters were written – *but by Miss van Allen herself*; a wedding was arranged; a story concocted of a non-existent carriage into which there climbed a non-existent groom – and that was the end of the charade. Now, it was you, Sherlock, who rightly asked the key question: *cui bono*? And you concluded that the real beneficiary was Wyndham. But exactly the contrary is the case! It was the mother and daughter who intended to be the beneficiaries, for they hoped to rid themselves of the rather wearisome Mr Wyndham – but not before he had been compelled, by moral and social pressures, to make some handsome money-settlement upon the pair of them – especially perhaps upon the young girl who, as Dr Watson here points out, could well have done with some decent earrings and a new handkerchief. And the *social* pressure I mention, Sherlock, was designed – carefully and cleverly designed – to come from *you*. A cock-and-bull story is told to you by some wide-eyed young thing, a story so bestrewn with clues at almost every point that even Lestrade – given a week or two! – would probably have come up with a diagnosis identical with your own. And why do you think she came to you, and not to Lestrade, say? Because "Mr Sherlock Holmes is the greatest investigator the world has ever known" – and his judgements are second only to the Almighty's in their infallibility. For if you, Sherlock, believed Wyndham to be guilty – then Wyndham *was* guilty in the eyes of the whole world – the whole world except for one, that is.'

'Except for two,' I added quietly.

Mycroft Holmes turned his full attention towards me for the

first time, as though I had virtually been excluded from his previous audience. But I allowed him no opportunity of seeking the meaning of my words, as I addressed him forthwith.

'I asked Holmes a question when he presented his own analysis, sir. I will ask you the same: have you in any way verified your hypothesis? And if so, how?'

'The answer, Dr Watson, to the first part of your question is, in large measure, "yes". Mr Wyndham, in fact, has quite enough money to be in no way embarrassed by the withdrawal of Miss van Allen's comparatively minor contribution. As for the second part . . .' Mycroft hesitated awhile. 'I am not sure what my brother has told you, of the various offices I hold under the British Crown—'

It was Holmes who intervened – and impatiently so. 'Yes, yes, Mycroft! Let us all concede immediately that the, shall we say, "unofficial" sources to which you are privy have completely invalidated my own reconstruction of the case. So be it! Yet I would wish, if you allow, to make one or two observations upon your own rather faithful interpretation of events? It is, of course, with full justice that you accuse me of having no first-hand knowledge of what are called "the matters of the heart". Furthermore, you rightly draw attention to the difficulties Mr Wyndham would have experienced in deceiving his stepdaughter. Yet how you under-rate the power of disguise! And how, incidentally, you *over*-rate the intelligence of Lestrade! Even Dr Watson, I would suggest, has a brain considerably superior—'

For not a second longer could I restrain myself. 'Gentlemen!' I cried, 'you are both – *both* of you! – most tragically wrong.'

The two brothers stared at me as though I had taken leave of my senses.

'I think you should seek to explain yourself, Watson,' said Holmes sharply.

'A man,' I began, 'was proposing to go to Scotland for a fortnight with his newly married wife, and he had drawn out one hundred pounds in cash – no less! – from the Oxford Street branch of the Royal National Bank on the eve of his wedding. The man, however, was abducted after entering a four-wheeler on the very morning of his wedding-day, was brutally assaulted, and then robbed of all his money and personal effects – thereafter being dumped, virtually for dead, in a deserted alley in Stepney. Quite by chance he was discovered later that same evening, and taken to the Whitechapel Hospital. But it was only after several days that the man slowly began to recover his senses, and some patches of his memory – and also, gentlemen, his *voice*. For, you see, it was partly because the man was suffering so badly from what we medical men term suppurative tonsillitis – the quinsy, as it is commonly known – that he was transferred to St Thomas's where, as you know, Holmes, I am at present engaged in some research on that very subject, and where my own professional opinion was sought only this morning. Whilst reading through the man's hospital notes, I could see that the only clue to his identity was a tag on an item of his underclothing carrying the initials "H. D." You can imagine my excitement—'

'Humphry Davy, perhaps,' muttered Mycroft flippantly.

'Oh no!' I replied, with a smile. 'I persisted patiently with the poor man, and finally he was able to communicate to me the name of his bank. After that, if I may say so, Holmes, it was almost child's play to verify *my* hypothesis. I visited the bank, where I learned about the withdrawal of money for the honeymoon, and the manager himself accompanied me back to St Thomas's where he was able to view the patient and to provide quite unequivocal proof as to his identity. I have to inform you, therefore, that not only does Mr Horatio Darvill exist, gentlemen; he is at this precise moment lying in a private ward on the second floor of St Thomas's Hospital!'

For some little while a silence fell upon the room. Then I saw Holmes, who these last few minutes had been standing by the window, give a little start: 'Oh, no!' he groaned. And looking over his shoulder I saw, dimly beneath the fog-beshrouded lamplight, an animated Mr Wyndham talking to a legal-looking gentleman who stood beside him.

Snatching up his cape, Holmes made hurriedly for the door. 'Please tell Mr Wyndham, if you will, Watson, that I have already written a letter to him containing a complete recantation of my earlier charges, and offering him my profound apologies. For the present, I am leaving – by the back door.'

He was gone. And when, a minute later, Mrs Hudson announced that two angry-looking gentlemen had called asking to see Mr Holmes, I noticed Mycroft seemingly asleep once more in his corner armchair, a monograph on polyphonic plainchant open on his knee, and a smile of vague amusement on his large, intelligent face.

'Show the gentlemen in, please, Mrs Hudson!' I said – in such peremptory fashion that for a moment or two that good lady stared at me, almost as if she had mistaken my voice for that of Sherlock Holmes himself.

DICK FRANCIS

The Gift

WHEN the breakfast-time Astrojet from La Guardia was still twenty minutes short of Louisville, Fred Collyer took out a block of printed forms and began to write his expenses.

Cab fare to airport, fifteen dollars.

No matter that a neighbour, working out on Long Island, had given him a free ride door to door: a little imagination in the expense department earned him half as much again (untaxed as the *Manhattan Star* paid him for the facts he came up with every week in his Monday racing column).

Refreshments on Journey, he wrote. *Five dollars.*

Entertaining for the purpose of obtaining information, six dollars fifty.

To justify that little lot he ordered a second double bourbon from the air hostess and lifted it in a silent good luck gesture to a man sleeping across the aisle, the owner of a third-rate filly that had bucked her shins two weeks ago.

Another Kentucky Derby. His mind flickered like a scratched print of an old movie over the days ahead. The same old slog out to the barns in the mornings, the same endless raking-over of past form, searching for a hint of the future. The same inconclusive work-outs on the track, the same slanderous rumours, same gossip, same stupid jocks, same stupid trainers, shooting their goddam stupid mouths off.

The bright, burning enthusiasm which had carved out his syndicated by-line was long gone. The lift of the spirit to the big occasion, the flair for sensing a story where no one else did, the sharp instinct which sorted truth from camouflage, all these he had had. All had left him. In their place lay plains of boredom and perpetual cynical tiredness. Instead of exclusives he nowadays gave his paper rehashes of other turfwriters' ideas, and a couple of times recently he had failed to do even that.

He was forty-six.

He drank.

Back in his functional New York office the Sports Editor of the *Manhattan Star* pursed his lips over Fred Collyer's account of the Everglades at Hialeah and wondered if he had been wise to send him down as usual to the Derby.

That guy, he thought regretfully, was all washed up. Too bad. Too bad he couldn't stay off the liquor. No one could drink and write, not at one and the same time. Write first, drink after; sure. Drink to excess, to stupor, maybe. But *after*.

He thought that before long he would have to let Fred go, that probably he should have started looking around for a replacement that day months back when Fred first turned up in the office too fuddled to hit the right keys on his typewriter. But that bum had had everything, he thought. A true journalist's nose for a story, and a gift for putting it across so vividly that the words jumped right off the page and kicked you in the brain.

Nowadays all that was left was a reputation and an echo: the technique still marched shakily on, but the personality behind it was drowning.

The Sports Editor shook his head over the Hialeah clipping and laid it aside. Twice in the past six weeks Fred had been incapable of writing a story at all. Each time when he had not phoned through they had fudged up a column in the office and stuck the Collyer name on it, but two missed deadlines were one more than forgivable. Three, and it would be all over. The management were grumbling louder than ever over the inflated expense accounts, and if they found out that in return they had twice received only sodden silence, no amount of for-old-times-sake would save him.

I did warn him, thought the Sports Editor uneasily. I told him to be sure to turn in a good one this time. A sizzler, like he used to. I told him to make this Derby one of his greats.

*

Fred Collyer checked into the motel room the newspaper had reserved for him and sank three quick mid-morning stiffeners from the bottle he had brought along in his briefcase. He shoved the Sports Editor's warning to the back of his mind because he was still sure that drunk or sober he could outwrite any other commentator in the business, given a story that was worth the trouble. There just weren't any good stories around any more.

He took a taxi out to Churchill Downs. (*Cab fare, four dollars fifty*, he wrote on the way; and paid the driver two seventy-five.)

With three days to go to the Derby the racecourse looked clean, fresh, and expectant. Bright red tulips in tidy columns pointed their petals uniformly to the blue sky, and patches of green grass glowed like shampooed rugs. Without noticing them Fred Collyer took the elevator to the roof and trudged up the last windy steps to the huge glass-fronted press room which ran along the top of the stands. Inside, a few men sat at the rows of typewriters knocking out the next day's news, and a few more stood outside on the balcony actually watching the first race, but most were engaged on the day's serious business, which was chat.

Fred Collyer bought himself a can of beer at the simple bar and carried it over to his named place, exchanging Hi-yahs with the faces he saw on the circuit from Saratoga to Hollywood Park. Living on the move in hotels, and altogether rootless since Sylvie got fed up with his absence and his drinking and took the kids back to Mom in Nebraska, he looked upon racecourse press rooms as his only real home. He felt relaxed there, assured of respect. He was unaware that the admiration he had once inspired was slowly fading into tolerant pity.

He sat easily in his chair reading one of the day's duplicated news releases.

'Trainer Harbourne Cressie reports no heat in Pincer Movement's near fore after breezing four furlongs on the track this morning.'

'No truth in rumour that Salad Bowl was running a temperature last evening, insists veterinarian John Brewer on behalf of owner Mrs L. (Loretta) Hicks.'

Marvellous, he thought sarcastically. Negative news was no news, Derby runners included.

He stayed up in the press room all afternoon, drinking beer, discussing this, that and nothing with writers, photographers, publicists and radio newsmen, keeping an inattentive eye on the racing on the closed-circuit television, and occasionally going out on to the balcony to look down on the anthill crowd far beneath. There was no need to struggle around down there as he used to, he thought. No need to try to see people, to interview them privately. Everything and everyone of interest came up to the press room sometime, ladling out info in spoonfed dollops.

At the end of the day he accepted a ride back to town in a colleague's Hertz car (*cab fare, four dollars fifty*) and in the evening having laid substantial bourbon foundations in his own room before setting out he attended the annual dinner of the Turfwriters' Association. The throng in the big reception room was pleased enough to see him, and he moved among the assortment of pressmen, trainers, jockeys, breeders, owners, and wives and girlfriends like a fish in his own home pond. Automatically before dinner he put away four doubles on the rocks, and through the food and the lengthy speeches afterwards kept up a steady intake. At half after eleven, when he tried to leave the table, he couldn't control his legs.

It surprised him. Sitting down, he had not been aware of being drunk. His tongue still worked as well as most around him, and to himself his thoughts seemed perfectly well organized. But his legs buckled as he put his weight on them, and he returned to his seat with a thump. It was considerably later, when the huge room had almost emptied as the guests went home, that he managed to summon enough strength to stand up.

'Guess I took a skinful,' he murmured, smiling to himself in self-excuse.

Holding on to the backs of chairs and at intervals leaning against the wall, he weaved his way to the door. From there he blundered out into the passage and forward to the lobby, and from there, looking as if he were climbing imaginary steps, out into the night through the swinging glass doors.

The cool May evening air made things much worse. The earth seemed literally to be turning beneath his feet. He listed sideways into a half circle and instead of moving forwards towards the parked cars and waiting taxis, staggered head-on into the dark brick front of the wall flanking the entrance. The impact hurt him and confused him further. He put both his hands flat on the rough surface in front of him and laid his face on it, and couldn't work out where he was.

Marius Tollman and Piper Boles had not seen Fred Collyer leave ahead of them. They strolled together along the same route making the ordinary social phrases and gestures of people who had just come together by chance at the end of an evening, and gave no impression at all that they had been eyeing each other meaningfully across the room for hours, and thinking almost exclusively about the conversation which lay ahead.

In a country with legalized bookmaking Marius Tollman might have grown up a respectable law-abiding citizen. As it was, his natural aptitude and only talent had led him into a lifetime of quick footwork which would have done credit to Muhammad Ali. Through the simple expedient of standing bets for the future racing authorities while they were still young enough to be foolish, he remained unpersecuted by them once they reached status and power; and the one sort of winner old crafty Marius could spot better even than horses was the colt heading for the boardroom.

The two men went through the glass doors and stopped just outside with the light from the lobby shining full upon them. Marius never drew people into corners, believing it looked too suspicious.

'Did you get the boys to go along, then?' he asked, standing on his heels with his hands in his pockets and his paunch oozing over his belt.

Piper Boles slowly lit a cigarette, glanced around casually at the star dotted sky, and sucked comforting smoke into his lungs.

'Yeah,' he said.

'So who's elected?'

'Amberezzio.'

'No,' Marius protested. 'He's not good enough.'

Piper Boles drew deep on his cigarette. He was hungry. One eleven pounds to make tomorrow, and only a five-ounce steak in his belly. He resented fat people, particularly rich fat people. He was putting away his own small store of fat in real estate and growth bonds, but at thirty-eight the physical struggle was near to defeating him. He couldn't face many more years of starvation, finding it worse as his body aged. A sense of urgency had lately led him to consider ways of making a quick ten thousand that once he would have sneered at.

He said, 'He's straight. It'll have to be him.'

Marius thought it over, not liking it, but finally nodded.

'All right, then. Amberezzio.'

Piper Boles nodded, and prepared to move away. It didn't do for a jockey to be seen too long with Marius Tollman, not if he wanted to go on riding second string for the prestigious Somerset Farms, which he most assuredly did.

Marius saw the impulse and said smoothly, 'Did you give any thoughts to a diversion on Crinkle Cut?'

Piper Boles hesitated.

'It'll cost you,' he said.

'Sure,' Marius agreed easily. 'How about another thousand, on top?'

'Used bills. Half before.'

'Sure.'

Piper Boles shrugged off his conscience, tossed out the last of his integrity.

'OK,' he said, and sauntered away to his car as if all his nerves weren't stretched and screaming.

Fred Collyer had heard every word, and he knew, without having to look, that one of the voices was Marius Tollman's. Impossible for anyone long in the racing game not to recognize that wheezy Boston accent. He understood that Marius had been fixing up a swindle and also that a good little swindle would fill his column nicely. He thought fuzzily that it was necessary to know who Marius had been talking to, and that as the voices had been behind him he had better turn round and find out.

Time however was disjointed for him, and when he pushed himself off the wall and made an effort to focus in the right direction, both men had gone.

'Bastards,' he said aloud to the empty night, and another late homegoer, leaving the hotel, took him compassionately by the elbow and led him to a taxi. He made it safely back to his own room before he passed out.

Since leaving La Guardia that morning he had drunk six beers, four brandies, one double Scotch (by mistake), and nearly three fifths of bourbon.

He woke at eleven the next morning, and couldn't believe it. He stared at the bedside clock.

Eleven.

He had missed the barns and the whole morning merry-go-round on the track. A shiver chilled him at that first realization, but there was worse to come. When he tried to sit up the room whirled and his head thumped like a pile driver. When he stripped back the sheet he found he had been sleeping in bed fully clothed with his shoes on. When he tried to remember how he had returned the previous evening, he could not do so.

He tottered into the bathroom. His face looked back at him like a nightmare in the mirror, wrinkled and red-eyed, ten years older overnight. Hungover he had been any number of times, but this felt like no ordinary morning-after. A sense of irretrievable disaster hovered somewhere behind the acute physical misery of his head and stomach, but it was not until he had taken off his coat and shirt and pants, and scraped off his shoes, and lain down again weakly on the crumpled bed, that he discovered its nature.

Then he realized with a jolt that not only had he no recollection of the journey back to his motel, he could recall practically nothing of the entire evening. Snatches of conversation from the first hour came back to him, and he remembered sitting at table between a cross old writer from the *Baltimore Star* and an earnest woman breeder from Lexington, neither of whom he liked; but an uninterrupted blank started from half-way through the fried chicken.

He had heard of alcoholic blackouts, but supposed they only happened to alcoholics; and he, Fred Collyer, was not one of those. Of course, he would concede that he did drink a little. Well, a lot, then. But he could stop any time he liked. Naturally he could.

He lay on the bed and sweated, facing the stark thought that one blackout might lead to another, until blackouts gave way to pink panthers climbing the walls. The Sports Editor's warning came back with a bang, and for the first time, uncomfortably remembering the twice he had missed his column, he felt a shade of anxiety about his job. Within five minutes he had reassured himself that they would never fire Fred Collyer, but all the same he would for the paper's sake lay off the drink until after he had written his piece on the Derby. This resolve gave him a glowing feeling of selfless virtue, which at least helped him through the shivering fits and pulsating headaches of an extremely wretched day.

Out at Churchill Downs three other men were just as worried. Piper Boles kicked his horse forward into the starting stalls and worried about what George Highbury, the Somerset Farms' trainer, had said when he went to scale at two pounds over-weight. George Highbury thought himself superior to all jocks and spoke to them curtly, win or lose.

'Don't give me that crap,' he said to Boles' excuses. 'You went to the Turfwriters' dinner last night, what do you expect?'

Piper Boles looked bleakly back over his hungry evening with its single martini and said he'd had a session in the sweat box that morning.

Highbury scowled. 'You keep your fat ass away from the table tonight and tomorrow if you want to make Crinkle Cut in the Derby.'

Piper Boles badly needed to ride Crinkle Cut in the Derby. He nodded meekly to Highbury with downcast eyes, and swung unhappily into the saddle.

Instead of bracing him, the threat of losing the ride on Crinkle Cut took the edge off his concentration, so that he came out of the stalls slowly, streaked the first quarter too fast to reach third place, swung wide at the bend and lost his stride straightening out. He finished sixth. He was a totally experienced jockey of above-average ability. It was not one of his days.

On the grandstand Marius Tollman put down his raceglasses shaking his head and clicking his tongue. If Piper Boles couldn't ride a better race than that when he was supposed to be trying to win, what sort of a goddam hash would he make of losing on Crinkle Cut?

Marius thought about the ten thousand he was staking on Saturday's little caper. He had not yet decided whether to tip off certain guys in organized crime, in which case they would cover the stake at no risk to himself, or to gamble on the bigger profit of going it alone. He lowered his wheezy bulk on to his seat and worried about the ease with which a fixed race could unfix itself.

Blisters Schultz worried about the state of his trade, which was suffering a severe recession.

Blisters Schultz picked pockets for a living, and was fed up with credit cards. In the old days, when he'd learned the skill at his grandfather's knee, men carried their billfolds in their rear pants' pockets, neatly outlined for all the world to see. Nowadays all these smash and grab muggers had ruined the market: few people carried more than a handful of dollars around with them, and those that did tended to divide it into two portions, with the heavy dough hidden away beneath zips.

Fifty-three years Blisters had survived: forty-five of them by stealing. Several shortish sessions behind bars had been regarded as bad luck, but not as a good reason for not nicking the first wallet he saw when he got out. He had tried to go straight once, but he hadn't liked it: couldn't face the regular hours and the awful feeling of working. After six weeks he had left his well-paid job and gone back thankfully to insecurity. He felt happier stealing two dollars than earning ten.

For the best haul at racemeets you either had to spot the big wads before they were gambled away, or follow a big winner away from the pay-out window. In either case, it meant hanging around the pari-mutuel with your eyes open. The trouble was, too many racecourse cops had cottoned to this modus op, and were apt to stand around looking at people who were just standing there looking.

Blisters had had a bad week. The most promisingly fat wallet had proved, after half an hour's careful stalking, to contain little money but a lot in pornography. Blisters, having a weak sex drive, was disgusted on both counts.

For his first two days' labour he had only twenty-three dollars to show, and five of these he had found on a stairway. His meagre room in Louisville was costing him eight a night, and with transport and eating to take into account, he reckoned he'd have to clear three hundred to make the trip worthwhile.

Always an optimist, he brightened at the thought of Derby Day. The pickings would certainly be easier once the real crowd arrived.

Fred Collyer's private Prohibition lasted intact through Friday. Feeling better when he woke, he cabbed out to Churchill Downs at seven-thirty, writing his expenses on the way. They included many mythical items for the previous day, on the basis that it was better for the office not to know he had been paralytic on Wednesday night. He upped the inflated total a few more dollars: after all, bourbon was expensive, and he would be off the wagon by Sunday.

The initial shock of the blackout had worn off, because during his day in bed he had remembered bits and pieces which he was certain were later in time than the fried chicken. The journey from dinner to bed was still a blank, but the blank had stopped frightening him. At times he felt there was something vital about it he ought to remember, but he persuaded himself that if it had been really important, he wouldn't have forgotten.

Out by the barns the groups of pressmen had already formed round the trainers of the most fancied Derby runners. Fred Collyer sauntered to the outskirts of Harbourne Cressie, and his colleagues made room for him with no reference to his previous day's absence. It reassured him: whatever he had done on Wednesday night, it couldn't have been scandalous.

The notebooks were out. Harbourne Cressie, long practised and fond of publicity, paused between every sentence to give time for all to be written down.

'Pincer Movement ate well last evening and is calm and cool this a.m. On the book we should hold Salad Bowl, unless the track is sloppy by Saturday.'

Smiles all round. The sky blue, the forecast fair.

Fred Collyer listened without attention. He'd heard it all before. They'd all heard it all before. And who the hell cared?

In a rival group two barns away the trainer of Salad Bowl was saying his colt had the beating of Pincer Movement on the Hialeah form, and could run on any going, sloppy or not.

George Highbury attracted fewer newsmen, as he hadn't much to say about Crinkle Cut. The three-year-old had been beaten by both Pincer Movement and Salad Bowl on separate occasions, and was not expected to reverse things.

On Friday afternoon Fred Collyer spent his time up in the press room and manfully refused a couple of free beers. (*Entertaining various owners at track, twenty-two dollars*.)

Piper Boles rode a hard finish in the sixth race, lost by a short head, and almost passed out from hunger-induced weakness in the jocks' room afterwards. George Highbury, unaware of this, merely noted sourly that Boles had made the weight, and confirmed that he would ride Crinkle Cut on the morrow.

Various friends of Piper Boles, supporting him towards a daybed, asked anxiously in his ear whether tomorrow's scheme was still on. Piper Boles nodded. 'Sure,' he said faintly. 'All the way.'

Marius Tollman was relieved to see Boles riding better, but decided anyway to hedge his bet by letting the syndicate in on the action.

Blisters Schultz lifted two billfolds, containing respectively fourteen and twenty-two dollars. He lost ten of them backing a certainty in the last race.

Pincer Movement, Salad Bowl, and Crinkle Cut, guarded by uniformed men with guns at their waists, looked over the stable doors and with small quivers in their tuned-up muscles watched other horses go out to the track. All three could have chosen to go. All three knew well enough what the trumpet was sounding for, on the other side.

Saturday morning, fine and clear.

Crowds in their thousands converged on Churchill Downs. Eager, expectant, chattering, dressed in bright colours and buying mint juleps in takeaway souvenir glasses, they poured through the gates and over the in-field, reading the latest sports columns on Pincer Movement versus Salad Bowl, and dreaming of picking outsiders that came up at fifty to one.

Blisters Schultz had scraped together just enough to pay his motel bill, but self-esteem depended on better luck with the hoists. His small, lined face with its busy eyes wore a look near to desperation, and the long predatory fingers clenched and unclenched convulsively in his pockets.

Piper Boles, with one-twenty-six to do on Crinkle Cut, allowed himself an egg for breakfast and decided to buy property bonds with the five hundred in used notes which had been delivered by hand the previous evening, and with the gains (both legal and illegal) he should add to them that day. If he cleaned up safely that afternoon, he thought, there was no obvious reason why he shouldn't set up the same scheme again, even after he had retired from riding. He hardly noticed the shift in his mind from reluctant dishonesty to habitual fraud.

Marius Tollman spent the morning telephoning to various acquaintances, offering profit. His offers were accepted. Marius Tollman felt a load lift from his spirits and with a spring in his step took his two-sixty pounds down town a few blocks, where a careful gentleman counted out ten thousand dollars in untraceable notes. Marius Tollman gave him a receipt, properly signed. Business was business.

Fred Collyer wanted a drink. One, he thought, wouldn't hurt. It would pep him up a bit, put him on his toes. One little drink in the morning would certainly not stop him writing a punchy piece that evening. *The Star* couldn't possibly frown on just *one* drink before he went to the races, especially not as he had managed to keep clear of the bar the previous evening by going to bed at nine. His abstinence had involved a great effort of will: it would be right to reward such virtue with just one drink.

He had however finished on Wednesday night the bottle he had brought with him to Louisville. He fished out his wallet to check how much he had in it: fifty-three dollars, plenty after expenses to cover a fresh bottle for later as well as a quick one in the bar before he left.

He went downstairs. In the lobby however his colleague Clay Petrovitch again offered a free ride in his Hertz car to Churchill Downs, so he decided he could postpone his one drink for half an hour. He gave himself little mental pats on the back all the way to the racecourse.

Blisters Schultz, circulating among the clusters of people at the rear of the grandstand, saw Marius Tollman going by in the sunshine, leaning backwards to support the weight in front and wheezing audibly in the growing heat.

Blisters Schultz licked his lips. He knew the fat man by sight: knew that somewhere around that gross body might be stacked enough lolly to see him through the summer. Marius Tollman would never come to the Derby with empty pockets.

Two thoughts made Blisters hesitate as he slid like an eel in the fat man's wake. The first was that Tollman was too old a hand to let himself be robbed. The second, that he was known to have friends in organized places, and if Tollman was carrying organization money Blisters wasn't going to burn his fingers by stealing it, which was how he got his nickname in the first place.

Regretfully Blisters peeled off from the quarry, and returned to the throng in the comforting shadows under the grandstand.

At twelve seventeen he infiltrated a close-packed bunch of people waiting for an elevator.

At twelve eighteen he stole Fred Collyer's wallet.

Marius Tollman carried his money in cunning underarm pockets which he clamped to his sides in a crowd, for fear of pickpockets. When the time was due he would visit as many different selling windows as possible, inconspicuously distributing the stake. He would give Piper Boles almost half of the tickets (along with the second five hundred dollars in used notes), and keep the other half for himself.

A nice tidy little killing, he thought complacently. And no reason why he shouldn't set it up some time again.

He bought a mint julep and smiled kindly at a girl showing more bosom than bashfulness.

The sun stoked up the day. The preliminary contests rolled over one by one with waves of cheering, each hard ridden finish merely a sideshow attending on the big one, the Derby, the roses, the climax, the ninth race.

In the jocks' room Piper Boles had changed into the silks for Crinkle Cut and began to sweat. The nearer he came to the race the more he wished it was an ordinary Derby day like any other. He steadied his nerves by reading the *Financial Times*.

Fred Collyer discovered the loss of his wallet upstairs in the press room when he tried to pay for a beer. He cursed, searched all his pockets, turned the press room upside down, got the keys of the Hertz car from Clay Petrovitch, and trailed all the way back to the car park. After a fruitless search there he strode furiously back to the grandstands, violently throttling in his mind the lousy stinking son of a bitch who had stolen his money. He guessed it had been an old hand, an old man, even. The new vicious lot relied on muscle, not skill.

His practical problems were not too great. He needed little cash. Clay Petrovitch was taking him back to town, the motel bill was going direct to the *Manhattan Star*, and his plane ticket was safely lying on the chest of drawers in his bedroom. He could borrow twenty bucks or so, maybe, from Clay or others in the press room, to cover essentials.

Going up in the elevator he thought that the loss of his money was like a sign from heaven; no money, no drink.

Blisters Schultz kept Fred Collyer sober the whole afternoon.

Pincer Movement, Salad Bowl, and Crinkle Cut were led from their barns, into the tunnel under the cars and crowds, and out again on to the track in front of the grandstands. They walked loosely, casually, used to the limelight but knowing from experience that this was only a foretaste. The first sight of the day's prices galvanized the crowds towards the pari-mutuel window like shoals of multicoloured fish.

Piper Boles walked out with the other jockeys towards the wire-meshed enclosure where horses, trainers and owners stood in a group in each stall. He had begun to suffer from a feeling of detachment and unreality: he could not believe that he, a basically honest jockey, was about to make a hash of the Kentucky Derby.

George Highbury repeated for about the fortieth time the tactics they had agreed on. Piper Boles nodded seriously, as if he had every intention of carrying them out. He actually heard scarcely a word; and he was deaf also to the massed bands and the singing when the Derby runners were led out to the track. 'My Old Kentucky Home' swelled the emotions of a multitude and brought out a flutter of eye-wiping handkerchiefs, but in Piper Boles they raised not a blink.

Through the parade, the canter down, the circling round, and even into the starting stalls, the detachment persisted. Only then, with the tension showing plain on the faces of the other riders, did he click back to realization. His heart-rate nearly doubled and energy flooded into his brain.

Now, he thought. It is now, in the next half-minute, that I earn myself one thousand dollars; and after that, the rest.

He pulled down his goggles and gathered his reins and his whip. He had Pincer Movement on his right and Salad Bowl on his left, and when the stalls sprang open he went out between them in a rush, tipping his weight instantly forward over the withers and standing in the stirrups with his head almost as far forward as Crinkle Cut's.

All along past the stands the first time he concentrated on staying in the centre of the main bunch, as unnoticeable as possible, and round the top bend he was still there, sitting quiet and doing nothing very much. But down the backstretch, lying about tenth in a field of twenty-six, he earned his thousand.

No one except Piper Boles ever knew what really happened; only he knew that he'd shortened his left rein with a sharp turn of his wrist and squeezed Crinkle Cut's ribs with his right foot. The fast-galloping horse obeyed these directions, veered abruptly left, and crashed into the horse beside him.

The horse beside him was still Salad Bowl. Under the impact Salad Bowl cannoned into the horse on his own left, rocked back, stumbled, lost his footing entirely, and fell. The two horses on his tail fell over him.

Piper Boles didn't look back. The swerve and collision had lost him several places which Crinkle Cut at the best of times would have been unable to make up. He rode the rest of the race strictly according to instructions, finishing flat out in twelfth place.

Of the one hundred and forty thousand spectators at Churchill Downs, only a handful had had a clear view of the disaster on the far side of the track. The buildings in the in-field, and the milling crowds filling all its furthest areas, had hidden the crash from nearly all standing at ground level and from most on the grandstands. Only the press, high up, had seen. They sent out urgent fact-finders and buzzed like a stirred-up beehive.

Fred Collyer, out on the balcony, watched the photographers running to immortalize Pincer Movement and reflected sourly that none of them would have taken close-up pictures of the second favourite, Salad Bowl, down on the dirt. He watched the horseshoe of dark red roses being draped over the winner and the triumphal presentation of the trophies, and then went inside for the re-run of the race on television. They showed the Salad

Bowl incident forwards, backwards and sideways, and then jerked it through slowly in a series of stills.

'See that,' said Clay Petrovitch, pointing at the screen over Fred Collyer's shoulder. 'It was Crinkle Cut caused it. You can see him crash into Salad Bowl . . . there! . . . Crinkle Cut, that's the joker in the pack.'

Fred Collyer strolled over to his place, sat down, and stared at his typewriter. Crinkle Cut. He knew something about Crinkle Cut. He thought intensely for five minutes, but he couldn't remember what he knew.

Details and quotes came up to the press room. All fallen jocks shaken but unhurt, all horses ditto; stewards in a tizzy, making instant enquiries and re-running the patrol-camera film over and over. Suspension for Piper Boles considered unlikely, as blind eye usually turned to rough riding in the Derby. Piper Boles had gone on record as saying 'Crinkle Cut just suddenly swerved. I didn't expect it, and couldn't prevent him bumping Salad Bowl.' Large numbers of people believed him.

Fred Collyer thought he might as well get a few pars down on paper: it would bring the first drink nearer, and boy how he needed that drink. With an ear open for fresher information he tapped out a blow-by-blow I-was-there account of an incident he had hardly seen. When he began to read it through, he saw that the first words he had written were 'The diversion on Crinkle Cut stole the post-race scene . . .'

Diversion on Crinkle Cut? He hadn't meant to write that . . . or not exactly. He frowned. And there were other words in his mind, just as stupid. He put his hands back on the keys and tapped them out.

'It'll cost you . . . a thousand in used notes . . . half before.'

He stared at what he had written. He had made it up, he must have. Or dreamt it. One or the other.

A dream. That was it. He remembered. He had had a dream about two men planning a fixed race, and one of them had been Marius Tollman, wheezing away about a diversion on Crinkle Cut.

Fred Collyer relaxed and smiled at the thought, and the next minute knew quite suddenly that it hadn't been a dream at all. He had heard Marius Tollman and Piper Boles planning a diversion on Crinkle Cut, and he had forgotten because he'd been drunk. Well, he reassured himself uneasily, no harm done, he had remembered now, hadn't he?

No he hadn't. If Crinkle Cut was a diversion, what was he a diversion *from*? Perhaps if he waited a bit, he would find he knew that too.

Blisters Schultz spent Fred Collyer's money on two hot dogs, one mint julep, and five losing bets. On the winning side, he had harvested three more billfolds and a woman's purse: total haul, ninety-four bucks. Gloomily he decided to call it a day and not come back next year.

Marius Tollman lumbered busily from window to window of the pari-mutuel and the stewards asked to see the jockeys involved in the Salad Bowl pile-up.

The crowds, hot, tired, and frayed at the edges, began to leave in the yellowing sunshine. The bands marched away. The stalls which sold souvenirs packed up their wares. Pincer Movement had his picture taken for the thousandth time and the runners for the tenth, last, and least interesting race of the day walked over from the barns.

Piper Boles was waiting outside the stewards' room for a summons inside, but Marius Tollman used the highest class messengers, and the package he entrusted was safely delivered. Piper Boles nodded, slipped it into his pocket, and gave the stewards a performance worthy of Hollywood.

Fred Collyer put his head in his hands, trying to remember. A drink, he thought, might help. Diversion. Crinkle Cut. Amberezzio.

He sat up sharply. *Amberezzio*. And what the hell did that mean? *It has to be Amberezzio*.

'Clay,' he said, leaning back over his chair. 'Do you know of a horse called Amberezzio?'

Clay Petrovitch shook his bald head. 'Never heard of it.'

Fred Collyer called to several others through the hub-bub, 'Know of a horse called Amberezzio?' And finally he got an answer. 'Amberezzio isn't a horse, he's an apprentice.'

'*It has to be Amberezzio. He's straight.*'

Fred Collyer knocked his chair over as he stood up. They had already called one minute to post time on the last race.

'Lend me twenty bucks, there's a pal,' he said to Clay.

Clay, knowing about the lost wallet, amiably agreed and slowly began to bring out his money.

'Hurry, for Chrissake,' Fred Collyer said urgently.

'OK, OK.' He handed over the twenty dollars and turned back to his own typewriter.

Fred Collyer grabbed his racecard and pushed through the post-Derby chatter to the pari-mutuel window further along the press room. He flipped the pages . . . Tenth race, Homeward Bound, claiming race, eight runners . . . His eye skimmed down the list, and found what he sought.

Phillip Amberezzio, riding a horse Fred Collyer had never heard of.

'Twenty on the nose, number six,' he said quickly, and received his ticket seconds before the window shut. Trembling slightly, he pushed back through the crowd, and out on to the balcony. He was the only pressman watching the race.

Those jocks did it beautifully, he thought in admiration. Artistic. You wouldn't have known if you hadn't known. They bunched him in and shepherded him along, and then at the perfect moment gave him a suddenly clear opening. Amberezzio won by half a length, with all the others waving their whips as if beating the last inch out of their mounts.

Fred Collyer laughed. That poor little so-and-so probably thought he was a hell of a fellow, bringing home a complete outsider with all the big boys baying at his heels.

He went back inside the press room and found everyone's attention directed towards Harbourne Cressie, who had brought with him the owner and jockey of Pincer Movement. Fred Collyer dutifully took down enough quotes to cover the subject, but his mind was on the other story, the big one, the gift.

It would need careful handling, he thought. It would need the very best he could do, as he would have to be careful not to make direct accusations while leaving it perfectly clear that an investigation was necessary. His old instincts partially re-awoke. He was even excited. He would write his piece in the quiet and privacy of his own room in the motel. Couldn't do it here on the racecourse, with every turfwriter in the world looking over his shoulder.

Down in the jockeys' changing room Piper Boles quietly distributed the pari-mutuel tickets which Marius Tollman had delivered: five hundred dollars' worth to each of the seven 'unsuccessful' riders in the tenth race, and one thousand dollars worth to himself. Each jockey subsequently asked a wife or girlfriend to collect the winnings and several of these would have made easy prey for Blisters Schultz, had he not already started home.

Marius Tollman's money had shortened the odds on Amberezzio, but he was still returned at twelve to one. Marius Tollman wheezed and puffed from pay-out window to pay-out window, collecting his winnings bit by bit. He hadn't room for all the cash in the underarm pockets and finally stowed some casually in more accessible spots. Too bad about Blisters Schultz.

Fred Collyer collected a fistful of winnings and repaid the twenty to Clay Petrovitch.

'If you had a hot tip, you might have passed it on,' grumbled Petrovitch, thinking of all the expenses old Fred would undoubtedly claim for his free rides to the racecourse.

'It wasn't a tip, just a hunch.' He couldn't tell Clay what the hunch was, as he wrote for a rival paper. 'I'll buy you a drink on the way home.'

'I should damn well think so.'

Fred Collyer immediately regretted his offer, which had been instinctive. He remembered that he had not intended to drink until after he had written. Still, perhaps one . . . And he did need a drink very badly. It seemed a century since his last, on Wednesday night.

They left together, walking out with the remains of the crowd. The racecourse looked battered and bedraggled at the end of the day: the scarlet petals of the tulips lay on the ground, leaving rows of naked pistils sticking forlornly up, and the bright rugs of grass were dusty grey and covered with litter. Fred Collyer thought only of the dough in his pocket and the story in his head, and both of them gave him a nice warm glow.

A drink to celebrate, he thought. Buy Clay a thank-you drink, and maybe perhaps just one more to celebrate. It wasn't often, after all, that things fell his way so miraculously.

They stopped for the drink. The first double swept through Fred Collyer's veins like fire through a parched forest. The second made him feel great.

'Time to go,' he said to Clay. 'I've got my piece to write.'

'Just one more,' Clay said. 'This one's on me.'

'Better not.' He felt virtuous.

'Oh come on,' Clay said, and ordered. With the faintest of misgivings Fred Collyer sank his third: but couldn't he still outwrite every racing man in the business? Of course he could.

They left after the third. Fred Collyer bought a fifth of bourbon for later, when he had finished his story. Back in his own room he took just the merest swig from it before he sat down to write.

The words wouldn't come. He screwed up six attempts and poured some bourbon into a tooth glass.

Marius Tollman, Crinkle Cut, Piper Boles, Amberezzio . . . It wasn't all that simple.

He took a drink. He didn't seem to be able to help it.

The Sports Editor would give him a raise for a story like this, or at least there would be no more quibbling about expenses.

He took a drink.

Piper Boles had earned himself a thousand bucks for crashing into Salad Bowl. Now how the hell did you write that without being sued for libel?

He took a drink.

The jockeys in the tenth race had conspired together to let

the only straight one among them win. How in hell could you say that?

He took a drink.

The stewards and the press had had all their attention channelled towards the crash in the Derby and had virtually ignored the tenth race. The stewards wouldn't thank him for pointing it out.

He took another drink. And another. And more.

His deadline for telephoning his story to the office was ten o'clock the following morning. When that hour struck he was asleep and snoring, fully dressed, on his bed. The empty bourbon bottle lay on the floor beside him, and his winnings, which he had tried to count, lay scattered over his chest.

JONATHAN GASH

The Julian Mondays

ELSA CHATTERTON'S mother had always accused her of misjudgement. Maybe Mother was right, because here Elsa was in Mrs Fairchild's grand Rolls-Royce, having to smile and make polite agreement all the way to London. And a calamitous misjudgement it was, the week after her fifty-fourth birthday. The offer of a lift was a makepeace on Mrs Fairchild's part; acceptance was Elsa's bit.

Normally she forgave herself all manner of errors, to keep intact the façade so necessary to a woman ensconced in village society. Like the particularly detestable error of allowing herself to be passed over for chairwoman of the Women's Guild two days previously – in favour of Mrs Fairchild. Elsa's condign get-out after that nasty business had been the weight which Squire Fairchild's name still carried in rural East Anglia. Her own husband Joseph's accidental death had fetched a fortune in industrial compensation and made her very comfortably off, thank you, but a deceased builder's reputation exercised no influence among the guild's wheeler-dealing cliques. No, this new misjudgement was different. No mental tricks to regain self-esteem here, for her own supporters in the guild would see this joint journey as sucking up to the new chairwoman. Needless to say, Mrs Fairchild knew all Elsa's reasons for a London trip, and gave it to her straight, as doubtless she said to her particular cronies.

'It's really not to be wondered at, Elsa,' she said as Thornton gentled the huge crimson motor through Brentwood. 'Joanne's going to that secretarial college was the catalyst, meeting people her own age.'

Catalyst, Elsa thought as she nodded and smiled. Another nowadays word. Not so terrible as that unspoken word *young*, though, for it was young Joanne who last Saturday steeled herself and broke the news that she was giving up Elsa's spare cottage and moving almost immediately to the Midlands.

For all her misjudgements, Elsa was never afraid of calamity; even calamity fell into its appointed square. But it was the end of those coffee Mondays in St Edmundsbury with Joanne, friendly listens to the BBC concert hour on her tenant's complicated wireless, the good-night sherry at half-past nine. What was Mrs Fairchild saying now, for heaven's sake? The horrid woman actually *knew* what estate agent she used, sheer insolence.

'. . . have no difficulty letting the cottage, Elsa. So rural.'

Miles from anywhere, Elsa angrily translated, saying, 'It isn't the money so much as having somebody in it.' There had been two break-ins recently, everybody said the Eldridge boy on account of his narrow eyes.

'And selling is so tiresome, probably people one doesn't know.'

Sell? Not to you, madam. Elsa remembered her husband's warning about the cottage and its patch: Squire Fairchild would give his eye teeth to buy it, to round off his estate.

'This journey *is* a treat,' she said brightly. The cottage was the last of Joseph's embryonic building schemes. She would see the Fairchilds to their grave with their rounding-off problems. 'How absolutely marvellous to do it every week. An excursion.'

Mrs Fairchild's glance was pleasant but oddly interrogative, seeing she must have got the point. 'Yes, well. As long as the traffic is light. Some Mondays are absolute hell, especially in winter. Thornton says it's to do with football.' The guild had agreed to change its meetings to Wednesdays because the new chairwoman Had Business on Mondays, never back before eight o'clock. The vote had been carried *nem con*. Elsa's clique believed it was only Harrods shopping and a hairdo; others said the Fairchilds owned a retail emporium. Thornton, who surely must know, was a Horkesley man and never spoke to Beckholt people.

For the rest of the journey they spoke of guild membership. 'Membership is influence,' Mrs Fairchild said several times, 'influence and achievement all in one.' Elsa remembered that tiresome deluge of details from Joanne. The new job came studded with scores of those nasty little two-worders which made Joanne's eyes glow (no, glitter): pension schemes, luncheon vouchers, inpaced increments, mortgage undercuts or whatever they were, quite ghastly. Listening to Mrs Fairchild's strength-through-joy membership sentences, Elsa mentally recorded her most recent misjudgement: young Joanne had endured an older woman for as long as it suited. Now Joanne had let her down, exposed the cottage as a needless extravagance vulnerable to the acquisitive Fairchilds. Joanne's betrayal had practically forced her into this tiresome journey, when you thought it out. Misjudgements everywhere.

The Rolls dropped her at St Giles, a bowshot from Oxford Street. Elsa was pleased by the looks that crimson elegance earned her, but less than happy at the more studied appraisals, as women with their slick minds priced her shoes, coat, handbag; she'd always found that irritating.

Travelling by tube was a treat. London pace, with its jaunty rockings and acceleration tugging your face. She brightened in the next hour among the crowds, straightened up her lordosis and decided to Live Through Posture (a guild lecture of three weeks gone) and move with alacrity. She brightened Mr Long's day through a rather difficult interview which tax came into quite needlessly – didn't she have Mr Jameson with his trustworthy tartan tie in Frinton? – and left him beaming his opaque smile after her down the stairs and out. Joseph would be looking down from Above, approving. At one fell swoop (she held the cliché in mind as a deliberate fiddlesticks to Joanne's dumb-belled words) she had solved all. Mr Long would immediately let the cottage, and satisfy the village's sense of thrift. Mrs Squire Fairchild's hints to sell would become ridiculous. Joseph could be smugly justified on his cloud, his scheme intact. With the cottage let, Joanne's letters would be forwarded most satisfyingly by a new tenant's hand, one in her eye, and the guild would realize it had passed up a superb organizer for a bossy meddler who'd changed the meeting day without so much as a by-your-leave.

In celebration Elsa spent some of this hectic Monday in the National Gallery, a nice walk, and then the Strand to look at the theatre posters. She was so thrilled when later, among the crowds in the Portrait Gallery, a clock chimed three. Three! In the afternoon! No wonder she felt shaky and even a little clammy in the press. She'd had nothing since breakfast.

However, still determinedly Living Through Posture, she decided to walk back through Soho to Tottenham Court Road and find some nice place for tea.

By now the pedestrians were tiring her. More pushchairs made for her ankles as she walked. There seemed more foreigners, all of them burly, all carless hurriers. Increasingly she found she had to halt, step aside. Indeed, once she was almost bundled off the pavement and only saved herself by a whisker. She felt hot and leant against a newspaper shop window for a moment, letting the crowds rush on by. The guild had lately had a lecture on hypoglycaemia. Sugar, a rest, a cup of tea, keep calm; there was a long list of remedies to be administered quick as you like or you toppled over or something; unthinkable, a disgrace. She drew breath and moved on.

The first three or four tea-likely places were mere sandwich bars with impossible stools and mounds of pâté in stone bowls. She counted the pavement's cracks – in childhood church one counted to prevent faints when kneeling on cold mornings. Walking with meticulous care she moved among the wretched Greek alphabets and shops selling suspect magazines, past the corner pub where the old street market flourished like some mad burgeoning garden. When she found the right place she was overwarm despite the bothersome wind. That it was unfortunately situated between a window display of impossible underclothing and a betting shop had to be ignored. Misjudgement again if you like, but the still interior was a haven. A dapper girl was at the counter within the curtained doorway. She wore a black tie over a lacy blouse, an expensive Laura Ashley; Elsa approved of the long sleeves. She welcomed Elsa with a remark about the blustery weather and let Elsa find a table. Elsa sank at the nearest with a shiver of gratitude.

Booths along one wall made the café seem long and thin. The lighting was unobtrusive. The ceiling mirrors could be called odd and the bamboo curtains possibly foreign, yet the two men at the serving counter were smiley. She observed with surprise that a fire was lit in the reassuringly rustic kitchen range which occupied the tearoom's far end. The tranquillity was spoiled by the brief anxiety about how to order. Did highly spirited waitresses lurk, giggling inanely as usual, behind the brick pillars? Fenestrated screens separated each booth, a mercy; Joseph would have tapped and found the mahogany genuine.

A few other customers chatted quietly, mostly ladies in ones and twos. She decided she must stop feeling so alone. Joanne's departure was now water under the bridge.

Then Julian slid into her booth, took a seat opposite, and the world changed.

Julian was slightly auburn, say twenty-five. His bright jacket was good Harris tweed, and the pale shirt with russet in his tie was a good mix. Later, she was to go over and over this encounter, who smiled first, said what. Definitely, she could recall Julian apologizing, something about did she mind, her being there first and everything. He meant sharing the table. Her own immortal response could have been the misjudgement of all time, but luckily he didn't seem to notice her absurd, 'Well, no,' though he made a token half-rise to go.

Refusal would have been cruel anyway as well as socially impossible. He'd obviously hastened from somewhere, maybe even raced against time. Why?

'Not at all,' she finally said. This would never happen in Jacklin's in the High Street, but mercifully this was only London. It would have been the subject of animated speculation, maybe become a permanent joke. The Day When That Total Stranger Sat At Mrs Chatterton's Table . . .

'Thanks so much.' He touched her hand, fingers so swiftly

withdrawn it was surely reflex gratitude. 'Only, you know what mothers are.'

His mother? He was possibly late. He described her – grey, stout, bespectacled, dark fur coat, torn leather handbag – and asked if she'd noticed such a lady. Elsa felt pleasure at the description. She herself was none of those things, still managed without glasses except for reading, was only just grey-touched, easily coped with. Through his winning smile he explained he was in trouble with his parents, who had very decided views, and ended, 'Do you think it's fair?'

'Well, how could I . . . ?' she was saying when one of the counter youths arrived to take their orders. Inevitably they became jumbled, one pot instead of two singles, so all Elsa could think was what if his mother arrived with her stern outlooks to find her son in the company of . . . Oh, God. She herself had somehow become the Total Stranger in the scenario, when it was really him. Her thoughts were all frayed ends, not a moment's rest in which to unravel and reknit.

Her alarm was stupid, for he was so charmingly hesitant about everything, even the milk, that they finished up laughing and having a mock battle over the biscuits. His chance remark about the cost of travel these days let her in easily and kept them going, cost of living, food, heavens the way fares have shot up and all that. Which led into his problem, to take a good job in banking or remain living in hopes as a writer. A gradual relief changed her Day-When-That-Total-Stranger guilt into pleasure. Only because this meeting was a fluke – could it be called that without making her out something unpleasant? – did she ignore her flustered inner self and chat on. Accidentally he disclosed his name. Julian suited him.

'That's what comes of being Scorpio,' he said with a comic face.

'I'm Scorpio, too!' she put in, surprised. They laughed a lot over his amused disbelief. She had to show him the Scorpio gemstone ring as proof that honestly she was Scorpio, no really, but even then he was unsure. She could tell. He held her hand to look the better at the turret-mounted aquamarine, hardly touching.

'You'll be saying we're neighbours next,' he joked. Fortunately – well, fortunate for her credibility – he lived in North London. They compared London with East Anglia, scores of differences, before she noticed the time and they had to part; wrong word of course: separate, go, leave. She found herself saying she occasionally dropped in on Mondays, because this tea house was still one of the reliable places hereabouts, and kept control when he said with obvious pleasure that he'd look out for her. With luck they'd meet again. They bickered over the bill; he lost and pretended anger. It actually eased things. It's difficult enough splitting a bill with another woman, let alone a man, especially with all the tip business. It was then that he asked her name. She glowed that he'd had to ask outright, though that was probably stupid of her in this day and age.

His last remark, half serious, gave her food for thought all the way home from Liverpool Street Station.

'I'll expect superb career advice next week, Elsa,' he said. 'Wrong of me to burden a new friend, but—'

'Not burden,' she cried. 'A career's a career, for Heaven's sake!'

They left the café together, and she did not look back. The implications of his words, so natural, left her mind roaring.

The following day was the oddest she'd ever experienced. She hardly noticed that Joanne had in fact left a goodbye note. She never could afterwards remember what it had said. Normally quite methodical, she began two letters and completed neither. She forgot to ring her friend in Polstead, Dora who always kept in touch. She missed the library van, got the time wrong for the lifeboats collection and had to send a neighbour's lad round with her contribution. Hopeless. Yet she buzzed, found herself singing along with the radio, some absurd country-style singer she hadn't a hope of enjoying. It was all quite silly.

To put it all in context, careers really were a problem. Look at Bernard's lad, shillyshallying over which college and barely eighteen. Of course, Julian's parents were utterly wrong to persuade him into banking when he was a born writer, with his artist's gentle hands. (Writers *were* artists, weren't they? She strove to remember a guild brains trust which had featured similar questions.) Parents shouldn't be so insistent. It was Julian's life, not theirs.

On Thursday morning she telephoned Mr Long. He would be pleased to discuss the cottage again, certainly. Monday morning was convenient, say noon? All arranged, a note in her handbag diary, so she'd have to go.

Curiously, during that Monday's journey in on the train, a number of new problems occurred to Elsa. For instance, what was Julian's present occupation? What was his last name? Would she recognize it, or had he not yet published? Why did he live in Muswell Hill, London, instead of with his opinionated parents? Did that mean – heavens – he was married? This last notion caused only the briefest flurry. No; any wife worth her salt would see off an intrusive mother-in-law. She herself had had bother with Joseph's bossy mother and knew.

London that second Monday was ridiculously over-crowded. She didn't care. Mr Long's preoccupation with the details of the cottage caused him to go into lengthy analyses of sales potentials, property redevelopment plans, such absurdities. She could not wait to get away. Guessing the time, she entered the Café Phryne and was hardly seated before Julian arrived. His transparent delight warmed her face, she felt it, and their hands reached each other's in genuine gladness.

He'd thought of her so often; he actually said so. That got them off to a fine start, and apart from a slight hesitation on her part when they ordered together they were into chatter and both – she couldn't get over it – so positively glad. As the hour went along, it transpired that Julian was working 'doing the money side' for a couple of small businesses actually here in Soho, to make ends meet. Needless to say those wretched parents, never far away it seemed, disapproved. How *blind*.

'Writing's in your blood or it isn't,' Julian explained. 'But banking's reliable. I was smothered at home so I got a place. It's lonely, but . . .'

'But it felt right?'

'That's it. All my writing needs is time.'

Of course she had to ask about his flat, a ghastly one-room affair with practically shared everything and him charged the earth. And the hours he had to put in at his part-time job!

'Being nice to everybody's a problem,' he confided at one point. 'Not that I don't like people. It's just that the women – most Soho restaurants are run by ladies; didn't you know? – are so practical-minded.' They expected him to be on hand almost continuously to do their sordid little accounts. He was delightfully good about the whole sorry business, not blaming anybody in the slightest and laughingly trying to deflect her attention from his plight, but she got it all out of him: impossible hours, a pittance, having to be smarmy to an endless stream of customers. Elsa knew how bitchy women could be when they had the upper hand; you hadn't to look further than dear Mrs Chairwoman Fairchild. She couldn't let him settle the bill after that, even though he protested. She could be quite firm when she wanted.

Going home that second Julian Monday she was mad with herself for mishandling their parting, so angry in fact that it worried her. He'd been reluctant to walk with her, having to get back to those people's wretched accounts, poor man, and she'd not had the wit to ask what he planned for later in the day. He might have suggested supper or something. However, he'd agreed to postpone the banking job decision to next Monday, which was certainly wise. They would then reconsider, three o'clock, so that was all right, but clearly her misjudgement was out marauding again. It needed serious watching.

The third Julian Monday went superbly. Julian, they decided together over a complicated layered apple cake, should reject banking. He would just have to face whatever parental wrath was going. They could lump it, Elsa told herself with satisfaction. Serve them right for interfering.

The fourth Julian Monday was a mixture. She invited him to dinner at Wheeler's. They met, and he outlined a lovely romantic novel he was planning; he gave her a telephone number. She phoned, late, from the public phone by platform nine while waiting for the ten-thirty train. It was an answering machine frightening her with Julian's recorded voice. She dropped the receiver, left no message.

The week stretched itself out with problems of its own. Mr Long was being tiresome, asking what exactly were Mrs Chatterton's intentions about the cottage please? Three potential rentals she'd spurned; two would-be buyers were ignored. Mrs Fairchild had called twice, pointedly remarking on the cottage's emptiness; vandals would soon be at it. Elsa placated everyone.

On the fifth Monday, it happened. Approaching from Brewer Street, Elsa saw the crimson Rolls edging away from the kerb near the Café Phryne. *Mrs Fairchild was entering the place* as if she owned it, bold as brass. Elsa almost staggered from astonishment, but had the presence of mind to turn aside. Thornton was at the wheel as the Rolls went in the underground car park. He didn't see her. She hung about for an hour, hoping to catch Julian, but must have missed him.

Agitation at this impossible coincidence compelled her to walk right past the curtained entrance, hoping that perhaps Julian had arrived early and she'd possibly be able to attract his attention somehow. Common sense finally calmed her. She went to a dingy café opposite the car park entrance, and at four-thirty saw the Rolls leave. Easy to watch it pick up Mrs Fairchild, and wait until it glided away. Courageously she went in to her usual booth table and ordered tea as though nothing had happened. Julian, a little dispirited this time, joined her after five minutes. He had been delayed by an accounts problem of exceptional difficulty.

It was during their conversation this fifth Monday that the penny dropped. Mrs Fairchild, it was widely known, had Business Interests in London – and Elsa had seen her enter this very café *as if she owned it*! And here was Julian looking *worn*, delayed by an accounting problem. All this was observed fact. The conclusion was inescapable: the squire's wife was one of the bitches who made Julian work so hard for starvation wages, and him possibly the new Charles Dickens. And that was the woman who'd done her out of the guild chair, and who wanted to get her hands on her Joseph's cottage! Her mind cooled to precision. She would make an instantaneous test.

'Julian,' she said, smiling. 'You're tired. All this work you're doing. Why don't we meet somewhere else for a change? The park, if it's fine—'

'I wish I could,' he said wistfully, poor lamb. 'But I have to phone in every so often, you see. There are sometimes urgent . . . bookings.'

'Is this one of the places where you do the accounts?' She came right out with it.

Julian gave an incredulous half laugh, recovered, then admitted it. 'Yes.' He hung his head. 'Here.'

'And the . . . owner is unkind?'

'It's that, a bit,' he said. 'And being so nice to all the owner's friends. They seem to think that because they own a place and pay you, you have to entertain anybody they send.'

'Free teas?' Elsa's shrewdness was certainly on form.

'Queening it over the waiters, making you an absolute slave.'

That Julian was trapped in his job called for all her sympathy. That he was trapped there by Mrs Fairchild called for decisive action. Why, even having afternoon tea at the Café Phryne was pouring money into the wretched woman's purse! The whole thing was intolerable. That evening she returned home wondering all the way how resolute she could become, a woman raised to believe infallibly in her own misjudgement.

Two days later, the Wednesday guild meeting was disturbed by a serious debate. A friend of Elsa's, Mrs Mullet from the shop, proposed that the guild's weekly meeting be moved back to Mondays. Mrs Fairchild was forced to concede a vote. Her vigorous defence kept the count in favour of no change, twenty to eleven, but there was a new mood, remembering the earlier *nem con* settlement.

All that night Elsa didn't sleep. Mrs Fairchild had shown real anger, even, one might think, distress during the discussion. Now Elsa knew one thing: her addiction to her Monday London jaunts was not on account of mere business. Women could be irritated, puzzled, baffled, angered, all those things, by commerce. But distress and anguish had showed through Mrs Fairchild's arguments. In fact, one or two questioning glances had been exchanged at the extent of the chairwoman's relief after the vote. Throughout the meeting Elsa kept remembering poor Julian's tiredness, his efforts to seem as buoyant as ever, once that cow had left in her showy motor. If a poor wage-slave had to be 'nice' to the owner's friends to keep his job, how 'nice' would he have to be to the owner herself? Mrs Fairchild must own the Café Phryne, and with it Julian.

She lay awake and listened to the birds come alive in the garden. In one way, there could be no risk of misjudgement in the matter. After all, Mrs Fairchild had suggested the lift to London – nay, pressed her. And dropped her near Soho. The straightest street through there simply happens to be Old Compton Street. The Café Phryne lay on the route. The car park Thornton used was a mere forty yards off. Inevitable, you could say. Right from the beginning it had been out of Elsa's hands entirely. Any misjudgement could be laid at the door of whoever had designed the entire scheme. She herself was free of all blame, no matter what the outcome.

There were questions to be asked, though. In particular, one: How far, dear Chairwoman Fairchild, cottage covetess, fascist oppressor, have you gone? Stating the question gave Elsa an odd confidence. By ten o'clock that morning she had decided.

By four o'clock, she had completed the letter, though that was easier said than done.

Anonymity didn't mean the letter was a poison pen, not really, for those were nasty, hideously underhand. No, this letter was a simple warning. Indeed, not even a warning; more guidance, a suggestion that Mrs Fairchild simply mend her ways. The clippings were glued with that common white gum typists used. Elsa had worn household gloves, carefully wetted the stamp with tap water in case they could trace a lick (these days anything was possible), and slipped the letter in the town's busy main post office. She deposited scissors and glue, in a plastic bag also free of her finger prints, into the bus depot's sordid dustbins.

Your double life in Soho will soon be revealed, she had compiled, *in letters and photographs sent to every East Anglian newspaper.* That was all. She'd considered adding some cant repent-ye phrase as diversion (they'd assume it was from a religious crank) but decided against it. Succinct, terse, direct. No mention of the Café Phryne, Julian, anything. Knowing Mrs Fairchild as she did, the letter would be burnt instantly. She would be compelled to put her business up for sale. Mr Long could handle its purchase, though he might be difficult about a country widow buying a Soho café. With a great sense of satisfaction Elsa sat and awaited results.

The first was that Mrs Fairchild killed herself. That is to say, fair's fair, she died in a mercifully swift accident driving her husband's Mini into a motorway bridge upright one evening. Great speed, no skid, and eventually not much of an inquest.

Secondly, Julian and the Café Phryne seemed astonishingly unaffected. Since the accident had occurred on a Friday, Elsa on her Monday visit expected the place to be shut and the sensitive Julian overcome by news of the tragedy, but no. She questioned him as closely as she was able, without even hinting about any recent sad calamity, but it appeared he was fixed in his plight – a creative genius, short on money. He seemed unaware of anything untoward.

'I've an idea, dear,' she said, skating as close to revelation as she dared. 'What if somebody else bought the business, from . . . the present owner. Would that be possible?'

'No, love.' He was so wistful, as he took her hand quite openly. 'Soho's so strict. Fixed licences, you see. Non-transferable. And look at the customers, darling. I had to countersign the lease. I'm a fixture, you see.'

Thrilled at the terms of endearment, she did as he said, surreptitiously inspected the other customers. She recognized one or two regular visitors. All were ladies, well-to-do. For the first time she began dimly to understand. The two men at the counter were not always the same. Sometimes one would actually sit with a customer, talk, light her cigarette. When that happened a replacement waiter would quietly appear within minutes, quite casual. The girl receptionist on the door never came into the tearooms. She seemed to have a separate entrance.

Elsa looked at Julian. He was untroubled, a natural you might say, in his element. She already knew he had to give advice to selected lady customers. He'd told her as much. Since advice on business matters had to be confidential, a special suite of rooms upstairs was provided. 'It's more or less usual round here,' he'd explained. 'Not the sort of . . . service you could supply in the open restaurant. Confidential. Risks of causing scandal, you see. There's always somebody willing to jump to the wrong conclusions. That's why the entire place is so gloomy, so intimate. It's also why we'd rather everybody came on fixed appointments.'

It was quite some time before Elsa spoke. 'What happens if somebody comes in by chance, simply for a snack?'

'This booth's left empty for them.' He was smiling, smoothing her hand. 'Of course, we hope she'll quite like the place, find something in it to her liking.' He gave her his look. 'And come again.'

The most suitable question took even longer this time. 'Do . . . customers sometimes, well, stay?'

'Clients, darling; we say clients because it's more professional. Yes, but very rarely. Would you like to see an apartment? We have two residentials, plus the temporary suites.'

'Are you allowed to show me? I'd hate you to get in trouble.'

He made a joke of it: 'For you, sweetheart, anything!' and ushered her the length of the tearoom into a plush foyer with carpeted stairs and two lifts. Music played, oil paintings gleamed as if burnished on the panelled walls. It was elegance at its most discreet. Greekish music softened the ride to the third floor, where discretion ruled in silence.

The apartments were unnumbered; Elsa took particular notice of the door.

'We vestibule the entrance,' Julian explained rather mysteriously, showing her in via a double porch. Seclusion, she supposed. An expert interior designer had expanded the lounge with clever wall furnishings. Other than that it was only marginally more gracious than her own cottage, which she had attended to herself. A relief, in a way. She had as much magic as they, and along the same lines.

'Who was the designer?' she asked, moving, apparently pleased, through the suite and pretending to admire the chintzy bedroom's pinkdom.

'Well, me, actually.'

'Aren't you wonderful!' she cried.

'It's what I'd really like to do full time,' Julian conceded wistfully.

She thought, as well as writing, banking, commercial counselling, café managing, and having regular appointments holding hands?

'Are the rates expensive?' she asked this interior decorator.

'In the hourly suites, or the apartments?'

'Both,' she said, and compared the sums he mentioned with those of a good London hotel. Say, half as much again as the Savoy's current rate. It could have been worse. And she'd come too far now to quibble.

'I'd quite like to stay here permanently,' Julian said, doing his wistful bit, which Elsa began to see might prove intensely irritating if it was allowed to continue unchecked. 'Save travelling.'

'And rent.' She added, when he looked surprised, 'You could hardly be charged rent here, since you do so much for them.'

'True.' Julian was wistful no longer.

'Plus there'd be the need to get away occasionally.' She closed the bedroom door firmly. 'Imagine living on top of the job night in, night out.'

'There is that.' He paused at the vestibule entrance. 'Do you have anything in mind, darling?'

'I have a quite idyllic cottage I want decorated.' She indicated her readiness and obediently he opened the door. 'It's beautifully situated. Once it's done you might like to use it, say once a week, as escape from all this.'

He murmured, 'What a marvellous idea!'

It seemed natural not to discuss things further until they went through into the tearoom. Julian agreed when Elsa told him to come and look at the cottage the following Monday – he was suddenly less tied down on Mondays – and again nodded when she instructed him to itemize his travel expenses and let her have the bill.

Someone less sure of her own sense of judgement than Elsa Chatterton would have been unnerved by the coincidence of Mrs Fairchild's funeral and Julian's first visit to the cottage. She felt she had to pay respects, she explained to her friends from the guild, which was the reason she'd dropped her nephew, Julian, at the cottage before hurrying on to St Mary's just in time before the coffin arrived. Afterwards she ferried Julian in her new Rover and gave him lunch at her own home. She was rather good at lunches, and driving him openly through the village was one way of reducing speculative gossip.

'The arrangement is that you will be my nephew, dear,' she told him when they were comfortable on the sofa afterwards. 'You are a struggling writer, after all. I'm helping you by letting you have that cottage rent free.'

'Darling,' Julian said doubtfully. 'The payment for my attendance has to be booked, back at the London end of things. It's too boring, I know, but that's how it operates.'

'Of course, dear.' She smiled, and went over the details. 'The payment *is* the cottage. You will have the deeds once you have made, paid, five hundred visits, staying overnight of course because it's a tiring journey. It's secluded. Eventually you will possess a highly valuable property which is appreciating every single minute. You come out and rest, once a week, from your hard work in London. You understand?'

He understood. 'Couldn't I have the deeds now, darling, and enjoy your company just as much?'

'You could, dear,' she said with the same sweet in-spite-of-myself smile with which she had recently accepted the guild chair. 'Except one has to guard against accidents. I'd hate there to be any fuss. I mean, we've lately had an example in this very village. A lady, not at all old, was driving along and accidentally . . .'

The arrival of a struggling romance writer was a nine-day wonder in the village. Being a barmy Londoner, he'd instantly ripped out the cottage interior, decorated so nicely by his auntie Elsa, and had it done up in mad fashionable colours, and landscaped its garden and acreage into an absolute mess. Mrs Chatterton kept house for him on his frequent visits, so anxious was she for his welfare, staying there and doing his washing, seeing he was fed with proper country food instead of that London muck. Mind you, the guild women said wisely to each other, the worry and responsibility of catering for her nephew actually seemed to be doing Elsa good. It'd given her something to do, made her feel needed, because she'd been at a loose end ever since her Joseph went. She'd blossomed. It did a woman good to feel properly used, so to speak. And that young Julian knew when he was on to a good thing, because his visits had become ever so much more frequent. At first, he'd only come out on Mondays. Now it was Mondays, Wednesdays, and Saturdays, six-eighteen train regular as clockwork.

The village was pleased and really rather proud to think that the countryside still had something even London did not possess.

MICHAEL GILBERT

The Jackal and the Tiger

ON THE evening of 15 April 1944, Colonel Hubert of Military Intelligence said to the Director of Public Prosecutions, 'The only mistake Karl made was to underestimate young Ronnie Kavanagh.'

That afternoon, Karl Muller, who sometimes called himself Charles Miller, had been shot in the underground rifle-range at the Tower of London, which was the place being used at that time for the execution of German spies.

'A fatal mistake,' agreed the Director.

Jim Perrot, late of the Military Police, wrote to his friend, Fred Denniston:

> Dear Denny,
> Do you remember those plans we talked over so often in North Africa and Italy? Well, I've got an option on a twenty-one-year lease of a nice first-floor office in Chancery Lane. That's bang in the middle of legal London, where the legal eagles are beginning to flap their wings and sharpen their claws again. Lots of work for an enquiry agency and not much competition – as yet. The lease is a snip. I've commuted my pension and got me a bit of capital. I reckon we'll have to put in about £2,000 each to get going. 'Denny's Detectives'! How about it?

And Denny's Detectives had turned out to be a success from the start.

As Perrot had said, there was no lack of work. Much of it was divorce work, the sad by-product of a long war. It was in connection with this branch of their activities, which neither of the partners liked, that they acquired Mr Huffin. He was perfectly equipped for the role he had to play. He was small, mild-looking, and so insignificant that many businessmen, departing to alleged conferences in the Midlands, had failed to recognize the little man who travelled in the train with them and occupied a table in an obscure corner of their hotel dining-room, until he stood up in court and swore to tell the truth, the whole truth, and nothing but the truth about the lady who had shared the businessman's table and later his bedroom.

Jim Perrot's job was the tracing of elusive debtors. His experience as a policeman was useful to him here. Fred Denniston, for his part, rarely left the office. His speciality was estimating the credit-worthiness of companies. He gradually became expert at reading between the lines of optimistic profit-and-loss accounts and precariously balanced balance sheets. He developed, with experience, a quite uncanny instinct for overvalued stocks and underdepreciated assets. Perrot would sometimes see him holding a suspect document delicately between his fingers and sniffing at it, as though he could detect by smell alone the odour of falsification.

One factor that helped them to show a steady profit was their absurdly small rent. When Perrot had described the lease as a 'snip' he was not exaggerating. At the end of the war, when no one was bothered about inflation, twenty-one-year leases could be had without the periodical reviews which are commonplace today. As the end of their lease approached, the partners did become aware that they were paying a good deal less than the market rent. Indeed, they could hardly help being aware of it. Their landlords, the Scotus Property Company, commented on it with increasing bitterness.

'It's no good complaining about it,' said Perrot genially. 'You should have thought about that when you granted the lease.'

'Just you wait till the end of the next year,' said Scotus.

Denniston said, 'I suppose we shall have to pay a bit more. Anyway, they can't turn us out. We're protected tenants.'

When a friendly valuer from the other end of Chancery Lane

learnt what their rent was, he struggled to control his feelings. 'I suppose you realize,' he said, 'that you're paying a pound a square foot?'

'Just about what I made it,' said Denniston.

'And that the going rate in this area is between five and six pounds?'

'You mean,' said Perrot, 'that when our lease comes to an end we'll have to pay five times the present rent?'

'Oh, at least that,' said the valuer cheerfully. 'But I imagine you've been putting aside a fund to meet it.'

The partners looked at each other. They were well aware that they had been doing nothing of the sort.

That was the first shock.

The second was Perrot's death. He had been putting on weight and smoking too much, but had looked healthy enough. One afternoon he complained of not feeling well, went home early, and died that night.

Denniston had been fond of him, and his first feelings were of personal loss. His next feeling was that he was going to need another partner and additional capital, and that fairly quickly.

He considered, and rejected, the idea of inviting Mr Huffin to become a partner. The main drawback was that he disliked him. And he was so totally negative. He crept into the office every morning on the stroke of nine and, unless he had some outside business, stayed in his room, which had been partitioned off from Denniston's, until half-past five. The partition was so thin that he could hear him every time he got up from his chair.

'Not partner material,' said Denniston to himself.

He tried advertising, but soon found that the limited number of applicants who had capital would have been unsuitable as partners, while the rather greater number, who might have been acceptable as partners, had no capital.

After some months of fruitless effort, he realized two other things. The first was that they were losing business. Jim Perrot's clients were taking their affairs elsewhere. The second was that the day of reckoning with his landlords was looming.

It was at this point that Andrew Gurney turned up. Denniston liked him at sight. He was young. He was cheerful. He seemed anxious to learn the business. And he made a proposal.

In about a year's time, when he attained the ripe old age of twenty-five, he would be coming into a bit of capital under a family trust. By that time he would have a fair idea whether the business suited him and he suited them. All being well, he was prepared to invest that capital in the firm.

They discussed amounts and dates, and came to a tentative agreement. Gurney took over Perrot's old room. Denniston breathed a sigh of relief and turned his mind to the analysis of a complex set of group accounts.

It was almost exactly a month later when Mr Huffin knocked on his door, put his head round, blinked twice, and said, 'If you're not too busy, I wonder if I might have a word with you?'

'I'm doing nothing that can't wait,' replied Denniston.

Mr Huffin slid into the room, advanced towards the desk, and then, as if changing his mind at the last moment, seated himself in the chair that was normally reserved for clients.

Denniston was conscious of a slight feeling of surprise. Previously when Mr Huffin had come to see him, he had stood in front of the desk and had waited, if the discussion was likely to be lengthy, for an invitation to sit down.

He was even more surprised when Mr Huffin spoke. He said, 'You're in trouble, aren't you?'

It was not only that Mr Huffin had omitted the 'sir' which he had previously used when addressing his employer. It was more than that. There was something sharp and cold in the tone of his voice. It was like the sudden unexpected chill which announces the end of autumn and the beginning of winter.

'You haven't seen fit to take me into your confidence,' Mr Huffin continued, 'but the wall between our offices is so thin that it's impossible for me not to hear every word that's said.'

Denniston had recovered himself sufficiently to say, 'The fact that you can overhear confidential matters doesn't entitle you to trade on them.'

'When the ship's sinking,' said Mr Huffin, 'etiquette has to go by the board.'

This was followed by a silence which Denniston found it difficult to break. In the end he said, 'It's true that Mr Perrot's death has left us in a difficult position. But, as it happens, I have been able to make arrangements which should tide us over.'

'You mean young Gurney? In the month he's been here he's earned less than half what you pay him. And speaking personally, I should have said that he's got no real aptitude for the work. What you need is someone without such nice manners, but with a thicker skin.'

Denniston said, 'Look here, Mr Huffin—' and stopped. He was on the point of saying, 'If you don't like the way I run this firm, we can do without you.'

But could they?

As though reading his thoughts Mr Huffin said, 'In the old days, Mr Perrot, you and I earned roughly equal amounts. Recently the proportions have been slipping. Last year I brought in half our fees. At least those were the figures you gave our auditor, so I assume they're correct.'

'You listened to that discussion also?'

'I felt I was an interested party.'

Mr Denniston said, 'All right. I accept that your services have been valuable. If that's your point, you've made it. I imagine it's leading up to something else. You want an increase in salary?'

'Not really.'

'Then perhaps you had it in mind that I should make you a partner?'

'Not exactly—'

'Then . . ?'

'My proposal was that I should take over the firm.'

In the long silence that followed, Denniston found himself revising his opinion of Mr Huffin. His surface meekness was, he realized, a piece of professional camouflage; as meaningless as the wigs of the barristers or the pin-striped trousers of the solicitors.

Mr Huffin continued, 'Have you thought out what would happen if I did leave? Maybe you could make enough to cover expenses. Until your lease expires. But what then? Have you, I wonder, overlooked one point? At the conclusion of a twenty-one-year lease, there is bound to be a heavy bill for dilapidations.'

'Dilapidations?' Denniston repeated slowly. The five syllables chimed together in an ominous chord. 'Surely there's nothing much to do?'

'I took the precaution of having a word with an old friend, a Mr Ellen. He's one of the surveyors used by the Scotus Property Company. He's a leading expert in his field and his calculations are very rarely challenged by the court. Last weekend I arranged for him to make an inspection. He thought that the cost of carrying out all the necessary work, in a first-class fashion, would be between six thousand pounds and eight thousand pounds.'

'For God's sake!' said Denniston. 'It can't be.'

'He showed me the breakdown. It could be more.'

To give himself time to think, Denniston said very slowly, 'If you have such a poor opinion of the prospects of the firm, why would you want to buy me out?'

'I'm sorry,' said Mr Huffin gently. 'You've misunderstood me. I wasn't proposing to pay you anything. After all, what have you got to sell?'

It was not Denniston's habit to discuss business with his wife. But this was a crisis. He poured out the whole matter to her as soon as he got home that evening.

'And I know damned well what he'll do,' he said. 'As soon as he's got me out, he'll bring in some accomplice of his own. They won't stick to divorce work. That's legal at least. The real money's in dirty work. Finding useful witnesses and bribing them to say what your client wants. Faking evidence. Fudging expert reports.'

'He seemed to be prepared to pay eight thousand pounds for the privilege of doing it,' his wife replied.

'Of course he won't. That's a put-up job between him and his old pal Mr Ellen of Scotus. He'll pay a lot less and be allowed to pay it in easy instalments.'

'What happens if you say no?'

'I'd have to challenge the dilapidations. It'd mean going to court and that's expensive.'

'If you used some of Gurney's money—' Mrs Denniston stopped.

They were both straightforward people. Denniston put what she was thinking into words: 'I can't take that boy's money and put it into a legal wrangle.'

'And there's no other way of raising it?'

'None that I can think of.'

'Then that's that,' said his wife. 'I'd say, cut your losses and clear out. We're still solvent. We'll think of something to do.'

It took a lot of talk to persuade him, but in the end he saw the force of her arguments. 'All right,' he said. 'No sense in dragging it out. I'll go in tomorrow and tell Huffin he can have the firm. I'll also tell him what I think of him.'

'It won't do any good.'

'It'll do me a lot of good.'

On the following evening he arrived back on the stroke of six. He kissed his wife and said to her, 'Whatever you were thinking of cooking for supper, think again. We're going out to find the best dinner London can provide. We'll drink champagne before it, Burgundy with it, and brandy after it.'

His wife, who had spent the day worrying about how they were going to survive, said, 'Really Fred. Do you think we ought—'

'Certainly we ought. We're celebrating.'

'Celebrating what?'

'A miracle!'

It had happened at nine o'clock that morning. Whilst Denniston was polishing up the precise terms in which he intended to say goodbye to Mr Huffin, his secretary came into his room. She was looking ruffled. She said, 'Could you be free to see Mr Kavanagh at ten?'

Denniston looked at his diary and said, 'Yes. That'll be all right. Who is Mr Kavanagh?'

'Mr Ronald Kavanagh,' said his secretary. As he was still

looking blank she added, 'Kavanagh Lewisohn and Fitch. He's the chairman.'

'Good God! How do you know that?' Denniston enquired.

'Before I came here, I worked in their head office.'

'Do you know Mr Kavanagh?'

'I was in the typing pool. I caught a glimpse of him twice in the three years I was there.'

'Did he say what he wanted?'

'He wanted to see you.'

'You're sure he didn't ask me to go and see him? He's coming here?'

'That's what he said.'

'It must be some mistake,' said Denniston.

Kavanagh Lewisohn and Fitch were so well known that people said KLF and assumed you would understand what they meant. They were one of the largest credit sale firms in London – so large that they rarely dealt with individual customers. They sold everything from computer banks to motor cars and from television sets to washing machines to middlemen, who, in turn, sold them to retailers. If Ronald Kavanagh was really planning to visit a small firm of enquiry agents, it could hardly be in connection with business matters. It must be private trouble. Something that needed to be dealt with discreetly.

When Kavanagh arrived, he turned out to be a slight, quiet, unassuming person in his early fifties. Denniston was agreeably surprised. Such managing directors of large companies as he had come across in the past had been intimidating people, assertive of their status and conscious of their financial muscle. A further surprise was that he really had come to talk business.

He said, 'This is something I wanted to deal with myself. Some time ago you did credit-rating reports for us on two potential customers.' He mentioned their names.

'Yes,' said Denniston, wondering what had gone wrong.

'We were impressed by the thorough way you tackled them. I assume, by the way, that you did the work yourself?'

Denniston nodded.

'You gave a good rating to one, although it was a new

company. The other, which was older and apparently sound, you warned us against. In both cases you were absolutely right. That's why I'm here today. Up to the present we've been getting the reports we needed from half a dozen different sources. This is now such an important part of our business that the board has decided that it would like to concentrate it in one pair of hands. Our first idea was to offer you the work on a retainer basis. Then we had a better idea.' Mr Kavanagh smiled. 'We decided to buy you. That is, of course, if you're for sale?'

Denniston was incapable of speech.

'We had it in mind to purchase your business as a going concern. We would take over the premises as they stand. There is, however, one condition. It's *your* brains and *your* flair that we're buying. We should have to ask you to enter into a service contract, at a fair salary, for five years certain, with options on both sides to renew. Your existing staff too, if they wish. But you are the one we must have.'

The room, which had shown signs of revolving on its axis, slowed down. Denniston took a grip of himself. He said, 'Your offer is more than fair, but there is one thing you ought to know. You spoke of taking over these premises. There is a snag . . .'

When Denniston had finished, Kavanagh said, 'It was good of you to tell me. It accords, if I may say so, with your reputation. We are not unacquainted with Scotus.' He smiled gently. 'We had some dealings with them over one of our branch offices last year. Fortunately we have very good solicitors and excellent surveyors. The outcome was a lot happier for us than it was for them. However, in this case it doesn't arise. Our own service department will carry out such repairs and redecoration as *we* consider necessary. If Scotus object, they can take us to court. I don't think they will. They're timid folk when they're up against someone bigger than themselves.'

'Like all bullies,' said Denniston. As he said it, he reflected with pleasure that Mr Huffin had undoubtedly got his ear glued to the wall.

*

It soon became apparent that Ronald Kavanagh was not a man who delegated to others things that he enjoyed doing himself.

On the morning after the deal had been signed he limped into the room, accompanied by the head of his service department and a foreman. They inspected everything and made notes. The next morning, a gang of workmen arrived and started to turn the office upside down.

Kavanagh arrived with the workmen. He said to Denniston, 'We'll start with your room. Strip and paint the whole place. They can do it in two days. What colours do you fancy?'

'Something cheerful.'

'I agree. My solicitor's office looks as if it hasn't been dusted since Charles Dickens worked there. What we want is an impression of cheerful reliability. Cream paint, venetian blinds, and solid-brass light fittings. And we'll need a second desk. I propose to establish a niche here for myself. I hope you don't mind?'

'I don't mind at all,' said Denniston. It occurred to him that one cause of his depression had been that since Perrot's death he had really had no one to talk to. 'I'll be glad of your company, though I don't suppose you'll be able to spare us a lot of time.'

'It's a common fallacy,' said Kavanagh, sitting on a corner of the table, swinging his damaged leg ('a relic of war service,' he explained), 'widely believed, but quite untrue, that managing directors are busy men. If they are, it's a sign of incompetence. I have excellent subordinates who do the real work. All I have to do is utter occasional sounds of approval or disapproval. It's such a boring life that a new venture like this is a breath of fresh air. Oh, you want to move this table. We'd better shift into young Gurney's office.'

'As I was saying,' Kavanagh continued when they had established themselves in Gurney's room, 'I have an insatiable curiosity about the mechanics of other people's business. When we went into a second-hand car market, we took over a motor-repair outfit. I got so interested that I put on overalls and started to work there myself. The men thought it was a huge joke, but they soon got used to it. And the things I learned about faking repair bills, you wouldn't believe. Oh, sorry, I'm afraid they want to start work in here too. Let's go to my club and get ourselves an early luncheon.'

Denniston found the new regime very pleasant. Kavanagh did not, of course, spend all his time with them, but he managed to put in a full hour on most days. His method of working was to have copies made, on the modern photocopying machine which had been one of his first innovations, of all of Denniston's reports. These he would study carefully, occasionally asking for the working papers. The questions he asked were shrewd and could not be answered without thought.

'Really,' he said, 'we're in the same line of business. Success depends on finding out who to trust. I once turned down a prosperous-looking televison wholesaler because he turned up in a Green Jackets' tie. I'm damned certain he'd never been near the brigade. Quite the wrong shape for a rifleman.'

'Instinct, based on experience,' agreed Denniston. He already felt years younger. It was not only the steady flow of new work and the certainty of getting a cheque at the end of each month. The whole office seemed to have changed. Even Mr Huffin appeared to be happy. Not only had his room been repainted, but it had been furnished with a new desk and a set of gleaming filing cabinets equipped with Chubb locks. These innovations seemed to have compensated him for the setback to his own plans, and he went out of his way to be pleasant to Kavanagh when he encountered him.

'Slimy toad,' said Denniston to his wife. 'When I asked Kavanagh if he planned to keep him, he laughed and said, "Why not? I don't much like the sort of work he's doing, but it brings in good money. As long as he keeps within the law. If you hear any complaints of sharp practice, that's another matter."'

'He sounds terrific.'

'Terrific's not quite the right word. He's honest, sensible, and unassuming. Also he's still a bit of a schoolboy. He likes to see the wheels go round.'

'I don't believe a single word of it,' said his wife.

*

'Well, Uncle,' said Andrew Gurney. 'What next?'

Kavanagh said, 'Next, I think, a glass of port.'

'Then it must be something damned unpleasant,' said Gurney.

'Why?'

'If it wasn't, you wouldn't be wasting the club port on me.'

'You're an irreverent brat,' said Kavanagh.

'When you wangled me into the firm, I guessed you were up to something.'

'Two large ports, please, Barker. Actually all I want you to do is to commit a burglary.'

'I said it was going to be something unpleasant.'

'But this is a very safe burglary. You are to burgle the offices of Denny's Detectives. Since the firm belongs to me, technically hardly a burglary at all, wouldn't you say?'

'Well . . .' said Gurney cautiously.

'I will supply you with the key to the outer door, the key of Mr Huffin's room, and a key for each of his new filing cabinets and his desk. Mr Huffin is a careful man. When these were installed, he asked for the duplicate keys to be handed to him. Fortunately I had had a second copy made of each. Neverthelesss, I was much encouraged by his request. It showed me that I might be on the right track.'

'What track?'

Kavanagh took a sip of his port and said, 'It's Warre '63. Don't gulp it. I suggest that you start around eleven o'clock. By that time Chancery Lane should be deserted except for the occasional policeman. In case you should run into trouble, I'll supply you with a note stating that you are working late with my permission.'

'Yes, Uncle, but—'

'When you get into Mr Huffin's room, take all the files from his cabinets and all the papers from his desk and photocopy them. Be very careful to put them back in the order you found them.'

'Yes, but—'

'I don't imagine you'll be able to finish the job in one night or even in two. When you leave, bring the photocopies round to my flat. You can use my spare room and make up for your lost nights by sleeping by day. I'll warn my housekeeper. As far as the office is concerned, you're out of town on a job for me. I think that's all quite straightforward.'

'Oh, quite,' said Gurney. 'The only thing is you haven't told me what you're up to.'

'When I've had a chance of examining Mr Huffin's papers, I may have a clearer idea myself. As soon as I do, I'll put you in the picture.'

Andrew sighed. 'When do you want me to start?'

'It's Monday today. If you start tomorrow night you should be through by the end of the week. I suggest you go home now and get a good night's rest.'

As his uncle had predicted, it took Andrew exactly four nights to finish the job. If he expected something dramatic to happen, he was disappointed. For a week his uncle failed to turn up at the office.

'Our owner,' said Mr Huffin, with a smirk, 'seems to have lost interest in us.'

Andrew smiled and agreed. He had just had an invitation to dinner at his uncle's flat in Albany and guessed that things might be moving.

During dinner his uncle spoke only of cricket. He was a devotee of the Kent team, most of whom he seemed to know by name. After dinner, which was cooked and served by the housekeeper, they retired to the sitting-room. Kavanagh said, 'And how did you enjoy your experience as a burglar?'

'It was a bit creepy at first. Chancery Lane seems to be inhabited after nightfall by howling cats.'

'They're not cats. They're the spirits of disappointed litigants.'

'Did I produce whatever it was you were looking for?'

'The papers from the cabinets related only to Mr Huffin's routine work. They showed him to be a thorough, if somewhat unscrupulous, operator. A model truffle-hound. Ninety-nine per cent of his private papers likewise. But the other one per cent – two memoranda and a bundle of receipts – were worth all the rest put together. They demonstrated that Mr Huffin has a second job. He's a moonlighter.'

'He's crooked enough for anything. What's his other job? Some sort of blackmail I suppose.'

'Try not to use words loosely, Andrew. Blackmail has become a portmanteau word covering everything from illegal intimidation to the use of lawful leverage.'

'I can't imagine Mr Huffin intimidating anyone.'

'Personally, probably not. But he has a partner. And that man we must now locate. Those scraps of paper are his footprints.'

Andrew looked at his uncle. He knew something of the work he had done during the war, but he found it hard to visualize this mild, grey-haired man pursuing, in peace, the tactics which had brought Karl Muller and others to the rifle-range in the Tower. For the first time he was striking the flint under the topsoil and it was a curiously disturbing experience.

He said, 'You promised—'

'Yes, I promised. So be it. Does the name David Rogerson mean anything to you?'

'I knew he was one of your friends.'

'More than that. During the retreat to Dunkirk he managed to extract me from a crashed and burning lorry. Which was, incidentally, full of explosives. That was when I broke my right leg in several places and contracted a limp which ended my service as an infanteer. Which was why I went into Intelligence. I kept up with David after the war. Not as closely as I should have liked. He had married a particularly stupid woman. However, we met once or twice a year for lunch in the City. We were both busy. I was setting up KLF, and he was climbing the ladder in Clarion Insurance. About six months ago he asked me to lend him some money. He wanted a thousand pounds. Of course I said yes and didn't ask him what he wanted it for. But I suppose he felt he owed me some sort of explanation. When he was leaving, he said, with something like a smile, "Do you play draughts?" I said I did when I was a boy. "Well," he said, "I've been huffed. By Mr Huffin." And that was all he did say. The next news I had was of his death.'

Gurney said, 'I read about that. No one seemed to know why he did it.'

'You may recall that at the inquest his wife was asked whether he had left a note. She said no. That was a lie. He did leave a note. As I discovered later. David had made me his executor. My first job was to look after his wife. I soon saw that Phyllis Rogerson had one objective. To live her own life on the proceeds of some substantial insurance policies which David had taken out – and to forget about him. I accepted that this was a natural reaction. Women are realists. It was when I was clearing up his papers that she told me the truth. He had left a letter. It was addressed to me. She said, "I guessed it was something to do with the trouble he'd been having. I knew that if you read it, all the unpleasantness would have to come out into the open. So I burnt it. I didn't even read it." I said, "If it was some sort of blackmailer, David won't have been his only victim. He must be caught and punished." She wouldn't listen. I haven't spoken to her since.'

'But you located Mr Huffin.'

'That wasn't difficult. The Huffin clan is not large. A clergyman in Shropshire, a farmer in Wales. A maiden lady in Northumberland. Little Mr Huffin of Denny's Detectives was so clearly the first choice that I had no hesitation in trying him first.'

'Clearly enough for you to spend your company's money in buying the agency.'

'We were on the lookout for a good credit-rating firm. My board was unanimous that Denniston was the man for the job. So I was able to kill two birds with one stone. Always an agreeable thing to do. My first idea was to expose Huffin as a blackmailer. I felt that there would be enough evidence in his files to convict him. I was wrong. What those papers show is that a second man is involved. Possibly the more important villain of the two. I see Huffin as the reconnaissance unit. The other man as the heavy brigade.'

'Do you know his name?'

'The only lead I have to him is that Mr Huffin used to communicate privately with a Mr Angus. The address he wrote to was a small newsagent's shop in Tufnell Park. An accommodation address, no doubt. Receipts for the payments he made to the shopkeeper were among his papers. I visualize Mr Angus calling from time to time to collect his letters. Or he may send a messenger. That is something we shall have to find out.'

'And you want me to watch the shop?'

'It's kind of you to offer. But no. Here I think we want professional help. Captain Smedley will be the man for the job. You've never heard of him? He's the head of a detective agency.' Rather unkindly, Kavanagh added, 'A *real* detective agency, Andrew.'

Captain Smedley said, 'I shall need exactly a hundred, in ones and fives. That's what it will cost to buy the man in the shop. I'll pay it to him myself. He won't play silly buggers with me.'

Kavanagh looked at Captain Smedley, who had a face like a hank of wire rope, and agreed that no one was likely to play silly buggers with him.

'I'll have a man outside. All the shopkeeper's got to do is tip him the wink when the letter's collected. Then my man follows him back to wherever he came from.'

'Might it be safer to have two men outside?'

'Safer, but more expensive.'

'Expense no object.'

'I see,' said the Captain. He looked curiously at Mr Kavanagh, whom he had known for some time. 'All right. I'll fix it up for you.'

On the Wednesday of the third week following this conversation Kavanagh got a thick plain envelope addressed to him at his flat. It contained several pages of typescript, which he read carefully. The look on his face was partly enlightenment and partly disgust.

'What a game,' he said. 'I wonder how they work it.'

After breakfast he spent some time in the reference section of the nearest public library browsing among civil service lists and copies of Whitaker's Almanack. Finally he found the name he wanted. Arnold Robbins. Yes, Arnold would certainly help him if the matter was put to him in the right way. But it would need devilish careful handling. 'A jackal,' he said, 'and a tiger. Now all we need is a tethered goat to bring the tiger under the rifle. But it will have to be tethered very carefully, in exactly the right spot. The brute is a man-eater, no question!'

A lady touched him on the shoulder and pointed to the notice which said SILENCE, PLEASE. He was not aware that he had spoken aloud.

During the months that followed, Kavanagh resumed his regular visits to the office in Chancery Lane, but Denniston noticed that his interest in the details of the work appeared to be slackening. He would still read the current reports and comment on them, but more of his time seemed to be spent in conversation.

In the old days Denniston might have objected to this as being a waste of time which could better have been spent in earning profits. Now it was different. He was being paid a handsome salary, and if it pleased the owner of the firm to pass an occasional hour in gossip, why should he object? Moreover, Kavanagh was an excellent talker, with a rich fund of experience in the byways of the jungle which lies between Temple Bar and Aldgate Pump. Politics, economics, finance. Honesty, dishonesty, and crime. Twenty years of cut-and-thrust between armies whose soldiers wore lounge suits and carried rolled umbrellas. Warfare in which victory could be more profitable, and defeat more devastating, than on any actual field of battle.

On one occasion, Kavanagh, after what must have been an unusually good luncheon, had devoted an entertaining hour to a dissertation on the tax system.

'At the height of their power and arrogance,' he said, 'the church demanded one-tenth of a man's income. The government of England exacts six times as much. The pirate who sank an occasional ship, the highwayman who held up a coach, was a child compared to the modern taxman.'

'You can't fight the state,' said Denniston.

'It's been tried. Poujade in France. But I agree that massive tax resistance is self-defeating. Each man must fight for himself. There are lawyers and accountants who specialize in finding loopholes in the tax laws, but such success can only be temporary. As soon as a loophole is discovered, the next finance act shuts it up. No. The essentials of guerrilla warfare are concealment and agility.'

Really interested now, Denniston said, 'Have you discovered a practical method of side-stepping tax? I've never made excessive profits, but I do resent handing over a slab of what I've made to a government who spend most of it on vote-catching projects.'

'My method is not one which would suit everyone. Its merit is simplicity. I arrange with my board that they will pay me only two-thirds of what I ought to be getting. The other third goes to charities nominated by me. They, of course, pay no tax. That part of it is quite legitimate. Our constitution permits gifts to charity.'

'Then how—'

'The only fact which is *not* known is that I set up and control the charities concerned. One is a local village affair. Another looks after our own employees. A third is for members of my old regiment. I am chairman, secretary, and treasurer of all three. Some of the money is devoted to the proper objects of the charity. The balance comes back, by various routes, to me. A lovely tax-free increment.'

'But,' said Denniston, 'surely—'

'Yes?'

'It seems too simple.'

'Simple, but, I assure you, effective.'

And later, to himself, 'I wonder if that was too obvious. I can only wait and see.'

'There's something stirring,' said Captain Smedley. 'My men tell me that those two beauties have got a regular meeting place. Top of the Duke of York's Steps. It isn't possible to get close enough to hear what they're saying. No doubt that's why they chose it. But they're certainly worked up about something. Licking their lips, you might say.'

'The bleating of the goat,' said Kavanagh. 'Excites the tiger.'

The letter which arrived at his flat a week later was in a buff envelope, typed on buff paper. It was headed, 'Inland Revenue Special Investigation Branch'. It said:

> Our attention has been drawn by the charity commissioners to certain apparent discrepancies in the latest accounts submitted to them of the undermentioned charities, all of which have been signed by you as treasurer. It is for this reason that we are making a direct approach to you before any further action is considered. The charities are the Lamperdown Village Hall Trust, the City of London Fusiliers' Trust, and the KLF Employees' Special Fund. You may feel that an interview would clarify the points at issue, in which case the writer would be happy to call on you, either at your place of business or at your residence, as you may prefer.

The writer appeared to be a Mr Wagner.

Kavanagh observed with appreciation the nicely judged mixture of official suavity and concealed threat. A queen's pawn opening.

Before answering it, he had a telephone call to make. The man he was asking for was evidently important, since he had to be approached through a secretary and a personal assistant, with suitable pauses at each stage. When contact had been made, a friendly conversation ensued, conducted on Christian-name terms. It concluded with Ronnie inviting Arnold to lunch at his club on the following Monday.

He then composed a brief letter to Mr Wagner, suggesting a meeting at his flat at seven o'clock in the evening on the following Wednesday. He apologized for suggesting such a late hour, but daytime commitments made it difficult to fix anything earlier.

'I wonder if it really is a tiger,' mused Kavanagh. 'Or only a second jackal. That would be disappointing.'

When he opened the door to his visitor, his fears were set to rest. Mr Wagner was a big man with a red-brown face. There was a tuft of sandy hair growing down each cheekbone. He had the broad, flattened nose of a pugilist. His eyes were so light as to be almost yellow, and a deep fold ran down under each eye to form a fence round the corners of an unusually wide mouth. His black coat was glossy, his legs decorously striped. He was a tiger. A smooth and shining tiger.

'Come in,' said Kavanagh. 'I'm alone this evening. Can I get you a drink?'

'Not just now,' said Mr Wagner.

He seated himself, opened his briefcase, took out a folder of papers, and laid it on the table. This was done without a word spoken. The folder was tied with tape. Mr Wagner's spatulate fingers toyed with the tape and finally untied it. With deliberation he extracted a number of papers and arranged them in two neat lines. Kavanagh, who had also seated himself, seemed hypnotized by this methodical proceeding.

When everything was to his satisfaction, Mr Wagner raised his heavy head, fixed his yellow eyes on Kavanagh, and said, 'I'm afraid you're in trouble.' An echo. Had not Mr Huffin said the same thing?

'Trouble?'

'You're in trouble, because you've been cheating.'

Kavanagh said, 'Oh!' Then, sinking a little in his chair, 'You've no right to say a thing like that.'

'I've every right to say it, because it's true. I've been studying the accounts of the three charities I mentioned in my letter. In particular, the accounts you submitted last month. They proved very interesting indeed.' The voice had become a purr. 'Previously your accounts were in such general terms that they might have meant – or concealed – anything. The latest accounts are, fortunately, much fuller and much more specific.'

'Well,' said Kavanagh, trying out a smile, 'the commissioners did indicate that they wanted rather more detail as to where the money went.'

'Yes, Mr Kavanagh. And where did it go?'

'It's—' Kavanagh waved a hand feebly towards the table. 'It's all there. In the accounts.'

'Then shall we look at them? These are the accounts of the Fusiliers' Trust. Previously the accounts only showed a lump sum, described as "grants to disabled Fusiliers and to the widows and dependants of deceased Fusiliers".'

'Yes. Yes. That's right.'

'In the latest accounts you supply a list of their names.' The voice deepened even further. The purr became a growl. The tiger was ready to spring. 'A very interesting list, because on reference to the army authorities, we have been unable to find any record of any of the people you mentioned as having served with the Fusiliers.'

'Possibly—'

'Yes, Mr Kavanagh?'

'Some mistake—'

'Thirty names. *All* of them fictitious?'

Kavanagh seemed incapable of speech.

'On the other hand, when we look at the KLF Fund, we find that the names you have given do correspond to the names of former employees of the firm. But a further question then presents itself. Have these people in fact received the sums shown against their names. Well? Well? Nothing to say? It would be very simple to find out. A letter to each of them—'

This seemed to galvanize Kavanagh into action for the first time. He half rose in his seat and said, 'No. I absolutely forbid it.'

'But are you in any position to forbid it?'

Kavanagh considered this question carefully, conscious that Mr Wagner's yellow eyes were watching him. Then he said, 'It does seem that there may have been some irregularity in the presentation of these accounts. I cannot attend to all these matters myself, you understand. Income may not always go where it should. There may be some tax which ought to have been paid . . .'

Mr Wagner had begun to smile. The opening of his lips displayed a formidable set of teeth.

'I had always understood,' went on Kavanagh, 'that in these circumstances, if the tax was paid, together with a sum by way of penalties—'

Mr Wagner's mouth shut with a snap. He said, 'Then you misunderstood the position. It is not simply a question of payment. When you sign your tax return, the form is so arranged that if you make a deliberate misstatement you can be charged before the court with perjury.'

There was a long silence. Kavanagh was thinking, 'So that's how he does it. Poor old David. I wonder what slip-up he made. I'm sure it was unintentional, but a charge of perjury. Goodbye to his prospects with the Clarion. And a lot of other things too.'

He said, in a voice which had become almost a bleat, 'You must understand how serious that would be for me, Mr Wagner. I'd be willing to pay any sum rather than have that happen. Is there no way . . .'

He let the sentence tail off.

Mr Wagner had taken a silver pencil from his pocket and seemed to be making some calculations. He said, 'If, in fact, the sums of money shown as going to the beneficiaries of these three trusts ended up in your own pocket, I would estimate – a rough calculation only – that you have been obtaining at least ten thousand pounds a year free of tax. I am not aware of how long this very convenient arrangement has been going on. Five years? Yes? Possibly more. Had you declared this income, you would have paid at least thirty thousand pounds of tax.'

'Exactly,' said Kavanagh eagerly. 'That is the point I was making. Isn't this something that could more easily be solved by a money payment? At the moment I have considerable resources. If a charge of perjury was brought, they would largely disappear. What good would that do to anyone?'

Mr Wagner appeared to consider the matter. Then he smiled. It was a terrible smile. He said, 'I have some sympathy with that point of view, Mr Kavanagh. Allow me to make a suggestion. It is a friendly suggestion. You can always refuse it. At the moment the file is entirely under my control. The information came from a private source. It is known only to me. You follow me?'

'I think so. Yes.'

Mr Wagner leaned forward and said with great deliberation, 'If you will pay me ten thousand pounds, the file will be destroyed.'

'Ten thousand pounds?'

'Ten thousand pounds.'

'How would the payment be made?'

'You would pay the money into an account in the name of M. Angus at the Westminster branch of the London and Home Counties Bank.'

'That should be enough for you,' said Kavanagh. He was addressing the door leading into the next room, which now opened to admit Sir Arnold Robbins, the deputy head of Inland Revenue and two other men. Robbins said, 'You are suspended from duty. These gentlemen are police officers. They will accompany you home and will impound your passport. It will be for the Director of Public Prosecutions to decide on any further action.'

Mr Wagner was on his feet. His face was engorged. A trickle of blood ran from one nostril down his upper lip. He dashed it away with the back of his hand and said in a voice thick with fury, 'So it was a trap.'

'You must blame your accomplice for that,' said Kavanagh. 'He saw the writing on the wall and sold you to save his own skin. There's not much honour among thieves.'

When Wagner had gone, Sir Arnold said, 'I apologize for not believing you. I suppose the fact is we give these special-investigation people too much rope. Incidentally, I've had a look at Rogerson's file. It was as you thought. A minor omission, not even his own income. Some money his wife got from Ireland. She may not even have told him about it.'

'Probably not,' said Kavanagh. 'She was a stupid woman.' He

switched off the microphone which connected with the next room. 'We've got all this on tape if you need it.'

'Good. And by the way, I take it those donations of yours are in order?'

'Perfectly. Every penny that went into those charities has gone to the beneficiaries. I'll show you the receipts. The only thing I fudged was that list of Fusilier names. I'll have to apologize to the charity commissioners and send them the correct list.'

As Sir Arnold was going, he said, 'Why did you tell Wagner it was his accomplice who had shopped him? Was it true?'

'No,' said Kavanagh. 'But I thought it might have some interesting results. It's going to be very difficult to get at Mr Huffin. He really was only the jackal. He picked up scraps of information when he was doing his job and fed them to Wagner, who moved in for the kill. Wagner will be at liberty until the director makes up his mind. I felt we should give him a chance to ask Mr Huffin for an explanation.'

'He didn't say anything,' said Captain Smedley. 'He just hit him. Huffin's not a big man. It lifted him off his feet and sent him backwards down the steps. Cracked his skull. Dead before he got to hospital.'

'And Mr Wagner?'

'I had a policeman standing by, like you suggested. I thought he was going to put up a fight, but he seemed dazed. When they got him to the station, he just keeled over. Some sort of cerebral haemorrhage.'

'So he's dead too?'

'No. But near enough. And if he does recover, he's in every sort of trouble. A good riddance to a nasty pair.'

But that was not their real epitaph. That had been spoken by Colonel Hubert on the evening of 15 April in the year 1944.

PAULA GOSLING

Killer

HE HATED her. He did.

Every morning when he left, she was there, staring out the window, waiting for him, watching him. And when he came home at night she was there again, black beady eyes following his every move. As if he would do anything to her.

As if he could.

They'd guess, wouldn't they?

Or would they?

Everybody thought he was so quiet, so polite. Hah!

Neighbours – what do they *really* know about one another? After all, they hadn't lived there long, he was still a mystery, he was sure of that.

Nobody knew his business. He kept to his routine, was always well mannered when he met one of them on the street. Some might know his name – the postman knew his name, of course – but not much else. He kept himself to himself and so did his woman. Dol knew her place.

She kept the house tidy, did the shopping, made sure he got his meals on time, made sure his life was comfortable, that was all he required of her. So she wasn't very pretty, and lacked imagination, so what? Dol suited him just fine. If home was dull, if the food was always the same on the same days, and the evenings decidedly lacking in novelty, what did it matter? It was a place to sleep.

And a place to hide, if necessary.

He had enough excitement outside home to satisfy him.

More than enough.

He was the Expert. He had a reputation downtown – where a

reputation counted. He was the one They turned to when some little rat fink had squealed once too often, or maybe caused Somebody Important some damage. They didn't like damage, downtown. They didn't like trouble. But they liked him. He worked fast. Neat and quiet, that was his style. In and out, nothing flashy – and he never talked. Not once. They liked that, too. He had plenty of work, one way and another. He kept in shape. He was in control.

Dol knew the consequences if she stepped out of line – he'd walked out before and he was quite prepared to do it again if she said anything he didn't like.

Or worse. He could do worse.

Doing worse was his business, after all.

And it *was* his business – nobody else's.

Especially not that nosy old hen next door.

He didn't know much about her, it was true, but she seemed to want to know all about him, the way she watched, the way she stared, the way she clocked his comings and goings.

It wasn't so bad, at first.

At first he'd even felt a little sorry for her.

After all, she was a shut-in, that was clear. Always in the same window during the day, keeping an eye on the street, probably making up stories about everyone, probably putting two and two together in her twisted little mind, maybe even coming to conclusions.

She might come to a conclusion about him.

That was the worry.

But who could she tell, shut up like that?

Her companion, he supposed.

Would she be believed? Dol said she was a gossipy, nervy thing. Drove her companion and just about everybody else on the street crazy. Always chattering in that cracked, cranky little voice that went through you like a rusty knife. Always complaining about something. Shut-ins got like that, he knew, went a little funny, got excited over nothing, made things up to liven their dull lives. Most of what she said was pure nonsense, of course. Probably nobody would believe her.

But they might.

Putting two and two together, she might hit on the truth. Stories got around, after all.

He tried varying his hours, changing his routine, but it didn't seem to make any difference, she was always there, watching, watching, watching.

And it played hell with his concentration. In a profession as specialized as his, you had to keep in touch with all the customers all the time, keep the territory covered. They wanted to know they could count on him, or they might turn to another Firm.

The Business might die on him.

Some joke.

But by the time they'd been in the new house a few months, he knew he was going to have to do something about Mrs Murgatroyd. That was her name. He didn't know her first name – probably nobody did except that poor, haggard woman who looked after her. He'd heard her companion speaking to her one day, when the window was open a crack and he was passing.

Just passing.

Mrs Murgatroyd had been eyeing him suspiciously from under her wrinkled eyelids when her companion had startled her by asking if she wanted something to drink. Well, the fuss that started! Talk about screeching, you'd think the poor woman had asked her if she wanted to be skinned alive!

And all the time she was complaining and crabbing, Mrs Murgatroyd was watching him out of the corner of her eye, watching to see if he reacted to her little performance.

Well, maybe she was a mind-reader.

Because the thought of breaking the bones in that scrawny little neck was beginning to haunt him. The thought of scaring the wits out of her, or even crushing the life right out of her body, kept him awake nights. He did it to others, in a professional way. Why not to her?

But it was only a thought.

Until she began to chatter at him through the glass, telling him off and screeching straight at him. That did it. That was the last straw. Staring was one thing, but jabbering at him another. It made him cringe every time he passed by.

What the hell would people think?

What was she saying?

What did she know?

He couldn't stand it. He knew he'd have to put a stop to it before it went on much longer. She was driving him crazy, and soon it might get back to Dol. He didn't want Dol upset.

Not again.

They'd had to move house twice before when neighbours got suspicious about him, began to point the finger or whisper behind their hands. They seemed to think he was bringing his work home, one way or another. As if he would. Dol had denied everything, of course, she was loyal through and through. She loved him. And he loved her, too, in his way.

But, in the end, they'd had to move.

Well, he was through moving. He liked it here, it was quiet and there were fields to walk in near by, and he'd really taken to it.

Except for Mrs Murgatroyd, of course.

The thing was, he'd have to wait his chance, move on impulse, trust his instinct. It wasn't professional, it was personal. Which meant no set-up, no back-up, no inside information. Not kill-to-order, and nothing to swell the kitty, afterwards. Not with this one. There had to be no connection with him, that was the thing. No way anyone could guess that he had anything to do with it.

Not easy.

Waiting never is, no matter how much of it you do.

But then, one morning, the moment arrived. All unexpected, the way these things do. He had slept a little late, and left the house just in time to see Mrs Murgatroyd's companion set out on a shopping expedition. She was running to catch the bus.

Which meant she'd left the house in a hurry.

On an impulse, he slipped up the path and went around the side of the house. Oh, Mrs Murgatroyd saw him, of course. Propped in the window, as usual, her little black eyes missing nothing that went on in the neighbourhood. She was agitated, she bobbed about frantically, she even called out for help – but there was no one to hear her, now.

No one to tell, now.

He'd been right. The companion had left the back door ajar. Just a bit. Just enough. He was in like a shadow – he was good at that – and savoured the moment.

Mrs Murgatroyd, you've poked your nosy little beak into a neighbour's business just once too often, he thought to himself. Now you'll find out just what I do, and how I do it.

Slowly, quietly, he moved across the kitchen and pushed open the door into the hall. The house smelled very different from his own. All houses had a characteristic smell, he was a connoisseur of smells, assigned personalities to houses on the basis of smells, knew what to expect the minute he was through a door. Some smelled richly of buttery meals and cream teas, some smelled rankly of cabbage and disinfectant. All of them smelled of death, after he'd dropped by.

This one would, too.

Moving stealthily, he slipped down the hall, his footsteps hardly making a whisper on the thick pile of the carpet. There – the sitting-room door was open, and he could hear Mrs Murgatroyd muttering to herself, alone in the room. She was talking about him. Words like 'murderer' and 'monster' rose above her inane jabbering.

He went in and she stopped her talk.

Gaped at him.

Moved back, as far back as she could.

She knew what he had come for, all right.

For all the good it would do her.

He thought it would be easy, but it wasn't. She *could* move, after all. She fled him, darting around the room, then making a frantic, scrabbling dash for the hall, screeching and flailing and jabbering.

But he got her.

And it was good, so good. She twisted and turned and

struggled but he got her, he finished her, and she would stare no more, jabber no more. Nasty, vicious, nosy little bag of bones.

Goodbye, Mrs Murgatroyd.

Now all he had to do was get out.

But luck wasn't with him.

Not this time.

The back door slammed – the companion was back! Too soon, too soon! Now she was in the doorway! Standing, staring, pointing at the scatter of green and blue on the carpet, and screaming!

Why did they all scream? Why were they so shocked?

What did they expect?

No other self-respecting cat would have put up with that damned budgie staring and screeching at him for another single day. Why should he?

He sighed and crawled under an armchair.

There'd be no pink salmon tonight.

PATRICIA HIGHSMITH

Those Awful Dawns

EDDIE's face looked angry and blank also, as if he might be thinking of something else. He was staring at his two-year-old daughter Francy who sat in a wailing heap beside the double bed. Francy had tottered to the bed, struck it, and collapsed.

'*You* take care of her,' Laura said. She was standing with the vacuum cleaner still in her hand. 'I've got things to do!'

'You hit her, f'Christ's sake, so *you* take care of her!' Eddie was shaving at the kitchen sink.

Laura dropped the vacuum cleaner, started to go to Francy whose cheek was bleeding, changed her mind and veered back to the vacuum cleaner and unplugged it, began to wrap the cord to put it away. The place could stay a mess tonight for all she cared.

The other three children, Georgie nearly six, Helen four, Stevie three, stared with wet, faintly smiling mouths.

'That's a cut, goddammit!' Eddie put a towel under the baby's cheek. 'Swear to God, that'll need stitches. Look at it! How'd you do it?'

Laura was silent, at least as far as answering that question went. She felt exhausted. The boys – Eddie's pals – were coming tonight at nine to play poker, and she had to make at least twenty liverwurst and ham sandwiches for their midnight snack. Eddie had slept all day and was still only getting dressed at seven.

'You taking her to the hospital or what?' Eddie asked. His face was half covered with shaving cream.

'If I take her again, they'll think it's always *you* smacking her. Mostly it is, frankly.'

'Don't give me that crap, not this time,' Eddie said. 'And "they", who the hell're "they"? Shove 'em!'

Twenty minutes later, Laura was in the waiting hall of St Vincent's Hospital on West 11th Street. She leaned back in the straight chair and half closed her eyes. There were seven other people waiting, and the nurse had told her it might be half an hour, but she would try to make it sooner because the baby was bleeding slightly. Laura had her story ready: the baby had fallen against the vacuum cleaner, must've hit the connecting part where there was a sliding knob. Since this was what Laura had hit her with, swinging it suddenly to one side because Francy had been pulling at it, Laura supposed that the same injury could be caused by Francy's falling against it. That made sense.

It was the third time they'd brought Francy to St Vincent's, which was four blocks from where they lived on Hudson Street. Broken nose (Eddie's fault, Eddie's elbow), then another time a trickling of blood at the ear that wouldn't stop, then the third time, the one time they hadn't brought her on their own, was when Francy had had a broken arm. Neither Eddie nor Laura had known Francy had a broken arm. How could they have known? You couldn't see it. But around that time Francy had had a black eye, God knew how or why, and a social worker had turned up. A neighbour must have put the social worker on their tail, and Laura was ninety per cent sure it was old Mrs Covini on the ground floor, damn her ass. Mrs Covini was one of those dumpy, black-dressed Italian mommas who lived surrounded by kids all their lives. Nerves of steel, who hugged and kissed the kids all day as if they were gifts from heaven and very rare things on Earth. The Mrs Covinis didn't go out to work, Laura had always noticed. Laura worked as a waitress five nights a week at a downtown Sixth Avenue diner. That plus getting up at 6 a.m. to fix Eddie's bacon and eggs, pack his lunchbox, feed the kids who were already up, and cope with them all day was enough to make an ox tired, wasn't it? Anyway, Mrs Covini's spying had brought this monster – she was five feet eleven if she was an inch – down on their necks three times. Her name, appropriately enough, was Mrs Crabbe. 'Four children are a lot to handle . . . Are you in the habit of using contraceptives, Mrs Regan?' Oh, crap. Laura moved her head from side to side on the back of the straight chair and groaned, feeling exactly as she had felt in high school when confronted by a problem in algebra that bored her stiff. She and Eddie were practising Catholics. She might have been willing to go on the Pill on her own, but Eddie wouldn't hear of it, and that was that. On her own, that was funny, because on her own she wouldn't have needed it. Anyway, that had shut old Crabbe up on the subject, and had given Laura a certain satisfaction. She and Eddie had some rights and independence left, at least.

'Next?' The nurse beckoned, smiling.

The young intern whistled. 'How'd this happen?'

'A fall. Against the vacuum cleaner.'

The smell of disinfectant. Stitches. Francy, who had been nearly asleep in the hall, had awakened at the anaesthetizing needle and wailed through the whole thing. The intern gave Francy what he called a mild sedative in a candy-covered pill. He murmured something to a nurse.

'What're these bruises?' he asked Laura. 'On her arms.'

'Oh – just bumps. In the house. She bruises easily.' He wasn't the same intern, was he, that Laura had seen three or four months ago?

'Can you wait just a minute?'

The nurse came back, and she and the intern looked at a card that the nurse had.

The nurse said to Laura, 'I think one of our OPTs is visiting you now, Mrs Regan?'

'Yes.'

'Have you an appointment with her?'

'Yes, I think so. It's written down at home.' Laura was lying.

Mrs Crabbe arrived at 7.45 p.m. the following Monday without warning. Eddie had just got home and opened a can of beer. He was a construction worker, doing overtime nearly every day in the summer months when the light lasted. When he got home he always made for the sink, sponged himself with a towel, opened a can of beer, and sat down at the oilcloth-covered table in the kitchen.

Laura had already fed the kids at 6 p.m., and had been trying to steer them to bed when Mrs Crabbe arrived. Eddie had cursed on seeing her come in the door.

'I'm sorry to intrude . . .' Like hell. 'How have you been doing?'

Francy's face was still bandaged, and the bandage was damp and stained with egg. The hospital had said to leave the bandage on and not touch it. Eddie, Laura and Mrs Crabbe sat at the kitchen table, and it turned into quite a lecture.

'. . . You realize, don't you, that you both are using little Frances as an outlet for your bad temper. Some people might bang their fists against a wall or quarrel with each other, but you and your husband are apt to whack baby Frances. Isn't that true?' She smiled a phoney, friendly smile, looking from one to the other of them.

Eddie scowled and mashed a book of matches in his fingers. Laura squirmed and was silent. Laura knew what the woman meant. Before Francy had been born, they had used to smack Stevie maybe a little too often. They damned well hadn't wanted a third baby, especially in an apartment the size of this one, just as the woman was saying now. And Francy was the fourth.

'. . . but if you both can realize that Francy *is – here* . . .'

Laura was glad that she apparently wasn't going to bring up birth control again. Eddie looked about to explode, sipping his beer as if he was ashamed to have been caught with it, but as if he had a right to drink it if he wanted to, because it was his house.

'. . . a larger apartment, maybe? Bigger rooms. That would ease the strain on your nerves a lot . . .'

Eddie was obliged to speak about the economic situation. 'Yeah, I earn fine . . . Riveter-welder. Skilled. But we got expenses, y'know. I wouldn't wanta go looking for a bigger place. Not just now.'

Mrs Crabbe lifted her eyes and stared around her. Her black

hair was neatly waved, almost like a wig. 'That's a nice TV. You bought that?'

'Yeah, and we're still paying on it. That's *one* of the things,' Eddie said.

Laura was tense. There was also Eddie's hundred-and-fifty-dollar wristwatch they were paying on, and luckily Eddie wasn't wearing it now (he was wearing his cheap one), because he didn't wear the good one to work.

'And the sofa and the armchairs, aren't they new . . . You bought them?'

'Yeah,' Eddie said, hitching back in his chair. 'This place is furnished, y'know, but you shoulda seen *that*.' He made a derisive gesture in the direction of the sofa.

Laura had to support Eddie here. 'What they had here, it was an old red plastic thing. You couldn't even sit on it.' It hurt your ass, Laura might have added.

'When we move to a bigger place, at least we've got those,' Eddie said, nodding at the sofa and armchairs section.

The sofa and armchairs were covered with beige plush that had a floral pattern of pale pink and blue. Hardly three months in the house, and the kids had already spotted the seats with chocolate milk and orange juice. Laura found it impossible to keep the kids off the furniture. She was always yelling at them to play on the floor. But the point was the sofa and the armchairs weren't paid for yet, and that was what Mrs Crabbe was getting at, not people's comfort or the way the house looked, oh no.

'Nearly paid up. Finished next month,' Eddie said.

That wasn't true. It would be another four or five months, because they'd twice missed the payments, and the man at the 14th Street store had come near taking the things away.

Now there was a speech from the old bag about the cost of instalment-plan buying. Always pay the whole sum, because if you couldn't do that, you couldn't afford whatever it was, see? Laura smouldered, as angry as Eddie, but the important thing with these meddlers was to appear to agree with everything they said. Then they might not come back.

'. . . if this keeps up with little Frances, the law will have to step in and I'm sure you wouldn't want that. That would mean taking Frances to live somewhere else.'

The idea was quite pleasant to Laura.

'Where? Take 'er where?' Georgie asked. He was in pyjama pants, standing near the table.

Mrs Crabbe paid him no mind. She was ready to leave.

Eddie gave a curse when she was out of the door, and went to get another beer. *'Goddam invasion of privacy!'* He kicked the fridge door shut.

Laura burst out in a laugh. 'That old sofa! Remember? *Jesus!*'

'Too bad it wasn't here, she coulda broke her behind on it.'

That night around midnight, as Laura was carrying a heavy tray of four superburgers and four mugs of coffee, she remembered something that she had put out of her mind for five days. Incredible that she hadn't thought of it for five whole days. Now it was more than ever likely. Eddie would blow his stack.

The next morning on the dot of nine, Laura called up Dr Weebler from the newspaper store downstairs. She said it was urgent, and got an appointment for 11.15. As Laura left for the doctor's, Mrs Covini was in the hall, mopping the part of the white tiles directly in front of her door. Laura thought that was somehow bad luck, seeing Mrs Covini now. She and Mrs Covini didn't speak to each other any more.

'I can't give you an abortion just like that,' Dr Weebler said, shrugging and smiling his awful smile that seemed to say, 'It's you holding the bag. I'm a doctor, a man.' He said, 'These things can be prevented. Abortions shouldn't be necessary.'

I'll damn well go to another doctor, Laura thought with rising anger, but she kept a pleasant, polite expression on her face. 'Look, Dr Weebler, my husband and I are practising Catholics, I told you that. At least my husband is and – you know. So these things happen. But I've already got four. Have a heart.'

'Since when do practising Catholics want abortions? No, Mrs Regan, but I can refer you to another doctor.'

And abortions were supposed to be easy lately in New York. 'If I get the money together— How much is it?' Dr Weebler was cheap, that was why they went to him.

'It's not a matter of money.' The doctor was restless. He had other people waiting to see him.

Laura wasn't sure of herself, but she said, 'You do abortions on other women, so why not me?'

'*Who*? When there's a danger to a woman's health, that's different.'

Laura didn't get anywhere, and that useless expedition cost her $7.50, payable on the spot, except that she did get another prescription for half-grain Nembutals out of him. That night she told Eddie. Better to tell him right away than postpone it, because postponing it was hell, she knew from experience, with the damned subject crossing her mind every half hour.

'Oh, *Chr–r–rist*!' Eddie said, and fell back on the sofa, mashing the hand of Stevie who was on the sofa and had stuck out a hand just as Eddie plopped.

Stevie let out a wail.

'Oh, shut up, that didn't kill you!' Eddie said to Stevie. 'Well, now what. Now what?'

Now what. Laura was actually trying to think *now what*. What the hell ever was there to do except hope for a miscarriage, which never happened. Fall down the stairs, something like that, but she'd never had the guts to fall down the stairs. At least not so far. Stevie's wailing was like awful background music. Like in a horror film. 'Oh, can it, Stevie!'

Then Francy started yelling. Laura hadn't fed her yet.

'I'm gonna get drunk,' Eddie announced. 'I suppose there's no booze.'

He knew there wasn't. There never was any booze, it got drunk up too fast. Eddie was going to go out. 'Don't you want to eat first?' Laura asked.

'Naw.' He pulled on a sweater. 'I just want to forget the whole damned thing. Just forget it for a *little* while.'

Ten minutes later, after poking something at Francy (mashed potatoes, a nippled bottle because it made less mess than a cup) and leaving the other kids with a box of fig newtons, Laura did the same thing, but she went to a bar farther down Hudson where she knew he didn't go. Tonight was one of her two nights off from the diner, which was a piece of luck. She had two whiskey sours with a bottle of beer as accompaniment, and then a rather nice man started talking with her, and bought her two more whiskey sours. On the fourth, she was feeling quite wonderful, even rather decent and important sitting on the bar stool, glancing now and then at her reflection in the mirror behind the bottles. Wouldn't it be great to be starting over again? No marriage, no Eddie, no kids? Just something new, a clean slate.

'I asked you – are you married?'

'No,' Laura said.

But apart from that, he talked about football. He had won a bet that day. Laura day-dreamed. Yes, she'd once had a marriage, love, and all that. She'd known Eddie would never make a lot of dough, but there was such a thing as living decently, wasn't there, and God knew her tastes weren't madly expensive, so what took all her money? The kids. There was the drain. Too bad Eddie was a Catholic, and when you marry a Catholic—

'Hey, you're not listening!'

Laura dreamed on with determination. Above all, she'd *had a dream* once, a dream of love and happiness and of making a nice home for Eddie and herself. Now the outsiders were even attacking her *inside her house*. Mrs Crabbe. A lot Mrs Crabbe knew about being woken up at five in the morning by a screaming kid, or being poked in the face by Stevie or Georgie when you'd been asleep only a couple of hours and your whole body ached. That was when she or Eddie was apt to swat them. In those awful dawns. Laura realized she was near tears, so she began to listen to the man who was still going on about football.

He wanted to walk her home, so she let him. She was so tipsy, she rather needed his arm. Then she said at the door that she lived with her mother, so she had to go up alone. He started getting fresh, but she gave him a shove and closed the front door, which locked. Laura hadn't quite reached the third floor when she heard feet on the stairs and thought the guy must've got in somehow, but it turned out to be Eddie.

'Well, how d'y'do?' said Eddie, feeling no pain.

The kids had got into the fridge. It was something they did about once a month. Eddie flung Georgie back and shut the fridge, then slipped on some spilled stringbeans and nearly fell.

'And lookit the *gas* f'Christ's sake!' Eddie said.

Every burner was on, and as soon as Laura saw it, she smelled gas, gas everywhere. Eddie flipped all the burners shut and opened a window.

Georgie's wailing started all the others.

'Shut up, shut up!' Eddie yelled. 'What the hell's the matter, are they hungry? Didn't you feed 'em?'

'Of course I fed 'em!' Laura said.

Eddie bumped into the door jamb, his feet slipped sideways in a funny slow-motion collapse, and he sat down heavily on the floor. Four-year-old Helen laughed and clapped her hands. Stevie was giggling. Eddie cursed the entire household and flung his sweater at the sofa, missing it. Laura lit a cigarette. She still had her whiskey-sour buzz and she was enjoying it.

She heard the crash of a glass on the bathroom floor, and she merely raised her eyebrows and inhaled smoke. Got to tie Francy in her crib, Laura thought, and moved vaguely towards Francy to do it. Francy was sitting like a dirty rag doll in a corner. Her crib was in the bedroom, and so was the double bed in which the other three kids slept. Goddam bedroom certainly was a bedroom, Laura thought. Beds were all you could see in there. She pulled Francy up by her tied-around bib, and Francy just then burped, sending a curdled mess over Laura's wrist.

'Ugh!' Laura dropped the child and shook her hand with disgust.

Francy's head had bumped the floor, and now she let out a scream. Laura ran water over her hand at the sink, shoving aside Eddie who was already stripped to the waist, shaving. Eddie shaved at night so that he could sleep a little longer in the morning.

'You're pissed,' Eddie said.

'And so what?' Laura went back and shook Francy to make

her hush. 'For God's sake, shut up! What've *you* got to cry about?'

'Give 'er an aspirin. Take some yourself,' Eddie said.

Laura told him what to do with himself. If Eddie came at her tonight, he could shove it. She'd go back to the bar. Sure. That place stayed open till three in the morning. Laura found herself pushing a pillow down on Francy's face to shut her up just for a minute, and Laura remembered what Mrs Crabbe had said: Francy had become the target – target? Outlet for both of them. Well, it was true, they did smack Francy more than the others, but Francy yelled more, too. Suiting action to the thought, Laura slapped Francy's face hard. That's what they did when people had hysterics, she thought. Francy did shut up, but for only a stunned couple of seconds, then yelled even louder.

The people below were thumping on their ceiling. Laura imagined them with a broom handle. Laura stamped three times on her floor in defiance.

'Listen, if you don't get that kid *quiet* . . .' Eddie said.

Laura stood at the closet undressing. She pulled on a night-gown, and pushed her feet into old brown loafers that served as house slippers. In the john, Eddie had broken the glass that they used when they brushed their teeth. Laura kicked some of the glass aside, too tired to sweep it up tonight. Aspirins. She took down a bottle and it slipped from her fingers before she got the top unscrewed. Crash, and pills all over the floor. Yellow pills. The Nembutals. That was a shame, but sweep it all up tomorrow. Save them, the pills. Laura took two aspirins.

Eddie was yelling, waving his arms, herding the kids toward the other double bed. Usually that was Laura's job, and she knew Eddie was doing it because he didn't want them roaming around the house all night, disturbing them.

'And if you don't stay in that bed, all of yuh, I'll *wham* yuh!'

Thump–thump–thump on the floor again.

Laura fell into bed, and awakened to the alarm clock. Eddie groaned and moved slowly, getting out of bed. Laura lay savouring the last few seconds of bed before she would hear the clunk that meant Eddie had put the kettle on. She did the rest, instant coffee, orange juice, bacon and eggs, instant hot cereal for the kids. She went over last night in her mind. How many whiskey sours? Five, maybe, and only one beer. With the aspirins, that shouldn't be so bad.

'Hey, what's with Georgie?' Eddie yelled. 'Hey, what the hell's in the john?'

Laura crawled out of bed, remembering. 'I'll sweep it up.'

Georgie was lying on the floor in front of the john door, and Eddie was stooped beside him.

'Aren't those Nembutals?' Eddie said. 'Georgie musta ate some! And lookit Helen!'

Helen was in the bathroom, lying on the floor beside the shower.

Eddie shook Helen, yelling at her to wake up. 'Jesus, they're like in a coma!' He dragged Helen out by an arm, picked Georgie up and carried him to the sink. He held Georgie under his arm like a sack of flour, wet a dishtowel and sloshed it over Georgie's face and head. 'You think we oughta get a doctor? – F'Christ's sake, move, will yuh? Hand me Helen.'

Laura did. Then she pulled on a dress. She kept the loafers on. She must phone Weebler. No, St Vincent's, it was closer. 'Do you remember the number of St Vincent's?'

'No,' said Eddie. 'What d'y do to make kids vomit? Anybody vomit? Mustard, isn't it?'

'Yeah, I think so.' Laura went out the door. She still felt tipsy, and almost tripped on the stairs. Good thing if she did, she thought, remembering she was pregnant, but of course it never worked until you were pretty far gone.

She hadn't a dime with her, but the newspaper-store man said he would trust her, and gave her a dime from his pocket. He was just opening, because it was early. Laura looked up the number, then in the booth she found that she had forgotten half of it. She'd have to look it up again. The newspaper-store man was watching her, because she had said it was an emergency and she had to call a hospital. Laura picked up the telephone and dialled the number as best she remembered it. Then she put the forefinger of her right hand on the hook (the man couldn't see the hook), because she knew it wasn't the right number, but because the man was watching her, she started speaking. The dime was returned in the chute and she left it.

'Yes, please. An emergency.' She gave her name and address. 'Sleeping pills. I suppose we'll need a stomach pump . . . Thank you. Goodbye.'

Then she went back to the apartment.

'They're still out cold,' Eddie said. 'How many pills're gone, do you think? Take a look.'

Stevie was yelling for his breakfast. Francy was crying because she was still tied in her crib.

Laura took a look on the bathroom tiles, but she couldn't guess at all how many pills were gone. Ten? Fifteen? They were sugar-coated, that's why the kids had liked them. She felt blank, scared, and exhausted. Eddie had put the kettle on, and they had instant coffee, standing up. Eddie said there wasn't any mustard in the house (Laura remembered she had used the last of it for all those ham sandwiches), and now he tried to get some coffee down Georgie's and Helen's throats, but none seemed to go down, and it only spilled on their fronts.

'Sweep up that crap so Stevie won't get any,' Eddie said, nodding at the john. 'What time're they coming? I gotta get going. That foreman's a shit, I told you, he don't want nobody late.' He cursed, having picked up his lunch-box and found it empty, and he tossed the lunch-box with a clatter in the sink.

Still dazed, Laura fed Francy at the kitchen table (she had another black eye, where the hell did *that* come from?), started to feed cornflakes and milk to Stevie (he wouldn't eat hot cereal), then left it for Stevie to do, whereupon he turned the bowl over on the oilcloth table. Georgie and Helen were still asleep on the double bed where Eddie had put them. *Well, after all, St Vincent's is coming*, Laura thought. But they weren't coming. She turned on the little battery radio to some dance music. Then she changed Francy's diaper. That was what Francy was howling about, her wet diaper. Laura had barely heard the howling this morning. Stevie had toddled over to Georgie and Helen and was poking them, trying to wake them up. In the john, Laura emptied the kids' pot down the toilet, and picked the pills out of the dustpan. She put the pills on a bare place on one of the glass shelves in the medicine cabinet.

At ten, Laura went down to the newspaper store, paid the man back, and had to look up the St Vincent number again. This time she dialled it, got someone, told them what was the matter and asked why no one had come yet.

'You phoned at seven? That's funny. I was on. We'll send an ambulance right away.'

Laura bought four quarts of milk, and more baby food at the delicatessen, then went back upstairs. She felt a little less sleepy, but not much. Were Georgie and Helen still breathing? She absolutely didn't want to go and see. She heard the ambulance arriving. Laura was finishing her third cup of coffee. She glanced at herself in the mirror, but couldn't face that either. The more upset she looked, the better, maybe. Two men in white came up, and went at once to the two kids. They had stethoscopes. They murmured and exclaimed. One turned and asked:

'*Wha'd* they take?'

'Sleeping pills. They got into the Nembutals.'

'This one's even cold. Didn't you notice that?'

He meant Georgie. One of the men wrapped the kids up in blankets from the bed, the other prepared a needle. He gave shots in the arm to both kids.

'No use telephoning us for another two three hours,' one of them said.

The other said, 'Never mind, she's in a state of shock. Better have some hot tea, lady, and lie down.'

They hurried off. The ambulance whined towards St Vincent's.

The whine was taken up by Francy, who was standing with her fat little legs apart, but no more apart than usual, while pee dripped from the lump of diaper between them. All the rubber pants were still dirty in the pan under the sink. It was a chore she should have done last night. Laura went over and smacked her on the cheek, just to shut her up for a minute, and Francy fell on the floor. Then Laura gave her a kick in the stomach, something she'd never done before. Francy lay there, silent for once.

Stevie stared wide-eyed and gaping, looking as if he didn't know whether to laugh or cry. Laura kicked her shoes off and went to get a beer. Naturally, there wasn't any. Laura combed her hair, then went down to the delicatessen. When she came back, Francy was sitting where she had lain before, and crying again. Change the diaper again? Stick a pair of dirty rubber pants on her? Laura opened a beer, drank some, then changed the diaper just to be doing something. Still with the beer beside her, she filled the sink with sudsy water and dumped the six pairs of rubber pants into it, and a couple of rinsed-out but filthy diapers as well.

The doorbell rang at noon, and it was Mrs Crabbe, damn her eyes, just about as welcome as the cops.

This time Laura was insolent. She interrupted the old bitch every time she spoke. Mrs Crabbe was asking how the children came to get the sleeping pills? What time had they eaten them?

'I don't know why any human being has to put up with intrusions like this!' Laura yelled.

'Do you realize that your son is dead? He was bleeding internally from glass particles.'

Laura let fly one of Eddie's favourite curses.

Then the old bag left the house, and Laura drank her beer, three cans of it. She was thirsty. When the bell rang again, she didn't answer it, but soon there was a knocking on the door. After a few minutes, Laura got so tired of it, she opened the door. It was old Crabbe again with two men in white, one carrying a satchel. Laura put up a fight, but they got a strait-jacket on her. They took her to another hospital, not St Vincent's. Here two people held her while a third person gave her a needle. The needle nearly knocked her out, but not quite.

That was how, one month later, she got her abortion. The most blessed event that ever happened to her.

She had to stay in the place – Bellevue – all that time. When she told the shrinks she was really fed up with marriage, her marriage, they seemed to believe her and to understand, yet they admitted to her finally that all their treatment was designed to make her go back to that marriage. Meanwhile, the three kids, Helen had recovered, were in some kind of free nursery. Eddie had come to see her, but she didn't want to see him, and thank God they hadn't forced her to. Laura wanted a divorce, but she knew Eddie would never say yes to a divorce. He thought people just didn't get divorced. Laura wanted to be free, independent, and alone. She didn't want to see the kids, either.

'I want to make a new life,' she said to the psychiatrists, who had become as boring as Mrs Crabbe.

The only way to get out of the place was to fool them, Laura realized, so she began to humour them, gradually. She would be allowed to go, they said, on condition that she went back to Eddie. But she wrung from a doctor a signed statement – she insisted on having it in writing – that she was to have no more children, which effectively meant that she had a right to take the Pill.

Eddie didn't like that, even if it was a doctor's orders. 'That's not marriage,' Eddie said.

Eddie had found a girlfriend while she was in Bellevue, and some nights he didn't come home, and went to work from wherever he was sleeping. Laura hired a detective for just one day, and discovered the woman's name and address. Then Laura sued for divorce on the grounds of adultery, no alimony asked, real Women's Lib. Eddie got the kids, which was fine with Laura because he wanted them more than she did. Laura got a full-time job in a department store, which was a bit tough, standing on her feet for so many hours, but all in all not so tough as what she had left. She was only twenty-five, and quite nice looking if she took the time to do her face and dress properly. There were good chances of advancement in her job, too.

'I feel peaceful now,' Laura said to a new friend to whom she had told her past. 'I feel different, as if I've lived a hundred years, and yet I'm still pretty young . . . Marriage? No, never again.'

She woke up and found it was all a dream. Well, not *all* a dream. The awakening was gradual, not a sudden awareness as in the morning when you open your eyes and see what's really in front of you. She'd been taking two kinds of pills on the doctor's orders. Now it seemed to her that the pills had been trick pills, to make the world seem rosy, to make her more cheerful – but really to get her to walk back into the same trap, like a doped sheep. She found herself standing at the sink on Hudson Street with a dishtowel in her hands. It was morning. 10.22 by the clock by the bed. But she *had* been to Bellevue, hadn't she? And Georgie had died, because now in the apartment there were only Stevie and Helen and Francy. It was September, she saw by a newspaper that was lying on the kitchen table. And – and where was it? The piece of paper the doctor had signed?

Where did she keep it, in her billfold? She looked and it wasn't there. She unzipped the pocket in her handbag. Not there either. But she'd had it. Hadn't she? For an instant, she wondered if she was pregnant, but there wasn't a sign of it at her waistline. Then she went as if drawn by a mysterious force, a hypnotist's force, to a bruised brown leather box where she kept necklaces and bracelets. In this box was a tarnished old silver cigarette case big enough for only four cigarettes, and inside this was a folded piece of crisp white paper. That was it. She had it.

She went into the bathroom and looked into the medicine cabinet. What did they look like? There was something called Ovral. That must be it, it sounded sort of eggy. Well, at least she was taking them, the bottle was half empty. And Eddie was annoyed. She remembered now. But he had to put up with it, that was all.

But she hadn't tracked down his girlfriend with a detective. She hadn't had the job in the department store. Funny, when it was all so clear, that job, selling bright scarves and hosiery, making up her face so she looked great, making new friends. Had Eddie had a girlfriend? Laura simply wasn't sure. Anyway, he had to put up with the Pill now, which was one small triumph for her. But it didn't quite make up for what she had to put up with. Francy was crying. Maybe it was time to feed her.

Laura stood in the kitchen, biting her underlip, thinking she had to feed Francy now – food always shut her up a little – and thinking she'd have to start thinking hard, now that she could think, now that she was fully awake. Good God, life couldn't just go on like this, could it? She'd doubtless lost the job at the diner, so she'd have to find another, because they couldn't make it on Eddie's pay alone. *Feed Francy*.

The doorbell rang. Laura hesitated briefly, then pushed the release button. She had no idea who it was.

Francy yelled.

'All *right*!' Laura snapped, and headed for the fridge.

A knock on the door.

Laura opened the door. It was Mrs Crabbe.

P. D. JAMES

A Very Desirable Residence

DURING and after Harold Vinson's trial, at which I was a relatively unimportant prosecution witness, there was the usual uninformed, pointless, and repetitive speculation about whether those of us who knew him would ever have guessed that he was a man capable of scheming to murder his wife. I was supposed to have known him better than most of the school staff and my colleagues found it irritatingly self-righteous of me to be so very reluctant to be drawn into the general gossip about what, after all, was the school's major scandal in twenty years. 'You knew them both. You used to visit the house. You saw them together. Didn't you guess?' they insisted, obviously feeling that I had been in some way negligent, that I ought to have seen what was going on and prevented it. No, I never guessed; or, if I did, I guessed wrong. But they were perfectly right. I could have prevented it.

I first met Harold Vinson when I took up a post as junior art master at the comprehensive school where he taught mathematics to the senior forms. It wasn't too discouraging a place as these teaching factories go. The school was centred on the old eighteenth-century grammar school, with some not too hideous modern additions, in a pleasant enough commuter town on the river about twenty miles south-east of London. it was a predominantly middle-class community, a little smug and culturally self-conscious, but hardly intellectually exciting. Still, it suited me well enough for a first post. I don't object to the middle-class or their habitats; I'm middle-class myself. And I knew that I was lucky to get the job. Mine is the usual story of an artist with sufficient talent but without enough respect for the fashionable idiocies of the contemporary artistic establishment to make a decent living. More dedicated men choose to live in cheap bed-sitting rooms and keep on painting. I'm fussy about where and how I live so, for me, it was a diploma in the teaching of art and West Fairing Comprehensive.

It only took one evening in Vinson's home for me to realize that he was a sadist. I don't mean that he tormented his pupils. He wouldn't have been allowed to get away with it had he tried. These days the balance of power in the classroom has shifted with a vengeance and any tormenting is done by the children. No, as a teacher, he was surprisingly patient and conscientious, a man with real enthusiam for his subject ('discipline' was the word he preferred to use being something of an intellectual snob and given to academic jargon) with a surprising talent for communicating that enthusiasm to the children. He was a fairly rigid disciplinarian, but I've never found that children dislike firmness provided a master doesn't indulge in that pedantic sarcasm which, by taking advantage of the children's inability to compete, is resented as particularly unfair. He got them through their examinations too. Say what you like, that's something middle-class kids and their parents appreciate. I'm sorry to have slipped into using the word 'kids', that modern shibboleth with its blend of condescension and sycophancy. Vinson never used it. It was his habit to talk about the alumni of the sixth. At first I thought it was an attempt at mildly pretentious humour, but now I wonder. He wasn't really a humorous man. The rigid muscles of his face seldom cracked into a smile and when they did it was as disconcerting as a painful grimace. With his lean, slightly stooping figure, the grave eyes behind the horn-rimmed spectacles, the querulous lines etched deeply from the nose to the corners of his unyielding mouth, he looked deceptively what we all thought he was – a middle-aged, disagreeable, and not very happy pedant.

No, it wasn't his precious alumni whom he bullied and tyrannized over. It was his wife. The first time I saw Emily Vinson was when I sat next to her at founder's memorial day, an archaic function inherited from the grammar school and regarded with such reverence that even those masters' wives who seldom showed their faces at the school felt obliged to make an appearance. She was, I guessed, almost twenty years younger than her husband, a thin, anxious-looking woman with auburn hair which had faded early and the very pale transparent-looking skin which often goes with that colouring. She was expensively and smartly dressed, too incongruously smartly for such a nondescript woman so that the ill-chosen too fashionable suit merely emphasized her frail ordinariness. But her eyes were remarkable, an unusual grey green, huge and slightly exophthalmic under the arched narrow eyebrows. She seldom turned them on me but when, from time to time, she gave me a swift elliptical glance it was as astounding as turning over an amateurish Victorian oil and discovering a Corot.

It was at the end of founder's memorial day that I received my first invitation to visit them at their home. I found that they lived in some style. She had inherited from her father a small but perfectly proportioned Georgian house which stood alone in some two acres of ground with lawns slanting green down to the river. Apparently her father was a builder who had bought the house cheaply from its impoverished owner with the idea of demolishing it and building a block of flats. The planning authority had slapped on a preservation order just in time and he had died in weeks, no doubt from chagrin, leaving the house and its contents to his daughter. Neither Harold Vinson nor his wife seemed to appreciate their possession. He grumbled about the expense; she grumbled about the housework. The perfectly proportioned façade, so beautiful that it took the breath, seemed to leave them as unmoved as if they lived in a square brick box. Even the furniture, which had been bought with the house, was regarded by them with as little respect as if it were cheap reproduction. When at the end of my first visit I complimented Vinson on the spaciousness and proportions of the dining-room he replied, 'A house is only the space between four walls. What does it matter if they are far apart or close together, or what they are made of? You're still in a cage.' His wife was carrying the plates into the kitchen at the time and didn't hear him. He spoke so low that I scarcely heard him myself. I am not even sure now that I was meant to hear.

Marriage is both the most public and the most secret of institutions, its miseries as irritatingly insistent as a hacking cough, its private malaise less easily diagnosed. And nothing is so destructive as unhappiness to social life. No one wants to sit in embarrassed silence while his host and hostess demonstrate their mutual incompatibility and dislike. She could, it seemed, hardly open her mouth without irritating him. No opinion she expressed was worth listening to. Her small domestic chat – which was, after all, all she had – invariably provoked him by its banality so that he would put down his knife and fork with a look of patient resigned boredom as soon as, with a nervous preparatory glance at him, she would steel herself to speak. If she had been an animal, cringing away with that histrionic essentially false look of piteous entreaty, I can see that the temptation to kick would be irresistible. And, verbally, Vinson kicked.

Not surprisingly they had few friends. Looking back it would probably be more true to say that they had no real friends. The only colleague of his who visited from the school, apart from myself, was Vera Pelling, the junior science teacher, and she, poor girl, was such an unattractive bore that there weren't many alternatives open to her. Vera Pelling is the living refutation of that theory so beloved, I understand, of beauty and fashion journalists in women's magazines that any woman if she takes the trouble can make something of her appearance. Nothing could be done about Vera's pig-like eyes and non-existent chin and, reasonably enough, she didn't try. I am sorry if I sound harsh. She wasn't a bad sort. And if she thought that making a fourth with me at an occasional free supper with the Vinsons was better than eating alone in her furnished flat I suppose she had her reasons, as I had mine. I never remember having visited the Vinsons without Vera although Emily came to my flat on three occasions, with Harold's approval, to sit for her portrait. It wasn't a success. The result looked like a pastiche of an early Stanley Spencer. Whatever it was I was trying to capture, that sense of a secret life conveyed in the rare grey-green flash of those remarkable eyes, I didn't succeed. When Vinson saw the portrait he said:

'You were prudent, my boy, to opt for teaching as a livelihood. Although, looking at this effort, I would say that the choice was hardly voluntary.' For once I was tempted to agree with him.

Vera Pelling and I became oddly obsessed with the Vinsons. Walking home after one of their supper parties we would mull over the traumas of the evening like an old married couple perennially discussing the inadequacies of a couple of relatives whom we actively disliked but couldn't bear not to see. Vera was a tolerable mimic and would imitate Vinson's dry, pedantic tones.

'My dear, I think that you recounted that not very interesting domestic drama last time we had supper together.'

'And what, my dear, have you been doing with yourself today? What fascinating conversation did you have with the estimable Mrs Wilcox while you cleaned the drawing-room together?'

Really, confided Vera, tucking her arm through mine, it had become so embarrassing that it was almost enough to put her off visiting them. But not quite enough apparently. Which was why she, too, was at the Vinsons' on the night when it happened.

On the evening of the crime – the phrase has a stereotyped but dramatic ring which isn't inappropriate to what, look at it as you will, was no ordinary villainy – Vera and I were due at the school at 7 p.m. to help with the dress rehearsal of the school play. I was responsible for the painted backcloth and some of the props and Vera for the make-up. It was an awkward time, too early for a proper meal beforehand and too late to make it sensible to stay on at school without some thought of supper, and when Emily Vinson issued through her husband an invitation to both Vera and me to have coffee and sandwiches at six o'clock it seemed sensible to accept. Admittedly, Vinson made it plain that the idea was his wife's. He seemed mildly surprised that she should wish to entertain us so briefly – insist on entertaining us, was the expression he used. Vinson himself wasn't involved with the play. He never grudged spending his private time to give extra tuition in his own subject but made it a matter of rigid policy never to become involved in what he described as extra-mural *divertissements* appealing only to the regressed adolescent. He was, however, a keen chess player and on Wednesday evenings spent the three hours from nine until midnight at the local chess club of which he was secretary. He was a man of meticulous habit and any school activity on a Wednesday evening would, in any case, have had to manage without him.

Every detail, every word spoken at that brief and unremarkable meal – dry ham sandwiches cut too thick and synthetic coffee – was recounted by Vera and me at the Crown Court so that it has always intrigued me that I can no longer visualize the scene. I know exactly what happened, of course. I can recount every word. It's just that I can no longer shut my eyes and see the supper table, the four of us seated there, imprinted in colours on the mind's eye. Vera and I said at the trial that both Vinsons seemed more than usually ill at ease, that Harold, in particular, gave us the impression that he wished we weren't there. But that could have been hindsight.

The vital incident, if you can call it that, happened towards the end of the meal. It was so very ordinary at the time, so crucial in retrospect. Emily Vinson, as if uneasily aware of her duties as hostess and of the unaccountable silence which had fallen on the table, made a palpable effort. Looking up with a nervous glance at her husband she said:

'Two such very nice and polite workmen came this morning—' Vinson touched his lips with his paper serviette then crumpled it convulsively. His voice was unusually sharp as he broke in: 'Emily my dear, do you think you could spare us the details of your domestic routine this evening? I've had a particularly tiring day. And I am trying to concentrate my mind on this evening's game.' And that was all.

The dress rehearsal was over at about nine o'clock, as planned, and I told Vera that I had left a library book at the

Vinsons' and was anxious to pick it up on the way home. She made no objection. She gave the impression, poor girl, that she was never particularly anxious to get home. It was only a quarter of an hour's brisk walk to the house and, when we arrived, we saw at once that something was wrong. There were two cars, one with a blue light on the roof, and an ambulance parked unobtrusively but unmistakably at the side of the house. Vera and I glanced briefly at each other then ran to the front door. It was shut. Without ringing we dashed round to the side. The back door, leading to the kitchen quarters, was open. I had an immediate impression that the house was peopled with large men, two of them in uniform. There was, I remember, a policewoman bending over the prone figure of Emily Vinson. And their cleaning woman, Mrs Wilcox, was there too. I heard Vera explaining to a plain-clothes policeman, obviously the senior man present, that we were friends of the Vinsons, that we had been there to supper only that evening. 'What's happened?' she kept asking. 'What's happened?' Before the police could answer Mrs Wilcox was spitting it all out, eyes bright with self-important outrage and excitement. I sensed that the police wanted to get rid of her, but she wasn't so easily dislodged. And, after all, she had been first on the scene. She knew it all. I heard it in a series of disjointed sentences:

'Knocked on the head – terrible bruise – marks all over the parquet flooring where he dragged her – only just coming round now – human fiend – head resting on a cushion in the gas stove – the poor darling – came in just in time at 9.20 – always come to watch colour TV with her on Wednesday night – back door open as usual – found the note on the kitchen table.' The figure writhing on the floor, groaning and crying in a series of harsh grunting moans like an animal in travail, suddenly raised herself and spoke coherently.

'I didn't write it! I didn't write it!'

'You mean Mr Vinson tried to kill her?' Vera was incredulous, head turning from Mrs Wilcox to the watchful, inscrutable faces of the police. The senior officer broke in:

'Now Mrs Wilcox, I think it's time you went home. The

ambulance is here. An officer will come along for your statement later this evening. We'll look after Mrs Vinson. There's nothing else for you to do.'

He turned to Vera and me. 'If you two were here earlier this evening, I'd like a word. We're fetching Mr Vinson now from his chess club. But if you two will just wait in the sitting-room please.'

Vera said: 'But if he knocked her unconscious and put her head in the gas oven, then why isn't she dead?'

It was Mrs Wilcox who replied, turning triumphantly as she was led out:

'The conversion, that's why. We're on natural gas from this morning. That North Sea stuff. It isn't poisonous. The two men from the Gas Board came just after nine o'clock.'

They were lifting Emily Vinson on to a stretcher now. Her voice came to us in a high querulous wail.

'I tried to tell him. You remember? You heard him? I tried to tell him.'

The suicide note was one of the exhibits at Vinson's trial. A document examiner from the forensic science laboratory testified that it was a forgery, a clever forgery but not Mrs Vinson's writing. He couldn't give an opinion on whether it was the work of the husband, although it was certainly written on a page taken from a writing pad found in the desk in the sitting-room. It bore no resemblance to the accused's normal writing. But, in his view, it hadn't been written by Mrs Vinson. He gave a number of technical reasons to support his view and the jury listened respectfully. But they weren't surprised. They knew that it hadn't been written by Mrs Vinson. She had stood in the witness box and told them so. And they were perfectly clear in their own minds who had written it.

There was other forensic evidence. Mrs Wilcox's 'Marks all over the parquet floor' were reduced to one long but shallow scrape, just inside the sitting-room door. But it was a significant scrape. It had been made by the heels of Emily Vinson's shoes. Traces of the floor polish which she used were found, not on the soles, but on the sides of the scraped heels, and there were minute traces of her shoe polish in the scrape.

The fingerprint officer gave evidence. I hadn't realized until then that fingerprint experts are mostly civilians. It must be a dull job, that constant and meticulous examination of surface for the tell-tale composites and whorls. Hard on the eyes, I should think. In this case the significance was that he hadn't found any prints. The gas taps had been wiped clean. I could see the jury physically perk up at the news. That was a mistake all right. It didn't need the prosecution to point out that the taps should have shown Mrs Vinson's prints. She, after all, had cooked their last meal. A cleverer murderer would merely have worn gloves, smudging any existing prints but ensuring that he left none of his own. It had been an over-precaution to wipe the gas taps clean.

Emily Vinson, quiet, distressed but gallant, obviously reluctant to testify against her husband, was remarkably competent in the witness box. I hardly recognized her. No, she hadn't told her husband that she and Mrs Wilcox had arranged to watch the television together shortly after nine o'clock. Mrs Wilcox, who lived near by, usually did come across to spend a couple of hours with her on Wednesday nights when Mr Vinson was at his chess club. No, she hadn't liked to tell Mr Vinson. Mr Vinson wasn't very fond of inviting people in. The message came over to the jury as clearly as if she had spelt it out, the picture of a downtrodden, unintellectual wife craving the human companionship which her husband denied her, guiltily watching a popular TV show with her cleaning woman at a time when she would be certain that her husband wouldn't catch them out. I glanced at his proud, unyielding mask, at the hands clutched over the edge of the dock, and imagined what he was thinking, what he would have said.

'Surely you have enough of domestic trivia and Mrs Wilcox's conversation, hardly exciting I should have thought, without inviting her into your drawing-room. The woman should know her place.'

The trial didn't take long. Vinson made no defence except to reiterate stubbornly, eyes fixed straight ahead, that he hadn't done it. His counsel did his best, but with the dogged persistence of a man resigned to failure, and the jury had the look of people glad to be faced, for once, with a clear-cut case they could actually understand. The verdict was inevitable. And the subsequent divorce hearing was even shorter. It isn't difficult to persuade a judge that your marriage has irretrievably broken down when your husband is serving a prison sentence for attempted murder.

Two months after the decree absolute we married and I took over the Georgian house, the river view, the Regency furniture. With the physical possessions I knew exactly what I was getting. With my wife, I wasn't so sure. There had been something disturbing, even a little frightening, about the competence with which she had carried out my instructions. It hadn't, of course, been particularly difficult. We had planned it together during those sessions when I was painting her portrait. I had written and handed her the fake suicide note on the paper she had supplied a few days before our plans matured. We knew when the gas was due to be converted. She had, as instructed, placed the note on the kitchen table before scraping the heels of her shoes across the polished floor. She had even managed beautifully the only tricky part, to bang the back of her head sufficiently hard against the kitchen wall to raise an impressive bruise but not sufficiently hard to risk bungling the final preparations; the cushion placed in the bottom of the oven for the head, the gas tap turned on and then wiped clean with her handkerchief.

And who could have imagined that she was such a consummate actress? Sometimes, remembering that anguished animal cry of 'I tried to tell him. I tried to tell him,' I wonder again what is going on behind those remarkable eyes. She still acts, of course. I find it remarkably irritating, that habit she has particularly when we are in company, of turning on me that meek, supplicating, beaten-dog expression whenever I talk to her. It provokes unkindness. Perhaps it's intended to. I'm afraid I'm beginning to get rather a reputation for sadism. People don't seem to want to come to the house any more.

There is one solution, of course, and I can't pretend that I haven't pondered it. A man who has killed another merely to get his house isn't likely to be too fastidious about killing again. And it was murder; I have to accept that.

Vinson only served nine months of his sentence before dying in the prison hospital of what should have been an uncomplicated attack of influenza. Perhaps his job really was his life and without his precious alumni the will to live snapped. Or perhaps he didn't choose to live with the memory of his wife's great betrayal. Beneath the petty tyranny, the impatience, the acerbity, there may have been love of a kind.

But the ultimate solution is barred to me. A month ago Emily explained, meekly, like a child propounding a problem, and with a swift sidelong glance, that she had written a confession and left it with her solicitor.

'Just in case anything happens to me, darling.'

She explained that what we did to poor Harold is preying on her mind but that she feels better now that all the details are written down and she can be sure that, after her death, the truth will at last be known and Harold's memory cleared. She couldn't have made it more plain to me that it is in my interest to see that I die first.

I killed Harold Vinson to get the house; Emily to get me. On the whole, she made the better bargain. In a few weeks I shall lose the house. Emily is selling it. After all, there's nothing I can do to stop her; the place belongs to her not me.

After we married I gave up the teaching post, finding it embarrassing to meet any colleagues as Emily's husband. It was not that anyone suspected. Why should they? I had a perfect alibi for the time of the crime. But I had a dream that, living in that perfection, I might become a painter after all. That was the greatest illusion of all.

So now they are taking down from the end of the drive the board which states 'This Desirable Residence For Sale'. Emily got a very good price for the house and the furniture. More than enough to buy the small but pretentious brick box on an executive estate in North London which will be my cage from now on. Everything is sold. We're taking nothing with us except the gas stove. But, as Emily pointed out when I remonstrated, why not? It's in perfectly good working order.

H. R. F. KEATING

The Evidence I Shall Give

SERGEANT MOOS was a dashed bore. Inspector Ghote thought he was actually the most boring person he had ever known, a one hundred and one per cent burden and bugbear. The trouble was the man could talk about just one thing only. His job, his kaam. Fingerprints.

Certainly there was no one to touch him in the entire Bombay Crime Branch as an expert. For that reason, though he was past the statutory age of retirement, he had somehow stayed on in his little cabin, its filing cabinets crammed with the prints of every miscreant who had ever come to police notice. He was, in fact, one famous fellow. It should have been a great honour even to know him. Except he was altogether unable to speak of anything else than his whorls, his loops, and his arches.

So, although from time to time Ghote felt obliged to allow himself to be caught by Moos, who seemed to know by some sort of telepathy if he had gone across for something to eat or was on the point of leaving for home, mostly he went to a good deal of trouble to keep out of his way. He had heard Moos's stories and accounts too often, each and every one of them.

'Ghote bhai, was I ever telling you one trick your clever badmash is sometimes trying? You know what it is such a fellow is attempting? He is presenting his fingers to be printed in wrong order only. Yes, yes, one devilish cunning move. He is thinking that when the said card is coming before me and I am seeing twinned loops and tented arches on third finger of right hand when on my records I have such on fourth finger I would be altogether deceived.'

At that point in this story – each time it was told – a glow of simple pleasure would come into the big, soft, brown eyes in Moos's round moon-like face and the cigarette that seemed to dangle permanently from his thickly loose lips would for a moment burn with a brighter light.

'But what a badmash like that is not at all counting on,' Moos would continue, filling in every possible corner of the picture, 'is that I am having a tip-top memory for any shape or form of fingerprint. Yes, tip-top, though I am saying it. So every time I am catching out such fellows. Never once failing.'

'Shabash, Sergeant, Shabash,' Ghote would dutifully offer congratulation.

But congratulations never brought to a halt the steady dribble of fingerprint fact and fingerprint theory, the be-all and end-all of Sergeant Moos's existence. He had no other interests. He was not married, and all he did when at last he left his cabin after a day's work was to get something to eat and then retire to his quarter where – Ghote had heard this at least a hundred times – he was collecting information to write the really definitive Indian book on – well, fingerprints.

So, when at the end of his own long day Ghote might be heading for home, thinking only of his Protima with his food waiting or ready if he was particularly tired to press his feet, and Moos would appear suddenly at his elbows with 'Inspector, what luck I am spotting you,' his first reaction would be to put up some excuse. Any excuse.

'Oh, hello, Moos bhai. Just off to . . . Well, I am in one devil of a hurry, you know.'

But then, more often than he could have wished, that excuse would fall away into nothingness. The look of pleading in Moos's big brown eyes would be too sad to ignore.

'But perhaps I can spare some minutes only.'

Then, over a cold drink at Moos's expense – he was punctilious about paying for his pleasure – there would come once again the story about how such-and-such a history-sheeter had failed to beat Moos's fabulous memory by presenting his fingers to an inexperienced print taker in the wrong order. Or perhaps it would be some other piece of oft-repeated information.

'Did I ever tell, Inspector – not many people are knowing this – it is between the third and fourth what they are calling foetal month that the fingerprints are formed on the unborn child. And those prints thereafter are remaining for the whole of the said person's life unchanged? Those unique prints. Did you know that?'

And Moos would lean back from the little round table with the two fizzing glasses of Thums Up or Limca on it and a look of sun-effulgent pleasure at the beauty of that fact would spread all over his round face. The wet-tipped cigarette between his lips would perk up till it was pointing straight out in front of him, jauntily.

How then could Ghote say, 'Yes, Sergeant, you have told me this already'? But after each such session he would say to himself that he was now entitled to adopt any evasive tactics that came to hand to prevent himself being caught again. For at least two weeks.

So it was with a feeling of entirely justified fury that late one afternoon he looked up from his desk to see Moos come bursting in. Only two days before had he not listened patiently for nearly three-quarters of an hour while he had been told – as if it wasn't something he had known since he had been probationary sub-inspector at Nasik Police Training School – that a workable method of classifying fingerprints had first been developed in India in 1897 by Mr Edward Henry, later Sir Edward, Commissioner of Police at Scotland Yard, and that his trusted assistant, Sub-Inspector Azizul Haque, had earned the title Rai Bahadur and an award of Rs 5,000?

'Oh, Ghote, you are here?'

'Yes. Why would I not be in my seat? Unless I was out on a case. As I have been till one hour past, and my report not yet finished.'

But the pointed remark went for nothing. Moos simply slouched forward, pulled away one of the chairs in front of the desk and slumped down on to it.

On his innocent typewriter Ghote took out the rage he felt at this blatant disregard of the unacknowledged agreement that he should be badgered by Moos only when he was not actually at work. He seized the wretched machine and dumped it on the floor beside his narrow desk with a crash that risked yet another key becoming appallingly stuck.

But then, as he looked across at Moos, something in the fellow's wide round face drained all his anger away. He did not look at all well. He looked, in fact, grey with illness, or with perhaps the effect of some catastrophic news. And, for surely the first time ever in his recollection of him, he was not mangling a cigarette between his lips.

'What is it you are wanting, bhai?' he asked then, fearing what he might hear in reply.

But to his surprise Moos answered with his usual request.

'I was wondering – if – if you have some minutes only to spare, Inspector, can we go for a cold drink?'

For a moment Ghote contemplated, in the face of this, saying straight out that they did have an arrangement, however much it had never been spoken of, that Moos would not get more than one chat per fortnight. But the grey look on the fellow's face was still there, undiminished. So, although this happened to be the first evening for a week that he was going to be able to get home at a decent hour, he yielded.

He received another surprise then. Moos, although scrupulous about standing treat, invariably took him to an Irani restaurant some way from Headquarters where the prices were moderate. Now unexpectedly he proposed a complete break with tradition.

'It is good of you to find some time, Inspector,' he said. 'I am well knowing you must be wanting to get back to your wife and child. But – but – well, shall we go to Badshah Juice Bar? You were once stating you were very much enjoying their Ganga Jamuna.'

It was true that the mixture of fresh lemon and orange juice, called in comparison with the confluence of the two holiest of India's rivers a Ganga Jamuna, was something, served deliciously chilled, that Ghote particularly delighted in on the rare occasions he felt he could allow himself to sample the air-conditioned luxury of the Badshah, just over the way from

Headquarters. But it was extraordinary that, since there could be no fingerprint link to that indulgence of his, Moos should ever have remembered it.

And why was Moos offering to take him to such a posh place at all?

Evidently he was not going to find the answer in a hurry. Once having secured himself the promise of an audience, Moos lapsed into heavy silence. Ghote rapidly cleared the papers from his desk, acknowledging to himself that he had had little intention of finishing his report that day, called to the office peon that he was leaving and made his way, with Moos a looming stone-like presence at his side, out and across the jostling, horn-hooting streams of traffic to the Badshah Juice Bar.

When at last he was seated in front of a tall condensation-pearled glass of Ganga Jamuna, and Moos, opposite, had a simple mosambi juice, which despite the fact that he was still not smoking it looked as if he had little intention of touching, he ventured to put a question.

'Well, Sergeant, what is it you are wanting to chat?'

But Moos did not answer.

Ghote shot him a glance in the cool dimness of the bar's upstairs room. Certainly, he did not look at all well.

'Bhai, are you ill itself? Is it serious?'

Thoughts of cancer – all those cigarettes – of leprosy even flashed into Ghote's mind.

'No, no,' Moos replied, however. 'I am hundred per cent fit, Inspector. You are knowing I have never had one day of sick leave in all my years of service?'

'Yes, yes. I remember you saying it. But – but, all the same, you look as if you are not keeping well, bhai.'

'Well?'

Moos sounded as if this was the first he had ever heard of any suggestion that he might be ill. But, if he was not so, what could be wrong with him? And this silence? He was hardly reluctant normally to talk, to talk and to talk, whenever he had secured a captive audience. So why was he saying nothing now?

Ghote took a sip of his Ganga Jamuna. It was, as ever, delicious. But somehow he could not quite savour it to the full.

He looked across at Moos.

'Inspector,' the old fellow said at last, seeming to drag the word syllable by syllable, letter almost by letter, from deep inside himself. 'Inspector, there is something I have to tell.'

'Yes? But that is what we have come here for, isn't it? For you to chat.'

Moos picked up his glass of mosambi juice, looked at it and put it down again.

'Inspector,' he asked, lowering his voice almost to a murmur. 'Inspector, you are knowing the Phalnikar case?'

'But yes, Sergeant. Of course. Up in court tomorrow, no? Plenty of kudos for Crime Branch there. Who would ever have thought we would be able to lay hands on the culprit when they were first finding His Honour's body in that flat that day? And your evidence will be the clincher, bhai. No getting past fingerprints.'

Sergeant Moos was famous, too, for his demeanour in the witness-box. No Defence pleader, however wily his tactics, however hectoring, had ever been known to shake Moos's simple certainties.

But, instead of the slow smile of satisfaction Ghote had hoped to call up on Moos's face by that tribute to the part he would play next day in bringing a murderer to justice, he replied only with a heaving groan.

'Moos? Moos bhai, what is it? What has happened?'

'It – it – it is this.'

But there followed only another groan. From the depths.

'Yes, bhai? What it is?'

'Inspector, I have found – I have found something.'

'Found something? What? Surely not that you have mis-identified that print from the Phalnikar flat? You were telling a fortnight ago how good it was.'

'No, no. It is not that.'

'But then what is it, bhai? It is to do with the Phalnikar case?

It cannot be anything too bad if it does not affect the evidence you would be giving.'

'Inspector, it is worse. Worse. Altogether worse.'

'No? What? Tell me, bhai. Tell me.'

'Inspector . . .'

Moos's voice had sunk yet lower. A mere sloshy whisper.

'Inspector, it is this. I have found – I have found one print that is altogether identical with the one belonging to the culprit in the Phalnikar case.'

'Identical?' Ghote repeated, struggling with bafflement. 'But – but that cannot be, bhai. So often you are telling. I was learning it at PTS even. No fingerprints are identical.'

Wearily, with bowed-under weariness, Moos wagged his head in negative.

'No, Ghote, that is not what I have ever said. It is not what you were truly taught at Training School either. What I have always stated is that chances of two prints being one and the same have been calculated from the number of variable factors to be found on each finger, ridge endings, islands, lakes, spurs, crossovers, and bifurcations, as coming out at one in one hundred thousand crores. It is because of this that it is always accepted that prints constitute infallible evidence.'

Figures slowly surfaced in Ghote's mind. 1:1,000,000,000,000. It was an incredibly small chance.

He looked at Moos across the narrow marble table.

'And you are telling that this fantastic chance has actually happened?' he asked. 'That you have seen a print that is cent per cent the same as the Phalnikar murderer's?'

'Yes.'

It was a whisper of a whisper.

'You are sure?'

The question was ridiculous, he knew. Moos, when it was anything at all to do with fingerprints, was always doubly, trebly, cast-iron sure.

'Yes, bhai. I am sure.'

The voice came as a series of small dull hammer-strokes.

After a moment Moos gave another of his beaten and battered groans.

'You are knowing, Inspector,' he went on ploddingly after a moment, 'that in different countries they have different standards of comparison for prints. It is something I must have told one lakh times. We are having different standards in the different states of India even. In Karnataka it is twelve points that must agree before identity is accepted. In the UP it is six only. While in France it is as many as seventeen. And in UK it is sixteen.'

'Yes, yes.'

It was true, as Moos had said, that he had produced these figures and others like them time and again in their chats. But never, till now, had he admitted by so much as a hint that the substance of their conversations had often been repeated and repeated.

'Well, Inspector, in these two prints I am telling you about I have checked, point for point, more than twenty-five agreeing. It was only this morning that I was going over my evidence for court tomorrow – I am liking to have everything clear in my head, you know – and, suddenly, looking at the Phalnikar culprit's print, something became triggered off in my mind. A similarity, a most close similarity. I thought for a few moments only, and then I was able to go straight to the file in question. It was that of one Ram Prasad, just only one conviction for HB.'

'One housebreaking conviction only, and you were remembering that print? Moos bhai, you are altogether a wonder.'

But the flattery did nothing for old Moos. He sat there at the table, his face still as grey as if he was working up to a dose of high fever. His expression, that of a man who has just learnt he is going to be hanged or shot.

'But,' Ghote said eventually, 'this is going to cast doubt upon all fingerprint evidences in each and every court, no? I mean, I can hear Defence pleaders one and all referring to this discovery which you are making and stating that someone other than the accused must have committed the crime.'

'Yes, yes. But it is worse, much worse. I have been sitting all day since I was checking and double-checking what I had found, and I have been thinking. It is not just only our cases, Inspector. It is worldwide also.'

'Worldwide?' Ghote thought. 'Yes,' he said. 'Yes, you are right. It would be worldwide. As soon as the news is getting out, everywhere in the world where a case is depending on fingerprint evidence your discovery will be brought in. You will be more famous, Moos bhai, than Rajiv Gandhi himself.'

But Moos was as stolidly unimpressed by this as ever he was in the witness-box by the bullying tactics of a Defence pleader.

'Soon there would be no more cases depending on fingerprint evidence,' he said. 'Before the year is out, I tell you, the fingerprint departments of every police force in the world will be closed down. All the science that has been accumulated since year 1897 is destined to be doomed. All the energies and efforts of nearly one hundred years will be like dew on the grass before the scorch of the sun itself.'

Now it was Ghote's turn to sit in silence. Moos, too, his terrible secret told, was again deprived of speech. His glass of mosambi juice remained untouched in front of him. Gote's Ganga Jamuna seemed equally now to be a mere token allowing him to sit in the dark, cool privacy of the almost empty upstairs room of the Badshah Bar. To sit and think.

Everything Moos had said was true. That single discovery of his, made thanks only to his phenomenal memory for every detail of his day-in, day-out study, was going to put paid for ever to a whole highly important branch of the science of criminal identification. Yes, the name of Moos would be heard on the lips of lawyers from the furthermost west of America to the easternmost parts of Japan. Of Moos, destroyer of Sir Edward Henry, of Sub-Inspector Azizul Haque, of all the scientists and police technicians who had ever worked to create the vast system of fingerprinting.

And then at last his slow-circling thoughts arrived at a conclusion.

He looked up.

'Moos bhai,' he said. 'There is one thing only for you to do.

You must forget what you have seen. You must put back into the files that fingerprint of Ram Prasad and forget that you were ever even suspecting that it was identically the same as that one of the Phalnikar culprit's.'

'No, Ghote bhai. Do not think I have not asked myself one lakh times if I should do that. If it was not my bounden duty even. But do it I cannot. It is there. I have seen it. I cannot persuade myself that I have not.'

'But, bhai, you must. You must. You know what would be the terrible consequences if you do not. You have yourself said it. Criminals by the thousand, by the lakh, by the crore, will escape justice if what you have found ever becomes—'

An appalling thought flashed into his mind.

'Moos bhai,' he said with frenzied intentness, 'have you already told any other person except myself?'

'No, no, Ghote bhai. You know you are the only man in entire Crime Branch who will ever listen to me.'

Ghote registered that, for the second time, Moos had admitted the inadmissible. So it was certain that only the two of them, Moos and himself, knew what had been discovered. Himself. He, too, now knew the world-shattering secret.

He sat in silence again, examining his conscience. What did he feel was his course in answer to the dilemma that now faced him and Moos equally?

Before long he found that his mind was made up. There must be some occasions in life when to lie, or at least to blot out the truth, was the one and only right thing to do. And this, beyond doubt, was one such occasion.

'Moos bhai,' he said with renewed earnestness, 'what you have found out must go no further. Not one inch. Ever.'

'But, Ghote, have you thought? I have been thinking and thinking all day, remember. It is not all so simple. I cannot, I cannot, forget what I have seen with my own two eyes. I have seen it. And you, you will not be able to forget either. Because I will show you the evidence. I must. That much I am owing you. And, once you have seen, you will have always before you the temptation to speak.'

'No,' Ghote jerked out in absolute denial. 'No, no, no.'

'Yes, my friend, you will. I have thought whether I would have this temptation, and I know that it would come to me. Perhaps on my death-bed only I will suddenly crave for that worldwide fame you have spoken of. Or when I am giving my bi-annual lecture at Nasik PTS, that lecture which Commissioner sahib himself was insisting I must give, perhaps then, even as I am explaining about odds of one hundred thousand crores to one, I would suddenly succumb to this temptation. Or what if I am one day getting drunk?'

'But, Moos bhai, you are never getting drunk.'

'Yes, yes. It is true I have never touched any kinds of wines. I have not dared. But in my remaining life who can say that I will not, and then . . .'

'But, no. No, that will not happen. It must not. It will not for me, I am promising. I will never fall to the temptation to speak of this. Never. I have decided. Already my mind is made up. Moos, old friend, I am going to forget we have ever met today.'

'Ghote bhai, you would not be able.'

'Yes. Yes, I shall. It is possible to forget as well as to remember. By one effort of will. From this moment on I am putting out of my mind each and every word that you have said. And I am telling you to do the same. Forget. Forget. Make yourself to forget.'

'No.'

'Yes. It can be done. It can. If you are willing. Go back to your cabin now. Take that card with the prints of Ram Prasad on it, and – yes, burn the same. Take out your lighter or your match-box, and then, better than putting the record of a two-per-paisa criminal back into the files, burn it. Just only burn it.'

'But, Ghote, tomorrow itself I am to give evidence. In the High Court. And when I am asked by the State pleader, as they are always asking as a matter of routine only, whether the fingerprint put in as evidence is that of the accused and the accused only, what am I to say?'

Ghote braced himself.

'You are going to say,' he ordered Moos with all the authority he could bring to bear, 'that the print put in as evidence is that of the accused. You know that this is so. Say it.'

'But, listen, the Phalnikar culprit committed his atrocity in the course of housebreaking, you remember that. And Ram Prasad, whose fingerprint is utterly the same as the one I myself was finding at the scene of the crime, has one conviction for HB itself.'

'Nevertheless,' Ghote answered, leaning forward and directing his full gaze into Moos's big round face, 'you are not going to remember that chance discovery you were making when tomorrow you are in the witness-box. You are not.'

'Ghote, I am. I will. I cannot help myself. Ghote bhai, fingerprints have been my whole life. Without my belief in the truth of them, where would I be? Ghote, on the matter of fingerprints I cannot lie.'

'But, Moos bhai, think. If tomorrow in court you come out with this, then from that moment on the whole of your beloved science of fingerprinting will begin to crumble into dust. Into dust of dust.'

'I know, Ghote, old friend, I know. But what to do? What to do?'

'Forget, bhai. I have said. Forget, forget, forget. Tell yourself that you have dreamt the whole damn thing. Tell yourself you were for two-three moments mad. One way or another, forget.'

'Well, I have wondered that: whether I had gone mad. But that record-sheet, that fingerprint, it is there, Ghote. It is there.'

Moos picked up the untouched glass of mosambi juice and banged it so emphatically on the surface of the table that a dollop of the pale lime slopped out over his hand. He failed to notice it.

'Listen,' he said, 'you must see that card also. Come now. Come and see with your own eyes.'

Ghote wriggled on his bench.

'But what else would that be?' he said, the thought of how long he had been delaying in going home suddenly blooming in his mind. 'I am not at all a fingerprint expert. I could not tell whether you are right or wrong, bhai.'

'No, please to come. Please. I want one more pair of eyes to see what I have seen.'

'No. No, sorry, bhai,' Ghote said, sweat springing up between his thighs despite the air-conditioned coolness all around. 'I must really be going home. Already I am behind schedule one half-hour. But I will come. First thing in the morning I will come to your cabin. I am promising.'

He drained in one long swallow all the rest of his big glass of Ganga Jamuna. It had lost its chill, and tasted only of sour sharpness.

'But, listen, bhai,' he said, looking across at Moos with all the seriousness he could command. 'Think about what I have been saying, yes? Just only forget what you saw. Burn that record card. Or at least put it back into the files. Or, better still, do what they are doing in Government offices with inconvenient letters. Mis-file same. And then forget. Forget it all.'

But Moos's big round face remained sullenly lugubrious.

'It has happened,' he said dully. 'It has happened, and I cannot forget it. I will remember all my life. In court also tomorrow I will not be able to forget.'

But he pushed himself to his feet, and Ghote knew with a wash of inner relief that he himself was free now to go home, to cast off if he could the image of Moos's woebegone face.

'Well, tomorrow we would see,' he said. 'Go back to your quarter now and get a good night's sleep. In the morning it would all look very much of rosier.'

'Yes, I will go. No. No, I will take one more look at those prints. One final-final check. Yes, I must. I must. Goodnight, bhai. And thank you for listening to me.'

Moos had never before offered a word of thanks for all the long hours Ghote had spent hearing his talk of radial loops, ulnar loops, twinned loops, and lateral pocket loops or whatever aspect of his obsession happened to come into his mind at any one time. And Ghote now was sharply conscious of the change. For an instant he wondered whether he ought after all to go back to Headquarters and let Moos show him the wretched, damnable record card, little though probably he would be able to make of it. But the thought of Protima waiting for him, or, more to the point, the thought of a wrathful Protima waiting deterred him.

'Goodnight then, bhai,' he said. 'See you first thing in the morning.'

In a way, however, Ghote saw Moos much sooner than first thing next morning. He saw him in his head through most of that night. He had been unable, indeed, to rid himself of the thought of Moos and his terrible discovery from the moment he had left him. He had been thoroughly poor company for Protima all the evening, till eventually she had said that if she was not going to get one word out of him she might as well go early to bed as she had done every night of the week.

And when, after sitting for half an hour trying to push from his mind every looming remembrance of Moos and his fearful horn-sharp dilemma and not succeeding, he went to bed himself, he found, tired though he had felt, bone-tired suddenly, that he still could not chase away the sight of Moos's round face, for once without a dangling wet-tipped cigarette at its centre, and the look of battered hopelessness in his eyes.

Wryly he thought of the advice he had offered with such conviction. To forget. To blot it all out. He had said to Moos he was going to do that himself, and here he was completely unable so much as to begin.

Was Moos really right in the discovery? Had he actually point by point seen incontrovertible evidence that the two fingerprints from the hands of different men were exactly and absolutely the same? Could he, despite his years-long reputation, have been mistaken?

Had he – this was a new, sudden thought – had he somehow desired to make his discovery, appalling though it had seemed to him? Had he in his innermost self wanted to make it? That chance of two prints being identical, however mathematically unlikely, might well be something that obscurely would haunt someone as obsessed with fingerprints as Moos. So had he, perhaps driven by that obsession to the point of madness, gone so far as actually to invent what he had most dreaded? It was possible. Possible.

Now, violently, he wished he had after all gone to see those two record cards. He would not have been able to make any expert comparison, but he might have been able to see enough to decide there was a prima-facie case. Or not. He might even with a single glance have realized that the prints on the two cards were in no way like each other, and then sadly have had to escort a mad Moos to the pagalkhana.

Then, lying there in the dark and biting his lower lip in vexation, he had told himself that this was the merest wishful thinking. Of course Moos, star witness in hundreds of cases involving fingerprints, never successfully challenged, never found wrong, was bound to be right in what he had seen with his own eyes. Yes, the whole huge edifice of fingerprinting was on the point of coming tumbling down. Tomorrow in the Bombay High Court when Sergeant Moos was called to give evidence a whole new era in criminology would begin. A black era.

At last sleep spread over him.

A sleep plagued with dreams. He saw Moos sitting opposite him in the Badshah Juice Bar and showing him all his fingers and thumbs, each one of them with the same pattern clear to be seen. Whirling, twirling question-marks. He saw Moos in the High Court witness-box, standing on his head. He saw the Judges themselves shrinking and shrinking away into nothingness. He saw his own fingers, and there were no tips to them at all.

He woke early, was as bad-tempered as he had been the evening before, pushed aside the beautifully crisp puris Protima had cooked for his breakfast, stamped out well before his accustomed time and rode his motor-scooter down to Headquarters with unaccustomed recklessness.

He had thought, on arriving, that he might even be too early for Moos. But it seemed not. There was a light on in his cabin, the lines of it bright above and below the door.

Strange, he thought.

But perhaps Moos was taking one more look at that fearful

evidence and had given himself the very strongest possible light to check on each and every one of those inescapable points of correspondence.

He turned the knob and opened the door.

The moment he stepped into the little crowded room, where the fan in the ceiling was whirring grindingly, he realized he was seeing something which at the back of his mind he had been expecting all along, for all that he had pushed the thought down.

Old Moos was slumped across his examination bench in a limp heap. Beside him was a small blue-glass bottle with squared-off ridged sides, its stopper out. Ghote, at that moment, was unable to recall the name of the liquid it had contained, though only a month earlier Moos had shown him the bottle and told him at length for what abstruse purpose he used minute quantities of its contents. 'I have to keep always under lock and key itself,' he had said. 'It is a Number One dangerous poison.'

On the table almost directly in front of the cabin's door there was a large, stiff brown envelope. On it, in staring block capitals, was his own name.

He took a step forward and picked it up. But for a moment he found himself totally incapable of opening it.

What if inside there were, as surely there were bound to be, two fingerprint record cards, each bearing a different name, each with one absolutely identical print? Had the burden, which Moos had found too much for him, been transferred to his own shoulders? Was he going to be left with the evidence, incontrovertible evidence, that there could be two totally identical fingerprints? And if he was, would he now be able to do what he had with such easy-come assurance said to Moos he would be able to do? To forget that he had ever known of their existence?

Yet, just possibly, one single glance at the cards might be enough to tell him that poor Moos had been driven by his obsession into the mere delusions of insanity.

With sweaty, trembling, useless fingers he tore away the top of the envelope, turned it upside-down and tipped its contents on to the table in front of him.

A small pile of grey ashes.

MICHAEL Z. LEWIN

Family Business

AT 0938 hours Gina heard footsteps on the stairs. She sat up from the typewriter and ran a hand through her hair. When the door opened, she was ready with businesslike attention.

In the old days the door had the words PLEASE KNOCK BEFORE ENTERING lettered at the bottom of the glass, but when Gina took over as receptionist-secretary she pointed out that nobody could come up the stairs without being heard and suggested that the door could do without being knocked on. The Old Man, of course, hadn't changed the door, but one of the first things Angelo had done was get the sign painter in to alter the lettering to NO NEED TO KNOCK BEFORE ENTERING. It was longer and that disturbed the symmetry and the Old Man didn't like it and Gina's idea had been to paint out all the stuff about knocking, but Angelo had gone one better and that was Angelo for you.

When the door opened, a woman looked hesitantly into the room.

'Hello,' Gina said. 'Come in.'

The woman was about forty with greying brown hair. Despite the invitation, she was still uncertain. 'Is this the detective agency?' she asked.

'That's right,' Gina replied. 'Can we help you?'

The woman looked as if she was reminding herself of a decision already made. She stepped in and closed the door carefully. Then she turned to face Gina. 'Is the detective in?'

'We have a number of operatives,' Gina said, 'but they are all out working at the moment.'

'Oh,' the woman said.

'Mr Angelo Lunghi is the head of the agency. I can ring him on his car phone if it is an emergency.'

'I know all about car phones,' the woman said. But it didn't sound like an emergency.

Gina said, 'Perhaps the best thing is if you sit down and tell me generally what the problem is.'

'You?' the woman said. Her face said, 'You? The receptionist?'

'That's right. What you say to me is entirely confidential, I promise you. And although Mr Lunghi supervises all our cases personally, I can certainly assess whether we are likely to be able to help you.'

'I see,' the woman said.

'As well as being receptionist and secretary here,' Gina said, 'I am also Mrs Lunghi.'

Dinner was served at 1910, the Lunghis' traditional Thursday evening meal, a hot curry made by Rosetta, Angelo's sister, whose domestic duties doubled with a part-time role as agency accountant. Thursday was a full family evening, which meant that the Old Man and Momma came down from their flat and that the two children, David and Marie, were expected to organize their school and social lives in such a way as to be there. Only Sal – Salvatore, Angelo's older brother, the painter – was not regularly there on Thursdays, Sunday afternoons, and Tuesdays. But sometimes he came and sometimes he brought one of his models, as he called them. It was not an issue.

Gina's parents lived in another city these days.

Tonight Angelo rubbed his hands together as he sat down. 'Good good good,' he said.

'Hey, and what's wrong with spaghetti?' the Old Man asked. But it was in a friendly way, and he said that sort of thing often. Spaghetti or some other pasta was on Sunday.

'Sorry I didn't get back to the office,' Angelo said.

'We coped,' Gina said.

'You know that guy Hardwick?'

They all knew that guy Hardwick, as various bits of investigation for Hardwick's solicitors had formed the major part of the agency's work for more than four weeks.

'Suddenly friend Hardwick decides that he *does* remember where he was on the night of 18 April.'

A groan went up from around the table.

'If he's going to be stupid enough to plead amnesia,' the Old Man said, 'then he ought to be smart enough to remember that he has amnesia.'

Everybody laughed.

'So what came into the office today?' Angelo asked.

'We were quite busy.'

'Good good good,' Angelo said and rubbed his hands.

David mimicked his father a moment after. 'Gooda gooda gooda.'

'Smart alec,' Angelo said, and swatted David on the top of the head. 'Tufty smart alec.'

David reconstructed his hair. It was all good humoured.

'The main thing was a woman whose son has too much money.'

'We should all have such a problem,' Momma said.

'But as far as the woman can tell, the son doesn't work for it. He doesn't have a regular job and won't explain where it comes from.'

Everyone was listening now. Most agency work was for solicitors or involved missing relatives or related to faithless spouses, though the Old Man had once had a murder and would only too happily tell the whole thing yet again. But a son with too much money was unusual. They began to vie gently for the chance to ask Gina questions.

Several began to speak. Angelo held up his hand and established chairmanship. 'Marie.'

'How old is the son?' Marie, fourteen, asked.

'Too old for you, my girl.'

Marie blushed, but smiled. She enjoyed her position as the family heartbreaker.

'The boy is twenty-two,' Gina said.

'And still lives at home?' Angelo asked.

'You still live at home,' the Old Man said.

'Our situation is not an ordinary one,' Momma said.

'That's right,' David said. They all looked at him. 'Our house is bigger than most people's.' They laughed. A pretender for 'family wit'.

'Twenty-two years of age.' The Old Man looked thoughtful. 'So what does he do that his mother doesn't know what he does?'

Gina said, 'Well, he's been on the social for fifteen months, though he stays up late and sleeps in the day a lot and he goes out evenings and nights. His last job was interior decorating.' Gina's face suggested that there was some unusual bit of information about the boy that was awaiting the right question.

'He's got boyfriends?' Momma asked.

'No.'

'He's a bloody artist?' This was the Old Man.

Gina shook her head.

'He's enrolled in the Open University and that's why he stays up at night, 'cause they don't have a video,' Rosetta, the accountant, offered.

'That's pretty tricky thinking,' David said.

Rosetta smiled.

Angelo considered, staring at his wife. 'So what's it going to be?' he asked himself aloud. 'So what's it going to be?'

'Give up?' Gina asked.

'Never,' the Old Man said.

Gina said, 'This unemployed-layabout kid has a one-year-old car and a car telephone. And when he goes out at night and his mother asks him what he's been doing, all he will say is, "Driving."'

'Well well well,' Angelo said. He looked around the table. Everyone else was looking at him. It was a matter of who had driving licences. And who could be asked to stay up all night following the son.

'We could ask Salvatore,' Momma said. She didn't like the Old Man to be out at night. There'd been enough of that, one way or another, when he was younger.

Gina said, 'Yes. He'd be interested in the work.'

'Work?' the Old Man said. 'He wants work, he can come here to work, he wants work. Right, Angelo?'

'Sally knows he's always got a place here if he wants it, Poppa,' Angelo said. 'But he'll never do it.'

'Never is a long time,' the Old Man said. 'But while I'm alive I think I agree with you.'

'That'll be for ever,' Marie said, and the Old Man – who doted on his only granddaughter – beamed and said, 'There. Now there's a child.'

'I'm glad you like my handiwork, Poppa,' Gina said.

The Old Man looked at Gina for a moment and then burst into loud laughter. He also liked his daughter-in-law.

'So how's it left with this woman?' Angelo asked.

'It's left I got the car and its registration number and the address, the car phone number, the names, all that.'

'You mean we're on tonight?'

'I already rang Salvatore. He's happy to do the night, or split shifts if you prefer. I didn't know exactly what you had to do tomorrow about the Hardwick.'

'Right,' Angelo said. 'Or we could use Max, or Johnny.'

'Outside ops are expensive,' Rosetta said.

'Salvatore ain't cheap,' Angelo said.

'At least he's in the family,' Momma said.

'*I*'m in the family,' the Old Man said. 'What's this you treat me like I couldn't follow a giraffe in a herd of mice? Am I not here or something? I got bad breath?'

'I haven't forgotten you, Poppa,' Angelo said.

'You're on shoplifting at Quicks again tomorrow,' Gina said.

'Cheaper to get a store detective replacement for me daytime than hire an outside op short-notice tonight.'

'We're not going to hire anybody tonight except Sal,' Angelo said. 'I don't know what all this is about. We can cover it. We can cover most things.'

'Dad?' David asked.

'Uh-huh?'

'Can I come out with you tonight?'

'I don't know I'm going out.'

'Can I go out with Uncle Sal, then?'

'Not on a school night,' Gina said.

David said, 'I could try to spin you a story about not having school, the teachers having one of those funny days they have or something, but it *is* a school day tomorrow.'

'Is that supposed to be news?' Angelo asked.

'But it's not an important day. No tests and I've got no homework. It's a good day for me to be out the night before.'

'Nice try,' Angelo said.

'Aw, Dad!'

'If we're still on it tomorrow night, maybe then. A Friday or a Saturday night.'

'Or both?'

'We'll see. We'll see.' Angelo turned back to Gina. 'What's the financial?'

'The mother has some money an aunt left her. She intended to fix the house up, but she's too worried about this kid. She's sure he's up to no good.'

'What's the name?'

'The boy is John Anson Hatwell.'

'Form?'

'I rang Charlie. It's mixed. He had some DC when he was sixteen, for some muggings, and he admitted two burglaries to be taken into account. He's been arrested twice again, for burglaries, but charges were dropped.'

'It sounds like a bit of a problem,' Angelo said.

'I asked her what she expected if we found out he was engaged in criminal activities. Of course, she wants a chance to "handle" it herself. I told her that really depended on what we found out, if we found out anything.'

'Sal will find out tonight whether the kid is going to be easy to tail or whether we'll need a team.'

'So you want Sally on all night? No shifts?'

'Not unless he needs it. If he does then maybe Poppa will cover it.' Angelo looked at his father. The Old Man looked at his wife. His wife looked at Gina. 'I'll talk to Sally,' Gina said, 'but we left it that he would do the night unless he heard different.'

'So,' Angelo said, 'you said it was busy. What else came in?'

'Well,' Gina said, 'there was this woman who found a comb in the back seat of her husband's car. She wanted *him* followed.'

'Suddenly it's follow follow follow,' Angelo said.

'But she didn't realize how expensive it was or how long it might take.'

'To follow a comb?' David asked.

'She went home to think about just how bad she wants to find out who belongs to the comb.'

'You should get a grant from the marriage guidance people,' Angelo said, 'the good advice you give out for free.'

'Free free free,' David said.

At 1055 the next morning Salvatore dropped in to report to Gina on his night's activities.

'The Big Man going to need me again tonight?'

'I don't know yet, Sal,' Gina said.

'It's just I got a model booked. I can unbook her if it's important.'

'I'll call him on the car phone.'

'Or leave a message in his Filofax?'

'Don't be naughty, Salvatore.'

Gina tried to ring Angelo, but he wasn't in his car. 'Sorry,' she said. 'I'll try him later.'

'I thought it through,' Sal said, 'and this one, it isn't that important I know ahead. Just let me know around dinnertime, eh?'

'You want to come over for dinner tonight?'

'No thanks, kid.' In a playful way he said, 'You ever done any modelling?'

'Only in my spare time.' An obvious joke, since everyone acknowledged that Gina never had spare time.

'Get hard up, give me a ring.'

'You want the money for last night now?'

'Yeah, I'll take it now, now you mention it.' He laughed. They both knew who was hard up for what.

Dinner was early on a Friday night to make it easier for David and Marie, who liked to go out. Rosetta went out Fridays too, with her fiancé of the last four years who was agonizing over the morality of divorce, if not necessarily over other moralities. Gina always cooked on Fridays, unless it was busy, in which case they went out for a pub meal.

Angelo was already in when Gina came home from the office. He had scrubbed some potatoes.

'So what did Sally have to say?' Angelo asked.

Normally they would have waited to talk about it till mealtime, but with the possibility that David would be riding if Angelo went out, they needed to plan ahead.

'Sally said that John Anson Hatwell didn't have a clue he was being followed and that he should be easy for one car.'

'That's something.'

'Sal got there about 2000. At 2135, Hatwell left his home address alone. He drove into the city and went to a backstreet café called Henry's. Do you know it?'

'That's on Morris Street, isn't it?'

'That's it. Do you know what it is?'

'Give me a clue.'

'Stays open all night.'

'Cabbies?'

Gina smiled.

Angelo considered the information. 'How long was Hatwell there?'

'Only about half an hour. Then drove around till 2 a.m.'

'Just drove around?'

'That's what Sally says. He took down the street names for a while, but the kid didn't stop anywhere. He just drove till 2:08. He might have been making calls from his car phone, but Sally didn't think so.'

'If he did, who to?'

Gina shrugged.

'And what happened then?'

'He picked up a prostitute at 2:08.'

'I see.'

'Dropped her off again at 2:32.'

'He may have too much money, but he doesn't like to waste it on frills, eh?'

'And then he went home,' Gina said.

'Hmmmm.'

'His mother says often he stays out till five or six, so this probably wasn't typical. I don't know what he does during the days. It was the evenings and nights that really worried her, and I told her that's what we would concentrate on.'

'I think we stick at that for the time being. What she's worried about is how he makes his money, not how he spends it.'

Gina nodded.

'I'll take him tonight. Maybe Sally again tomorrow.'

'And David?'

They looked at each other. Angelo said, 'I more or less promised him.'

'Yes,' Gina said. 'All right.'

Angelo and David arrived at Hatwell's house at 1830. Their car was well stocked for a long night. Thermos flasks, cassette tapes, food, blankets. Specimen jars in case of emergency. David had been out before and knew the drill.

'Which car is it, Dad?'

'The Opel across the street. Under the light.'

'I see.'

'How're your eyes these days, son? Can you read the number plate?'

David read the number plate. Then he said, 'Grandad told Mum that he wanted to come along tonight.'

'She didn't say anything to me.'

'I think Gran talked him out of it.'

'More likely there's a private-eye film on TV. He loves to pick holes in the stories.'

'Coincidences like that don't happen in real life,' David said, mimicking his grandfather.

Angelo smiled. 'That's it.'

'Did you ever think of being something other than a private detective, Dad?'

'I didn't get much choice once Uncle Sal went to art college.'

'Do you mind?'

'I don't think about it.'

'What else would you have wanted to do?'

Angelo considered. 'I don't know.'

'A painter like Uncle Sal?'

'You got to be able to draw,' he said.

'Uncle Sal's stuff doesn't look like you have to draw so well.'

'You've got to be able to draw to make it look like you can't,' Angelo said.

'Oh,' David said. Then, 'What time do you think this Hatwell bloke is going to come out of his house?'

'Not for a while yet,' Angelo said. 'He didn't go out till 2130 last night.'

But Angelo was wrong, because three minutes later, at 1922, John Anson Hatwell left his mother's house and got into his car.

'Write it down,' Angelo said to David as he started his car.

David took up the clipboard and wrote a note of the time that they had begun the active phase of their surveillance.

Hatwell's night began much as the previous night had begun. He drove to Henry's Café, parked, and went in.

The windows of the café were large and clear enough that Hatwell could be seen going to the counter, placing an order, and then moving to a table where another man already sat. Hatwell had entered the café at 1949.

The man behind the counter carried a tray to Hatwell at 1953. The man sitting with Hatwell rose and left the café at 1959. This man got into one of the taxis up the street.

'Binoculars,' Angelo said with some urgency, but David already had the large-lens binoculars out of the case and resting on the dashboard for support.

When the man pulled his taxi into the road, David read out the vehicle's registration number and the name of the taxi company. Angelo recorded these on the clipboard sheet.

The binoculars intensified light from dim images. It was as if one's eyes were suddenly five times as big: more light from the object was caught.

At 2006 Angelo took some money from his coin purse. 'What say you go in and ask for a couple of doughnuts?'

'Really?'

'See whether Hatwell is talking to anybody else, but if he gets up to leave, just walk back to the car.'

'OK, Dad.'

'And don't tell your mother.'

David winked and put out his hand for the money.

By 2013 he was back in the car. 'Hatwell isn't talking to anybody else. What he's got left is some chips on a small plate, and he took a drink from whatever he had a cup of.'

Angelo began to speak, but David interrupted him. 'There was a mirror behind the counter,' he said. 'I watched him in that.'

'Good boy,' he said. Then, 'Hang on. I think we're rolling.'

Hatwell had risen from his table and was walking towards the café door.

'Got a time for me, Dad?' David asked.

Hatwell drove to a petrol station. Angelo pulled into a street on the opposite side of the road, turned around, and waited, ready to go in whichever direction Hatwell chose after his stop.

Hatwell filled his Opel with petrol. David practised with the binoculars and saw that the car had taken 41.42 litres.

'Litres?' Angelo asked. 'How much is that in real?'

'A bit more than nine gallons,' David said.

'Oh,' Angelo said, not having expected an answer. He wrote it down.

Hatwell left the petrol station and drove around for about half an hour. Then, at 2102, he pulled to the side of the road and stopped suddenly. Angelo had to drive past him. David turned to see what was happening to the Opel.

'It looks like he's talking on the phone, Dad,' David said.

Angelo again used a side-street and turned around quickly. They could just make out Hatwell's car.

After another minute on the phone, Hatwell put it away and made a squealing U-turn. Angelo pulled out to follow him, and already it was obvious that the car was being driven in a much more positive manner than before.

This went on for thirteen minutes as they followed the Opel across town. Then suddenly Hatwell slowed down. Taking a chance, Angelo – who felt he was lucky still to be with the car – slowed down too, rather than overtake it as he had done the time before.

Hatwell did not *seem* to notice them.

'If he'd been looking for us,' Angelo said to his quiet son, 'he'd have spotted us a dozen times.'

Hatwell appeared instead to be intent on finding a house number. After a few moments of slow cruising, he parked. Angelo pulled past him and parked on the other side of the street.

'Stay here and stay low,' he said to David.

Angelo got out of his car. As he pretended to lock the vehicle door, he saw which way Hatwell had turned. Angelo turned in the other direction and walked till he found a telephone pole. In a sideways movement he dropped into its shadow and turned back to watch Hatwell.

Hatwell had not moved far. For several seconds he studied the front of a semi-detached house. Then he began to walk. Angelo followed unseen.

Hatwell walked around the block. When he got to the front of the semi again, he walked up the path and then through the gate between the house and its garage.

Angelo slipped back into his car, where David waited eagerly.

'What's up, Dad?'

'I think he's committing a burglary,' Angelo said. 'If I had to guess, that would be it.' He started his car.

'Where are we going?'

'I want to get in a better position in case he leaves fast.'

Angelo turned around in the street and reparked several yards behind Hatwell's Opel.

They waited for nearly an hour, but eventually Hatwell reappeared. He carried two suitcases and was not in any apparent hurry.

'A cool son of a bitch,' Angelo said tensely.

David was pleased that his father used such language with him. Gina would have disapproved.

Hatwell did not have to unlock his boot. A push of a button and the lid flew up. In a moment the cases were in and the lid back down. Hatwell got into his car then, and still without seeming to rush, he drove away.

'What do we do now, Dad?'

'Follow follow follow,' Angelo said. He pulled out to do just that, but he was in deep thought.

Angelo and David came home when Hatwell finally returned to his mother's house, parked, and went in. David, who knew he had been along for something unusual, *said* he was too excited to sleep. But when Angelo sent him upstairs, he went with a yawn, not a murmur. He was too tired to be too excited to sleep.

Angelo left a note on the kitchen table for Gina to wake him at 0800 and to get the Old Man down. On another day Rosetta would have been summoned, but normally she stayed out on a Friday night and did not return on Saturday until noon.

At 0822, when everyone was together and Angelo had had a cup of coffee, he said, 'It's tough to know exactly what to do.'

He explained what they had done and seen. That Hatwell had pulled up to use his car phone a second time and had driven to look for and find a second address after that. But something had perhaps looked wrong to him. He had not stayed long and had not gone on to the property at the second address.

'And then,' Angelo said, 'cool as can be, he drives back to Henry's and has some more food. This is at 3:12 in the morning.

He's got two suitcases of stolen goods in the boot of his car and he still hasn't locked it because when he finally went back to his mother's house, he locked it before he went inside. We have to decide what to do.'

'What does the client want you to do?' the Old Man asked.

Gina said, 'She said she wanted to know if there was anything criminal before we told the police.'

'How much money have you had?' the Old Man asked.

'Fee for three nights, but no expenses.'

'She seem flush?'

'She didn't hesitate writing the cheque,' Gina said.

'Our responsibility is to her,' the Old Man said.

'I am tempted to follow Hatwell this morning,' Angelo said. 'To find out what he does with it all. He must be going to take it to a fence today.'

'Who's paying you to do that?' the Old Man asked. 'Suddenly you're an independent working on commission from the police?'

'I know I know I know, Pop,' Angelo said. 'All I said was that I am tempted. How often do we get something like this?'

'Not often, but so what?'

'Who paid you to solve the murder of Norman Stiles?'

'At least I was being paid to check a suspect's alibi. So I stumbled on to a different way to alibi him. At least I was being paid.'

'You never got paid.'

'So at least I was owed,' the Old Man said with dignity.

'I know I know I know,' Angelo said. 'But I am still tempted.'

'I think we should contact Mrs Hatwell,' Gina said. 'She is the client.'

The Old Man looked at Gina fondly.

'I was also tempted to try to look in the boot while Hatwell was in Henry's.'

'Not with David there!'

'But Hatwell parked right in front of the café the second time.'

They sat quietly for a moment. 'We have an obligation to the client,' Angelo said. 'And an obligation to the police. But if it came to it, I think I could deal with the police.'

At the time, they didn't ask him what he meant by that.

Instead, Gina said, 'How tired are you?'

'I'm all right.'

'This is what we do,' Gina said. 'We drive two cars to the Hatwells'. I go up to the door to see if I can talk to Mrs Hatwell myself. You wait outside and you follow the son if he goes anywhere. Poppa mans the office.'

'Who's paying, he goes anywhere?' the Old Man demanded again.

'Maybe if we recover what's in the suitcases, the owners will pay us,' Gina said.

Gina and Angelo arrived at 0949. Before Gina went in, Angelo slipped into her passenger seat. 'I'm not that happy about you going in cold,' Angelo said.

'I'll be all right.'

He raised his eyebrows. 'Tell her you're there only as a courtesy. We have to tell the police. We have no choice.'

She nodded and got out.

And it was true enough. Police everywhere are territorial. It is not enough that justice be done in the end. If it's their justice, they are loath for anybody else to administer it. The bulk of a detective agency's business does not require direct involvement in, or knowledge of, illegality; but to be in the bad books of the local police can obstruct detective work a hundred times in a year. It is not something to risk casually.

But Angelo was still tempted to let Hatwell have a little rope and to see where he would take the suitcases.

In the end, however, stronger forces determined his actions.

Gina went to the door of the house at 0954. She was admitted to the house at 0955 by Mrs Hatwell.

By 1015, Angelo was tired of waiting. He sorely wished he had put a wire on her. Or at least a call device, a button to be pushed in case of emergency. They had relied too much on the assumption that the young Hatwell's routine of sleeping late would be followed. Angelo felt he had been careless from fatigue. He felt that he had put Gina at risk. He began to think that he should go to the house himself.

Having begun to think that, he began to decide to do it.

He got out of his car. He walked towards the house. He stood by the Opel. Gina did not emerge.

Angelo looked at the house. Then he began to walk up the path.

Suddenly the front door burst open. John Anson Hatwell ran out.

Angelo froze. He was in no-man's-land. He couldn't get back to his own car to follow without it being obvious. And Gina still did not appear.

So Angelo tackled Hatwell himself as the young man ran by.

The act was a surprise to both of them. But with Hatwell on the ground, Angelo knew enough to be able to keep him there.

Hatwell swore and spluttered and made enquiries as to what Angelo thought he was doing.

Angelo informed him that he was making a citizen's arrest, something he was perfectly entitled to do as long as he was willing to take the consequences of false citizen's arrest.

Angelo fretted, however, because all he could do was sit there holding Hatwell immobile when what he wanted to do was go into the house to make sure Gina was all right.

Why had Hatwell come out running? What had he done? What had happened to the two women inside? Angelo at first *asked* for answers from Hatwell. Then he screamed at his prisoner.

Rosetta served Sunday dinner at 1400 sharp. It was an even-numbered Sunday in the month so her 'fiancé', Walter, was in attendance. Salvatore was there too, having brought a model named Carol.

'This is my father,' Sal said, introducing her to the Old Man. 'And my mother. And this is Carol. She models for me.'

'Hello,' Momma said tersely. Carol didn't *look* like a potential wife.

'Welcome and make yourself at home,' the Old Man said. He shook Carol's hand warmly.

'My niece and nephew, Marie and David.'

'Hello.'

'Hello.'

'Hcllo.'

'Gina you met at the door. That's Rosetta behind the salad bowl and Walter next to her. And the man with the black eye is my brother Angelo. He's about to tell us how he got it.'

Carol exchanged greetings with the rest of the family and everyone sat down.

In fact, the one thing that Angelo didn't remember was when he had been hit in the eye. 'I was just worried that the creep had done something to my Gina.'

Gina said, 'The boy's mother was crying. I was trying to console her. She was a client after all.'

'But I didn't know.'

'No.'

'So there I was sitting on this kid,' Angelo began, 'having made a citizen's arrest.'

'Tricky,' the Old Man said. 'Very tricky.'

'I thought I had him bang to rights,' Angelo said. 'I thought he had two suitcases of stolen goods locked in the boot of his car. I had seen him put them there. I had seen him lock it. I thought—'

'But it was four hours later.'

'I know I know I know. Nobody was more surprised than me when the police opened the boot and it was flaming empty.'

'That was a very tense moment,' Gina agreed.

'I was thinking I'm going to go down for GBH,' Angelo said. 'A friend, Charlie, may be over there, but he's not going to be able to get me off GBH.'

Angelo paused to look around the room.

'So come on,' Salvatore said. 'Get on with it. How come you're here and smiling instead of being held on remand in a tin hut somewhere out in the country?'

Gina said, 'My Angelo did say before we went out that he thought he could deal with the police.'

Angelo said, 'I was bothered by this Hatwell's car telephone.'

'He didn't use it the night I was out,' Sal said.

'But with David and me . . .' Angelo turned to David who beamed at the guests. 'With David and me he used it twice. Each time he then goes to a house somewhere. First time it's suitcases. Second time nothing. But it bothered me. And then I'm thinking, each night he's down at this taxi drivers' café. First night he eats alone. Second night he eats with a cabby. You see, the problem about these phone calls is, who is it he's talking to?'

'So my boy puts two and two together,' the Old Man said to Carol proudly.

'And he got twenty-two,' David said.

'And this time I am lucky,' Angelo said.

'Who was it then?' Carol asked.

'What I decided was that Hatwell was working with a taxi driver. The driver picked up fares from a house. He noticed whether they locked up when they left, whether it looked like it was empty. Then after he took them to their destination, he telephoned Hatwell. Gave him the address. Hatwell went to the address, confirmed to his own satisfaction that the house was empty. And burgled it if he thought it was right.'

'Gosh,' Carol said.

'Some nights the driver got no appropriate fares or maybe he was just off work – that's what I think happened your night, Sal.'

Salvatore nodded.

'But Friday night they had a big hit. The police figured there was nearly two grand's worth in the suitcases when they recovered them from the cabby. Who drove home at the end of his shift via Hatwell's house. Duplicate key to Hatwell's boot. Takes the cases at six in the morning. Who sees?'

'They were still in his taxi when the police got there,' Gina said.

'And how did you know who the taxi driver was?' Carol asked.

'Ah, that was down to David,' Angelo said. 'He was the one who spotted the man's registration number when he went on shift. A word with his dispatcher and he was dispatched.'

'All in a night's work, ma'am,' David said.

Carol smiled.

'The police say they think it will resolve about forty outstanding burglaries,' Gina said.

'Well done, brother,' Salvatore said with genuine pride.

'Thanks.'

'Are people ready to eat?' Rosetta asked.

'So what's today?' the Old Man asked.

'Linguini, with my special sauce,' Rosetta said.

'That's Italian for "little tongues",' the Old Man said.

'Oh,' Carol said.

'So,' the Old Man said to Rosetta, 'what's wrong with some curry?'

There was a quiet groan from several places around the table.

'A family joke,' Salvatore explained.

'You know, Carol,' the Old Man said, 'one time, one time only, I was involved in an actual *murder* case.'

'Gosh!' Carol said.

'The man's name was Norman Stiles and he was a small-time bookmaker.'

A second, louder groan was heard. But not by the Old Man.

PETER LOVESEY

A Case of Butterflies

BEFORE calling the police, he had found a butterfly in the summerhouse. It had unsettled him. The wings had been purple, a rich, velvety purple. Soaring and swooping, it had intermittently come to rest on the wood floor. His assumption that it was trapped had proved to be false, because two of the windows had been wide open and it had made no move towards the open door. He knew what it was, a Purple Emperor, for there was one made of paper mounted in a perspex case in his wife Ann's study. As a staunch conservationist, Ann wouldn't have wanted to possess a real specimen. She had told him often enough that she preferred to see them flying free. She had always insisted that Purple Emperors were in the oak wood that surrounded the house. He had never spotted one until this morning, and it seemed like a sign from her.

'You did the right thing, sir.'

'The right thing?'

'Calling us in as soon as you knew about this. It takes courage.'

'I don't want your approval, Commander. I want my wife back.'

'We all want that, sir.'

Sir Milroy Shenton made it plain that he didn't care for the remark, mildly as it was put. He rotated his chair to turn his back on the two police officers and face the view along King's Reach where the City skyline rises above Waterloo Bridge. He stared at it superficially. The image of the butterfly refused to leave his mind, just as it had lingered in the summerhouse. Less than an hour ago he had called the emergency number from his house in Sussex. The police had suggested meeting in London in case the house was being observed, and he had nominated the Broad Wall Complex. He had the choice of dozens of company boardrooms across London and the Home Counties that belonged in his high-tech empire. The advantage of using Broad Wall was the proximity of the heliport.

He swung around again. 'You'll have to bear with me. I'm short of sleep. It was a night flight from New York.'

'Let's get down to basics, then. Did you bring the ransom note?'

Commander Jerry Glazier was primed for this. He headed the Special Branch team that was always on stand-by to deal with kidnapping incidents. International terrorism was so often involved in extortion that a decision had been taken to involve Special Branch from the beginning in major kidnap inquiries. Captains of industry like Shenton were obvious targets. They knew the dangers, and often employed private bodyguards. Not Shenton: such precautions would not square with his reputation in the City as a devil-may-care dealer in the stock market, known and feared for his dawn raids.

Glazier was assessing him with a professional eye, aware how vital in kidnap cases is the attitude and resolve of the 'mark'.

First impressions suggested that this was a man in his forties trying to pass for twenty-five, with a hairstyle that would once have been called short back and sides and was now trendy and expensive. A jacket of crumpled silk was hanging off his shoulders. The accent was Oxford turned cockney, a curious inversion Glazier had noted lately in the business world. Scarcely ten minutes ago he had read in *Who's Who* that Shenton's background was a rectory in Norfolk, followed by Winchester and Magdalen. He had married twice. The second wife, the lady now abducted, was Ann, the only daughter of Dr Hamilton Porter, deceased. Under *Recreations*, Shenton had entered *Exercising the wife*. It must have seemed witty when he thought of it.

Now he took a package from his pocket. 'Wrapped in a freezer bag, as your people suggested. My sweaty prints are all over it, of course. I didn't know it was going to be evidence until I'd read the bloody thing, did I?'

'It isn't just the prints.' Glazier glanced at the wording on the note. It read IF YOU WANT HER BACK ALIVE GET ONE MILLION READY. INSTRUCTIONS FOLLOW. 'There's modern technology for you,' he commented. 'They do the old thing of cutting words from the papers, but now they dispense with paste. They use a photocopier.' He turned it over to look at the envelope. 'Indistinct postmark, wouldn't you know.'

'The bastards could have sent it any time in the last six days, couldn't they?' said Shenton. 'For all I know, they may have tried to phone me. She could be dead.'

Glazier wasn't there to speculate. 'So you flew in from New York this morning, returned to your house, and found this on the mat?'

'And my wife missing.'

'You've been away from the house for how long, sir?'

'I told you – six days. Ann had been away as well, but she should have been back by now.'

'Then I dare say there was a stack of mail waiting.'

'Is that relevant?'

The pattern of the interview was taking shape. Shenton was using every opportunity to assert his status as top dog.

'It may be,' Glazier commented, 'if you can remember what was above or below it in the stack.' He wasn't to be intimidated.

'I just picked everything up, flipped through what was there and extracted the interesting mail from the junk.'

'*This* looked interesting?'

'It's got a stamp, hasn't it?'

'Fair enough. You opened it, read the note, and phoned us. Did you call anyone else?'

'Cressie.'

'Cressie?'

'Cressida Concannon, Ann's college friend. The two of them were touring.'

'Touring where, sir?'

'The Ring of Kerry.'

'*Ireland?*' Glazier glanced towards his assistant, then back to Shenton. 'That was taking a chance, wasn't it?'

'With hindsight, yes. I told Ann to use her maiden name over there.'

'Which is . . ?'

'Porter.'

'So what have you learned from her friend?'

'Cressie's still over there, visiting her sister. She last saw Ann on Wednesday at the end of their holiday, going into Cork airport.'

'Have you called the airline to see if she was on the flight?'

Shenton shook his head. 'Tracing Cressie took the best part of half an hour. I flew straight up from Sussex after that.'

'Flew?'

'Chopper.'

'I see. Did your wife have a reservation?'

'Aer Lingus. The two-fifteen flight to Heathrow.'

Glazier nodded to his assistant, who left the room to check. 'This holiday in Ireland – when was it planned?'

'A month ago, when New York came up. She said she deserved a trip of her own.'

'So she got in touch with her friend. I shall need to know more about Miss Concannon, sir. She's an old and trusted friend, I take it?'

'Cressie? She's twenty-four carat. We've known her for twelve years, easily.'

'Well enough to know her political views?'

'Hold on.' Shenton folded his arms in a challenging way. 'Cressie isn't one of that lot.'

'But does she guard her tongue?'

'She's far too smart to mouth off to the micks.'

'They met at college, you say. What were they studying?'

'You think I'm going to say politics?' Shenton said as if he were scoring points at a board meeting. 'It was bugs. Ann and Cressie's idea of a holiday is kneeling in cowpats communing with dung-beetles.'

'Entomology,' said Glazier.

'Sorry, I was forgetting some of the fuzz can read without moving their lips.'

'Do you carry a picture of your wife, sir?'

'For the press, do you mean? She's been kidnapped. She isn't a missing person.'

'For our use, Sir Milroy.'

He felt for his wallet. 'I dare say there's one I can let you have.'

'If you're bothered about the media, sir, we intend to keep them off your back until this is resolved. The Press Office at the Yard will get their co-operation.'

'You mean an embargo?' He started to remove a photo from his wallet and then pushed it back into its slot. Second thoughts, apparently.

Glazier had glimpsed enough of the print to make out a woman in a see-through blouse. She seemed to be dancing. 'I mean a voluntary agreement to withhold the news until you've got your wife back. After that, of course . . .'

'If I get her back unharmed I'll speak to anyone.'

'Until that happens, you talk only to us, sir. These people, whoever they are, will contact you again. Do you have an answer-phone at your house?'

'Of course.'

'Have you played it back?'

'Didn't have time.' Shenton folded the wallet and returned it to his pocket. 'I don't, after all, happen to have a suitable picture of Ann on me. I'll arrange to send you one.'

'Listen to your messages as soon as you get back, sir, and let me know if there's anything.'

'What do you do in these cases – tap my phone?'

'Is that what you'd recommend?'

'Commander Glazier, don't patronize me. I called you in. I have a right to know what to expect.'

'You can expect us to do everything within our powers to find your wife, sir.'

'You don't trust me, for God's sake?'

'I didn't say that. What matters is that you put your trust in us. Do you happen to have a card with your Sussex address?'

Shenton felt for the wallet again and opened it.

Glazier said at once, 'Isn't that a picture of your wife, sir, the one you put back just now?'

'That wasn't suitable. I told you.'

'If it's the way she's dressed that bothers you, that's no problem. I need the shot of her face, that's all. May I take it?'

Shenton shook his head.

'What's the problem?' asked Glazier.

'As it happens, that isn't Ann. It's her friend Cressida.'

Between traffic signals along the Embankment, Glazier told his assistant, Inspector Tom Salt, about the photograph.

'You think he's cheating with his wife's best friend?'

'It's a fair bet.'

'Does it have any bearing on the kidnap?'

'Too soon to tell. His reactions are strange. He seems more fussed about how we intend to conduct the case than what is happening to his wife.'

'High-flyers like him operate on a different level from you and me, sir. Life is all about flow-charts and decision making.'

'They're not all like that. Did you get anything from the airline?'

'Everything he told us checks. There was a first-class reservation in the name of Ann Porter. She wasn't aboard that Heathrow flight or any other.'

The next morning Glazier flew to Ireland for a meeting with senior officers in the *gardaí*. Cork airport shimmered in the August heat. At headquarters they were served iced lemonade in preference to coffee. A full-scale inquiry was authorized.

He visited Cressida Concannon at her sister's, an estate house on the northern outskirts of Cork, and they talked outside, seated on patio chairs. She presented a picture distinctly different from the photo in Shenton's wallet; she was in a cream-coloured linen suit and brown shirt buttoned to the top. Her long brown hair was drawn back and secured with combs. Like

Lady Ann, she was at least ten years younger than Shenton. She had made an itinerary of the tour around the Ring of Kerry. She handed Glazier a sheaf of hotel receipts.

He flicked through them. 'I notice you paid all of these yourself, Miss Concannon.'

'Yes. Ann said she would settle up with me later. She couldn't write cheques because she was using her maiden name.'

'Of course. Porter, isn't it? So the hotel staff addressed her as Mrs Porter?'

'Yes.'

'And was there any time in your trip when she was recognized as Lady Shenton?'

'Not to my knowledge.'

'You remember nothing suspicious, nothing that might help us to find her?'

'I've been over it many times in my mind, and I can't think of anything, I honestly can't.'

'What was her frame of mind? Did she seem concerned at any stage of the tour?'

'Not once that I recall. She seemed to relish every moment. You can ask at any of the hotels. She was full of high spirits right up to the minute we parted.'

'Which was . . ?'

'Wednesday, about twelve-thirty. I drove her to the airport and put her down where the cars pull in. She went through the doors and that was the last I saw of her. Surely they won't harm her, will they?'

Glazier said, as if he hadn't listened to the question, 'Tell me about your relationship with Sir Milroy Shenton.'

She drew herself up. 'What do you mean?'

'You're a close friend, close enough to spend some time alone with him, I believe.'

'They are both my friends. I've known them for years.'

'But you do meet him, don't you?'

'I don't see what this has to do with it.'

'I'll tell you,' said Glazier. 'I'm just surprised that she went on holiday with you and relished every moment, as you expressed it. She's an intelligent woman. He carries your picture fairly openly in his wallet. He doesn't carry one of Lady Ann. Her behaviour strikes me as untypical, that's all.'

She said coolly, 'When you rescue her from the kidnappers, you'll be able to question her about it, won't you?'

Before leaving Ireland, Glazier had those hotels checked. Without exception the enquiries confirmed that the two women had stayed there on the dates in question. Moreover, they had given every appearance of getting on well. One hotel waiter in Killarney recalled that they had laughed the evenings away together.

Within an hour of Glazier's return to London, there was a development. Sir Milroy Shenton called on the phone. His voice was strained. 'I've heard from them. She's dead. They've killed her, the bastards, and I hold you responsible.'

'Dead? You're sure?'

'*They're* sure.'

'Tell me precisely how you heard about this.'

'They just phoned me, didn't they? Irish accent.'

'A man?'

'Yes. Said they had to abort the operation because I got in touch with the filth. That's you. They said she's at the bottom of the Irish Sea. This is going to be on your conscience for the rest of your bloody life.'

'I need to see you,' said Glazier. 'Where are you now?'

'Manchester.'

'How do they know you're up there?'

'It was in the papers. One of my companies has a shareholders' meeting. Look, I can't tell you any more than I just did.'

'You want the killers to get away with it, sir?'

'What?'

'I'll be at Midhurst. Your house.'

'Why Midhurst?'

'Get there as soon as you can, Sir Milroy.' Glazier put an end to the call and stabbed out Tom Salt's number. 'Can you lay on a chopper, Tom?'

*

'What's this about?' Salt shouted over the engine noise after they were airborne.

'Shenton. His wife is dead.'

'Why would they kill her? While she was alive she was worth a million.'

'My thought exactly.'

Salt wrestled with that remark as they followed the ribbon of the Thames southwards, flying over Richmond and Kingston. 'Don't you believe what Shenton told you?'

'She's dead. I believe that much.'

'No kidnap?'

'No kidnap.'

'We're talking old-fashioned murder, then.'

'That's my reading of it.'

There was a break in the conversation that brought them across the rest of Surrey before Salt shouted, 'It's got to be Cressie Concannon, hasn't it?'

'Why?'

'She wasn't satisfied with her status as the mistress, so she snuffed her rival and sent the ransom note to cover up the crime.'

Glazier shook his head. 'Cressie is in Ireland.'

'What's wrong with that? Lady Shenton was last seen in Ireland. We know she didn't make the flight home.'

'Cressie didn't send the ransom note. The postage stamp was British.'

The pilot turned his head. 'The place should be coming up any minute, sir. Those are the South Downs ahead.'

Without much difficulty they located Shenton's house, a stone-built Victorian mansion in a clearing in an oak wood. The helicopter wheeled around it once before touching down on the forecourt, churning up dust and gravel.

'We've got at least an hour before he gets here,' Glazier said.

'Is there a pub?' asked Salt, and got a look from his superior that put him off drinking for a week.

Rather less than the estimated hour had passed when the

clatter of a second helicopter disturbed the sylvan peace. Glazier crossed the drive to meet it.

'No more news, I suppose?' Sir Milroy Shenton asked as he climbed out. He spoke in a more reasonable tone than he'd used on the phone. He'd had time to compose himself.

'Not yet, sir.'

'Found your way in?'

'No, we've been out here in the garden.'

'Not much of a garden. Ann and I preferred to keep it uncultivated except for the lawns.'

'She must have wanted to study the insect life in its natural habitat.'

Shenton frowned slightly, as if he'd already forgotten about his wife's field of study. 'Shall we go indoors?'

A fine curved staircase faced them as they entered. The hall was open to three floors. 'Your wife had a study, I'm sure,' said Glazier. 'I'd like to see it, please.'

'To your left – but there's nothing in there to help you,' said Shenton.

'We'll see.' Glazier entered the room and moved around the desk to the bookshelves. 'Whilst we were waiting for you I saw a couple of butterflies I'd never spotted before. I used to collect them when I was a kid, little horror, before they were protected. Did you know you had Purple Emperors here?'

Shenton twitched and swayed slightly. Then he put his hand to his face and said distractedly, 'What?'

'Purple Emperors. There were two in the summerhouse just now. The windows were open, but they had no desire to leave. They settled on the floor in the joints between the boards.' Glazier picked a book off the shelf and thumbed through the pages, finally turning them open for Shenton's inspection. 'How about that? Isn't it superb? The colour on those wings! I'd have sold my electric train-set for one of these in my collection.' He continued to study the page.

'You must have lived in the wrong area,' said Shenton, with an effort to sound reasonable.

'I wouldn't say that,' said Glazier. 'There were oaks in the park where I played. They live high up in the canopy of the wood. You never see them normally, but they are probably more common than most of us realized then.'

'This isn't exactly helping to find my wife,' said Shenton.

'You couldn't be more wrong,' said Glazier. 'How long ago did you kill her, Sir Milroy?'

Shenton tensed. He didn't respond.

'She's been dead a few weeks, hasn't she, long before your trip to New York. She didn't visit Ireland at all. That was some friend of Cressida Concannon's, using the name of Ann Porter. A free trip around the Ring of Kerry. No wonder the woman was laughing. She must have thought the joke was on you, just as the expenses were. I don't suppose she knew that the real Lady Ann was dead.'

'I don't have to listen to this slanderous rubbish,' said Shenton. He'd recovered his voice, but he was ashen.

'You'd better. I'm going to charge you presently. Miss Concannon will also be charged as an accessory. The kidnapping was a fabrication. You wrote the ransom note yourself some time ago. You posted envelopes to this address until one arrived in the condition you required – with the indistinct date-stamp. Then all you had to do was slip the ransom note inside and hand it to me when you got back from New York and alerted us to your wife's so-called abduction. How long has she been dead – four or five weeks?'

Shenton said with contempt, 'What am I supposed to have done with her?'

'Buried her – or tried to. You weren't the first murderer to discover that digging a grave isn't so easy if the ground is unhelpful. It's always a shallow grave in the newspaper reports, isn't it? But you didn't let that defeat you. You jacked up the summerhouse and wedged her under the floorboards – which I suppose was easier than digging six feet down. The butterflies led me to her.'

Shenton latched on to this at once. Turning to Tom Salt he said, 'Is he all right in the head?'

Salt gave his boss a troubled glance.

Shenton flapped his hand in derision. 'Crazy.'

'You don't believe me?' said Glazier. 'Why else would a Purple Emperor come down from the trees? Listen to this.' He started reading from the book. "They remain in the tree-tops feeding on sap and honeydew unless attracted to the ground by the juices of dung or decaying flesh. They seldom visit flowers."' He looked up, straight into Shenton's stricken eyes. 'Not so crazy after all, is it?'

JAMES McCLURE

Scandal at Sandkop

UNCLE DARVIE was the progressive of Sandkop, a remote village in the bushveld north of Johannesburg. He believed that the Earth was round. And although many argued with him, and made him climb windmills to see how flat the horizon stayed, they could not alter his conviction.

Yet this did not mean he was an irreligious man, as a stranger might have supposed. Far from it: the Dominee regarded Uncle Darvie – whom he alone called Doctor Kruger, out of one professional's respect for another – as the fat-tailed ram of his flock. Some said that Uncle Darvie had not missed a single service in forty-three years, which went back before the Dominee's own time, but it was certainly true that he never missed a funeral, and that showed how clear his conscience was. In short, Uncle Darvie's devotion to both God and man so moved the Dominee that he was prompted to one of his rare smiles whenever they met over a deathbed.

Hettie Kruger, however, treated her husband with the loving contempt she thought he deserved.

'It's a scandal!' she said at the supper table one winter evening. 'Call yourself a doctor and a Christian and yet you let this happen!'

'Oh, ja?'

'Let a man murder his wife under your very eyes!'

Uncle Darvie nibbled off a whole row of pips from his mealie cob before bothering to look up. When he did, the melted butter ran down his chin and into his beard, which was modelled on that of his namesake.

'And you eat like a kaffir who doesn't wear shoes. Sis!'

'What did you say before that?' he asked, having only half-heard her because she began everything by saying what a scandal it was. Even the colour of a woman's hat would make her do it.

'Murder his wife.'

'Who?'

'Faanie Vermaak, that's who. And don't say I haven't told you this before.'

'I won't, love of my life, I won't.'

He began trimming the cob like a lathe.

'Well, Uncle Darvie?'

'Mmmm.'

'Motive. Faanie has a motive. When he was caught with that girl from the town who was staying at Uncle Jacobus's place, he said that one day he would find her. Do you remember that? When they put her in the Scotch cart and had the kaffir drive her away? Little hussy!'

'Spoken in the heat of the moment. Faanie's told me himself; he's very ashamed of the whole matter and just wants to forget it.'

'Huh!'

'A man can understand why he took a liking to her, she being of his own kind.'

'And young! And pretty! And as shameless as they come! A man may understand that, yes – but a woman wouldn't!'

'Mmmm.'

'And how do you think Emily Vermaak feels? Being told a thing like that? That he preferred one of his own kind?'

'You were the one so against him marrying her in the first place, woman. It was you who said no good could come of it if he took up with an English-speaker.'

'A long time ago, that was. Five years. Don't be unfair. How was I to know that Emily would learn to talk the *taal* so nice you need never worry she was English? And that's another mistake you keep making: she is real English, not just English-speaking. And what happens? She goes to all the trouble to be a proper wife to him and he wants to run away with—'

'He didn't run away,' said Uncle Darvie, tossing his cob over a shoulder and reaching for another.

'But he wants to – oh, ja. I know men. Secretly, that's what he wants. And the reason he's trying to poison poor Emily so an old fool like you won't notice.'

'What with?'

'Arsenic.'

'So, arsenic is it? We make progress.'

'Evidence,' said Hettie firmly, removing the pips from her cob with a knife which she had been taught by Emily Vermaak was more ladylike. 'We have *evidence* it's happening.'

'Evidence? Arsenic? Motive? Where have you been learning all these big lawyer's words? Has Sergeant Poolman been in Sandkop for the day again? For coffee and a show-off?'

'No. From Emily herself. Auntie Tina went to call on her again yesterday, to see if she was getting any better. She actually said she thought Faanie was trying to kill her.'

'It makes a good story.'

'Auntie Tina also points out,' Hettie continued icily, 'that Emily's sickness began when Faanie was found in that barn with Petronella Swart. From that very day.'

'But we locked him up in the pig sty for two nights.'

'All right then, but almost from that very day. Do you remember how she ran home and went to bed? Have you seen her out of it since? Have you?'

'Consumption,' said Uncle Darvie, picking his teeth with a chew of fingernail. 'That's the trouble with your Mrs Vermaak.'

'She says different. She says—'

'How come she knows what arsenic can do? Did you ask her that? What are the signs?'

'She knows them.'

'Ha, and I also know Faanie Vermaak. Don't forget, I brought him into this world. Never was a more honest boy born.'

'That sinner!'

'Almighty God, Hettie, we didn't catch him *doing* anything with Petronella, they were just *talking*. And he's repented. You'll see, given a little time—'

'And Emily will be dead! Ja, and Faanie can run off to his slut. Men! You are all the same, siding with each other.'

'Women,' he sighed, 'women talk far too much about things that aren't their business.'

'So it isn't our business that one of us is being slowly done to death?'

'No.'

'I wonder if the Dominee would agree?'

He knew he had given a silly answer, and now waited to pay for it. Reaching out for his snuff horn on the dresser.

'Have you forgotten what day it is?'

He had: it was the Sabbath. Divine retribution, no less.

'Why not tell me then?' he asked irritably. 'Why doesn't she? God in heaven, don't I ride out to Welkom once a fortnight to see how she is getting on?'

'What she said to Auntie Tina was in strictest confidence.'

'In other words, she wanted the whole of Sandkop to know.'

'Uncle Darvie! Shame on you! You, an elder of the church, casting slander on a good woman like Auntie Tina! Three husbands she's had!'

He very nearly made a joking rejoinder, with a dark hint at who the real poisoner in their midst might be, but wisely checked himself in time.

'And so? What must I do about it?'

'You're to go and take a proper look at Emily. And then, if you see anything suspicious, you've got to tell the Dominee and Sergeant Poolman and—'

'I'll ride out tomorrow.'

'I'll see you do. And that's another thing: when are you going to get yourself a motor car like Dr Steenkamp in Blikkiesdorp? No wonder people are talking. No wonder.'

'I don't much mind,' replied Uncle Darvie, escaping on to the stoep.

He was too old a dog to learn new tricks, and besides, he was quite sure they were wrong about Emily Vermaak and poor old Faanie.

*

Being a man of his word, he was on the dirt track to Welkom soon after breakfast. As he passed over the cattle-grid at the gate, he felt the usual sadness come upon him. Even after a two-year drought, the place should not have been in such a state. Barbed-wire fences falling down all over, and cattle roaming where they liked. If it had not been for the thorn trees, he would have had difficulty in making out where the pastures ended and the veld began.

Not that anything like two years had passed since the scene at the barn – a matter of six months at most. But it was land that had been fought for, and land that you had to fight in turn, and keep on fighting, or the whole battle might as well have never begun. It was shocking, really.

Only the ridgeback bitch came out to greet him when he reached the long, low homestead built of mud bricks, with its tin roof that would rust if it was not painted again soon. Then, as he was tethering his horse, the Hottentot maid, whose face was truly like a yellow monkey's, appeared.

She told him her master was probably down at the dam, throwing sticks in the water. He told her to fetch him up directly as he wanted a word. He would find his own way in.

The Vermaak family bed almost filled the dim back room. It had been brought up from the Cape on the Great Trek itself, they said. A gigantic bed, made with stinkwood and leather thongs, that was ideal for the conception and delivery of gigantic sons – as Faanie had been. Yet he and Emily were still to be blessed, and that, Uncle Darvie considered, was at least half of their problem.

The farmer's wife looked very small and bony in it – like a panting springbok lying on its side at a dry waterhole. She had her back to him and was staring at a scruffy cat on the other pillow.

'Morning, Emily! How goes it? Just I was passing by and I thought I'd stop in for a minute.'

She ignored him.

'It's all right then if I examine you?'

'What's left of me, you mean,' she said bitterly.

Uncle Darvie had been in half a mind to confront her outright with what had been reported to him, but now he was actually at her bedside, the very thought of it made him feel ridiculous. It was only hearsay, after all, and that from Auntie Tina, who was notoriously inventive.

So he elected to complete his observations first, and then see if there was any point in causing an upset. Everything he noted down had a simple, straightforward explanation without any sinister undertones – just as he had supposed. A layman, of course, with a list of symptoms for only one thing, and thinking they could therefore mean only one thing, might have been misled. But not Uncle Darvie, who already had a lifetime of successful doctoring behind him.

And so, when it came to inspecting the scalp, he paused. Emily Vermaak was still English enough to practise a modesty uncommon among his own womenfolk of her years, and was wearing a night cap. Then, on the evidence already before him, he decided that asking her to remove it would be very unnecessary.

'Aren't you finished yet?'

'I am, I am – so sorry. Well, have you got anything to tell me? About how you are? Coughing much?'

'No more than you'd expect.'

'Good, good. Taking your medicine?'

'Of course.'

She still lay with her back to him – there was not really room around the other side of the bed for a man of his bulk. This was disconcerting, and made it difficult to find the right words for the question Hettie would undoubtedly expect him to ask. Then he had it.

'No special worries? You don't think something's – er, poisoning your system?'

She turned over to face him then, her brown eyes huge in the gaunt, spotty face.

'That's a funny thing to ask, Uncle Darvie. Isn't it you who's supposed to tell me what is the matter?'

How very right she was. He grunted apologetically, picked up his bag and stood a moment trying to think of something soothing to say. He felt a floorboard dip under the shift of his weight, and looked down to see they were all in bad condition – Faanie had even allowed the termites to make a start on his house. Disgraceful.

'God bless, Emily Vermaak,' said Uncle Darvie, and went outside to see if the erring husband had been found. He was glad to leave the room with all its smells, the sort you get with a very sick person, faintly rotten and sweet, and to which he had never grown accustomed. He was out in the fresh air too often for that.

Faanie was talking to Uncle Darvie's horse. Standing a good head above its own head, which just showed what a big fellow he was. Yet there was a stoop to his broad shoulders, and his mouth, pinky-grey in the black bush of his beard, was curiously slack.

'Uncle Darvie? How is—'

'No better, no worse, trust in the Lord, Faanie. But you, man, what is happening to you? Do you want me to give you something – a tonic?'

Faanie smiled crookedly. 'I'm all right, Uncle. There's nothing you can give me that will help. I'll get better when my love gets better – if she can, after what I've done to her.'

'And in the mean time?' Uncle Darvie said, hearing his own echo of Hettie's words. 'What happens to Welkom? Are you giving it back to the kaffirs or what? I saw some just now, sitting on their backsides, doing no work—'

'It is my fault, not theirs,' Faanie replied with his customary honesty – which not many men would have done where there were kaffirs concerned.

'Ja, maybe, but this is your heritage, man! You fully understand? It was Almighty God who led our forebears to this place, He who gave it to His Chosen People. To ignore the Will of the Lord is no light matter!'

'No, it isn't. I will try tomorrow.'

'May God give you a tomorrow, Faanie Vermaak.'

Uncle Darvie was pleased with the way he said this, from

down deep in his chest, for it seemed to strike home at last. Faanie took his hand off the horse's nose and nervously picked his own.

'Petronella Swart. Is she what fills your mind night and day?'

'No, Uncle! That is not true! I know they say so in Sandkop, and I know Emily can never really believe me it was nothing, but—'

'What were you talking to her about?' asked Uncle Darvie, giving the foolish man his first-ever invitation to explain himself.

'About? About nothing. We were looking at the moon and wondering if—'

'It's round,' Uncle Darvie broke in. 'Round-shaped like the world we live on. But what sort of talk was this for a married man?'

'I don't understand.'

'These are scientific things you should say to your wife.'

'She was never interested. Whenever I wonder about anything, Emily says there are professors in England who already know—'

'Faanie, take a pull at yourself, man! Stop moping. Get Welkom back on its legs. And the Dominee and me want to see you in church this Sunday.'

Uncle Darvie brushed him aside and mounted his horse, heaving himself up in only one attempt. Then he remembered his original mission.

'Tell me, Faanie, do you take your wife her meals?'

The farmer reddened.

'Of course not! That's the Hott'not girl's work! I serve from the table and she takes them through.'

'I was just wanting to know if she eats properly, man.'

'Oh, I see. Usually the plate is empty when it comes back.'

'One more question, Faanie: do you hold any grudges about what happened at Uncle Jacobus's place? Are you sure? Not deep inside?'

There was a pause, and then Faanie Vermaak said: 'No, it was a just punishment you and the elders gave me in the sty.'

Which allowed Uncle Darvie to ride off in a much happier

frame of mind than he had arrived in, feeling more convinced than ever that nothing untoward was taking place at Welkom – except to the land itself. And he had even done something about that.

Hettie Kruger, however, was not so easily persuaded. But that was her way.

'Of course, Emily wouldn't tell you what she told Auntie Tina,' she scoffed on his return. 'Trust a man to be so stupid and ask her outright.'

'I didn't exactly, I—'

'What if she was wrong? What if harm came to Faanie he did not deserve? She still loves that rubbish of a man or why would—'

'Last night, last night it was different, Hettie Kruger. Last night you said she actually told—'

'It seems all you care about is the farm!'

'Don't try to wriggle out of it, woman.'

'Me? Who's this doing the wriggling, may I ask? Tonight Auntie Tina can herself tell you of what passed between them.'

'No, I will not see her. I can't have my name—'

'Your name is in enough trouble already. We're trying to help you.'

'No.'

'Anyway, you can't refuse to see her.'

'Oh, no?'

'She has already made an appointment for her piles. That is something you cannot cancel.'

Uncle Darvie knew he was beaten. And for the rest of the day, went about his rounds with a face that intimated to his patients that they were not alone in their troubles. Several kindly offered him spoonfuls of their most dependable patent medicines, and one old dear tried to press on him a purge she had bought from a witchdoctor.

His surgery that evening was an equally gloomy business. Folk kept asking him how *he* was. What made it particularly difficult to bear was the fact that although Auntie Tina had been entered at the top of his list, she did not appear when he rang his small bell. The second person came instead, then the third, and so on. Finally, between acne and roundworm, he put his stethoscope to the wall and confirmed his worst suspicions: Hettie and Auntie Tina were engaged in preliminary discussions in the front room.

He was devoutly praying for an emergency call as his last patient withdrew, when in she came with her usual vigour.

'Evening, you old layabout!'

'Auntie Tina. We must make haste, hey? I've just remembered noticing Gert van der Merwe wasn't looking too—'

Auntie Tina turned her back on him, hoisted up her black dress, bent over and backed towards the paraffin lamp shining on his desk.

'Emily Vermaak has all the symptoms, you know,' Auntie Tina stated with confidence, from round the other side.

'Feet a little wider apart, please.'

'She is wasting away, she vomits a lot and has diarrhoea, there's spots on her face, and her hands and feet itch. Also she feels sick all the time, her hair drops out in lumps – I've seen it – and her skin is that funny dark colour. Can you see them?'

'Man, I don't like talking like this,' Uncle Darvie protested plaintively.

With a delighted laugh, Auntie Tina dropped her skirt and turned around.

'I – I didn't mean—'

'Well? What do you think now? Haven't you even got a book that knows what it's doing?'

He had, right there on the desk before him, with the place marked. There was no need for him to open it though, because he could recall the paragraph vividly – especially now Auntie Tina had reminded him of its contents, virtually word for word.

'You have allowed yourself to become constipated again. I want you to take—'

'Well?' she repeated.

'Emily said nothing to me of vomiting and diarrhoea.'

'She's a lady, that's why. Haven't you smelled her room?'

'Ja, but—'

'Didn't she keep scratching while you were there?'

'No, not once.'

'It comes and goes; I've noticed. Saturday wasn't the only time I've been to Welkom, you know. Oh, no! *I* do what little I can for those who need help.'

That was very unjust of Auntie Tina.

'Spots can come from what you're eating!' he snapped.

'Exactly!'

Uncle Darvie glared at her.

'Her skin was always doing strange things. Remember how it burned when she first came here to work in Gert's shop? There is no sun in England, so they tell me.'

'Nor is there any in that room of hers. Besides, it's got a strange reddish tint that isn't natural.'

Uncle Darvie opened his book and looked again at the line referring to skin colour. A tanned, weatherbeaten appearance could be observed, it said, which was why it was put in some tonics. However, such a characteristic could place the entire community under suspicion of arsenical poisoning – the writer had not reckoned on the South African sun.

'And what about the hair, Uncle Darvie?'

'Look, you listen to me, there are many diseases that can—'

'My backside,' interrupted Auntie Tina. 'What are you going to do about it?'

For one joyous moment, Uncle Darvie thought she had changed subjects, reverting her concern to her own well-being. Then he saw the steely, selfless look in her eye.

'Emily told you these were the symptoms?'

'She read them to me out of a newspaper. It was all about a man who murdered his wife and nearly didn't get found out. They had even buried her first.'

'And why did he murder her?'

'Because of another woman he wanted to—'

'I thought so. And he used?'

'A white powder called arsenic he got from the chemist.'

'There is no chemist in Sandkop.'

Auntie Tina shrugged. Quite rightly – there were chemists in other places. Although Uncle Darvie could not imagine Faanie Vermaak leaving the farm in his condition.

'Where was this? I haven't seen such a story and—'

'It was a very old paper. Going a bit yellow.'

He decided against arguing this point any further. The truth was buying a paper was a recent thing in his life, which had started only when his name began to appear in a weekly list of contributors to the Blikkiesdorp Voortrekker Memorial Fund.

'Has it not occurred to you that this story in the paper is simply giving a poor, sick woman ideas?'

He had not consciously formulated that thought before uttering it, and sat back very proud to think his mind could be so brilliant.

'Er, come again?'

Uncle Darvie was pleased to: 'Seeing herself as the wife in the way of a man's desires, she begins to imagine—'

'Nobody can imagine their body wasting away!'

'What happened to Auntie Rentia when she thought she had pregnancy? Didn't she swell right up?'

'Huh! There is still the danger you could be wrong.'

'But—'

'Words, words, words! Men will play with words all day, thinking they are magic. We want to know what you intend to *do*.'

'We?'

The door opened without a knock first, and Hettie stumped in, halting at her friend's heaving side, arms akimbo.

'Well,' she asked, unabashed by what he might be thinking, 'what are you going to do, Darvie Kruger?'

They made a daunting couple. It had been only with women such as these in their laagers that his forebears managed to keep off otherwise overwhelming hordes of savages. Uncle Darvie wished that he, too, could turn and run.

'I tell you what, ladies,' he said, improvising desperately, 'if Emily Vermaak is indeed being given poison, then it is reaching her in her food.'

'He is quick, this one,' murmured Hettie.

'Tomorrow morning I will ride again to the farm. There I will speak to the Hott'not maid and give her special instructions. From now on, she must serve the food straight from the pot on to the plate in the kitchen – and then take it direct to her missus. Then, if we see an improvement in Emily's condition, I will see what steps must be taken to go more deeply into this matter.'

They looked at each other.

'What if Faanie wants to know why?' objected Auntie Tina.

'Then I tackle him there and then, face to face.'

'You will note,' muttered Hettie drily, 'that he has already found the courage to ask the *woman* straight out. But not the man, oh no.'

'It's different actually accusing—'

'The idea is good,' said Auntie Tina, giving one of those nods when she also sucked in her moustache. 'How long though will this take?'

'I would say a week from now. And "you will note", no harm can come to Emily in the mean time, not with this plan.'

'A week?' queried Hettie. 'Much can happen in a week. What if he tries some other way?'

Uncle Darvie had not thought of that, but somehow he had been given the gift of tongues.

'What is a poisoner – a *slow* poisoner? Someone who does not want to be found out. If she died any other way, there would be immediate suspicion – and, as you say, motive. He wants to dance with a pretty girl, not a rope.'

It was artful that, seeming to side with them. And his ploy clinched the matter. Without further ado, they plodded off to make some coffee.

And the following morning, Uncle Darvie did as he had promised. Putting the fear of God into the Hottentot maid, and not hearing a squeak out of Faanie whom he told it was for dietary reasons.'

Not unnaturally, the news of sudden and violent death at Welkom proved a tremendous shock.

Uncle Darvie and the Dominee were walking home together after the second service that very next Sunday, speaking with humble pride of having had Faanie Vermaak among the congregation again that morning, when the farm's head boy came staggering towards them.

At first, they both thought he was drunk, as most kaffirs were on the Lord's Day, and merely readied themselves to belabour him with their sticks.

Then the man, coughing and gasping, near-winded by his long run, managed to say enough for them to realize there had been shooting.

'Come, come in my motor car!' urged Gert van der Merwe, who was the only other person still abroad in the street, it being a very hot afternoon for winter. 'I can get you there much faster than the Devil can ride!'

The Dominee looked doubtful, and Uncle Darvie hesitated. Neither was very happy about motor cars. But then neither was dressed for riding, being in their long black frock-coats and white ties.

So off they went with Gert, who charitably allowed the head boy to stand on the back bumper, which pleased the simple creature immensely until he lost his grip going over the cattle grid.

The Dominee smiled his rare smile.

And Uncle Darvie drew the blanket up over the bloodied head of Faanie Vermaak whose soul had to be already well on its way to Hell by then. Faanie had died before they got to him, killed by his own hand.

'Man, may I see the note again?' Uncle Darvie asked politely, wiping his hand on the wall of the storeroom first.

'Certainly, my friend, but I say he does not repent in it.'

Uncle Darvie took the scrap of paper, torn from a crops ledger, and read the words scrawled across it:

To whom It May Concern

Almighty God have Mercy on Me. I do not know what to

say so You will Understand. But I do know I Cannot Live with This Guilt. I cannot Live while I can hear my Brethren Accuse me Behind My Back as they did in Church Today. They Say I am killing My Love. Even Uncle Darvie and the Dominee ask Strange Question when a man Thinks about them. I know None of it is True when I walk on my lands but I have Terrible Terrible Dreams when it seem to I wish harm to the Star in my Night Sky. Take Care of Her. I must Know the Truth of my Guilt and the Lord Will Tell Me. Please Forgive me. I remain, Your Obedient servant,
F. J. Vermaak.

'He does ask us to forgive him,' Uncle Darvie murmured. 'Is that not repentance?'

'Well . . .'

'Dominee? Was it something else you had in mind? A full confession, maybe?'

'So, you have heard.'

'Of course.'

With the return of conversation, the air in that tiny room with its corrugated-iron walls baking under the sun, suddenly became almost as stifling as smoke. It also smelled like Swart's Flesh Shop, which was making the Dominee restless.

'Shall we talk on the stoep, Doctor?' he suggested, leading the way with a heavy clump of his boots. 'Or maybe you can wait in the kitchen while I first go and see how Gert is getting on with Mrs Vermaak.'

'Fine, tell her I'll be in again by and by.'

But Uncle Darvie did not go straight indoors; he had spotted the Hottentot maid standing drunkenly against the rainwater tank.

'Hey, where were you this afternoon?' he demanded,

'Making merry in my hut, baasie.'

'Oh, ja? Have you been doing as I told you?'

'True's God, baasie!'

'Take not the Name—' Uncle Darvie began, then found

himself distracted. His mind filled with the horrific effect of a shotgun fired inside a man's mouth.

'Hey? When did you last give your missus a meal then?'

'Lunchtime, my baas. Then she say I must go off same as all servants on Sunday afternoon time.'

The maid scuttled away as the Dominee came out of the house again.

'The widow is very calm,' he said. 'Gert is happy to stay with her while we decide what there is to do.'

'Shock,' grunted Uncle Darvie. 'That it should come to this.'

'You cannot blame yourself, Doctor.'

'Who told him to come to church? Who? It was me.'

'Perhaps this was the best way for it to end. The Almighty has in His Wisdom decided—'

'You can't say that until there's proof . . .' began Uncle Darvie, as they were walking into the kitchen, but his sentence remained for ever unfinished.

There was the proof. Right there on the kitchen table: a large tin of sheep dip with its screw-top off. And beside it, a cup of coffee filled to the brim.

'Sheep dip!' exclaimed the Dominee. 'I thought I noticed something darker than blood on his clothes.'

'Sheep dip,' mourned Uncle Darvie. 'Now, why didn't I think of that? All the time I had in mind the white powder. Yes, it says so here on the label: Beware – Sodium Arsenite.'

He pressed the palm of his hand against the coffee-pot.

'Still warm, Dominee. He must have been preparing it for her at tea time. Yes, the cup stinks of it.'

'But look here – and here, Doctor!'

Uncle Darvie's attention had been so taken up with the sheep dip, he had failed to note what else lay on the table top. There was a cut-throat razor, a short length of binding cord, and a stick of dynamite which Faanie must have had left over from blasting the dam. Even their separate properties as instruments of destruction were enough to make Uncle Darvie shudder – their combined effect so weakened his knees he had to sit down.

'What can this mean?' he said softly.

The Dominee picked up the cut-throat and turned to him, even more grim-faced than usual.

'I take it you do not miss its overall significance, Doctor, which is simply that the Lord God spared the life of Emily Vermaak this day not once but, in a manner of speaking, four times.'

'Five,' corrected Uncle Darvie, with whom accurate arithmetic was a habit. 'There's the gun.'

'Quite so, even more for us to give thanks for. But to return to your question: you have been called to look into men's bodies; I, to look into their souls. And what I see here is one of those terrible dreams Faanie talks about in his letter to us. Only he woke up just in time, saw what he was about to do, wrote the note and very decently shot himself.'

'But *why*? Why all of a sudden?'

There was an odd glint in the Dominee's eye as he replied: 'Because all of a sudden, this slow poisoner was being thwarted by someone. He was being stopped from killing his victim, and could think of no other way except putting an end to her once and for all!'

'Which he realized he could no longer do with the sheep dip, because she'd smell it if he put in enough to kill her outright?'

'Right again, Doctor. So he explored what other means he had at his disposal, and I would suggest that slicing open, strangling—'

'Ja, ja, please—'

'The horror of it brought him to his senses,' the Dominee added, a little peevish at being cut short. 'Shall I sent Gert for Sergeant Poolman to come now?'

Uncle Darvie stood up and barred his way to the bedroom, motioning with his hand for the right to think a moment before they did anything.

'Would it not be best,' he said, 'if we did not make our discoveries public?'

'That Faanie was poisoning his wife? Why, Doctor, I'm surprised at you! Anyone can make a mistake.'

'No, no, it wasn't that. I mean, in Heaven's Name, what good will it do? The Almighty has ordained that this should happen to spare Emily Vermaak suffering – but won't we be going against His Will in telling the police about the poison?'

'I cannot see how.'

'Sergeant Poolman can be trusted to be discreet in cases of simple suicide, as we both know from the past. But mention attempted murder, and those other ones, in the ordinary clothes who smoke cigarettes, will come down like vultures on Sandkop. Think of the distress that could cause Emily – all the pain and indignity of her having to tell strangers, outsiders, even newspaper reporters about what came between her and Faanie. Has the woman not suffered enough?'

The Dominee gave a little shrug.

'What will she feel if she *knows* Faanie was trying to kill her? We don't know, she might change her mind in time and think fondly of him – for her own sake, mind.'

Uncle Darvie was speaking with a desperation that he knew took its strength from the guilt large inside him. He tried once more to win his colleague round.

'All right, what about our part in this? Are you looking forward to seeing me admit at the inquest I made a mistake? Do you want to explain, under oath, how it was you, a leader of the community, disregarded the facts and treated them as gossip – thus endangering a woman's life?'

That was better. The Dominee closed his eyes and seemed to pray for a moment.

'Ja, I can see how this could be the Will of God also,' he said. 'What do we do? Destroy the note?'

'No, that would arouse suspicion. Few men don't explain their self-inflicted ends. The beauty of this one is that it can be read the other way – if you don't know about the poison, as the Sergeant doesn't, because Auntie Tina always insists that no outsider ever hears her stories, then it just sounds as if it's about Petronella Swart.'

'But—' began the Dominee.

'The Sergeant knows that already and can be discreet. No, all we do is put all this back where it belongs and say nothing.'

Uncle Darvie began to screw the lid on the can of sheep dip. He would put it back in the storeroom and perhaps sprinkle a little round to explain how it got on the clothes.

'Yes, this *is* right,' said the Dominee, coming to his side and coiling up the cord.

'You know, it's a funny thing,' Uncle Darvie murmured, happy that they were once again in accord, 'but I still can't believe this of Faanie. Truly, in my heart, that is. I still see him as the honest boy I pulled out backwards, and when I first saw him in the storeroom I thought—'

'What, old friend?'

'That – that he'd been murdered.'

'Doctor Kruger,' replied the Dominee, sparing one more smile, 'if ever a man was born stubborn and pigheaded, it was you! Only this time I don't have to make you go up a tree to see that.'

Two weeks later, Uncle Darvie suddenly rushed out of his surgery in the middle of rummaging for an ear syringe in a drawer, and went across to the manse.

Several things had happened since that dreadful Sunday afternoon out at Welkom. An inquest had been opened and closed on Faanie Vermaak, being held with unusual dispatch as it was important to know where to bury him. He had gone down deep into unconsecrated ground, and that had been one funeral both Uncle Darvie and even the Dominee missed, only Sergeant Poolman and two kaffirs with spades attended it. While Emily Vermaak had moved in with Uncle Jacobus and his family and was showing remarkable signs of recovery without any treatment at all, eating everything they put in front of her. There had been no buyer as yet for the farm, but hopes of a stranger becoming interested ran high.

Less happy had been Uncle Darvie's loss of the peace of his mind. Which had given him no respite until he put his hand in that drawer.

Within minutes, the Dominee had been roused from his afternoon nap and bundled into Gert's Model T. Where he sat almost as bemused as Gert himself, while all three of them drove out to Welkom.

'I'm saying nothing,' Uncle Darvie informed them, 'nothing till I look in the dressing-table!'

Which he did shortly afterwards, with the Dominee peering over and seeing that it was naturally quite empty, save for its linings in each drawer.

'Right, that's one,' said Uncle Darvie, then began pulling up the floorboards on the far side of the big bed where a man could not fit himself unless it was moved.

'Sis!' said Gert, pinching his nose. 'What's down there?'

It was dark under the house, but soon a pale wriggle of maggots showed up, crawling over a mess of grey, slimy heaps sprinkled with sweet papers.

'So that's why he couldn't kill her – she was throwing her food away for fear of poison!' gasped the Dominee. 'No wonder she is fattening up so nicely.'

'No wonder,' echoed Uncle Darvie, his smile crooked as he noticed the other's air of romantic interest.

Then he dived for the door.

'Hey, but where are we going now?' Gert pleaded.

'To pay a call on a *very poisonous woman*,' Uncle Darvie said over his shoulder.

The Dominee cringed. That could mean only one person he knew. They were bound for Auntie Tina.

She sat very still, hands in her lap, as she listened to what her principal guest had to say. The Dominee, who found even a temporary boudoir an unnerving place to be, kept his eyes fixed out of the window.

'Isn't that a bit much?' Emily Vermaak asked Uncle Darvie.

'That is precisely my point. Does a man care very much how he kills, providing the killing is effective? Does he not just grab up the first thing that will do the job? Why should he care? It's not him that's going to suffer – to feel the pain.'

'Unless, of course, he means to kill himself.'

'Man,' Uncle Darvie said to her, 'I must say you are a very

cool personality. Ja, that's the meaning of all those things on the kitchen table – Faanie was trying to decide which would be best for *him*.'

'Not for . . .' mumbled the Dominee, glancing across for a moment.

'Faanie Vermaak never ever intended his wife any harm,' Uncle Darvie growled. 'It was just the opposite: I let a woman murder a man under my nose! And how? By not seeing those symptoms were also symptoms of acute malnutrition, self-imposed, and helped along – in the case of the face sores – by too many of Auntie Tina's sweets!'

'She was very useful,' said Emily Vermaak.

'I'll say. Just a hint and you were vomiting all over the place in her mind. And the way she remembered the symptoms off pat. But that was where you made your big mistake!'

'Oh? Do tell me.'

'You missed one thing – you missed that when Auntie Tina tells a story that has scandal in it, she never leaves out a single detail.'

'Such as?'

'The fact you read aloud from the newspaper. When you want to convince somebody of something, you get them to read it themselves so they can see it down in black and white. You didn't because you knew she couldn't read English and so you translated.'

'And we don't get English papers in Sandkop?'

'Ja, but first I thought of her saying it was "old and going yellow". What farmer's wife ever keeps a newspaper for so long as that without tearing it up to line her drawers and shelves? What other use is there for newspapers once you've read them – unless they're kept specially to remind you of something? Most probably something with which *you've* been connected.'

'I thought I'd never know why I did,' she said, pulling the paper out from under the cushion and handing it to him. 'Although now I wouldn't be without it.'

'The hair – how did you do that though?'

'Ringworm. The cat had it. I would have thought Sherlock of the Bushveld would have spotted that.'

'The *Hereford Times*,' Uncle Darvie read out. 'Major Herbert Rouse Armstrong T.D., sentenced to death for killing his wife in the Welsh border town of – hey, I see the date is 1922, five years ago. That's a coincidence, ja? Are you this Madame X involved?'

For the first time, Emily Vermaak showed emotion. She jumped up and kicked Uncle Darvie on the shins.

'You bastard! You bloody old peasant! I'll give you the "other woman"! I met the little rat at a Whitney dance, didn't I? Said he was a poor lonely widower. Said I was such a comfort to him in his grief – and that was *before* . . . Can't you see? I just wanted to get away as far as possible and find someone who would love me and—'

She slumped on her bed and began to cry.

The Dominee fled. Uncle Darvie, knowing there was no useful way of pursuing the matter, got wearily to his feet. Words were magic, but she could deny every last one used in her deadly spell.

'At least I kept my promise,' Emily Vermaak snuffled.

'Of sacred fidelity?'

'I mean when I promised Faanie he would *rot in Hell* for what he'd done to me! It wasn't hard to pretend I was dying – I'd died a little that night already. Then, when I saw what refusing my food was doing to me . . .'

'But you, woman,' Uncle Darvie said softly, 'won't you have to join him there some day? For what you've done?'

'I never thought of that,' she said in English. 'You're a funny old duffer. What really started you thinking there could be another side to it?'

'Ah,' said Uncle Darvie, taking off his hat again. 'All my life I've believed there was more to this world than meets the eye. Now, you tell me, my dear, what does an oblate spheroid mean to you?'

JILL McGOWN

A Fine Art

GERALD got off the bus and stepped out into the sultry morning. He waited for a lull in the Monday traffic which streamed past, and took deep breaths of air already heavy with exhaust fumes. Perhaps he gripped the briefcase too tightly as he crossed the road to the station, but he looked just like everyone else. Just like any other successful young City gent. And until Friday evening, that was just what he had been. Until Friday evening.

'Surely you're not doing that *now*?' asked Paula. 'You'll be late for your concert.'

'Of course I won't,' said Gerald, as he began to piece the light fitting together again. The early evening news was just starting; he wouldn't have begun the job if he hadn't had time to complete it. 'It had to be done,' he said, stepping off the stool, and going over to the switch. 'So it might as well be done straight away.' The light came on, and he smiled at Paula. 'Never put off . . .' he said.

'Please don't start quoting maxims, Gerald.'

There was a silence after she had spoken, broken by the TV newsreader, who said that there were fears of terrorist activity in the capital over the weekend.

'I wasn't aware that quoting maxims was something I was given to doing,' he said.

'And don't be so pompous!'

Pompous? For a moment, he felt a little hurt. But she wasn't feeling well, of course. That would explain it. Though she had seemed a little cool lately. Ever since the party, really. He frowned. Perhaps she hadn't been well for some time, and hadn't wanted to worry him with it.

'Maybe I shouldn't go,' he said.

'Oh no. I don't want to spoil your evening too,' she said. 'You go. You've been looking forward to it for ages.'

She didn't look too bad, he thought. In fact, she looked her usual, healthy, pretty self. It was probably just the thundery weather, as she had said. He smiled again. 'If you're sure,' he said. 'I'll go and change.'

No one joined him at his table for two as he dined alone, permitting himself a small sherry beforehand. But a last-minute concert-goer had his optimism rewarded by getting Paula's seat, and Gerald felt vaguely contemptuous of him as he settled himself down. Totally disorganized. Coming on spec to a concert like this. Gerald shifted a little in his seat, crossing his legs away from his neighbour, in unconscious rejection of this lack of discipline incarnate.

The orchestra and the audience waited for the conductor, but he didn't arrive. Instead, the sober-faced manager walked on to the podium; there was a smattering of applause from people who didn't know any better.

Groans greeted the announcement that the evening's programme had had to be cancelled because of a bomb threat; there was much scepticism and no panic as they filed out obediently. Gerald felt the pang of guilt that he always felt when his countrymen were active on the mainland. Guilt that his compatriots blew people up? Or guilt that he had opted out of the unpleasantness altogether? He wasn't sure. But he didn't like it when he couldn't place the Irish Sea firmly between him and them. Not that he would ever have become involved, even if he had stayed; his mother had always hurried him past the tough little boys with the toy guns, who played at soldiers. He had followed her example as he grew up, and perhaps, he thought, that was where this odd sense of guilt sprang from. It had been a hoax, anyway, according to the car radio.

Dusk was falling as he arrived home. Downstairs was in darkness, but a light was on in the bedroom. Gerald cut the engine and coasted down the incline. He didn't put the car away, because the garage door made such a whine, and he didn't want to waken her if she had managed to get to sleep. Worriedly, he dug in his pocket for his door key. It wasn't like Paula to go to bed early, even when she was one degree under. She was a night owl, and he had long ago given up trying to reform her. He usually went up a full two hours before she did; he had to have a decent night's sleep. So she must feel really bad if she had gone to bed. He opened the door carefully, silently, and closed it without letting it so much as click.

His foot was on the bottom tread when he heard what sounded like a moan. But even in the instant that he took to gather himself to run up to her, he heard a corresponding, unmistakably masculine grunt, and he froze. His foot on the stair, his hand on the banister, poised ready to run to his wife's sick bed, he listened in paralysed horror as the sounds increased in intensity. When he at last moved, it was to cover his ears. Then, slowly, he took his hands away and left the house as silently as he had entered.

He sat in the car and looked up at the lit bedroom window. Who was he? Where did she meet him? Why, *why*? Would she go off with him, whoever he was? Was he going to lose her? He couldn't, he couldn't lose her. It had never occurred to him to consider the possibility before. But whoever that was up there was going to take her from him; she was having an affair with someone else, had fallen in love with someone else.

He got out of the car, easing the door shut, and stood in the shadow of the garage. Eventually, the hall light went on, and he emerged, a slight figure in dark clothes. Gerald frowned, momentarily unable to place the thin, handsome face. Paula didn't come out with him, and he closed the front door, standing irresolutely for a moment, looking at Gerald's car.

John Sheldon, of course. Sheldon, who lived his life with all the arrogance that his inherited wealth allowed. A friend of the famous and infamous, who boasted of his connections with the underworld, of his spell in prison for possession of marijuana, of the driving ban that he'd just completed, of the women that he'd had. But Paula? Paula had been distant, polite, when they'd met him. A mutual friend had invited them to one of Sheldon's parties, where every other face was well known; Gerald and Paula had left when their overgrown schoolboy of a host had produced the cocaine. Paula had found him just as appalling as he had.

The evidence argued against that. And Gerald was forced to concede that the man did have a kind of superficial attraction. The attraction of the rebel, he supposed. Gerald came from a background where it was almost rebellious simply to conform. But there was nothing glamorous about observing speed limits and working a ten-, often twelve-hour day. It had produced the trappings of wealth in Gerald's case, but no time to enjoy them.

Sheldon turned back towards the house, then shrugged slightly, turned again, and walked away. Gerald watched his retreating figure, and he could see how it had happened. Sheldon had never come across a woman who hadn't fallen at his feet, so he'd made it his business to see that Paula was no exception. He'd seduced her with glitz and glamour, and made her see how boring and uneventful her life with Gerald was. A rebel who cocked a snook at authority – he could see that Paula could be attracted by that. Easy enough to be a rebel if you didn't have to work. But Paula had fallen for it, fallen for *him*. And what could he do against someone like Sheldon? Someone who had had everything Gerald worked so hard for handed to him on a plate and didn't have to conform to anyone's rules? What if she went away with him? His hands went to his ears again, as though he could block out the memory of what he had overheard.

He was reversing the car out of the driveway, driving off after Sheldon. He didn't know what he was going to do – talk to him, plead with him. Anything. He had to stop him stealing Paula from him. The car nosed its way down the narrow street to the building site, alongside which Sheldon was walking. There was no point in appealing to the man's sense of honour, because he didn't have one. He had broken up other marriages; he would take Paula away from him, and Paula was why Gerald lived. He couldn't bear to lose her.

He could see Sheldon's car, parked on the opposite side of the road from the building site. And Sheldon, sauntering along, stepping off the pavement. He hated him for existing; Gerald's foot went down on the accelerator, and a sudden, breathtaking surge of power pumped through his whole body as the car went straight and true for Sheldon.

He scrambled out and ran back to his victim, kneeling down, feeling for signs of life. There were none. It had been swift and efficient. And he had made certain that Sheldon could never take Paula away, God forgive him. Gerald crossed himself. And God bless the money-grubbing property developers who knocked down the mean little houses and built homes fit for yuppies. For no one had seen, no one had heard.

He walked back to the car, sizing up the boot. Just about. Sheldon presented little difficulty to Gerald, even as a dead weight, and he hoisted the body on to his shoulder and tipped it into the boot like a sack of the cement that had made Sheldon senior's original profits. Sheldon's keys lay in the road, and Gerald stooped to pick them up. He had to go to Sheldon's place; he had to make sure that there was nothing of Paula's there. Nothing to connect him to Sheldon. Then, he'd sort out what to do with the body.

He should be feeling frightened, he told himself. He was driving along with a man's body in the boot of his car. But he felt exhilarated, almost jubilant, as he at last arrived at the quiet private mews where Sheldon lived. On a Friday evening, only one or two incurious lights glowed in the windows, and no one saw him let himself in with Sheldon's key.

As he searched the rooms, he was only barely aware of the car, *his* car, parked outside with a body in its boot. He was still on a high from the power-surge. And he found nothing. No sign, no trace of Paula's presence. He began to think of his next move. Dump the body? Or just report the car stolen? Leave it there, complete with body, and report it stolen. Yes. Yes, he'd probably do that. He opened the door to leave and found himself face to face with two men. His heart stopped beating.

'Vinny sent us,' said the first, a small man with wiry hair.

'Who are you?' Gerald heard himself saying.

'Never mind names.'

Gerald swallowed.

'He said to make sure you wasn't stoned,' said the other.

Gerald's eyes widened slightly. They thought he was Sheldon.

'He said we had to give you your instructions,' said the first.

'You . . . you'd better come in.' Gerald stood aside.

'He looks a bit windy to me,' observed the second man, a tall, gaunt figure in black. 'Will he be OK?'

'Vinny says he's OK.'

It irritated Gerald, even under these bizarre circumstances, to be talked about as though he wasn't there.

'Is that your car outside?' asked the tall one.

'Yes.' There seemed little point in lying, whoever they were.

'Where's the other one?' asked the small man.

'What?'

'You were supposed to be getting a car. Where is it?'

Gerald's working life was spent thinking quickly, acting quickly. And bluffing.

'You don't need to know where it is,' he said calmly.

The small man nodded, and a glimmer of something like respect came into his eye. And then he began, as promised, to give Gerald his instructions. Sheldon's instructions.

My God, they were going to rob a bank. Not an ordinary bank. One which only existed to provide safety-deposit boxes for its customers. And Vinny, it seemed, had spent a great deal of money working out how to break into it without anyone being any the wiser until the bank opened again on Monday. Sheldon's job didn't sound too arduous. He had to keep lookout, tell them if it was safe to come up, open the boot, and be ready to drive off once the others were in the car. If there was trouble, he would have to outdrive the police, but there would be no trouble. Sheldon was to meet the small man at seven o'clock on Saturday morning, and he would take him to the tunnel exit. It was a long way away from the bank, away from anywhere. Sheldon would be home in time for lunch. Sweet as a nut it would be.

The small man gestured to the door, and they seemed to be leaving. Outside, the thin one ran a hand over Gerald's car. 'Nice motor,' he said.

Gerald stiffened slightly. Go on, he thought. Get your fingerprints on it. Then they'll believe me that it was stolen. He reached into his pocket, and took out his own keys. 'Here,' he said; holding them out. 'Have a drive, if you like.'

'Can I?'

'No!' barked the small man. 'If you're seen riding around in one of them . . .'

The other took Gerald's keys. 'Just a look,' he assured his companion. Gerald watched, tense, as he opened the door, sat in the car, touched the steering wheel, the dash, everything.

'I'm for one of these,' he said. 'When we've done.' He put the keys in the ignition.

'Out,' said the boss, and reluctantly the other man eased his tall frame out of the car.

'Just leave the keys,' Gerald said, striving to sound unconcerned. 'I'm going out.'

And there it was, after they'd gone. Covered with fingerprints almost certainly known to the police. Covered with someone *else*'s fingerprints at any rate. Gerald felt cock-a-hoop as he left Sheldon's place, walking a long, safe distance before hailing a taxi.

'Did you enjoy the concert?' Paula asked.

'It was cancelled,' he said. 'Bomb scare.'

He had gone for a drive, he explained, intending to go back to the hall in case they had given the all-clear for the concert to start after all. But the car had packed up on him, and it took for ever to get a taxi.

'I thought I heard your car earlier,' she said.

'No. Must have been someone turning in the road.'

It was perfect. Perfect. God was on his side.

But the supercharge didn't last for ever, and as he lay in bed, his belief in God's partisanship waned with it. It was still his car. It had still killed someone, someone who was still in the boot. Someone known to Gerald. Vinny, he had been told, would have Sheldon's legs broken if he fouled up this job. But murder? And anyway, if the job didn't take place, then the police could hardly connect Sheldon's death to it, could they? So what would make Vinny move on to murder from grievous bodily harm? Being double-crossed, Gerald supposed. If the job *did* take place, and Sheldon . . .

Gerald sat up, sweating in the oppressive, thundery heat. Suppose Sheldon did turn up? Turned up, but then robbed them of the loot? Then Vinny could well get murderous. And there would be a moment. Just a single moment, when the haul would be in the boot, and the others not yet in the car. If he could just put his foot down again. Like he had with Sheldon. But he needed a car. A car, a car – Sheldon's car, of course. Parked across from the building site, powerful as his own. Gerald remembered the sensation of all that power transferring itself from the engine to him, and he wanted to feel it again.

He wore a business suit, because he would be carrying a briefcase, and he mustn't look odd. He wore driving gloves. And he had a plan, a plan that would put all these crooks behind bars where they belonged, and leave him in the clear.

It took longer than they thought, and it was well after lunchtime when Gerald finally heard the tapped signal. There was no one around; there had been no one all morning, in this unlovely, unproductive, uninhabited cul-de-sac. Gerald dragged away the manhole cover and opened the boot, as instructed. He watched, revving the engine nervously, as the small man emerged and the sack was handed up to him by the other. The tall man was pushing back the manhole cover, the other dropped the sack in the boot.

Again, the growling power of the engine charged into Gerald's body as he roared away, the boot still open. His only regret was that he couldn't see them in the mirror as he disappeared from their view. He stopped, slammed down the boot with his gloved hand, and drove off again, this time within the speed limit. And it was difficult, keeping to the snail's pace laid down, when he knew that he had all that potency inside him. But he drove like the model driver he was, back to the building site. Back to where he had rid himself of the threat to his security. They were working on the site, taking no notice of him as he opened the boot. They didn't know that he was emptying jewellery and cash from a sack to a briefcase. All of it, except one particularly beautiful diamond ring. For that was going to be in Sheldon's pocket when they found him. Along with the key to a left-luggage locker.

Gerald walked home, unremarkable in his pin-striped suit, carrying his briefcase. He had to wait until tomorrow to carry on with his plan. Tomorrow, when he would know for certain that the bank really was unaware that a robbery had taken place, and it would be safe for him to use Sheldon's car again. And safe to plant the ring on Sheldon. Right now, Vinny's boys would be there, tearing the place apart. When they found nothing, they'd go looking for Sheldon. And if they looked in the boot of the car, what they would find there would scare them off for good.

He went straight upstairs and hid the briefcase in the spare room. He felt good; it was only when he walked into the living-room and saw Paula reading, curled up in an armchair, that the power suddenly drained away, and he began to shake uncontrollably.

A drink. A drink would steady him. He walked almost blindly to the sideboard, and half filled a tumbler with whisky, drinking it down like lemonade. It hurt; it knocked his breath away.

'Gerald?' Paula twisted round. 'Gerald, for God's sake! What's wrong?'

'Nothing,' he croaked. He poured another as he spoke, the bottle rattling against the glass. He had to stop the shaking, drown the terrible dread in the pit of his stomach. How long did it take to work? *Did* it work? He'd never tried it before.

'Gerald, what are you doing? Where have you been?'

'To the car,' he said, the lines that he had rehearsed surfacing through the fog of panic. 'It's been stolen.'

'I thought it wouldn't go,' she said.

'It obviously went for them,' said Gerald. He drained his glass again, the liquor burning his throat, and poured another, bringing the bottle with him as he sat down.

'Gerald, what are you *doing*?' she asked again. She looked at the bottle at his feet, her face bewildered. 'What did the police say?'

'I haven't told them yet,' he said, desperately trying to stop his hand shaking as he lifted the glass to his lips.

'Gerald – it's just a car. It's insured.' She frowned. 'Was there something in it?' she asked. 'Something important?'

There was something in it, all right, he thought. But he was prepared for that question too, and he told her what he would tell the police when they asked. 'Just my briefcase,' he said, gulping down half of what was in the glass. Come on, come on. Work.

'Gerald – you can't drink whisky like that! You'll make yourself ill!'

No. It would make him better. At last there was a numbing sensation round his mouth. It was working, and it wasn't burning his throat any more. It was going down smoothly and sweetly, like fresh water.

'Gerald, stop that!' She scrambled to her feet. 'You can kill yourself doing that!' She came over to him and took away his empty glass, picking up the bottle. She looked at it, then at him. 'Oh God!' she said. 'This isn't about the car, is it?'

His head was beginning to feel a bit muzzy, and that line hadn't been in the script that he'd rehearsed all morning.

'It *was* you I heard last night, wasn't it?' she said. 'You did come home. When the concert was cancelled. You came home, didn't you?'

He looked up at her. She was beautiful. Really, really beautiful. No wonder Sheldon had wanted to add her to his collection. And he didn't blame her for falling for Sheldon. Sheldon had seduced her. He was glamorous, exciting. He lived on the edge of disaster all the time. And it ought to be distasteful, but it wasn't. It was exciting. Exciting to feel the rush of adrenalin, even exciting not to know how long it would last. Oh, Paula should have seen him when he drove off, leaving Vinny's stooges standing.

'That's all it was,' she was saying. 'I'm sorry. But that's what happened, and I can't change it. I wish to God I could.'

He had been aware that she had been speaking; he had heard her voice, the rise and fall. No words. He couldn't understand the words. He couldn't see her properly. He felt very strange. 'I love you, Paula,' he said, his voice thick and hoarse. 'I don't blame you.' His head swam.

'No. No, Gerald. Get up. Get up – you can't pass out. Gerald, get *up*!'

She was pulling at him, putting her arms round him, pulling him off the sofa. She couldn't lift a big man like him, he thought. He'd have to help. And he staggered to his feet, leaning on her, as she slid open the door, taking him out on to the patio, telling him to breathe fresh air, walking him up and down in the tiny space. In a moment of clarity, he knew what was going to happen and broke away from her just before he was violently and painfully sick.

She must have put him to bed. He couldn't remember. He hadn't known that it was possible to have so much pain in your head. He still felt sick. And he had things to do . . . He stumbled as he got up, shakily righting himself. It was morning. What time was it? Only ten o'clock. It was all right. If he lived, he'd got plenty of time. If he died, then none of it mattered.

The pain had gone by the time he heard Paula's key in the door. He felt hollow and weak, and the smell and taste of the whisky still clung to him through a bath and several brushings of his teeth. Paula didn't speak; she made coffee and brought it to him, sitting beside him on the sofa.

'Are you better?' she asked softly.

He nodded. 'Where have you been?' he asked.

'Mass.'

Paula hadn't been to church for years. That was another thing he'd nagged her about.

'Good for the soul and all that,' she said, almost in tears. 'I explained to Father Gallagher that you weren't well.' She took his hands in hers. 'I'm so sorry, Gerald.'

'He wouldn't have made a fool of himself,' Gerald said. 'He wouldn't have thrown up on the patio.'

'Father Gallagher?' she asked, startled.

'Sheldon!'

'Oh.' She gave a short sigh. 'I imagine he has, in his time,' she said.

'Paula,' he said. 'I understand, you know. I understand why you had an affair with him. But . . .' He looked at her. 'I can't live like he does. I have to—'

'Gerald,' she said, interrupting him. 'I told you yesterday. John Sheldon doesn't mean a thing to me.'

'What?' He stared at her, bemused.

'Please believe me, Gerald. I know why I did it. I was angry with you. Because you . . . you're so straight. So rigid. You made me leave the party, and I didn't *want* to leave.'

His eyes widened. 'You wanted to stuff cocaine up your nose?'

'No! But I didn't want to leave just because other people were going to. I felt . . . I felt humiliated, Gerald. It was ridiculous and childish, I know. But I was angry, and that's why I rang him up. That's why it happened. There was nothing more to it than that.'

'What?' he said again, his mouth dry.

'Please believe me. It wasn't an affair, Gerald. It was a one-night stand. I felt that I had something to prove, I suppose. But it didn't mean a thing, I swear.'

His mouth hung open as he looked at her. 'But . . .' he began, wanting to tell her what he had done. Tell her that Sheldon was dead. Because of her. Dead in the boot of his car. But he couldn't tell her that he was a murderer. So he told her what she was, instead. Using words that he had never uttered before. Words that once he wouldn't have tolerated being spoken in her presence. And when he had run out of names to call her, he stood up. 'I'm going,' he said, his back to her. He couldn't look at her.

'All right.' She sounded hurt and angry and frightened. 'If that's what you think of me, maybe you should go.' Her voice shook. 'But I love you, Gerald. And I wish you could forgive me.'

'I do,' he said, still not looking at her. 'I have.' He sighed. 'I have things to do.'

'Can't they wait?'

'What for?'

She touched his shoulder, and he turned to her. He had something to prove too. To himself, to Paula. Now. Now, while he could still remember the tremendous sensation of power surging through him, as he killed for her. *Killed* for her. Boring, straight, staid old Gerald would prove that Sheldon wasn't the only one who could excite her. Now. Everything else could wait. He'd go afterwards.

He woke to darkness, alone in the bed, and fumbled for the clock. The glowing digits told him it was half-past nine, and he lay back, telling himself that he must get up. He must go and put the finishing touches to this whole ghastly business. But he didn't move.

Because all that their brief, unsatisfactory union had proved was that even his normal reserves of energy were exhausted. He had fallen into a defeated sleep, with Paula assuring him that it didn't matter, while the sounds of Sheldon's successful trespass echoed in his memory, mocking him. It mattered. It *mattered*.

He was tired. He didn't want to go out. His limbs ached, and he just wanted to stay there, alone in the darkness. If he went early enough in the morning, he could still beat the bank to it. It would take time to discover the robbery, time to call the police, time to alert everyone.

Yes, he thought. Monday morning. That would be even better. No one would look twice at him leaving something in a left-luggage locker, putting something in the boot of a car. He couldn't use Sheldon's car, though. It would be too risky tomorrow. But he could get the bus. His car had been stolen, hadn't it? What more natural? Yes, he thought, closing weary eyes again. Tomorrow would be time enough.

Gerald woke again at ten past five, when a peal of distant thunder disturbed the air. He gently eased himself out of bed so as not to disturb the sleeping Paula and prepared to complete his plan.

Gerald stepped on to the pavement and could see a newsagent's billboard for the evening paper on the streets already. Something big must have happened, and Gerald's heart pumped as he drew closer to it. Not the robbery. Please God, not the robbery.

BOMB BLAST AT VICTORIA – TWO DEAD, it read.

The thunder that had wakened him had not been thunder; it had been a bomb which had claimed lives. There was no guilt. Perhaps it never had been guilt. All that the bomb meant to him was that the robbery would be playing second fiddle to it as far as the police were concerned.

And now, all he had to do was walk into the station, leave the briefcase, then come out again, joining the commuters as they made their way to the tubes. On to Sheldon's place, where he would open the boot of his car, plant the ring and the key, go to work as normal, and report his car missing. The confidence was back in Gerald's step as he walked on towards the station, tingling with anticipation, living on the edge.

The robbery would be discovered, and sooner or later so would Sheldon's body. The key would be traced, and the loot would be found. The fingerprints on his car would lead them to Vinny and his cronies, and their ridiculous protestations that Sheldon was *not* the man who had run off with their loot would be treated with derision. The perfect murder. And that thought gave Gerald intense pleasure.

As he entered the station, Gerald felt the charge go through his body without 2000 c.c. of engine providing it. *He* was providing it. And he'd show Paula what he could do when he wasn't hung-over and exhausted.

'Security check,' said the policewoman. 'Could you open your briefcase, please?'

But Gerald couldn't even move.

'If once a man indulges himself in murder, very soon he comes to think little of robbing; and from robbing he comes next to drinking and sabbath-breaking, and from that to incivility and procrastination.'

Thomas De Quincey
Murder Considered as One of the Fine Arts

JOHN MALCOLM

Dinah, Reading

AT BREAKFAST on Saturday morning Sue expressed a hope that I could keep out of trouble while she was away visiting her mother in Bath. I grunted some reply or another whilst I looked at the auction catalogues and price lists that had come in the morning post. She was only going to be away for one night and it seemed unnecessary to respond to that sort of provocation; I perused the illustrations patiently while she got herself ready and then took her to Paddington in a taxi to catch the mid-morning train. Men are seldom as innocently employed as when among books so, as I walked back along Praed Street, I popped into Mr Goodston's shop to look for a read I'd promised myself. It started just as simply as that.

Mr Goodston was sitting behind his desk studying racing form. Sporting papers were propped up on the teetering stacks of books in front of him. Around the dingy shop ranks of subfusc bindings darkened the dusty air. I don't know why I like Mr Goodston, who is a cautious fat man of great professionalism, but I suspect that it is because he flatters me with help and encouragement in a way that suggests that the younger generation are not prominent among his clients. In my work for the Art Investment Fund of White's Bank I have had to do much research, not just of an art-historical nature, and Mr Goodston is both a well of information and a rich source of background anecdote. At home and in my office are the catalogues that trace the auction sale prices and the commercial movement of art; here lay countless volumes of memoir and social record that put life into the tableaux we purchase on behalf of our investors.

'Mr Simpson!' His eyes rolled up above the level of his half-moons. 'This is indeed an honour and a pleasure. The only rugby blue amongst my clientele. I have admirals, generals, and masters of foxhounds in plenty but of rugby men, alas, only one: yourself.' He smiled a trifle sadly and moved his papers to one side. Mr Goodston did not convey his usual bright impression and I suspected the papers in front of him. Mr Goodston has a weakness for the horses which consumes his literary profits. He is a punter. If his shop is closed you know that he is either in a nearby betting shop or on his way to one of the classic meetings. He cannot help it; Mr Goodston is a racing man.

'To what do I owe the pleasure?' He peered at me expectantly. 'Is it the stage again? Ellen Terry? Or a more sporting affair? Lillie Langtry and Mr Moreton Frewen perhaps?' He put his finger up waggishly to tap the side of his nose.

'Not this time, Mr Goodston.'

'Aha! The plot thickens. Well, you know me, my dear sir.' He waved an expansive arm. 'Sporting, Military, and Thespian specialities. Under what heading can I be of assist, as they say?'

'Naval, I think, Mr Goodston.'

'Naval? Naval! There you touch upon a chord, my dear young man. You touch a chord! Naval matters are dear to my heart. But not after the invention of steam. The Royal Navy was never quite the same after the invention of steam. I am purely a sailing man.'

'This would be eighteenth century, Mr Goodston. I was walking down the Portobello Road the other day, debating a holiday in Cartagena with Sue. The Portobello Road, as I'm sure you know, was named after a farm in that area which, in turn, was named, like the Scottish town, after—'

'Vernon's victory! My dear Mr Simpson! Old Grog! The hero of Porto Bello! Bells were rung up and down the country. Countless inns were renamed the Admiral Vernon. But a holiday in Cartagena? In Colombia? Is that not a fearsome prospect? Is that not dangerous?'

'Good gracious no, Mr Goodston. Colombia isn't all cocaine barons blazing machine-guns down the main streets. Cartagena is a wonderful example, a unique example of Spanish Colonial

South America. It is a must on any professional tourist's list. Superb. I've always wanted to go there and see where Vernon failed. Never had the chance. Actually, it would probably be more dangerous to go to Porto Bello just now. You'd have to fly to Panama, nip up to Colon, and then go by road out along the coast, with a pretty fair chance of being mugged or robbed along the way. I wouldn't mind seeing it, though. Beautiful harbour, I believe. The old forts are still there.'

Mr Goodston gazed at me fondly. 'Porto Bello,' he murmured. 'Vernon. Around 1739? Very exaggerated at the time, but the nation needed a victory over the Spanish. War of Jenkins's Ear. It wasn't that great a capture, really. Morgan had taken Porto Bello with his pirates sixty years earlier, but Morgan was a filthy rascal. Welsh. As cruel as Satan. The rich ladies of Porto Bello were strapped naked to red-hot baking ovens and roasted until they gave up their valuables. Filthy beast. Did worse things at Panama.'

I blinked. The dusty antiquarian bookshop of Mr Goodston in Praed Street is an odd place in which to conjure up visions of plump, rich, naked ladies being baked on stoves by roaring pirates but the imaginative mind needs no geographical movement for its stimulation. Bookshops exist for that reason. I cleared my throat.

'Is there a book on Vernon I could get hold of? There isn't one in print 'cos I've tried. I'd like to read about him and the great failure at Cartagena before I go there.'

Mr Goodston gave me a triumphant stare. 'Of course there is. And let me say that you have come to the right place because, by an extraordinary coincidence, I got a copy in a consignment of books, very valuable books, that came in after cataloguing this very morning. Look not so alarmed, dear boy. The Vernon book is not itself valuable. I had to take the er, chaff with the wheat, you might say. It can be had for a modest sum. *The Angry Admiral* by Cyril Hughes Hartmann. Heinemann, 1953. Vernon was not really so bad-tempered, you know, and his dispositions saved the country from invasion by the French in

1745, but Anson took the credit. Poor old Grog.' He hauled himself to his feet. 'The books are upstairs. Let me show you.'

I felt flattered. Mr Goodston had never before taken me up to his inner sanctum. I followed him obediently as he squeezed through a door at the back of the shop and we creaked up a staircase to the first floor. He fumbled with a key and we went into another book-lined room. Tea-chests on the floor were full of books; Mr Goodston rummaged among them and emerged, triumphant, holding a red cloth volume.

'The very item! *The Angry Admiral.* I – is something the matter?'

He peered at me reproachfully, my attention having been diverted. His gaze followed mine to a painting hanging on the wall. It depicted a girl of perhaps eight or nine years old sitting at a kitchen table. She looked wistfully out of the canvas over a bowl of cereal.

'That's a Dod Proctor,' I said. 'I didn't know you had a Dod Proctor.'

A fond smile appeared on his lips. 'That is indeed a Dod Proctor. My late wife bought it many years ago. It is an odd item because there is a portrait of her husband Ernest on the back. I imagine it came from her studio – a sort of working canvas used on both sides. I am very fond of it. My goodness. I had no idea that your stewardship of White's Art Fund took your artistic interests so wide.'

I smiled back at him. 'White's Art Fund specializes in modern British painting. It is my business to know of such fine painters as Dod Proctor. She is unmistakable. And my goodness—'

Downstairs the shop doorbell rang, cutting me off. Mr Goodston made a noise indicating irritation at the possible arrival of more custom.

'If you will excuse me for one moment?'

'Of course.'

I trod carefully over the piles of books on the floor while he disappeared downstairs. The painting had an appeal that is difficult to describe. The child had thin arms and was dressed in a collared frock of the 1930s. The china on the table was blue with white spots, probably from the T. H. Green pottery. Dod Proctor deserved to be represented among the Art Fund's range of paintings well ahead of other, more fashionable women artists.

Downstairs there was a crack and a scuffle, resulting in a heavy thumping cascade of books. A voice bellowed in anger.

'Pay up! Now! Or else!'

I nipped back over the books, down the staircase and into the shop. Mr Goodston was pinned to the wall behind his desk, spectacles askew, by a fattish man in a stained suit who grasped his lapels. Another thick-set bloke stood leaning with his back to the door, hard against it so that no one could get in.

'Here, here,' I said mildly. 'What's all this about?'

Fatty let go of Mr Goodston and turned towards me with a nasty scowl. 'It's about money owing. That's what it's about. Who are you, then? The new minder?'

I raised my eyebrows at Mr Goodston, who was getting his breath back.

'Injudicious,' he gasped, ' – unfortunate – betting shop – poor horses – a temporary embarrassment—'

'Temporary!' The fat man curled his lip. 'You owe my guvnor a lot of cash and have done for a long time. Now you pay up, see, or else.'

'Or else what?' I enquired, bristles starting on the back of my neck.

The fat man faced me with a sneer. 'Or else people will get hurt. Got me, squire? Yourself included.'

My dear old father used to say that the essence of success in war is to use the utmost brutality. A military man would have added that an element of surprise helps a lot. Fatty was standing all wrong for a real professional: legs apart, arms akimbo, head thrust forward aggressively. I leant my back against a bookcase and brought my right foot up sharply, like a man punting a good up-and-under for a scrum to chase, straight into the place it would hurt most. There was a great choked-off screech and he doubled up in the middle of the floor. His chum on the door bounded forward predictably on to a straight left to the end of the nose, with gratifyingly sanguinary results. I wrenched the door open while he clasped bloodied hands to his injured hooter and propelled him through.

'Out,' I said. 'Both of you.'

The doubled-up fat one managed to hit his head on the door-jamb as I shoved him out. He turned to snarl at me painfully.

'You haven't heard the last of this,' he wheezed. 'We'll be back.'

'You tell your guvnor to collect his money legally or next time I'll shove you under a bus.' I gestured at a large red one hammering its way down Praed Street. 'Without the slightest compunction.' With a glance at a couple of entranced passers-by I went back in and slammed the door. Mr Goodston had slid down on to the chair behind his desk. Distress emanated from him.

'My dear Mr Simpson! The shame! The humiliation! I am mortified! Your kind efforts – much appreciated – awful – what would I have done – you are a dangerous man when roused, sir. But I am done, Mr Simpson, done.' He waved a hopeless hand at his desk and the racing papers. 'My downfall, sir. My downfall. Since my dear wife died . . .' He gestured vaguely and let his hand fall dramatically to the crowded surface. It was clear that even in his financial extremities Mr Goodston had been unable to resist the lure of the turf. A detailed programme for the day's racing at Haydock Park was carefully marked in red pencil. I shook my head sadly as I picked it up.

'Mr Goodston, it is not for me to criticize your pastimes. I do not gamble, myself. I may have related to you that once, during a heavy downpour in the Nathan Road, Hong Kong, I had my palm read by an Indian. He took one look at my hand and advised me never to gamble. Nevertheless, it is an excitement I think I can understand . . .'

I let my voice trail off. My eye had inevitably caught sight of the lists of runners. Prickles went down my spine. Fate was staring me in the eye.

'What is it, Mr Simpson?'

'It's incredible! There's a horse called Dainty Dinah running in the five thirty at Haydock Park! Fifty to one against. You haven't marked it.'

'Indeed I have not. It is a rank outsider. Rank.'

I put the paper down. I felt feverish. 'Is there a betting shop near here that you can use? I mean one where you are not a major debtor?'

He gaped at me. 'Near the station. But—'

'But me no buts, Mr Goodston. We are going to that shop now. I shall put down, on your behalf, three hundred quid on Dainty Dinah to win.'

'Mr Simpson! What is this?'

'Actually – no – yes, damn it – I shall also put fifty quid on it for myself as well. It will pay for my holiday in Cartagena with Sue.'

'Mr Simpson! Mr Simpson, please! What has possessed you? I cannot allow it! The horse cannot win! I couldn't repay you!'

'Ah, yes you could. Because the horse will win. And' – I held up a hand to restrain him – 'even if it doesn't win, you will be able to recoup the loss. It can be a loan against the books I shall buy from you. Look upon it as a payment on account. I shall easily purchase that value of books in a relatively short period. But it will be unnecessary. The horse will win.'

Mr Goodston paused. Mr Goodston is a gambling man. He blinked at me. 'But – but Mr Simpson, why? Why this sudden urge?' His expression became anxious. 'Did you sustain a knock in your imbroglio just now? You are not a gambler. I can confirm that you have told me that many times. I would never forgive myself if I were to be the cause of a horrible stumble in your forward and distinguished career. Please, Mr Simpson, why? Why?'

'I cannot tell you that just now, Mr Goodston, because I am superstitious. It would spoil the chance. Come, let us place our bets. I take it that your obligations do not amount to more than fifteen thousand pounds?'

He shook his head dumbly. My glance fell on the red cloth Vernon book, now lying on the floor. 'How much do I owe you for that?'

He picked it up and handed it to me. 'With my compliments, my dear sir. With my compliments, in return for your, er, assistance just now.'

'Thank you, Mr Goodston, but I do not expect you to give me your stock. However, there's no time to lose. We must go and place our bets quickly, before the odds shorten in.'

He gave me a wondering look. 'There is no danger of that. No danger at all.'

I practically ran him from the shop and we placed the bets. We got fifty to one without demur. Mr Goodston pocketed his receipts and I took mine for my fifty-pound flutter. I promised to phone him after the horse had won and arrange to celebrate. He looked at me strangely but said nothing; gamblers have superstitions about chains of events.

I spent that afternoon inside watching television. It was the longest afternoon of my life. By the time the five thirty at Haydock Park came on I felt as though I had been waiting in the changing-room at Twickenham before the Oxford match for five years. Dainty Dinah was a small brown horse the cameras barely noticed. They concentrated on three others. At the first bend Dainty Dinah was well back. On the far leg of the course she made up a few places. On the last bend she moved into third place. I knocked my mug of tea over on to the carpet. Down the final straight she sailed past the favourite and the second favourite. She won by three clear lengths with no possible challenges or infringements. I found that I was hoarse and must have been shouting; I rushed to the telephone but Mr Goodston's phone rang without reply. I guessed that he would have watched the race in the betting shop and was now either being given sal volatile or was in the pub, buying drinks. I downed a large gin and tonic myself. I felt like going out and kicking a hole in the big drum. I thought of Sue and decided to give her a big surprise when she got back. I was restless.

I managed to calm myself by reading the book on Vernon. It was gripping stuff. If Vernon hadn't been hampered by a blockheaded redcoat general called Wentworth he would have captured Cartagena and Latin America might have fallen into

British hands. I decided that the cloth-headed Wentworth might have done us an unintentional good turn. Vernon ended up, just like Cochrane after him, at odds with the Board of Admiralty, who struck him off. I finished the book late at night; it was in good condition except for some jottings – a name and two telephone numbers – on the map endpapers, which was irritating. People mistreat books.

In the morning I breakfasted cheerfully and then nipped over to Praed Street. Mr Goodston keeps a bottle of Celebration Cream sherry in his desk for special occasions and I rather fancied a glass with him in view of events. There was a policeman standing by the door of the shop and I bade him an affable good morning. It wasn't until I'd passed him and was inside that I noticed that he'd followed me and that the interior was unaccountably full for a Sunday.

I first sighted the two bookie's men. They stood against a bookcase looking a bit sheepish. Facing them was a sturdy plain-clothes man whose occupation was obvious. Next to him stood an athletic-looking ginger-haired man who let out an exclamation at the sight of me.

'Good Heavens,' I said. 'Hello, Nobby. How are you today?'

'That's 'im.' The fat heavy one pointed at me excitedly, as though justifying himself.

'Who are you?' the uniformed policeman demanded.

'It's all right,' I answered him, 'I am well acquainted with Chief Inspector Roberts.'

'That's him,' Fatty insisted again, self-righteously. 'Violent bastard, he is. Dangerous. He's your man.'

The plain-clothes man spoke. 'Are you saying that this is the man involved in your affray yesterday?'

'Yeah. That's him. Nasty piece of work. I told you. Look at him.'

The ginger-haired man let out an audible groan. I have known Nobby Roberts since we were at college together, where he played on the wing while I was a front-row man, usually a prop. When he left college he went into the police force to satisfy a strong sense of social and judicial vocation. He is a very serious police officer and tends to get pompous but he's a close friend.

'Dear God,' he now said, in stricken tones, 'I don't believe it. Tim, are you really the man involved in a punch-up with these two yesterday morning on these premises? Witnessed by several passers-by?'

'I wouldn't have called it an affray, Nobby. Just seeing them off the premises, you know. They have unpleasant methods of debt collection.'

'For Heaven's sake,' he snapped, 'I've just circulated your description to the entire Metropolitan Police Force.'

'You didn't have to do that, Nobby. All you had to do was phone me. I would have confessed to everything.'

He opened his mouth, closed it, opened it again, then closed it.

'Where's Mr Goodston?' I demanded.

'Mr Goodston,' the plain-clothes man said, 'was the subject of a severe attack yesterday afternoon, late, here. It was fortunate that his assailants were interrupted. As it is, he is in hospital under sedation.'

'Oh dear. Oh dear, oh dear.' I bit my lip.

Nobby Roberts glared at me before turning to the plain-clothes man. 'Take these two and get their statements,' he ordered. To the uniformed man he said, 'You stay here. Let no one in. They're still searching upstairs.' Then he wheeled on me with a grim expression. 'You – you follow me.' He stalked out of the shop and I followed him meekly down the street until we got to an Italian café where he marched in and ordered two coffees. His eyes were tinged with pink. We took a table to ourselves and I leaned across to him, confidentially.

'I say, Nobby, are things a bit quiet down at the Yard? I mean why is a big-time rozzer like you called out on a Sunday morning for a bookshop break-in? Don't suppose Gillian can be very pleased, can she?'

His eyes got a bit pinker. 'Suppose you do some explaining first, for a change? What the bloody hell are you up to? Eh?'

'Keep calm, old friend. I saw Sue off to her mother's yesterday morning and then popped in to ask for a book. While we were talking those two thugs came in and started leaning on Mr Goodston for a gambling debt. So I ejected them.'

He stared at me distractedly. 'I sometimes wonder if it's possible for me to investigate any crime in London without you getting in the way. What in hell were you after with Mr Goodston? I didn't know that front-row men could read.'

'There is no need to be offensive, Nobby. I am one of Mr Goodston's regulars. I have had stuff from him on Ellen Terry and Whistler and Moreton Frewen—'

'Oh no! Oh no! The mere mention of those names fills me with dread. Not another? Oh, please. Not another?'

'Nobby, control yourself. Get a grip, man. I just wanted a book. Anyway, that was in the morning. You say he was attacked again late yesterday?'

'Yes.' He picked up his coffee and took a swig of it.

'Was that before or after he won his fifteen thousand pounds?'

Coffee spurted from him. I managed to get some napkins and mop him up while a clucking Italian matron, who had run out from behind her Gaggia machine, clapped him on the back. After he'd stopped choking and cleaned himself he glared at me, eyes red, face suffused. 'What fifteen thousand pounds?'

'The fifteen thousand he won on Dainty Dinah. The horse I backed for him in the five thirty at Haydock Park.'

A look of the most intense suspicion combined with an unattractive scarlet scowl came over his face. 'You did what?'

'I made him back a horse. It was a cert. I lent him three hundred and it came in at fifty to one. I went with him to the betting shop to put it on. The horse won. Actually, Nobby, I had fifty quid on it myself. It'll pay for me and Sue to go on holiday. Cartagena. I'm looking forward to that. Do you know—'

'Stop! Stop right there! You never bet on horses! Never! I've been to countless dinner parties you've bored to death with that story of yours about a palm reader in Hong Kong. He told you never to gamble and you never do.'

'There is no need to be offensive, Nobby. People enjoy that story. Anyway, this was different.'

'Why?'

'Well—'

I was fated to be interrupted that weekend. A burly bloke with short hair barged in through the café door and addressed Nobby from the side of our table.

'No go, Chief. We've checked right through.' He handed Nobby a paper with a list on it. 'Still missing. And we've gone through the lot with a fine-tooth comb. Page by page.'

Nobby gave him a look that was not at all complimentary. 'It has to be there. Check again.'

'But, sir—'

'Check again! You've got to find it. Go back to the hospital as well and see if you can question Goodston. There's no time!'

The burly bloke withdrew, looking sullen. I raised my eyebrows in query but got no response from across the table. I sipped my coffee whilst thoughts could be detected seething across Nobby's face.

'God damn it,' he said, eventually.

'Anything I can help with at all?'

He gave me a sour look. Various bitter expressions distorted his features until, at last, a resigned demeanour came over him. He muttered to himself for a moment and then spoke out loud.

'Mullarkey,' he said.

'I beg your pardon?'

'Barry Mullarkey. You may not have heard of him. He lives in St John's Wood. He's a fence. A dealer. A villain. He deals in all things illegal and stolen. Including drugs. He skipped it to Spain last week. We had an agent – a cleaner – working on the inside, in his flat. We were poised to go. The key to Mullarkey's dealings is his Swiss bank account. The Swiss have promised to co-operate but they need the details of his account. Under current drug law we can confiscate the lot. Mullarkey memorized the numbers but our agent heard that Mullarkey had written the details down in case he forgot them or for his wife to find. He is a great collector of books; every year he has to cull his collection by about a hundred volumes to allow room for new ones. Your Mr Goodston buys the cull. He did it again this year, the deal being set up just before Mullarkey skipped it. The books are upstairs in the shop right now.'

'Ah. Nobby—'

'Wait! Will you let me finish! By mistake, Mullarkey's henchman, a dumb cluck called Foster, let go the book that contains the details of the Swiss account written in it. Mullarkey gave him hell on the phone from Spain. Hence the attack on Mr Goodston: to get the book back. We scared them off but they got away. We need those account numbers and we've no time to lose.'

'So the fifteen thousand pounds was nothing to do with it?'

'Of course not! Stop interrupting! As far as I know Mr Goodston must still have his betting receipts safe and sound. He seems to be very meticulous; his records and cataloguing are good enough to satisfy even a VAT inspector. All those books of Mullarkey's are listed and we've been through every page of every one of them without success. All except one, that is. There's one missing.'

'Ah. That would be *The Angry Admiral*, by Cyril Hughes Hartmann, Nobby. Published by Heinemann in 1953.'

This time I thought the coffee was going to spurt from his ears. The Italian matron rushed out from behind her Gaggia machine in quite a state to thump him on the back as I mopped him up. The gist of her comments was that he was giving her coffee a bad name. That didn't please him, either.

'How the hell did you know that was the missing title? We've been combing that bloody shop all morning. We need those numbers! Only we have the list of books that Goodston bought off Mullarkey. My men went to hospital with him and he told them where to find it, even though he was very shaky. You can't have seen it!'

'Of course I haven't seen it. I bought the book off Mr Goodston yesterday. At least, technically I haven't actually bought it because I haven't paid for it yet, so I don't suppose Mr

Goodston has registered the sale in his books. What with two assaults in one day I expect he forgot to tell you, but I've got it.'

'Why? *For Pete's sake, why?*'

'Nobby, you must calm yourself. I keep trying to tell you, I'm going to Cartagena on holiday. So—'

'Where the hell is that book?' he shouted. His eyes were bright red.

'At home. And it's funny you should mention it because someone has spoiled the endpapers by putting a name and two sets of numbers right in the old map of the Caribbean that—'

I got no further. He was on his feet, bellowing. He grabbed me by the lapels. He ran me from the shop whilst hurling money at the Italian matron. He bellowed even louder when he got outside and a police car came squeaking up like a terrified pet. He roared the address of my flat in Onslow Gardens at the driver and his mate before we were scattered across the back seat as the car shot off. I had to grab a handle to steady myself.

'Cartagena.' His voice was thick. 'Cartagena? What do you keep raving on about Cartagena for?'

'A holiday, Nobby. I was interested in the Vernon connection. *The Angry Admiral* is a book about Admiral Vernon. I've been trying to explain to you. Remember Jeremy White's uncle, Sir Richard? His hobby was visiting the sites of the battles of the Hundred Years War. A perfectly innocent pastime with gastronomic perks. I thought I might do something similar in South America. It's not unknown, you know. An ambassador called John Ure did a book on Morgan—'

'Eccentric.' His furious voice cut me off. 'No, not just eccentric, mad. You're mad. Cartagena? In Colombia? You'll get yourself and Sue slaughtered.'

The car careered into the Old Brompton Road on two wheels. I shot him a glance. 'What about you? I fear for your health, you know, Nobby. If you go cutting short your coffee breaks and being driven like this you'll get severe dyspepsia and—'

'Shut up! Just shut up!'

We hurtled to a halt outside my flat. He and the front man were out before we stopped moving. They shot up the stairs three at a time. I skipped along behind thinking they'd have to wait for me to open up but I was wrong. The door was open and they shot through like a pair of ferrets. I heard a great bellow from Nobby.

'Foster!'

The inside of my flat was somewhat deranged. Most of my books were on the floor. By the time I entered four men were struggling fiercely across the centre carpet. Nobby was twisting the arm behind a medium-sized fellow in a sweater and jeans whilst his uniformed man was having a lot of trouble with a bigger bloke in a corduroy jacket. I leapt in to help before the flat got wrecked. I have to admit that I was very indignant; when the two men were handcuffed and out of the place I addressed Nobby with some irritation.

'Who gave them my address? Eh?'

'You idiot! That was Mullarkey's dumb assistant, Foster, but the other one is his very dangerous right-hand man. With the spectacle you made of yourself at Goodston's yesterday it can't have been all that difficult for them to trace you. Now – where the *hell* is that book?'

It was by the bedside, where I'd left it. I handed it to Nobby and he stared at the name and numbers in the back until, for the first time that day, his face started to relax. 'Thank the Lord for that,' he said. 'I'll keep this.'

'Hang on! That's my book! I want it for my holiday. You've got your numbers.'

He stuck his face close to mine. 'This book,' he said, 'is evidence. You can have it back once a successful prosecution and sequestration of funds has taken place.'

'Oh, that's great! I like that! That's the thanks I get, is it? A wrecked flat and my book purloined by ungrateful policemen. I don't suppose you'll even offer to help clear this up before Sue gets back this afternoon?'

He grinned savagely. 'The rest of my Sunday is going to be quite busy enough without helping poor little Timmy to hide this lot from Sue. Serves you right. Teach you to keep out of trouble and not to hit bookies' men, not even in a good cause.'

And with that the ungrateful blighter went out. I sat down to survey the mess until his head popped round the door again.

'By the way,' he said, 'you never told me how you knew that horse was going to win.'

'That,' I replied, with some hauteur, 'is between Mr Goodston and me. You've behaved very badly and since you find my stories so boring you can jolly well wait until you hand over that book before you hear this one.'

He made a face at me and left. It didn't take me all that long to clear up because most of the displacement was books. I picked up an auction catalogue and went off to Mr Goodston's well before Sue's train was due back. Knowing how most hospitals work these days I guessed he'd be home again and he was. He sat behind his desk with a piece of sticking plaster gummed to his forehead and a bruise below one eye, but his manner was jaunty.

'My very dear Mr Simpson! My saviour!' He waved his betting slips at me. 'You are incredible, sir! A maestro! How did you do it?'

'Are you all right, Mr Goodston?'

'As you see: battered but unbowed. And much wealthier. Thanks to you.'

'Good.' I sat down next to him.

'Please, Mr Simpson, can you now tell me? Please? Why that horse?'

I grinned at him. 'It was extraordinary. That Dod Proctor of yours upstairs of the little girl; she features in several of her paintings. I have often wondered who that wistful child was. Until this week.' I held up a Christie's catalogue and opened it in front of him. 'Sold for £46,000 on 2 March 1989. Lot 95. A painting by Dod Proctor, RA. Possibly a record price.' I opened the pages further so that he could see the coloured illustration of a painting of an adolescent girl sitting by a window, looking at a red book, with cloth binding. His eyes bulged a little before he glanced involuntarily up to the ceiling, in the direction of the room upstairs where his painting of the same girl, somewhat younger, hung on the wall. Then he looked down to the title of the painting sold at Christie's:

Dinah, Reading.

'It came in yesterday morning. The catalogue and price list, sent on from the office. I never saw such a cert in my life, not in a bookshop or anywhere else.'

Mr Goodston reached into his desk. Mr Goodston pulled out a full bottle of Celebration Cream sherry.

'Mr Simpson,' he croaked, 'would you care for a glass – no, damn it, for a beaker at least – of Celebration Cream?'

ELLIS PETERS

The Trinity Cat

HE WAS sitting on top of one of the rear gateposts of the churchyard when I walked through on Christmas Eve, grooming in his lordly style, with one back leg wrapped round his neck, and his bitten ear at an angle of forty-five degrees, as usual. I reckon one of the toms he'd tangled with in his nomad days had ripped the starched bit out of that one, the other stood up sharply enough. There was snow on the ground, a thin veiling, just beginning to crackle in promise of frost before evening, but he had at least three warm refuges around the place whenever he felt like holing up, besides his two houses, which he used only for visiting and cadging. He'd been a known character around our village for three years then, ever since he walked in from nowhere and made himself agreeable to the vicar and the verger, and, finding the billet comfortable and the pickings good, constituted himself resident cat to Holy Trinity church, and took over all the jobs around the place that humans were too slow to tackle, like rat-catching, and chasing off invading dogs.

Nobody knows how old he is, but I think he could only have been about two when he settled here, a scrawny, chewed-up black bandit as lean as wire. After three years of being fed by Joel Woodward at Trinity Cottage, which was the verger's house by tradition, and flanked the lich-gate on one side, and pampered and petted by Miss Patience Thomson at Church Cottage on the other side, he was double his old size, and sleek as velvet, but still had one lop ear and a kink two inches from the end of his tail. He still looked like a brigand, but a highly prosperous brigand. Nobody ever gave him a name, he wasn't the sort to get called anything fluffy or familiar. Only Miss Patience ever dared coo at him, and he was very gracious about that, she being elderly and innocent and very free with little perks like raw liver, on which he doted. One way and another, he had it made. He lived mostly outdoors, never staying in either house overnight. In winter he had his own little ground-level hatch into the furnace-room of the church, sharing his lodgings matily with a hedgehog that had qualified as assistant vermin-destructor around the churchyard, and preferred sitting out the winter among the coke to hibernating like common hedgehogs. These individualists keep turning up in our valley, for some reason.

All I'd gone to the church for that afternoon was to fix up with the vicar about the Christmas peal, having been roped into the bell-ringing team. Resident police in remote areas like ours get dragged into all sorts of activities, and when the area's changing, and new problems cropping up, if they have any sense they don't need too much dragging, but go willingly. I've put my finger on many an astonished yobbo who thought he'd got clean away with his little breaking-and-entering, just by keeping my ears open during a darts match, or choir practice.

When I came back through the churchyard around half-past two, Miss Patience was just coming out of her gate, with a shopping bag on her wrist, and heading towards the street, and we walked along together a bit of the way. She was getting on for seventy, and hardly bigger than a bird, but very independent. Never having married or left the valley, and having looked after a mother who lived to be nearly ninety, she'd never had time to catch up with new ideas in the style of dress suitable for elderly ladies. Everything had always been done mother's way, and fashion, music and morals had stuck at the period when mother was a carefully-brought-up girl learning domestic skills, and preparing for a chaste marriage. There's a lot to be said for it! But it had turned Miss Patience into a frail little lady in long-skirted black or grey or navy blue, who still felt undressed without hat and gloves, at an age when Mrs Newcombe, for instance, up at the pub, favoured shocking pink trouser suits and red-gold hair-pieces. A pretty little old lady Miss Patience was, though, very straight and neat. It was a pleasure to watch her walk. Which is more than I could say for Mrs Newcombe in her trouser suit, especially from the back!

'A happy Christmas, Sergeant Moon!' she chirped at me on sight. And I wished her the same, and slowed up to her pace.

'It's going to be slippery by twilight,' I said. 'You be careful how you go.'

'Oh, I'm only going to be an hour or so,' she said serenely. 'I shall be home long before the frost sets in. I'm only doing the last bit of Christmas shopping. There's a cardigan I have to collect for Mrs Downs.' That was her cleaning-lady, who went in three mornings a week. 'I ordered it long ago, but deliveries are so slow nowadays. They've promised it for today. And a gramophone record for my little errand-boy.' Tommy Fowler that was, one of the church trebles, as pink and wholesome-looking as they usually contrive to be, and just as artful. 'And one mustn't forget our dumb friends, either, must one?' said Miss Patience cheerfully. 'They're all important, too.'

I took this to mean a couple of packets of some new product to lure wild birds to her garden. The Church Cottage thrushes were so fat they could hardly fly, and when it was frosty she put out fresh water three and four times a day.

We came to our brief street of shops, and off she went, with her big jet-and-gold brooch gleaming in her scarf. She had quite a few pieces of Victorian and Edwardian jewellery her mother'd left behind, and almost always wore one piece, being used to the belief that a lady dresses meticulously every day, not just on Sundays. And I went for a brisk walk round to see what was going on, and then went home to Molly and high tea, and took my boots off thankfully.

That was Christmas Eve. Christmas Day little Miss Thomson didn't turn up for eight o'clock Communion, which was unheard-of. The vicar said he'd call in after matins and see that she was all right, and hadn't taken cold trotting about in the snow. But somebody else beat us both to it. Tommy Fowler! He was anxious about that pop record of his. But even he had no chance until after service, for in our village it's the custom for the choir to go and sing the vicar an aubade in the shape of 'Christians, Awake!' before the main service, ignoring the fact that he's then been up four hours, and conducted two Communions. And Tommy Fowler had a solo in the anthem, too. It was a quarter-past twelve when he got away, and shot up the garden path to the door of Church Cottage.

He shot back even faster a minute later. I was heading for home when he came rocketing out of the gate and ran slam into me, with his eyes sticking out on stalks and his mouth wide open, making a sort of muted keening sound with shock. He clutched hold of me and pointed back towards Miss Thomson's front door, left half-open when he fled, and tried three times before he could croak out:

'Miss Patience . . . She's there on the floor – she's bad!'

I went in on the run, thinking she'd had a heart attack all alone there, and was lying helpless. The front door led through a diminutive hall, and through another glazed door into the living-room, and that door was open, too, and there was Miss Patience face-down on the carpet, still in her coat and gloves, and with her shopping-bag lying beside her. An occasional table had been knocked over in her fall, spilling a vase and a book. Her hat was askew over one ear, and caved in like a trodden mushroom, and her neat grey bun of hair had come undone and trailed on her shoulder, and it was no longer grey but soiled, brownish black. She was dead and stiff. The room was so cold, you could tell those doors had been ajar all night.

The kid had followed me in, hanging on to my sleeve, his teeth chattering. 'I didn't open the door – it was open! I didn't touch her, or anything. I only came to see if she was all right, and get my record.'

It was there, lying unbroken, half out of the shopping-bag by her arm. She'd meant it for him, and I told him he should have it, but not yet, because it might be evidence, and we mustn't move anything. And I got him out of there quick, and gave him to the vicar to cope with, and went back to Miss Patience as soon as I'd telephoned for the outfit. Because we had a murder on our hands.

So that was the end of one gentle, harmless old woman, one of the very many these days, battered to death because she walked in on an intruder who panicked. Walked in on him, I judged, not much more than an hour after I left her in the street. Everything about her looked the same as then, the shopping-bag, the coat, the hat, the gloves. The only difference, that she was dead. No, one more thing! No handbag, unless it was under the body, and later, when we were able to move her, I wasn't surprised to see that it wasn't there. Handbags are where old ladies carry their money. The sneak-thief who panicked and lashed out at her had still had greed and presence of mind enough to grab the bag as he fled. Nobody'd have to describe that bag to me, I knew it well, soft black leather with an old-fashioned gilt clasp and a short handle, a small thing, not like the hold-alls they carry nowadays.

She was lying facing the opposite door, also open, which led to the stairs. On the writing-desk by that door stood one of a pair of heavy brass candlesticks. Its fellow was on the floor beside Miss Thomson's body, and though the bun of hair and the felt hat had prevented any great spattering of blood, there was blood enough on the square base to label the weapon. Whoever had hit her had been just sneaking down the stairs, ready to leave. She'd come home barely five minutes too soon.

Upstairs, in her bedroom, her bits of jewellery hadn't taken much finding. She'd never thought of herself as having valuables, or of other people as coveting them. Her gold and turquoise and funereal jet and true-lover's-knots in gold and opals, and mother's engagement and wedding rings, and her little Edwardian pendant watch set with seed pearls, had simply lived in the small top drawer of her dressing-table. She belonged to an honest epoch, and it was gone, and now she was gone after it. She didn't even lock her door when she went shopping. There wouldn't have been so much as the warning of a key grating in the lock, just the door opening.

Ten years ago not a soul in this valley behaved differently from Miss Patience. Nobody locked doors, sometimes not even overnight. Some of us went on a fortnight's holiday and left the doors unlocked. Now we can't even put out the milk money until the milkman knocks at the door in person. If this generation likes to pride itself on its progress, let it! As for me, I thought suddenly that maybe the innocent was well out of it.

We did the usual things, photographed the body and the scene of the crime, the doctor examined her and authorized her removal, and confirmed what I'd supposed about the approximate time of her death. And the forensic boys lifted a lot of smudgy latents that weren't going to be of any use to anybody, because they weren't going to be on record, barring a million to one chance. The whole thing stank of the amateur. There wouldn't be any easy matching up of prints, even if they got beauties. One more thing we did for Miss Patience. We tolled the dead-bell for her on Christmas night, six heavy, muffled strokes. She was a virgin. Nobody had to vouch for it, we all knew. And let me point out, it is a title of honour, to be respected accordingly.

We'd hardly got the poor soul out of the house when the Trinity cat strolled in, taking advantage of the minute or two while the door was open. He got as far as the place on the carpet where she'd lain, and his fur and whiskers stood on end, and even his lop ear jerked up straight. He put his nose down to the pile of the Wilton, about where her shopping-bag and handbag must have lain, and started going round in interested circles, snuffing the floor and making little throaty noises that might have been distress, but sounded like pleasure. Excitement, anyhow. The chaps from the CID were still busy, and didn't want him under their feet, so I picked him up and took him with me when I went across to Trinity Cottage to talk to the verger. The cat never liked being picked up, after a minute he started clawing and cursing, and I put him down. He stalked away again at once, past the corner where people shot their dead flowers, out at the lich-gate, and straight back to sit on Miss Thomson's doorstep. Well, after all, he used to get fed there, he might well be uneasy at all these queer comings and goings. And they don't say 'as curious as a cat' for nothing, either.

I didn't need telling that Joel Woodward had had no hand in

what had happened, he'd been nearest neighbour and good friend to Miss Patience for years, but he might have seen or heard something out of the ordinary. He was a little, wiry fellow, gnarled like a tree-root, the kind that goes on spry and active into his nineties, and then decides that's enough, and leaves overnight. His wife was dead long ago, and his daughter had come back to keep house for him after her husband deserted her, until she died, too, in a bus accident. There was just old Joel now, and the grandson she'd left with him, young Joel Barnett, nineteen, and a bit of a tearaway by his grandad's standards, but so far pretty innocuous by mine. He was a sulky, graceless sort, but he did work, and he stuck with the old man when many another would have lit out elsewhere.

'A bad business,' said old Joel, shaking his head. 'I only wish I could help you lay hands on whoever did it. But I only saw her yesterday morning about ten, when she took in the milk. I was round at the church hall all afternoon, getting things ready for the youth social they had last night, it was dark before I got back. I never saw or heard anything out of place. You can't see her living-room light from here, so there was no call to wonder. But the lad was here all afternoon. They only work till one, Christmas Eve. Then they all went boozing together for an hour or so, I expect, so I don't know exactly what time he got in, but he was here and had the tea on when I came home. Drop round in an hour or so and he should be here, he's gone round to collect this girl he's mashing. There's a party somewhere tonight.'

I dropped round accordingly, and young Joel was there, sure enough, shoulder-length hair, frilled shirt, outsize lapels and all, got up to kill, all for the benefit of the girl his grandad had mentioned. And it turned out to be Connie Dymond, from the comparatively respectable branch of the family, along the canal-side. There were three sets of Dymond cousins, boys, no great harm in 'em but worth watching, but only this one girl in Connie's family. A good-looker, or at least most of the lads seemed to think so, she had a dozen or so on her string before she took up with young Joel. Big girl, too, with a lot of mauve eye-shadow and a mother-of-pearl mouth, in huge platform shoes and the fashionable drab granny-coat. But she was acting very prim and proper with old Joel around.

'Half-past two when I got home,' said young Joel. 'Grandad was round at the hall, and I'd have gone round to help him, only I'd had a pint or two, and after I'd had me dinner I went to sleep, so it wasn't worth it by the time I woke up. Around four, that'd be. From then on I was here, watching the telly, and I never saw nor heard a thing. But there was nobody else here, so I could be spinning you the yarn, if you want to look at it that way.'

He had a way of going looking for trouble before anybody else suggested it, there was nothing new about that. Still, there it was. One young fellow on the spot, and minus any alibi. There'd be plenty of others in the same case.

In the evening he'd been at the church social. Miss Patience wouldn't be expected there, it was mainly for the young, and anyhow, she very seldom went out in the evenings.

'*I* was there with Joel,' said Connie Dymond. 'He called for me at seven, I was with him all the evening. We went home to our place after the social finished, and he didn't leave till nearly midnight.'

Very firm about it she was, doing her best for him. She could hardly know that his movements in the evening didn't interest us, since Miss Patience had then been dead for some hours.

When I opened the door to leave the Trinity cat walked in, stalking past me with a purposeful stride. He had a look round us all, and then made for the girl, reached up his front paws to her knees, and was on her lap before she could fend him off, though she didn't look as if she welcomed his attentions. Very civil he was, purring and rubbing himself against her coat sleeve, and poking his whiskery face into hers. Unusual for him to be effusive, but when he did decide on it, it was always with someone who couldn't stand cats. You'll have noticed it's a way they have.

'Shove him off,' said young Joel, seeing she didn't at all care for being singled out. 'He only does it to annoy people.'

And she did, but he only jumped on again, I noticed as I closed the door on them and left. It was a Dymond party they were going to, the senior lot, up at the filling station. Not much point in trying to check up on all her cousins and swains when they were gathered for a booze-up. Coming out of a hangover, tomorrow, they might be easy meat. Not that I had any special reason to look their way, they were an extrovert lot, more given to grievous bodily harm in street punch-ups than anything secretive. But it was wide open.

Well, we summed up. None of the lifted prints was on record, all we could do in that line was exclude all those that were Miss Thomson's. This kind of sordid little opportunist break-in had come into local experience only fairly recently, and though it was no novelty now, it had never before led to a death. No motive but the impulse of greed, so no traces leading up to the act, and none leading away. Everyone connected with the church, and most of the village besides, knew about the bits of jewellery she had, but never before had anyone considered them as desirable loot. Victoriana now carry inflated values, and are in demand, but this still didn't look calculated, just wanton. A kid's crime, a teenager's crime. Or the crime of a permanent teenager. They start at twelve years old now, but there are also the shiftless louts who never get beyond twelve years old, even in their forties.

We checked all the obvious people, her part-time gardener – but he was demonstrably elsewhere at the time – and his drifter of a son, whose alibi was non-existent but voluble, the window-cleaner, a sidelong soul who played up his ailments and did rather well out of her, all the delivery men. Several there who were clear, one or two who could have been around, but had no particular reason to be. Then we went after all the youngsters who, on their records, were possibles. There were three with breaking-and-entering convictions, but if they'd been there they'd been gloved. Several others with petty theft against them were also without alibis. By the end of a pretty exhaustive survey the field was wide, and none of the runners seemed to be ahead of the rest, and we were still looking. None of the stolen property had so far showed up.

Not, that is, until the Saturday. I was coming from Church Cottage through the graveyard again, and as I came near the corner where the dead flowers were shot, I noticed a glaring black patch making an irregular hole in the veil of frozen snow that still covered the ground. You couldn't miss it, it showed up like a black eye. And part of it was the soil and rotting leaves showing through, and part, the blackest part, was the Trinity cat, head down and back arched, digging industriously like a terrier after a rat. The bent end of his tail lashed steadily, while the remaining eight inches stood erect. If he knew I was standing watching him, he didn't care. Nothing was going to deflect him from what he was doing. And in a minute or two he heaved his prize clear, and clawed out to the light a little black leather handbag with a gilt clasp. No mistaking it, all stuck over as it was with dirt and rotting leaves. And he loved it, he was patting it and playing with it and rubbing his head against it, and purring like a steam-engine. He cursed, though, when I took it off him, and walked round and round me, pawing and swearing, telling me and the world he'd found it, and it was his.

It hadn't been there long. I'd been along that path often enough to know that the snow hadn't been disturbed the day before. Also, the mess of humus fell off it pretty quick and clean, and left it hardly stained at all. I held it in my handkerchief and snapped the catch, and the inside was clean and empty, the lining slightly frayed from long use. The Trinity cat stood upright on his hind legs and protested loudly, and he had a voice that could outshout a Siamese.

Somebody behind me said curiously: 'Whatever've you got there?' And there was young Joel standing open-mouthed, staring, with Connie Dymond hanging on to his arm and gaping at the cat's find in horrified recognition.

'Oh, no! My gawd, that's Miss Thomson's bag, isn't it? I've seen her carrying it hundreds of times.'

'Did *he* dig it up?' said Joel, incredulous. 'You reckon the chap who – you know, *him*! – he buried it there? It could be anybody, everybody uses this way through.'

'My gawd!' said Connie, shrinking in fascinated horror against his side. 'Look at that cat! You'd think he *knows* . . . He gives me the shivers! What's got into him?'

What, indeed? After I'd got rid of them and taken the bag away with me I was still wondering. I walked away with his prize and he followed me as far as the road, howling and swearing, and once I put the bag down, open, to see what he'd do, and he pounced on it and started his fun and games again until I took it from him. For the life of me I couldn't see what there was about it to delight him, but he was in no doubt. I was beginning to feel right superstitious about this avenging detective cat, and to wonder what he was going to unearth next.

I know I ought to have delivered the bag to the forensic lab, but somehow I hung on to it overnight. There was something fermenting at the back of my mind that I couldn't yet grasp.

Next morning we had two more at morning service besides the regulars. Young Joel hardly ever went to church, and I doubt if anybody'd ever seen Connie Dymond there before, but there they both were, large as life and solemn as death, in a middle pew, the boy sulky and scowling as if he'd been press-ganged into it, as he certainly had, Connie very subdued and big-eyed, with almost no make-up and an unusually grave and thoughtful face. Sudden death brings people up against daunting possibilities, and creates penitents. Young Joel felt silly there, but he was daft about her, plainly enough, she could get him to do what she wanted, and she'd wanted to make this gesture. She went through all the movements of devotion, he just sat, stood and kneeled awkwardly as required, and went on scowling.

There was a bitter east wind when we came out. On the steps of the porch everybody dug out gloves and turned up collars against it, and so did young Joel, and as he hauled his gloves out of his coat pocket, out with them came a little bright thing that rolled down the steps in front of us all and came to rest in a crack between the flagstones of the path. A gleam of pale blue and gold. A dozen people must have recognized it. Mrs Downs gave tongue in a shriek that informed even those who hadn't.

'That's Miss Thomson's! It's one of her turquoise earrings! *How did you get hold of that, Joel Barnett?*'

How, indeed? Everybody stood staring at the tiny thing, and then at young Joel, and he was gazing at the flagstones, struck white and dumb. And all in a moment Connie Dymond had pulled her arm free of his and recoiled from him until her back was against the wall, and was edging away from him like somebody trying to get out of range of flood or fire, and her face a sight to be seen, blind and stiff with horror.

'You!' she said in a whisper. 'It was you! Oh, my God, *you* did it – *you* killed her! And me keeping company – how could I? How could *you*!'

She let out a screech and burst into sobs, and before anybody could stop her she turned and took to her heels, running for home like a mad thing.

I let her go. She'd keep. And I got young Joel and that single earring away from the Sunday congregation and into Trinity Cottage before half the people there knew what was happening, and shut the world out, all but old Joel who came panting and shaking after us a few minutes later.

The boy was a long time getting his voice back, and when he did he had nothing to say but, hopelessly, over and over: 'I didn't! I never touched her, I wouldn't. I don't know how that thing got into my pocket. I didn't do it. I never . . .'

Human beings are not all that inventive. Given a similar set of circumstances they tend to come out with the same formula. And in any case, 'deny everything and say nothing else' is a very good rule when cornered.

They thought I'd gone round the bend when I said: 'Where's the cat? See if you can get him in.'

Old Joel was past wondering. He went out and rattled a saucer on the steps, and pretty soon the Trinity cat strolled in. Not at all excited, not wanting anything, fed and lazy, just curious enough to come and see why he was wanted. I turned him loose on young Joel's overcoat, and he couldn't have cared less. The pocket that had held the earring held very little interest for him. He didn't care about any of the clothes in the wardrobe, or on the pegs in the little hall. As far as he was concerned, this new find was a non-event.

I sent for a constable and a car, and took young Joel in with me to the station, and all the village, you may be sure, either saw us pass or heard about it very shortly after. But I didn't stop to take any statement from him, just left him there, and took the car up to Mary Melton's place, where she breeds Siamese, and borrowed a cat-basket from her, the sort she uses to carry her queens to the vet. She asked what on earth I wanted it for, and I said to take the Trinity cat for a ride. She laughed her head off.

'Well, *he's* no queen,' she said, 'and no king, either. Not even a jack! And you'll never get that wild thing into a basket.'

'Oh, yes, I will,' I said. 'And if he isn't any of the other picture cards, he's probably going to turn out to be the joker.'

A very neat basket it was, not too obviously meant for a cat. And it was no trick getting the Trinity cat into it, all I did was drop in Miss Thomson's handbag, and he was in after it in a moment. He growled when he found himself shut in, but it was too late to complain then.

At the house by the canal Connie Dymond's mother let me in, but was none too happy about letting me see Connie, until I explained that I needed a statement from her before I could fit together young Joel's movements all through those Christmas days. Naturally I understood that the girl was terribly upset, but she'd had a lucky escape, and the sooner everything was cleared up, the better for her. And it wouldn't take long.

It didn't take long. Connie came down the stairs readily enough when her mother called her. She was all stained and pale and tearful, but had perked up somewhat with a sort of shivering pride in her own prominence. I've seen them like that before, getting the juice out of being the centre of attention even while they wish they were elsewhere. You could even say she hurried down, and she left the door of her bedroom open behind her, by the light coming through at the head of the stairs.

'Oh, Sergeant Moon!' she quavered at me from three steps up. 'Isn't it *awful*? I still can't believe it! *Can* there be some mistake? Is there any chance it *wasn't* . . . ?'

I said soothingly, yes, there was always a chance. And I slipped the latch of the cat basket with one hand, so that the flap fell open, and the Trinity cat was out of there and up those stairs like a black flash, startling her so much she nearly fell down the last step, and steadied herself against the wall with a small shriek. And I blurted apologies for accidentally loosing him, and went up the stairs three at a time ahead of her, before she could recover her balance.

He was up on his hind legs in her dolly little room, full of pop posters and frills and garish colours, pawing at the second drawer of her dressing-table, and singing a loud, joyous, impatient song. When I came plunging in, he even looked over his shoulder at me and stood down, as though he knew I'd open the drawer for him. And I did, and he was up among her fancy undies like a shot, and digging with his front paws.

He found what he wanted just as she came in at the door. He yanked it out from among her bras and slips, and tossed it into the air, and in seconds he was on the floor with it, rolling and wrestling it, juggling it on his four paws like a circus turn, and purring fit to kill, a cat in ecstasy. A comic little thing it was, a muslin mouse with a plaited green nylon string for a tail, yellow beads for eyes, and nylon threads for whiskers, that rustled and sent out wafts of strong scent as he batted it around and sang to it. A catmint mouse, old Miss Thomson's last-minute purchase from the pet shop for her dumb friend. If you could ever call the Trinity cat dumb! The only thing she bought that day small enough to be slipped into her handbag instead of the shopping-bag.

Connie let out a screech, and was across that room so fast I only just beat her to the open drawer. They were all there, the little pendant watch, the locket, the brooches, the true-lover's-knot, the purse, even the other earring. A mistake, she should have ditched both while she was about it, but she was too greedy. They were for pierced ears, anyhow, no good to Connie.

I held them out in the palm of my hand – such a large haul they made – and let her see what she'd robbed and killed for.

If she'd kept her head she might have made a fight of it even then, claimed he'd made her hide them for him, and she'd been afraid to tell on him directly, and could only think of staging that public act at church, to get him safely in custody before she came clean. But she went wild. She did the one deadly thing, turned and kicked out in a screaming fury at the Trinity cat. He was spinning like a humming-top, and all she touched was the kink in his tail. He whipped round and clawed a red streak down her leg through the nylon. And then she screamed again, and began to babble through hysterical sobs that she never meant to hurt the poor old sod, that it wasn't her fault! Ever since she'd been going with young Joel she'd been seeing that little old bag going in and out, draped with her bits of gold. What in hell did an old witch like her want with jewellery? She had no *right*! At her age!

'But I never meant to hurt her! She came in too soon,' lamented Connie, still and for ever the aggrieved. 'What was I supposed to do? I had to get away, didn't I? *She was between me and the door!*'

She was half her size, too, and nearly four times her age! Ah, well! What the courts would do with Connie, thank God, was none of my business. I just took her in and charged her, and got her statement. Once we had her dabs it was all over, because she'd left a bunch of them sweaty and clear on that brass candlestick. But if it hadn't been for the Trinity cat and his single-minded pursuit, scaring her into that ill-judged attempt to hand us young Joel as a scapegoat, she might, she just might, have got clean away with it. At least the boy could go home now, and count his blessings.

Not that she was very bright, of course. Who but a stupid harpy, soaked in cheap perfume and gimcrack dreams, would have hung on even to the catmint mouse, mistaking it for a herbal sachet to put among her smalls?

I saw the Trinity cat only this morning, sitting grooming in the church porch. He's getting very self-important, as if he knows he's a celebrity, though throughout he was only looking after the interests of Number One, like all cats. He's lost interest in his mouse already, now most of the scent's gone.

ANTHONY PRICE

The Berzin Lecture

(*Tape Commences*)

Fred, you will have had the papers on the debriefing of Colonel Gorbatov by now, but there's one thing that isn't in them. It's no more than a footnote to the important stuff really, but it's not uninteresting in its way, and perhaps it's significant.

As you know, Gorbatov came across with a briefcase of assorted documents as well as what was in his head. It was only a job lot – he more or less cleared out his desk, I think – but it included one curiosity: a bound collection of lectures given by none other than old Berzin at a seminar for middle-ranking KGB hopefuls at the Dzershinsky Centre a few years ago. And one of the papers concerns our own dear David, no less, who stars in a cautionary case study illustrating 'The Dialectic of Failure', or some such rubbishy jargon of Berzin's.

The case study dates from a good few years back and actually concerns the 'Rickmansworth Scandal' as we called it, which you may not remember well, as it took place when you were spending a lot of time in the States and old Colonel Henderson was standing in for you.

You will recall, though, that this was when the Russians were hell-bent on getting in on American computer technology (then, as now!), and one of their methods (also then, as now!) was to find a careless European company with the right links, and enter the States by the back door through personnel exchange.

Well, what happened here was they recruited a bright young chap – 'Dr Singer' – who was going places in this commercial research establishment at Rickmansworth, with a useful American transfer in prospect. Only just as he was due to pack up the Americans acquired a KGB defector in West Berlin who had done some of the early spade-work at Rickmansworth – he didn't know Singer's identity, but when he was de-briefed the Yanks would surely know someone was singing there. Then, at best, there'd be some in-depth vetting (the vetting at Rickmansworth had been as superficial as you'd expect), and Singer's Russian control reckoned he didn't have the balls for that – he'd cut and run.

The trouble was there wasn't much time and the Russians had to choose between lifting Singer at once or taking 'appropriate corrective action'; and as they didn't want to abort, and the late unlamented Abakumov was in overall charge, that bloody-minded fellow Beletsky was told to go in and win by 'acting correctly'.

Beletsky came up with a typically simple and cold-blooded solution: the Americans would soon be looking for a traitor at Rickmansworth, so he'd give them one in advance to satisfy them.

What he did was to infiltrate a low-grade operative into the sub-contracting company responsible for the outside security at Rickmansworth, by name (appropriately) Blackman.

Blackman started on late-night duty, which was unpopular, but at the first opportunity he volunteered for Sunday duty, which was even more unpopular because it didn't count as overtime for some reason.

What happened on that particular Sunday in due course was that a phone message was made to a colleague of Dr Singer's, a perfectly innocent bachelor scientist by the name of Cousins, urgently summoning him to the director's office at the Research Centre.

Shortly after Cousins arrived at the centre, Blackman phoned up his boss Williamson at his home and said that while doing his rounds in the car park outside he'd looked through the window of the director's office – the centre was a newish single-storey building, mostly plate-glass, pretty much like a goldfish bowl – and he'd seen Dr Cousins acting suspiciously there. It seemed to him, in fact, that Dr Cousins was photographing something on the director's desk, but he hadn't gone in close for fear of being spotted. So what should he do now, because Dr Cousins had just come out and was getting into his car to leave?

Blackman's boss lived only fifteen minutes away from the research centre, and – as Beletsky expected (although it wouldn't have mattered either way) – he told Blackman to hold Cousins at the gate on some pretext and wait for his arrival, he'd be there directly.

What Blackman did (on Beletsky's orders) was to refuse in the most rudely officious manner to open the gate for Cousins. The bewildered Cousins then got out of his car to remonstrate with him. As he did so a big black Jaguar – which had been lurking rather ostentatiously and suspiciously just down the road outside – accelerated into the entrance of the centre. Inside this Jag there was what Blackman believed to be a KGB snatch-squad, whose job – so he also fondly believed – was to 'rescue' Dr Cousins, leaving a heroic Blackman bloody but unbowed.

Actually, it wasn't a KGB operation at all at this point – and it wasn't a snatch-squad either: it was a Bulgarian crew carefully and deliberately sub-contracted for the job, because with what he had in mind Beletsky didn't want the Russians directly involved – he wanted the crew to be identified, and he didn't mind the Bulgars getting all the stick for what followed.

So . . . what *actually* happened was that Blackman pretended to try and grab – or grapple with – the unfortunate Cousins (for the benefit of the second man on the gate) when the Bulgars roared up.

And what the dreadful Bulgars then did – following their orders to the letter – was to shoot both Blackman and Cousins dead on the spot: Blackman as though to protect Cousins, and Cousins as though by accident . . . Bulgars being traditionally ham-fisted in such matters, as well as identifiable.

Blackman's boss arrived on the scene a few minutes later, to find one heroically dead security man and one accidentally dead traitor . . . Because when he searched Cousins' car he found a set of duplicate keys to the director's desk and a Minox camera complete with Singer's latest pictures, which Blackman had earlier planted in it. And when Cousins' cottage was searched it contained more incriminating material – also planted, of course – to complete the picture. The subsequent identification of the Bulgars, who flew out of Heathrow the same evening, merely added a little window-dressing to the scene.

Beletsky's scenario was swallowed by our people, hook, line, and sinker – one dead hero, one dead traitor – all neatly tied and parcelled. Several Bulgarian diplomats were duly declared *persona non grata* and there were some sighs of embarrassed relief that the treacherous Dr Cousins wasn't around for a trial, only an inquest. All that remained was a routine check-out of security at Rickmansworth, to appease the Americans.

And that's where both Berzin and David – codenamed by Berzin 'The Leopard' – came in.

Of course, David shouldn't have been sent to Rickmansworth on a routine job, he was supposed to be handling only the difficult and complicated ones. To understand why he was dispatched there you have to remember how very badly he got on with Colonel Henderson in your absence, Fred. Henderson disliked David intensely: 'irresponsible, unreliable, arrogant, self-opinionated and unsuitable for promotion' – remember his famous final fitness report? And David, for his part, shrugged off Henderson as a temporary inconvenience. He knew you were coming back eventually, so he did his best to ignore Henderson meanwhile, and made no secret of it – which of course only irritated Henderson even more.

It seems to me that this is where the ironies of the Rickmansworth affair really started to pile up. Because Berzin, who was running their 'Enemy Personnel Evaluation' section then, had marked David as one of our coming men and had already done a special study of him. You might even say that Berzin and David were brothers under the skin – each just a bit too clever for his own good.

Anyway, Singer transmitted a minor panic to Beletsky when David arrived at Rickmansworth, and Beletsky consulted

Abakumov as to the next 'appropriate corrective action', and Abakumov passed the buck to Berzin.

Left to himself Beletsky would probably have trotted out some more of his murderous Bulgars to arrange for David to have an accident. But Berzin was totally against that for two reasons. Firstly, an accident to someone as well-regarded as David (by you, Fred, if not by Henderson) might well stir up a full-scale investigation. And secondly, in any case, he assessed the likelihood of David making trouble as very low. It was just a routine job, there was no evidence that the official version was incorrect, and David had more interesting fish to fry back in London.

Where he miscalculated was that David *was* – and of course still *is* – an arrogant bugger (Henderson's fitness report was entirely correct, except that it omitted David's virtues, which outweigh his vices). It simply never occurred to him that Henderson had sent him off on a pure routine job: his jobs were the difficult ones, where something wasn't quite right . . . *ipso facto*, something wasn't quite right about Rickmansworth.

The result was that he soon smelt a rat there: it was all just too neat. After which he managed to offend nearly everyone in the research centre – from the director downwards – by treating them as a bunch of careless twits. The only person he really got on with down there was Blackman's boss Williamson (the man in charge of external security), who happened to be an ex-sergeant-major from his old armoured regiment, with whom he'd served in Normandy. But Williamson didn't carry much weight with the director and, above all, there just wasn't any evidence to support his suspicions.

Nevertheless, he finally sent back a recommendation to Henderson that all the research personnel should be vetted again in-depth by a full-strength team and they should also take a much closer look at the deceased hero Blackman.

When Singer heard about this from his angry director, who'd received a copy of the recommendation, he produced a much bigger panic for Beletsky, and once again Berzin was consulted.

But once again Berzin counselled inaction. Nothing, he said, had really changed: *firstly*, for a fact, he knew that Henderson had a low opinion of Audley; *secondly*, the director of the research centre agreed with Henderson, and didn't want his staff unnecessarily ruffled by more vetting; *thirdly*, Henderson's budget and his manpower were already overstrained, and in-depth vetting takes a lot of time and money; and *fourthly*, David still hadn't got one single piece of evidence to discredit the official version – and that, to his mind, clinched matters.

Berzin's judgement was at first vindicated: Henderson turned down the recommendation, and announced that he was coming down personally to Rickmansworth to smooth the director's feathers and read the riot act to David.

But then, just as the sighs of relief were dying away in Moscow Centre, the bombshell exploded: Henderson had changed his mind – a programme of full-scale in-depth vetting was to be instituted, including Blackman.

Well, you know the rest of that part of it: Singer cracked up even before we got to him; took a plane to Paris and from there to Moscow.

All this, more or less, is in *our* records, Fred. What *isn't* in our records – and what *is* in old Berzin's seminar lecture – is what happened next . . . in Moscow.

Because Berzin was then in dead trouble: he'd given the wrong advice not once but twice, and he was supposed to be the great expert in the affair.

Logically, he was for the chop. But just as David always had you to bail him out of his troubles, so Berzin had Platov in the Second Directorate. And although Platov wasn't ready to swing for him, he was able to buy him time – and it was out of this that Berzin cobbled 'The Dialectic of Failure'.

The first element of this is that 'failures should never be written off, they should be correctly appreciated and acted on'.

Berzin simply couldn't see where he had gone wrong. Which, refined down, led him to devote considerable effort and resources to finding out why Henderson had changed his mind.

And in the end he cracked the problem.

Henderson had driven down to Rickmansworth from London to be nice to the director and to humiliate David.

When he arrived at the main gate of the research centre he was met by one of Williamson's men, Robson, also an ex-armoured corps NCO.

Robson explained that the visitors' car park was closed for repairs, but he would personally take Henderson round the back, to the director's own car park outside his office, where there was a space beside the director's own Daimler.

As Henderson got out of the car, he found himself looking straight at the director's office. The only trouble was *he couldn't see into it – all he could see was himself, reflected as though in a mirror*.

He walked up and down outside of the building for a few yards each way, and found that the big plate-glass windows for about twenty yards had this mirror-like quality. Then they became ordinary windows again.

At this point, up walked David.

'Where's the director's office?' asked Henderson.

'Just there on the corner, Colonel,' said David. 'But we'll have to go round the side to get in.'

'Do you realize that it's impossible to see into the director's office from the car park?' snapped Henderson.

'But you can,' said David. 'I've looked into it myself – I did that the evening I arrived, it was one of the first things I checked. There aren't even any blinds.'

'Well, you go and look now,' said Henderson. 'All you'll see is yourself, damn it!'

'But that's impossible,' said David. 'I've been in that office a dozen times—'

And then, equally conveniently, up comes Williamson, to solve the problem.

'Oh yes,' said he, 'the windows of the director's office and the adjacent computer room are covered with Anti-Glare plastic sheeting, which reduces sunlight by twenty per cent – the director's office was just like an oven in summer before that was installed and the computers next door were over-heating.'

So it all came out: 'Anti-Glare' sheeting is in common use on windows in such goldfish bowls. And one curious side-effect of it is to turn plate-glass into a mirror from outside during the daylight hours, so that you cannot see *in*, though you can see *out* from inside almost normally, just without any external glare. But when it gets dark, the effect is reversed: you can see *in* from outside, but there's a mirror-effect inside and you can't see *out* . . .

'Why, you pair of bloody fools!' said Henderson. 'Don't you see what this means?'

The pair of bloody fools looked at each other.

'I looked in after dark, that first time,' said David, staring accusingly at Williamson. Then he looked at Henderson. 'And so did Blackman, by God! He was always on night duty until that Sunday – it wouldn't have occurred to him to check, if he didn't know about the Anti-Glare . . . He'd never been inside the building . . . Christ! He *couldn't* have seen Dr Cousins at all!'

It was a moment of pure triumph for Henderson: at one glance he had spotted what clever David had missed, and even though his powers of observation had thereby vindicated David's recommendation, it did so in the most humiliating way imaginable, proving that David was not nearly as clever as he thought he was.

That was how it seemed to Henderson anyway – quite irresistibly, in his moment of triumph. But to Berzin, sweating in Dzershinsky Street, it didn't seem like that at all once he'd tracked down a third-hand account of it – as gleefully retold in the Reform Club by one of David's innumerable enemies – to him it simply didn't ring true. Because if there was one thing Berzin reckoned he knew, it was that David was no such bloody fool. And if there was another thing he was sure of, it was that neither David nor Williamson, never mind Blackman himself, would have left the director's window unchecked like that.

All he needed for proof was a sight of the appropriate Anti-Glare sheeting sales records, either from the retailer or the wholesaler, and that was a routine task. In fact, just a little research established that the windows of the computer area had been covered eighteen months before, but that a further quantity of sheeting had been purchased more recently – it seems that ex-Sergeant-Major Williamson and ex-Sergeant Robson had installed it themselves the Sunday before Henderson's arrival, with David keeping *cave*: they had done the do-it-yourself job between them.

The sum total of the risk David had taken was that Henderson wouldn't detail the circumstances of his triumph publicly to anyone at the research centre, least of all to the director, but would keep it to himself as an after-dinner story. But then just as Berzin knew David, so David knew Henderson: he reckoned the old boy would not admit that he'd been about to turn the vetting recommendation down, or certainly not to a mere civilian. And that was all that was needed to make the fraud stick.

So there it was: David had beaten Berzin by a mixture of cheating and psychology, and he was laughing and Berzin was in the hot seat.

But that was where the second element of the dialectic came in:

> a correctly appreciated failure can confer an advantage on the defeated party, since a victorious enemy is often peculiarly vulnerable to resolute counterattack at his weakest point.

In fact Berzin survived simply by convincing Abakumov that while Singer was really pretty small beer – there'd be other Singers; he was no great loss; he had always been a potential liability – David *was* a very dangerous enemy. And to discredit him, which would be an important success by any standards, all they had to do was to let slip to Colonel Henderson how he'd been shamefully and disgracefully deceived and manipulated by his own man, and into doing the right thing too, and that would actually make it even more irritating.

Which is what they did – and which resulted in Henderson's

final adverse report on David, and Berzin's summation of the dialectic:

> The Leopard, who is a man of the highest capacity and most remarkable intuitive faculty, is today a senior officer in his service. But, as a result of our corrective action, he has failed to achieve promotion appropriate to his ability; which, taking the longer view, must be accounted a much more notable success than the minor failure of the Singer Operation.

Of course, you and I, Fred, know that David's real trouble is not Henderson's fitness report, but his own lamentable lack of ambition. But in the light of Berzin's dialectic perhaps we ought to have a look at some of our other high-flyers who have come unstuck over recent years, don't you think? Just in case the blighter has been applying his theories to screw up their career prospects, eh?

(*Tape ends*)

IAN RANKIN

Playback

IT WAS the perfect murder.

Perfect, that is, so far as the Lothian and Borders Police were concerned. The murderer had telephoned in to confess, then had panicked and attempted to flee, only to be caught leaving the scene of the crime. End of story.

Except that now he was pleading innocence. Pleading, yelling, and screaming it. And this worried Detective Inspector John Rebus, worried him all the way from his office to the four-storey tenement in Leith's trendy dockside area. The tenements here were much as they were in any working-class area of Edinburgh, except that they boasted colour-splashed roller blinds at their windows, or Chinese-style bamboo affairs. And their grimy stone façades had been power-cleaned, their doors now boasting intruder-proof intercoms.

A far cry from the greasy venetian blinds and kicked-in passageways of the tenements in Easter Road or Gorgie, or even in nearby parts of Leith itself, the parts the developers were ignoring as yet.

She had worked as a legal secretary, this much Rebus knew. She had been twenty-four years of age. Her name was Moira Bitter. Rebus smiled at that. It was a guilty smile, but at this hour of the morning any smile he could raise was something of a miracle.

He parked in front of the tenement, guided by a uniformed officer who had recognized the badly dented front bumper of Rebus's car. It was rumoured that the dent had come from knocking down too many old ladies, and who was Rebus to deny it? It was the stuff of legend. And gave him prominence in the fearful eyes of the younger recruits.

A curtain twitched in one of the ground-floor windows, and Rebus caught a glimpse of an elderly lady. Every tenement, it seemed, tarted up or not, boasted its elderly lady. Living alone, with one dog or four cats for company, she was her building's eyes and ears. As Rebus entered the hallway, a door opened and the old lady stuck out her head.

'He was going to run for it,' she whispered. 'But the bobby caught him. I saw it. Is the young lass dead? Is that it?' Her lips were pursed in keen horror.

Rebus smiled at her but said nothing. She would know soon enough. Already she seemed to know as much as he did himself. That was the trouble with living in a city the size of a town, a town with a village mentality.

He climbed the four flights of stairs slowly, listening all the while to the report of the constable who was leading him inexorably towards the corpse of Moira Bitter. They spoke in an undertone: stairwell walls had ears.

'The call came at about five a.m., sir,' explained PC MacManus. 'The caller gave his name as John MacFarlane, and said he'd just murdered his girlfriend. He sounded distressed by all accounts, and I was radioed to investigate. As I arrived, a man was running down the stairs. He seemed in a state of shock.'

'Shock?'

'Sort of disorientated, sir.'

'Did he say anything?' asked Rebus.

'Yes, sir, he told me, "Thank God you're here. Moira's dead." I then asked him to accompany me upstairs to the flat in question, called in for assistance, and the gentleman was arrested.'

Rebus nodded. MacManus was a model of efficiency, not a word out of place, the tone just right. Everything by rote, and without the interference of too much thought. He would go far as a uniformed officer, but Rebus doubted the young man would ever make CID. They had reached the fourth floor. Rebus paused for breath, then walked into the flat.

The hall's pastel colour scheme extended to the living-room and bedroom. Mute colours, subtle and warming. There was nothing subtle about the blood though. The blood was copious. Moira Bitter lay sprawled across her bed, her chest a riot of colour. She was wearing apple-green pyjamas, and her hair was silky blonde. The police pathologist was examining her head.

'She's been dead about three hours,' he informed Rebus. 'Stabbed three or four times with a small sharp instrument, which, for the sake of convenience, I'm going to term a knife. I'll examine her properly later on.'

Rebus nodded, and turned to MacManus, whose face had a sickly grey tinge to it.

'Your first time?' Rebus asked.

The constable nodded slowly.

'Never mind,' Rebus continued. 'You never get used to it anyway. Come on.'

He led the constable out of the room and back into the small hallway. 'This man we've arrested, what did you say his name was?'

'John MacFarlane, sir,' said the constable, taking deep breaths. 'He's the deceased's boyfriend apparently.'

'You said he seemed in a state of shock. Was there anything else you noticed?'

The constable frowned, thinking. 'Such as, sir?' he said at last.

'Blood,' said Rebus coolly. 'You can't stab someone in the heat of the moment without getting blood on you.'

MacManus said nothing. Definitely not CID material, and perhaps realizing it for the very first time. Rebus turned from him and entered the living-room. It was almost neurotically tidy. Magazines and newspapers in their rack beside the sofa. A chrome and glass coffee table bearing nothing more than a clean ashtray and a paperback romance. It could have come straight from an Ideal Homes exhibition. No family photographs, no clutter. This was the lair of an individualist. No ties with the past, and a present ransacked wholesale from Habitat and Next. There was no evidence of a struggle. No evidence of an encounter of any kind: no glasses or coffee cups. The killer had not loitered, or else had been very tidy about his business . . .

Rebus went into the kitchen. It, too, was tidy. Cups and plates stacked for drying beside the empty sink. On the draining-board were knives, forks, teaspoons. No murder weapon. There were spots of water in the sink and on the draining-board itself, yet the cutlery and crockery were dry. Rebus found a dish-towel hanging up behind the door and felt it. It was damp. He examined it more closely. There was a small smudge on it. Perhaps gravy or chocolate. Or blood. Someone had dried something recently, but what?

He went to the cutlery drawer and opened it. Inside, amidst the various implements was a short-bladed chopping knife with a heavy black handle. A quality knife, sharp and gleaming. The other items in the drawer were bone dry, but this chopping knife's wooden handle was damp to the touch. Rebus was in no doubt: he had found his murder weapon.

Clever of MacFarlane, though, to have cleaned and put away the knife. A cool and calm action. Moira Bitter had been dead three hours. The call to the police station had come an hour ago. What had MacFarlane done during the intervening two hours? Cleaned the flat? Washed and dried the dishes? Rebus looked in the kitchen's swing bin, but found no other clues, no broken ornaments, nothing that might hint at a struggle. And if there had been no struggle, if the murderer had gained access to the tenement and to Moira Bitter's flat without forcing an entry . . . if all this were true, Moira had known her killer.

Rebus toured the rest of the flat, but found no other clues. Beside the telephone in the hall stood an answering machine. He played the tape, and heard Moira Bitter's voice.

'Hello, this is Moira. I'm out, I'm in the bath, or I'm otherwise engaged.' (A giggle.) 'Leave a message and I'll get back to you, unless you sound boring.'

There was only one message. Rebus listened to it, then wound back the tape and listened again.

'Hello, Moira, it's John. I got your message. I'm coming over. Hope you're not "otherwise engaged". Love you.'

John MacFarlane: Rebus didn't doubt the identity of the caller. Moira sounded fresh and fancy-free in her message. But did MacFarlane's response hint at jealousy? Perhaps she *had* been otherwise engaged when he'd arrived. He'd lost his temper, blind rage, a knife lying handily . . . Rebus had seen it before. Most victims knew their attackers. If that were not the case, the police wouldn't solve so many crimes. It was a blunt fact. You double-bolted your door against the psychopath with the chain-saw, only to be stabbed in the back by your lover, husband, son, or neighbour.

John MacFarlane was as guilty as hell. They would find blood on his clothes, even if he'd tried cleaning it off. He had stabbed his girlfriend, then calmed down and called in to report the crime, but had grown frightened at the end and had attempted to flee.

The only question left in Rebus's mind was the why? The why, and those missing two hours.

Edinburgh in the early hours. The occasional taxi rippling across cobblestones, and lone shadowy figures slouching home with hands in pockets, shoulders hunched. During the night hours, the sick and the old died peacefully, either at home or in some hospital ward. Two in the morning until four: the dead hours. And then some died horribly, with terror in their eyes. The taxis still rumbled past, the night people kept moving. Rebus let his car idle at traffic lights, missing the change to green, only coming to his senses as amber turned red again. Glasgow Rangers were coming to town on Saturday. There would be casual violence. Rebus felt comfortable with the thought. The worst football hooligan could probably not have stabbed with the same ferocity as Moira Bitter's killer. Rebus lowered his eyebrows. He was rousing himself to fury, keen for confrontation. Confrontation with the murderer himself.

John MacFarlane was crying as he was led into the interrogation room, where Rebus had made himself look comfortable, cigarette in one hand, coffee in the other. Rebus had expected a lot of things, but not tears.

'Would you like something to drink?' he asked.

MacFarlane shook his head. He had slumped into the chair on the other side of the desk, his shoulders sagging, head bowed, and the sobs still coming from his throat. He mumbled something.

'I didn't catch that,' said Rebus.

'I said I didn't do it,' MacFarlane answered quietly. 'How could I do it? I love Moira.'

Rebus noted the present tense. He gestured towards the tape machine on the desk. 'Do you have any objection to my making a recording of this interview?'

MacFarlane shook his head again.

Rebus switched on the machine. He flicked ash from his cigarette on to the floor, sipped his coffee, and waited. Eventually, MacFarlane looked up. His eyes were stinging red. Rebus stared hard into those eyes, but still said nothing. MacFarlane seemed to be calming. Seemed, too, to know what was expected of him. He asked for a cigarette, was given one, and started to speak.

'I'd been out in my car. Just driving, thinking.'

Rebus interrupted him. 'What time was this?'

'Well,' said MacFarlane, 'ever since I left work, I suppose. I'm an architect. There's a competition on just now to design a new art gallery and museum complex in Stirling. Our partnership's going in for it. We were discussing ideas most of the day, you know, brainstorming.' He looked up at Rebus again, and Rebus nodded. Brainstorm: now there was an interesting word . . .

'And after work,' MacFarlane continued, 'I was so fired up I just felt like driving. Going over the different options and plans in my head. Working out which was strongest . . .'

He broke off, realizing perhaps that he was talking in a rush, without thought or caution. He swallowed and inhaled some smoke. Rebus was studying MacFarlane's clothes. Expensive leather brogues. Brown corduroy trousers. A thick white cotton shirt, the kind cricketers wore, open at the neck. And a tailor-made tweed jacket. MacFarlane's 3-Series BMW was parked in the police garage, and being searched. His pockets had been emptied, a Liberty-print tie confiscated in case he had ideas about hanging himself. His brogues, too, were without their laces, these having been confiscated along with the tie. Rebus had gone through the belongings. A wallet, not exactly bulging with money but containing a fair spread of credit cards. There were more cards, too, in MacFarlane's personal organizer. Rebus flipped through the diary pages, then turned to the sections for notes and for addresses. MacFarlane seemed to lead a busy but quite normal life.

Rebus studied him now, across the expanse of the old table. MacFarlane was well built, handsome if you liked that sort of thing. He looked strong, but not brutish. Probably he would make the local news headlines as 'Secretary's Yuppie Killer'. Rebus stubbed out his cigarette.

'We know you did it, John. That's not in dispute. We just want to know why.'

MacFarlane's voice was brittle with emotion. 'I swear I didn't, I swear.'

'You're going to have to do better than that.' Rebus paused again. Tears were dripping on to MacFarlane's corduroys. 'Go on with your story,' he said.

MacFarlane shrugged. 'That's about it,' he said, wiping his nose with the sleeve of his shirt.

Rebus prompted him. 'You didn't stop off anywhere for petrol or a meal or anything like that?' He sounded sceptical.

MacFarlane shook his head. 'No, I just drove until my head was clear. I went all the way to the Forth Road Bridge. Turned off and went into Queensferry. Got out of the car to have a look at the water. Threw a few stones in for luck.' He smiled at the irony. 'Then drove round the coast road and back into Edinburgh.'

'Nobody saw you? You didn't speak to anyone?'

'Not that I can remember.'

'And you didn't get hungry?' Rebus sounded entirely unconvinced.

'We'd had a business lunch with a client. We took him to the Eyrie. After lunch there, I seldom need to eat until the next morning.'

The Eyrie was Edinburgh's most expensive restaurant. You didn't go there to eat, you went to spend money. Rebus was feeling peckish himself. The canteen did a fine bacon buttie . . .

'When did you last see Miss Bitter alive?'

At the word 'alive', MacFarlane shivered. It took him a long time to answer. Rebus watched the tape revolving. 'Yesterday morning,' MacFarlane said at last. 'She stayed the night at my flat.'

'How long have you known her?'

'About a year. But I only started going out with her a couple of months ago.'

'Oh? And how did you know her before that?'

MacFarlane paused. 'She was Kenneth's girlfriend,' he said at last.

'Kenneth being . . ?'

MacFarlane's cheeks reddened before he spoke. 'My best friend,' he said. 'Kenneth was my best friend. You could say I stole her from him. These things happen, don't they?'

Rebus raised an eyebrow. 'Do they?' he said.

MacFarlane bowed his head again. 'Can I have a coffee?' he asked quietly.

Rebus nodded, then lit another cigarette.

MacFarlane sipped the coffee, holding it in both hands like a shipwreck survivor. Rebus rubbed his nose and stretched, feeling tired. He checked his watch. Eight in the morning. What a life. A string of bacon rind curled across the plate in front of him. He had eaten two bacon rolls. MacFarlane had refused food, but finished the first cup of coffee in two gulps, and gratefully accepted a second.

'So,' Rebus said, 'you drove back into town.'

'That's right.' MacFarlane took another sip of coffee. 'I don't know why, but I decided to check my answering machine for calls.'

'You mean when you got home?'

MacFarlane shook his head. 'No, from the car. I called home from my car phone and got the answering machine to play back any messages.'

Rebus was impressed. 'That's clever,' he said.

MacFarlane smiled again, but the smile soon vanished. 'One of the messages was from Moira,' he said. 'She wanted to see me.'

'At that hour?' MacFarlane shrugged. 'Did she say why she wanted to see you?'

'No. She sounded . . . strange.'

'Strange?'

'A bit . . . I don't know, distant maybe.'

'Did you get the feeling she was on her own when she called?'

'I've no idea.'

'Did you call her back?'

'Yes, I think so. Her answering machine was on. I left a message.'

'Would you say you're the jealous type, Mr MacFarlane?'

'What?' MacFarlane sounded surprised by the question. He seemed to give it serious thought. 'No more so than the next man,' he said at last.

'Why would anyone want to kill her?'

MacFarlane stared at the table, shaking his head slowly.

'Go on,' said Rebus, sighing, growing impatient. 'You were saying how you got her message.'

'Well, I went straight to her flat. It was late, but I knew if she was asleep I could always let myself in.'

'Oh?' Rebus was interested. 'How?'

'She gave me a spare key,' MacFarlane explained.

Rebus got up from his chair and walked to the far wall and back, deep in thought. 'I don't suppose,' he said, 'you've got any idea *when* Moira made that call?'

MacFarlane shook his head. 'But the machine will have logged it,' he said. Rebus was more impressed than ever. Technology was a wonderful thing. What's more, he was impressed by MacFarlane. If the man was a murderer, then he was a very good one, for he had fooled Rebus into thinking him innocent. It was crazy. There was nothing to point to him *not* being guilty. But all the same, a feeling was a feeling, and Rebus most definitely had a feeling.

'I want to see that machine,' he said. 'And I want to hear the message on it. I want to hear Moira's last words.'

It was interesting how the simplest cases could become so complex. There was still no doubt in the minds of those around Rebus – his superiors and those below him – that John MacFarlane was guilty of murder. They had all the proof they needed, every last bit of it circumstantial.

MacFarlane's car was clean: no bloodstained clothes stashed in the boot. There were no prints on the chopping-knife, though MacFarlane's prints were found elsewhere in the flat – not surprising given that he'd visited that night, as well as on many a previous one. No prints either on the kitchen sink and taps, though the murderer had washed a bloody knife. Rebus thought that curious . . . And as for motive: jealousy, a falling-out, a past indiscretion. The CID had seen them all.

Murder by stabbing was confirmed, and the time of death narrowed down to a quarter of an hour either side of three in the morning. At which time MacFarlane claimed he was driving towards Edinburgh, but with no witnesses to corroborate the claim. There was no blood to be found on MacFarlane's clothing, but, as Rebus himself knew, that didn't mean the man wasn't a killer.

More interesting, however, was that MacFarlane denied making the call to the police. Yet someone – in fact, whoever murdered Moira Bitter – *had* made it. And more interesting even than this was the telephone answering machine.

Rebus went to MacFarlane's flat in Liberton to investigate. The traffic was busy coming into town, but quiet heading out. Liberton was one of Edinburgh's many anonymous middle-class districts, substantial houses, small shops, a busy thoroughfare. It looked innocuous at midnight, and was even safer by day.

What MacFarlane had termed a 'flat' comprised, in fact, the top two storeys of a vast detached house. Rebus roamed the building, not sure if he was looking for anything in particular. He found little. MacFarlane led a rigorous and regimented life, and had the home to accommodate such a lifestyle. One room had been turned into a makeshift gymnasium, with weightlifting equipment and the like. There was an office for business use, and a study for private use. The main bedroom was decidedly masculine in taste, though a framed painting of a naked woman had been removed from one wall and tucked behind a chair. Rebus thought he detected Moira Bitter's influence at work.

In the wardrobe were a few pieces of her clothing and a pair of her shoes. A snapshot of her had been framed and placed on MacFarlane's bedside table. Rebus studied the photograph for a long time. Then sighed and left the bedroom, closing the door after him. Who knew when John MacFarlane would see his home again . . .

The answering machine was in the living-room. Rebus played the tape of the previous night's calls. Moira Bitter's voice was clipped and confident, her message to the point: 'Hello.' Then a pause. 'I need to see you. Come round as soon as you get this message. Love you.'

MacFarlane had told Rebus that the display unit on the machine showed time of call. Moira's call registered at 3.50 a.m., about forty-five minutes after her death. There was room for some discrepancy, but not three-quarters of an hour's worth. Rebus scratched his chin and pondered. He played the tape again. 'Hello,' then the pause. 'I need to see you.' He stopped the tape and played it again, this time with the volume up and his ear close to the machine. That pause was curious, and the sound quality on the tape was poor. He rewound and listened to another call from the same evening. The quality was better, the voice much clearer. Then he listened to Moira again. Were these recording machines infallible? Of course not. The time display could have been tampered with. The recording itself could be a fake. After all, whose word did he have that this *was* the voice of Moira Bitter? Only John MacFarlane's. But John MacFarlane had been caught leaving the scene of a murder. And now here Rebus was being presented with a sort of an alibi for the man. Yes, the tape could well be a fake, used by MacFarlane to substantiate his story, but stupidly not put into use until after the time of death. Still, from what Rebus had heard from Moira's own answering machine, the voice was certainly similar to her own. The lab boys could sort it out with their clever machines. One technician in particular owed him a rather large favour . . .

Rebus shook his head. This still wasn't making much sense. He played the tape again and again.

'Hello.' Pause. 'I need to see you.'

'Hello.' Pause. 'I need to see you.'

'Hello.' Pause. 'I need—' . . .

And suddenly it became a little clearer in his mind. He ejected the tape and slipped it into his jacket pocket, then picked up the telephone and called the station. He asked to speak to Detective Sergeant Brian Holmes. The voice, when it came on the line, was tired, but amused.

'Don't tell me,' Holmes said, 'let me guess. You want me to drop everything and run an errand for you.'

'You must be psychic, Brian. Two errands really. Firstly, last night's calls. Get the recording of them and search for one from John MacFarlane, claiming he'd just killed his girlfriend. Make a copy of it and wait there for me. I've got another tape for you, and I want them both taken to the lab. Warn them you're coming—'

'—and tell them it's priority, I know. It's *always* priority. They'll say what they always say: give us four days.'

'Not this time,' Rebus said. 'Ask for Bill Costain and tell him Rebus is collecting on his favour. He's to shelve what he's doing. I want a result today, not next week.'

'What's the favour you're collecting on?'

'I caught him smoking dope in the lab toilets last month.'

Holmes laughed. 'The world's going to pot,' he said.

Rebus groaned at the joke and put down the receiver. He needed to speak with John MacFarlane again. Not about lovers this time, but about friends . . .

Rebus rang the doorbell a third time, and at last heard a voice from within.

'Jesus, hold on! I'm coming.'

The man who answered the door was tall, thin, wire-framed glasses perched on his nose. He peered at Rebus and ran his fingers through his hair.

'Mr Thomson?' Rebus asked. 'Kenneth Thomson?'

'Yes,' said the man, 'that's right.'

Rebus flipped open his ID. 'Detective Inspector John Rebus,' he said by way of introduction. 'May I come in?'

Kenneth Thomson held open the door. 'Please do,' he said. 'Will a cheque be all right?'

'A cheque?'

'I take it you're here about the parking tickets,' said Thomson. 'I'd have got round to them eventually, believe me. It's just that I've been hellish busy, and what with one thing and another . . .'

'No, sir,' said Rebus, his smile as cold as a church pew, 'nothing to do with parking fines.'

'Oh?' Thomson pushed his glasses back up his nose and looked at Rebus. 'Then what's the problem?'

'It's about Miss Moira Bitter,' said Rebus.

'Moira? What about her?'

'She's dead, sir.'

Rebus had followed Thomson into a cluttered room overflowing with bundles of magazines and newspapers. A hi-fi sat in one corner, and covering the wall next to it were shelves filled with cassette tapes. These had an orderly look to them, as though they had been indexed, each tape's spine carrying an identifying number.

Thomson, who had been clearing a chair for Rebus to sit on, froze at the detective's words.

'Dead?' he gasped. 'How?'

'She was murdered, sir. We think John MacFarlane did it.'

'John?' Thomson's face was quizzical, then sceptical, then resigned. 'But why?'

'We don't know that yet, sir. I thought you might be able to help.'

'Of course I'll help if I can. Sit down, please.'

Rebus perched on the chair, while Thomson pushed aside some newspapers and settled himself on a sofa.

'You're a writer, I believe,' said Rebus.

Thomson nodded distractedly. 'Yes,' he said. 'Freelance journalism, food and drink, travel, that sort of thing. Plus the occasional commission to write a book. That's what I'm doing now, actually. Writing a book.'

'Oh? I like books myself. What's it about?'

'Don't laugh,' said Thomson, 'but it's a history of the haggis.'

'The haggis?' Rebus couldn't disguise the smile in his voice, warmer this time: the church pew had been given a cushion. He cleared his throat noisily, glancing around the room, noting the piles of books leaning precariously against walls, the files and folders and newsprint cuttings. 'You must do a lot of research,' he said appreciatively.

'Sometimes,' said Thomson. Then he shook his head. 'I still can't believe it. About Moira, I mean. About John.'

Rebus took out his notebook, more for effect than anything else. 'You were Miss Bitter's lover for a while,' he stated.

'That's right, Inspector.'

'But then she went off with Mr MacFarlane.'

'Right again.' A hint of bitterness had crept into Thomson's voice. 'I was very angry at the time, but I got over it.'

'Did you still see Miss Bitter?'

'No.'

'What about Mr MacFarlane?'

'No again. We spoke on the telephone a couple of times. It always seemed to end in a shouting match. We used to be like . . . well, it's a cliché, I suppose, but we used to be like brothers.'

'Yes,' said Rebus, 'so Mr MacFarlane told me.'

'Oh?' Thomson sounded interested. 'What else did he say?'

'Not much really.' Rebus rose from his perch and went to the window, holding aside the net curtain to stare out on to the street below. 'He said you'd known each other for years.'

'Since school,' Thomson added.

Rebus nodded. 'And he said you drove a black Ford Escort. That'll be it down there, parked across the street.'

Thomson came to the window. 'Yes,' he agreed uncertainly, 'that's it. But I don't see what—'

'I noticed it as I was parking my own car,' Rebus continued, brushing past Thomson's interruption. He let the curtain fall and turned back into the room. 'I noticed you've got a car alarm. I suppose you must get a lot of burglaries around here?'

'It's not the most salubrious part of town,' Thomson said. 'Not all writers are Jeffrey Archer.'

'Did money have anything to do with it?' Rebus asked.

Thomson paused. 'With what, Inspector?'

'With Miss Bitter leaving you for Mr MacFarlane. He's not short of a bob or two, is he?'

Thomson's voice rose perceptibly. 'Look, I really can't see what this has to do with—'

'Your car was broken into a few months ago, wasn't it?' Rebus was examining a pile of magazines on the floor now. 'I saw the report. They stole your radio and your car phone.'

'Yes.'

'I notice you've replaced the car phone.' He glanced up at Thomson, smiled, and continued browsing.

'Of course,' said Thomson. He seemed confused now, unable to fathom where the conversation was leading.

'A journalist would need a car phone, wouldn't he?' Rebus observed. 'So people could keep in touch, contact him at any time. Is that right?'

'Absolutely right, Inspector.'

Rebus threw the magazine back on to the pile and nodded slowly. 'Great things, car phones.' He walked over towards Thomson's desk. It was a small flat. This room obviously served a double purpose as study and living-room. Not that Thomson entertained many visitors. He was too aggressive for many people, too secretive for others. So John MacFarlane had said.

On the desk sat more clutter, though in some appearance of organization. There was also a neat word processor, and beside it a telephone. And next to the telephone sat an answering machine.

'Yes,' Rebus repeated. 'You need to be in contact.' Rebus smiled towards Thomson. 'Communication, that's the secret. And I'll tell you something else about journalists.'

'What?' Unable to comprehend Rebus's direction, Thomson's tone had become that of someone bored with a conversation. He shoved his hands deep into his pockets.

'Journalists are hoarders.' Rebus made this sound like some great wisdom. His eyes took in the room again. 'I mean, near-pathological hoarders. They can't bear to throw things away, because they never know when something might become useful. Am I right?'

Thomson shrugged.

'Yes,' said Rebus, 'I bet I am. Look at these cassettes, for example.' He went to where the rows of tapes were neatly displayed. 'What are they? Interviews, that sort of thing?'

'Mostly, yes,' Thomson agreed.

'And you still keep them, even though they're years old?'

Thomson shrugged again. 'So I'm a hoarder.'

But Rebus had noticed something on the top shelf, some plain brown cardboard boxes. He reached up and lifted one down. Inside were more tapes, marked with months and years. But these tapes were smaller. Rebus gestured with the box towards Thomson, his eyes seeking an explanation.

Thomson smiled uneasily. 'Answering machine messages,' he said.

'You keep these, too?' Rebus sounded amazed.

'Well,' Thomson said, 'someone may agree to something over the phone, an interview or something, then deny it later. I need them as records of promises made.'

Rebus nodded, understanding now. He replaced the brown

box on its shelf. He still had his back to Thomson when the telephone rang, a sharp electronic sound.

'Sorry,' Thomson apologized, going to answer it.

'Not at all.'

Thomson picked up the receiver. 'Hello?' He listened, then frowned. 'Of course,' he said finally, holding the receiver out towards Rebus. 'It's for you, Inspector.'

Rebus raised a surprised eyebrow, and accepted the receiver. 'Hello?'

It was, as he had known it would be, Detective Sergeant Holmes.

'OK,' Holmes said. 'Costain no longer owes you that favour. He's listened to both tapes. He hasn't run all the necessary tests yet, but he's pretty convinced.'

'Go on.' Rebus was looking at Thomson, who was sitting, hands clasping knees, on the arm of the chair.

'The call we received last night,' said Holmes, 'the one from John MacFarlane admitting to the murder of Moira Bitter, originated from a portable telephone.'

'Interesting,' said Rebus, his eyes on Thomson. 'And what about the other one?'

'Well, the tape you gave me seems to be twice-removed.'

'What does that mean?'

'It means,' said Holmes, 'that according to Costain it's not just a recording, it's the *recording* of a recording.'

Rebus nodded, satisfied. 'OK, thanks, Brian.' He put down the receiver.

'Good news or bad?' Thomson asked.

'A bit of both,' answered Rebus thoughtfully.

Thomson had risen to his feet. 'I feel like a drink, Inspector. Can I get you one?'

'It's a bit early for me, I'm afraid,' Rebus said, looking at his watch. It was eleven o'clock: opening time. 'All right,' he said, 'just a small one.'

'The whisky's in the kitchen,' Thomson explained. 'I'll just be a moment.'

'Fine, sir, fine.'

Rebus listened as Thomson left the room and headed off towards the kitchen. He stood beside the desk, thinking through what he now knew. Then, hearing Thomson returning from the kitchen, floorboards bending beneath his weight, he picked up the wastepaper basket from below the desk, and, as Thomson entered the room, proceeded to empty the contents in a heap on the sofa.

Thomson stood in the doorway, a glass of whisky in each hand, dumbstruck. 'What on earth are you doing?' he spluttered at last. But Rebus ignored him and started to pick through the now strewn contents of the bin, talking as he searched.

'It was pretty close to being foolproof, Mr Thomson. Let me explain. The killer went to Moira Bitter's flat, and talked her into letting him in, despite the late hour. He murdered her quite callously, let's make no mistake about that. I've never seen so much premeditation in a case before. He cleaned the knife and returned it to its drawer. He was wearing gloves, of course, knowing John MacFarlane's fingerprints would be all over the flat, and he cleaned the knife precisely to disguise the fact that he *had* worn gloves. MacFarlane, you see, had not.'

Thomson took a gulp from one glass, but otherwise seemed rooted to the spot. His eyes had become vacant, as though picturing Rebus's story in his mind.

'MacFarlane,' Rebus continued, still rummaging, 'was summoned to Moira's flat. The message *did* come from her. He knew her voice well enough not to be fooled by someone else's voice. The killer sat outside Moira's flat, sat waiting for MacFarlane to arrive. Then the killer made one last call, this one to the police, and in the guise of an hysterical MacFarlane. We know this last call was made on a car phone. The lab boys are very clever that way. The police are hoarders, too, you see, Mr Thomson. We make recordings of emergency calls made to us. It won't be hard to voice-print that call, and try to match it to John MacFarlane. But it won't be John MacFarlane, will it?' Rebus paused for effect. 'It'll be you.'

Thomson gave a thin smile, but his grip on the two glasses

had grown less steady, and whisky was dribbling from the angled lip of one of them.

'Ah-ha.' Rebus had found what he was looking for in the contents of the bin. With a pleased-as-punch grin on his unshaven, sleepless face, he pinched forefinger and thumb together and lifted them for his own and Thomson's inspection. He was holding a tiny sliver of brown recording tape.

'You see,' he continued, 'the killer had to lure MacFarlane to the murder scene. Having killed Moira, he went to his car, as I've said. There he had his portable telephone, and a cassette recorder. He was a hoarder, and had kept all his answering machine tapes, including messages left by Moira at the height of their affair. He had found the message he needed, and had spliced it. It was this message that he played, having dialled John MacFarlane's answering machine. All he had to do after that was wait. The message MacFarlane received was, 'Hello, I need to see you.' There was a pause after the 'hello'. And that pause was where the splice was made in the tape, excising this.' Rebus looked at the sliver of tape. 'The one word "Kenneth". "Hello, Kenneth, I need to see you." It was Moira Bitter talking to you, Mr Thomson, talking to you a long time ago.'

Thomson hurled both glasses at once, so that they arrowed in towards Rebus, who ducked. The glasses collided above his head, shards raining down on him. Thomson had reached the front door, had hauled it open even before Rebus was on him, lunging, pushing the younger man forward through the doorway and on to the tenement landing. Thomson's head hit the metal rails with a muted chime, and he let out a single moan before collapsing. Rebus shook himself free of glass, feeling one or two tiny pieces nick him as he brushed a hand across his face. He brought a hand to his nose and inhaled deeply. His father had always said whisky would put hairs on his chest. Rebus wondered if the same miracle might be effected on his temples and the crown of his head . . .

It had been the perfect murder.

Well, almost. But Kenneth Thomson had reckoned without

Rebus's ability actually to believe someone innocent despite the evidence against them. The case against John MacFarlane had been overwhelming. Yet Rebus, feeling it to be wrong, had been forced to invent other scenarios, other motives, and other means to the fairly chilling end. It wasn't enough that Moira had died – died at the hands of someone she knew. MacFarlane had to be implicated in her murder. The killer had been out to tag them both. But it was Moira the killer hated, hated because she had broken up a friendship as well as a heart.

Rebus stood on the steps of the police station. Thomson was in a cell somewhere below his feet, somewhere below ground level. Confessing to everything. He would go to jail, while John MacFarlane, perhaps not realizing his luck, had already been freed.

The streets were busy now. Lunchtime traffic, the reliable noises of the everyday. The sun was even managing to burst from its slumber. All of which reminded Rebus that his day was over. Time, all in all he felt, for a short visit home, a shower and change of clothes, and, God and the Devil willing, some sleep . . .

RUTH RENDELL

A Drop Too Much

You won't believe this, but last Monday I tried to kill my wife. Yes, my wife, Hedda. And what a loss that would have been to English letters! Am I sure I want to tell you about it? Well, you're not likely to tell her, are you? You don't know her. Besides, she wouldn't believe you. She thinks I'm the self-appointed president of her fan club.

The fact is, I'm heartily glad the attempt failed. I don't think I've got the stamina to stand up to a murder inquiry. I'd get flurried and confess the whole thing. (Yes, thanks, I will have a drink. My back's killing me – I think I've slipped a disc.)

Hedda and I have been married for fifteen years, and I can't complain she hasn't kept me in the lap of luxury. Of course, I've paid my own price for that. To a sensitive man like myself, it is a little humiliating to be known as Hedda Hardy's husband. And I don't really care for her books. It's one thing for a man to write stuff about soldiers of fortune and revolutions in South American republics and jet-set baccarat games and seductions on millionaires' yachts, but you expect something a little more – well, delicate and sensitive from a woman. Awareness, you know, the psychological approach. I've often thought of what Jane Austen said about the way she wrote, on a little piece of ivory six inches wide. With Hedda it's more a matter of bashing away at a bloody great rock face with a chisel.

Still, she's made a fortune out of it. And I will say for her, she's generous. Not a settlement or a trust fund though, more's the pity. And the property's all in her name. There's our place in Kensington – Hedda bought that just before house prices went sky-high – and the cottage in Minorca, and now we've got this farmhouse in Sussex. You didn't know about that? Well, that's crucial to the whole thing. That's where I made my abortive murder attempt.

Hedda decided to buy it about six months ago. Funnily enough, it was the same week she took Lindsay on as her secretary. Of course she's had secretaries before, must have had half a dozen, and they've all worshipped the ground she trod on. To put it fancifully, they helped fill my cup of humiliation. (And while on the subject of cups, old man, you may refill my glass. Thank you.)

I'll tell you what I mean. They were all bitten by the bug of this Women's Lib rubbish, so you can imagine they were falling about with glee to find a couple like us. And though I manage to be rather vague about my financial position with most of our friends, you can't keep things like that dark from the girl who types the letters to your accountant, can you? The fact is, Hedda's annual income tax amounts to – let me see – yes, almost six times my annual income.

They were mistresses of the snide comment. What did you say? All right, I don't mind admitting it, a couple of them were my mistresses too. I had to prove myself a man in some respects, didn't I? But Lindsay . . . Lindsay's different. For one thing, she'd actually heard of *me*.

When Hedda introduced us, Lindsay didn't come out with that It-must-be-wonderful-to-be-married-to-such-a-famous-writer bit. She said, 'You write that super column for *Lady of Leisure*, don't you? I always read it. I'm crazy about gardening.'

My heart warmed to her at once, old man. And when Hedda'd finished making the poor sweet type about twenty replies to her awful fan letters, we went out into the garden together. She's really very knowledgeable. Imagine, she was living with her parents in some ghastly suburban hole and doing their whole garden single-handed. Mind you, though, it's living in the suburbs that's kept her so sweet and unspoiled.

Not that it was just that – I mean the gardening bit – that started our rapport. Lindsay is just about the most beautiful girl I ever saw. I adore those tall delicate blondes that look as if a puff of wind would blow them away. Hedda, of course, is handsome after a fashion. I dare say anyone would get a battered look churning out stuff about rapes and massacres year after year between breakfast and lunch.

The long and short of it is that by the end of a week I was head over heels in love with Lindsay. And she feels the same about me. A virgin too, old man. What did you say? You should be so lucky? I reckon I deserved every bit of luck I could get in those utterly bloody weeks while Hedda was buying the farmhouse.

Honestly, Hedda treats me the way some men treat their wives. Pours out all her troubles, and if I don't grovel at her feet telling her how wonderful she is she says I don't know what it is to have responsibilities and that, anyway, I can't be expected to understand business. And all this because the house agent didn't phone her at the precise time he'd promised and the vendor got a bit bolshie about the price. I don't blame him, the way Hedda drives a bargain.

(Another Scotch? Oh, well, if you twist my arm.) Hedda got possession of the place in March and she had an army of decorators in and this firm to do the carpets and that one to do the furnishings. Needless to say, I wasn't consulted except about the furniture for what she calls my 'den'. Really, she ought to remember it isn't lap dogs who live in dens.

It's an extraordinary thing how mean rich people can be. And quixotic. Thousands she spent on that wallpaper and Wilton, but when it came to the garden she decided I could see to all that on my own, if you please. Hedda really has no idea. Just because I happen to know the difference between a calceolaria and a cotoneaster and am able (expertly, if I may for once blow my own trumpet) to instruct stockbrokers' wives in rose-pruning, she thinks I enjoy nothing better than digging up half an acre of more or less solid chalk. However, when I said I'd need to hire a cultivator and get God knows how much top soil and turfs, she was quite amenable for her and said she'd pay.

'I don't suppose it'll come to more than a hundred or so, will it?' she said. 'With the Stock Market the way it is, I don't want to sell any more shares.' Just as if she was some poor little housewife having to draw it out of the Post Office. And I knew for a fact – Lindsay had told me – she was getting fifty thousand for her latest film rights.

She'd had the old stables at the end of the garden converted into a double garage. You can't park on the road itself, there's too much through traffic, but there's a drive that leads down to the garage between the garden and a field. Not another house for miles, by the way. But the garden was a bloody wilderness and at that time you had to plough through brambles and really noxious-looking giant weeds to get from the garage to the house. Taking care, I may add, not to fall down the well on the way. Oh, yes, there's a well. Or there was.

'I suppose that'll have to be filled in?' I said.

'Naturally,' said Hedda. 'Or are you under the impression I'm the sort of lady who'd want to drop a coin down it and make a wish?'

I was going to retort that she'd never dropped a coin in her life without knowing she'd get a damn sight more than a wish for it, but she'd just bought me a new car so I held my tongue.

I decided the best thing would be to fill the well up with hardcore, concrete the top and make a gravel path over it from the garage entrance to the back kitchen door. It wasn't going to be a complicated job – just arduous – as the brick surround of the well lay about two inches below the level of the rest of the garden. The well itself was very deep, about forty feet, as I know from measuring with a plumb line.

However, I postponed work on the well for the time being. Hedda had gone off to the States on a lecture tour, leaving mountains of work for poor little Lindsay, a typescript to prepare about a million words long, and God knows how many dreary letters to write to publishers and agents and all those people for whom the world is expected to stop when Hedda Hardy is out of the country.

Still, since Hedda had now established her base in Sussex and had all her paraphernalia there, Lindsay was down there too and we had quite a little honeymoon. I can't begin to tell you what a marvel that girl is. What a wife she'll make! – for some other lucky guy. I can only say that my wish is her command. And I don't even have to express my wish. A hint or a glance is enough, and there's the drink I've just been beginning to get wistful about, or a lovely hot bath running or a delicious snack on a tray placed right there on my lap. It makes a change for me, old man, the society of a really womanly old-fashioned woman. D'you know, one afternoon while I happened to be taking a little nap, she went all the way into Kingsmarkham – that's our neighbouring burg – to collect my car from being serviced. I didn't have to ask, just said something about being a bit weary. And when I woke up, there was my vehicle tucked away in the garage, and Lindsay in a ravishing new dress tip-toeing about getting our tea so as not to disturb me . . .

But I mustn't get sidetracked like this. Inevitably, we began to talk of the future. Women, I've noticed, always do. A man is content to take the goods the gods provide and hope the consequences won't be too bloody. It's really quite off-putting the way women, when one has been to bed with them once or twice, always say:

'What are we going to do about it?'

Mind you, in Lindsay's case I felt differently. There's no doubt, marriage or not, she's the girl for me. I'm not used to a sweet naïvety in the female sex – I thought it had died with the suffrage – and to hear the assumptions Lindsay made about my rights and my earning power et cetera really did something for my ego. To hear her talk – until I put her right – you'd have thought I was the breadwinner and Hedda the minion. Well, you know what I mean. Unfortunate way of putting it.

We were bedding out plants one afternoon – yes, I said 'plants', there's no need to be coarse – when Lindsay started discussing divorce.

'You'd divide your property, wouldn't you?' she said. 'I mean, split it down the middle. Or, if you didn't think that quite fair on her, she could keep this place and that sweet cottage in wherever it is, and we could have the Kensington house.'

'Fair on her?' I said. 'My dear girl, I adore you, but you don't know you're born, do you? All these hereditaments or messuages or whatever the lawyers call them are *hers*. Hers, lovey, in *her* name.'

'Oh, I know that, darling,' she said. (By the way, she really has the most gorgeous speaking voice. I can't wait for you to meet her.) 'I know that. But when you read about divorce cases in the papers, the parties always have to divide the property. The judge makes a – a whatsit.'

'An order,' I said. 'But in those cases the money was earned by the husband. Haven't you ever heard of the Married Women's Property Act?'

'Sort of,' she said. 'What is it?'

'I'll tell you what it *means*,' I said. 'It means that what's mine is hers and what's hers is her own. Or, to enlarge, if she fails to pay her Income Tax I'm liable, but if I fail to pay mine nobody can get a bean out of her. And don't make me laugh, sweetheart,' I said, warming to my theme, 'but any idea you may have about division of property – well, that's a farce. There's nothing in English law to make her maintain me. If we got divorced I'd be left with the clothes I stand up in and the pittance I get from *Lady of Leisure*.'

'Then what are we going to do about it?' she said.

What a question! But, to do her justice, she didn't make any silly suggestions as to our living together in a furnished room. And she was even sweeter to me than before.

Of course, she loves me so she doesn't feel it a hardship to run around laying out my clean clothes and emptying my ashtrays and fetching the car round to the front door for me when it's raining. But I know she thought I'd have a go at Hedda, ask her to let me go and make a settlement on me. I could picture Hedda's face! Having a deeply rooted idea that she's the most dynamic and sexy thing since Helen of Troy, my wife has never suspected any of my philanderings and she hasn't an inkling of what's in the wind with Lindsay. The funny thing is, I had an idea that if I did tell her she'd just roar with laughter and then say something cutting about church mice and beggars who can't be choosers. Hedda's got a very nasty tongue. It's been sharpened up by writing all that snappy dialogue, I suppose.

Anyway when she got back she wasn't interested in me or Lindsay or all those petunias and antirrhinums we'd planted. The first thing she wanted to know was why I hadn't filled in the well.

'All in good time,' I said. 'It's a matter of priorities. The well can get filled in any time, but the only month to plant annuals is May.'

'I want the well filled in now,' said my wife. 'I'm sick of that bloody great heap of hardcore out there. If I wanted to look at rocks I'd have bought a house in the Alps.'

What I'd said about priorities wasn't strictly true. (Thanks, I will have that topped up, if you don't mind.) I didn't want to fill the well in because I'd already started wondering if there was any possible way I could push Hedda down it. It had become a murder weapon, and to fill it up with hardcore now would be like dropping one's only gun into the Thames off Westminster Bridge.

Hedda hadn't made a will, but so what? As her widower, I'd get the lot. All through those hot weeks of summer while I stalled about the well, I kept thinking of Lindsay in a bikini on Hedda's private beach in Minorca – only it'd be my private beach – Lindsay entertaining guests in the drawing-room in Kensington, Lindsay looking sweet among the herbaceous borders at the farm, *my* farm. And never a harsh word from her or a snide crack. I'd never again be made to feel that somehow I'd got an invisible apron on. Or be expected to – well, accede to distasteful demands when I'd got a headache or was feeling tired.

But how do you push an able-bodied woman of thirty-eight, five feet ten, a hundred and fifty-two pounds, down a well? Hedda's an inch taller than I am and very powerful. Bound to be, I suppose, the T-bone steaks she eats. Besides, she never goes into the garden except to walk across it from the garage to the back kitchen door when she's put her Lincoln Continental away. I thought vaguely of getting her drunk and walking her out there in the dark. But Hedda doesn't drink much and she can hold her liquor like a man.

So the upshot of all this thinking was – nothing. And at the beginning of this month Lindsay went off for her three weeks' holiday to her sister in Brighton. I'd no hope to give her. Not that she'd a suspicion of what was going on in my mind. I wouldn't have involved a sweet little innocent like her in what was, frankly, a sordid business. As we kissed goodbye, she said:

'Now, remember, darling, you're to be extra specially loving to Hedda and get her to settle a lump sum on you. Then afterwards, when it's all signed, sealed, and settled, you can ask for a divorce.'

I couldn't help smiling, though I felt nearer to tears. When you come across ingenuousness like that, it revives your faith in human nature. And when you come to think of it, old man, what an angel! There she was, prepared to endure agonies of jealousy thinking of me making love to Hedda, and all for my sake. I felt pretty low after she'd gone, stuck at the farm with Hedda moaning about not knowing how to get through all her work without a secretary.

However, a couple of days bashing away at the typewriter with two fingers decided her. She couldn't get a temp typist down in Sussex, so she'd go back to Kensington and get a girl at vast expense from the nearest agency. I wasn't allowed to go with her.

She stuck her head out of the Lincoln's window as she was going off up the drive and pointed to the heap of hardcore.

'Faith doesn't move mountains,' she bawled. 'The age of miracles is past. So let's see some goddamned action!'

Charming. I went into the house and got myself a stiff drink. (Thanks, I don't mind if I do.) It was fair enough being alone at the farm, though painful in a way after having been alone there with Lindsay. A couple of postcards came from her – addressed to us both, for safety's sake – and then, by a bit of luck, she phoned. Of course, I was able to tell her I was going to be alone for the next three weeks, and after that she phoned every night.

Remember how marvellous the weather was last week and

the week before? Not too hot, but ideal for a spot of heavy engineering in the open air. I was just resigning myself to the fact that I couldn't put off filling in the well a day longer when I got this brilliant idea.

Oddly enough, it was television that inspired me. Hedda doesn't care for watching television, though we've got two big colour sets which she says, if you please, that she bought for my benefit. I hardly think it becomes her to turn up her nose at the medium considering what a packet she's made out of getting serials on it. Be that as it may, I don't much enjoy watching it with her supercilious eye on me, but I'm not averse to a little discriminating viewing while she's away. It must have been the Friday night I saw this old Hollywood film about some sort of romantic goings-on in the jungle. Dorothy Lamour and Johnny Weissmuller, it was that old. But the point was, there was a bit of wild animal trapping in it, and the way the intrepid hunter caught this puma thing was by digging a trough right on the path the hapless beast frequented and covering it up rather cunningly with branches and leaves.

It struck me all of a heap, I don't mind telling you. The occasion called for opening a bottle of Hedda's Southern Comfort. In the morning, a wee bit the worse for wear, I spied out the land. First of all I needed a good big sheet of horticultural polythene, but we'd already got plenty of that for the cloches in which I was going to have a stab at growing melons. Next the turfs. I drove over to Kingsmarkham and ordered turfs and the best-quality gravel. The lot was delivered on Monday.

By that time I'd got all the surrounding ground levelled and raked over, smooth as a beach after the tide's gone out. The worst part was getting rid of the hardcore. Hedda was damned right about faith not moving mountains. It took me days. I had to pick up every chunk by hand, load it on to my wheelbarrow and cart it about a hundred yards to the only place where it could be reasonably well concealed, in a sort of ditch between the greenhouse and the boundary wall. Must have been Thursday afternoon before I got it done to my satisfaction. I remember reading somewhere that the human hand is a precision instrument that some people use as a bludgeon. I wish I could use mine as bludgeons. By the time I was done, they looked like they'd been through a mincing machine.

I waited till nightfall – not that it mattered, as there wasn't an observer for miles apart from a few owls and so on – and then I spread the polythene over the mouth of the well, weighting it down not too firmly at the edges with battens. The lot was then covered with a thin layer of earth so that all you could see was smoothly-raked soil, bounded by the house terrace, the really lovely borders of annuals Lindsay and I had made, and the garage at the far end.

I was pretty thankful I'd got those turfs and that gravel well in advance, I can tell you, because the next day when I went to start my new car, I couldn't get a squeak out of it. Moxon's, who service it for me, had to come over from Kingsmarkham and collect it. Some vital part had packed up, I don't know what, I leave all that mechanical stuff to Hedda. But the thing was, I was stranded without a vehicle which rather interfered with my little plan to surprise Lindsay by popping down to Brighton for her last week.

She, of course, was dreadfully disappointed that she wasn't going to get her surprise. 'Why don't I come back and join you, darling?' she said when she phoned that Saturday night.

And get wind of what was going on down the garden path?

'I'd much rather be with you by the sea,' I said. 'No, I'll give Moxon's a ring Monday morning. If the car's ready I'll just have to stagger in to Kingsmarkham on the eleven-fifteen bus and collect it. It's only an hour's run to Brighton. I could be with you by lunchtime.'

'Heaven,' said Lindsay, and so it would have been if Hedda hadn't sprung a little surprise of her own on me. Luckily – with my heavenly week ahead in view – I'd laid all those turfs and made a neat gravel path from the garage to the back kitchen door when, on Sunday night, Hedda phoned. She'd got all her work done, thanks to the efficiency of the temp girl, and she was coming down in the morning for a well-earned rest. By twelve noon she'd be with me.

But I didn't feel dispirited and there didn't seem any point in phoning Lindsay. After all, we were soon going to be together for ever and ever. Before I went to bed I made a final survey of the garden. The path looked perfect. No one would have dreamt it hid a forty-foot death trap going down into the bowels of the earth.

That was last Sunday night, the night the weather broke, if you remember. It was pelting down with rain in the morning, but I had to go out to establish my alibi. I caught the ten-fifteen bus into Kingsmarkham to be on the safe side. When Hedda says twelve noon, she means twelve noon and not a quarter past. But, by God, I was nervous, old man. I was shaking and my heart was drumming away. As soon as the Olive and Dove opened I went in and had a couple of what the doctor would have ordered if he'd been around to do an electrocardiogram. And I chatted up the barmaid to make sure she'd know me again.

At twelve sharp I beetled down to Moxon's. Couldn't have given a damn whether the car was ready or not, but if Moxon's people were talking to me face to face at noon, the police would know I couldn't have been at the farm pushing my wife down a well, wouldn't they? The funny thing was this mechanic chappie said my vehicle had been taken back to the farm already. The boss had driven it over himself, he thought, though he couldn't be sure, having only just got in. Well, that gave me a bit of a turn and I had a very nasty vision of poor old Moxon walking up to the house to find me and . . . However, I needn't have worried. I was just getting on the bus that took me back when I saw Moxon himself zoom by in the Land Rover with the towrope.

It was still pouring when I reached home. I nipped craftily round the back way and in via the garage. Hedda's Lincoln and my little Daf were there all right, the two of them snuggled up for all the world like a couple of cuddly creatures in the mating season.

Out of the garage I went on to my super new path. And it was as I had planned, a big, sagging hole edged with sopping wet turf where the well mouth was. I crept up to it as if something or someone might pop out and bite me. But nothing and no one did, and when I looked down I couldn't see a thing but a bottomless pit, old boy. Never mind the rain, I thought. I'll get into my working togs, clear the well mouth of polythene and other detritus, and call the police. Here is my wife's car, officer, but where is my wife? I suspect a tragic accident. Ah, yes, I have been out all the morning in Kingsmarkham as I can prove to you without the slightest difficulty.

I was fantasizing away like this, with the rain trickling down between my raincoat collar and my sweater, when there came – my God, I'll never forget it – the most ear-splitting bellow from the house. In point of fact, from the kitchen window.

'Where the flaming hell have you been?' Only she didn't say 'flaming', you know. 'Are you out of your goddamned mind? I come here to find the place covered with your filthy fag-ends and not a duster over it for a fortnight. Where have you been?'

Hedda.

I nearly had a coronary. No, I'm not kidding. I had the first symptoms. Dizziness and pain up my left side and in my arm. I thought I'd had it. I suppose the fact is Hedda and I do have a perfect diet, the very best of protein and vitamins, and that stood me in good stead when it came to the nitty-gritty. Well, I sort of staggered up the path and into the kitchen. There she was, hands on hips, looking like one of those whatsits – Furies or Valkyries or something. (Sorry, I've had a drop too much of your excellent Scotch.)

I could have done with a short snort at that moment. I didn't even get a cup of coffee.

'One hell of a landscape gardener you are,' Hedda yelled at me. 'A couple of drops of rain and your famous path caved in. Lucky for you it happened before I got here. I might have broken my leg.'

Her leg, ha ha! Of course I saw what had happened. The water had collected in a pool till the polythene sagged and the battens finally gave way. I would have to run into a wet spell, wouldn't I, after the heatwave we'd been having?

'You didn't put enough of that hardcore down,' said my wife in her psychopathic-bird-of-prey voice. 'Christ, you live in the lap of luxury, never do a hand's turn but for that piddling around the peonies column of yours, and you can't even fill in a goddamned well. You can get right out there this minute and start on it.'

So that's what I did, old man. All that hardcore had to be humped back by the barrow-load and tipped down the well. I worked on it all afternoon in the rain and all yesterday, and this morning I remade the path. It's messed up my back properly, I can tell you. I felt the disc pop out while I was dropping the last hundredweight in.

Still, Hedda had bought me that German hi-fi equipment I've been dreaming of for years, so I mustn't grumble. She's not a bad sort really, and I can't complain my every wish isn't catered for, provided I toe the line. (No, I'd better not have any more. I'm beginning to get double vision, thanks all the same.)

Lindsay? I expect her back on Monday and I suppose we'll just have to go on as before. The funny thing is, she hasn't phoned since last Saturday, though she doesn't know Hedda's back. I called her sister's place this morning and her sister went into a long involved story about Lindsay going off on Monday morning, full of something about a surprise for someone – but then Hedda came in and I had to ring off.

I can use your phone, old man? That's most awfully nice of you. I don't want the poor little sweet thinking I've dropped her out of my life for ever . . .

JULIAN SYMONS

The Birthmark

IT IS often said that doctors know of several undetectable poisons which they never mention in the presence of patients, but in truth these reports are much exaggerated, for they generally refer to beneficial medicines that may have a deadly effect if wrongly used. Insulin injections, for instance, are vital for diabetics but can cause death through hypoglycaemia if injected into a perfectly healthy person. The truly undetectable poisons are discovered by research chemists, and the secrets of them remain buried in their laboratories. Or at least, that is where they should remain.

The use of such a poison was the undoing of Courtney Vance. After the trial and sentence he freely admitted his guilt, complaining to prisoners and warders alike about his bad luck. 'It was perfect, really perfect,' he would say. 'Nothing could possibly go wrong.' Then he would launch into a lengthy account of the affair and just what did, unbelievably, go wrong. Courtney got a life sentence, which with remission generally means nine years in Britain, but he served only three of them. Another prisoner, who had slaughtered his wife and three children with an axe and suffered agonies of remorse ever since, was enraged by the endless repetition of the tale, and Courtney's callousness about the crime. He stabbed Courtney fatally with a shiv made in the prison craft shop where they worked side by side. The axe murderer was sent to Broadmoor, where he in turn bored his doctors with an endless recital of grief about his lost family.

Courtney Vance was in his late thirties at the time of the murder, a senior sales representative for DPN Medical Supplies. The term *salesman* was deprecated, but he was in fact a salesman and a very good one. His manner with the wholesale chemists on whom he called was confident but deferential, impressive both through his grasp of medical detail and his refusal to oversell any product. 'This is something that our wise men think may be helpful in certain arthritic cases,' he would say. 'But they do acknowledge it has limitations, and frankly my own feeling is that there *may* be side effects in certain conditions, although of course I'm not a doctor.'

His smile conveyed, what was already known to many of his customers, that he might have been – could have been – a doctor if mysterious family troubles had not prevented him from taking the final examinations. In fact he had failed his prelims twice, and then given up. Or rather his father, an assistant bank manager, had been told that it would be a waste of money for him to continue.

'They say you've got no application. "Not too bright and lacks application", that was the story at school, and it's the same now. I don't know what you're fitted for, Bill, except to sweep the streets.'

Courtney said truthfully that it had been his father who wanted him to be a doctor, and he hoped it would not come to sweeping the streets. What did he feel inclined for? Some kind of journalism perhaps, certainly something that wasn't tied down to regular hours in an office or a doctor's surgery. He had half a dozen jobs in as many years after giving up medicine, and left or failed at all of them, before being taken on for a trial period by DPN. There he was a success from the start, and at the time of the murder had been with them for ten years. He worked from home, which was an outer suburb of London called Warners Green, although he was required to spend four weeks each year at the laboratories outside Northampton where new products were tested, and another four at conferences where selling points were emphasised. He much enjoyed these occasions, when he impressed everybody by his authoritative manner, which was combined always with deference to superiors.

It was shortly after he got the DPN job that he married

Evelyn Bridges, whom he had known at school. Her father was understood to be something influential in the City. Certainly he always wore a bowler hat when he drove up every day from Warners Green to town in his Mercedes, except on days when the Mercedes was to be seen outside the local golf club. His wife drove a small Lancia. 'They're a two-car family,' Mr Vance senior said when his son told him he had been accepted by Evelyn. 'It's a good marriage, son.' His wife wiped her eye, and said it seemed like fate that they should have met again. Evelyn, like Courtney (who had by now discarded his first name of William, always detestably abbreviated to Bill) was an only child.

In fact fate had received some assistance from Courtney. After that first chance renewal of acquaintance at a local Conservative Club dance he had sensed that Evelyn was his for the taking, and had courted her assiduously. He was in his late twenties, and had been thinking that it was time for marriage. This was even truer of Evelyn, who was a couple of years older, plump, placid, and plain. In a physical sense she was hardly a catch, but there was the Mercedes, the Lancia, that 'something in the City' aura of money. It was a church wedding, the reception for a hundred and fifty people was held at the best local hotel, Mr Bridges paid for a honeymoon in Paris. He waved aside Courtney's thanks. 'You're one of the family now, m'boy.'

Being one of the family, however, did not bring the benefits Courtney had hoped for, even expected. When Mr Bridges had a heart attack and died on the golf course a couple of years later, the bowler hat proved to have been, as one might say, a deception. Whatever Mr Bridges had been in the City it was something not very important, or not very profitable. He had lived consistently above his income. The house had to be sold, the Mercedes went of course, the Lancia was replaced by a Mini, the widow settled down in a small flat. For Courtney and Evelyn there was nothing at all.

It was true, as she said, that they had each other, and by now Courtney had received promotion at DPN. They lived in a neat little semi-detached house in a row of almost exactly similar houses, with a pocket handkerchief garden in front and a bigger patch behind. There were in the first years no children, something which Evelyn regretted but which secretly pleased Courtney. He was a careful, cautious man, and regarded a child as an expense which they really could not afford. This was something Evelyn knew, as she seemed mysteriously to know everything about him. He realized the depth of her understanding when she suggested he should have a vasectomy.

'You know you don't want children,' she said. 'Admit it.'

He found that difficult. 'It isn't exactly that I don't want them, it's what they cost. I've worked it out, and the annual expense when you take everything into account—'

'It doesn't matter. I want us to be happy, Court, that's all.'

'I should like you just to look at these figures, they show the situation so clearly . . .'

Evelyn looked at the figures and said yes, he had the vasectomy, and felt distinctly relieved. They had quite a busy social life. The senior Vances and Mrs Bridges came round to Sunday lunch or supper at regular intervals, and both Courtney and Evelyn were pillars of the local Conservatives. There were socials and bazaars, at homes, tea and supper parties. Evelyn made little scones and cakes and home-made jams, and was an excellent housekeeper, working always within the agreed sum he gave her each month. 'She's just a wonderful little wife, son,' the now retired Mr Vance senior said after a supper party of beef olives, potatoes done in some French manner with cream or butter, and a green salad, all washed down with cheap but flavoursome supermarket wine. Courtney did not dissent, although 'little' was by now a misnomer, for Evelyn enjoyed her own cooking and was distinctly big.

It was because of her size, Courtney told himself, that he indulged in occasional peccadilloes. His success as a salesman for DPN products had led to an extension of his territory, so that he often spent a night or two away from home. On these occasions he looked deliberately for one-night stands, and often found them. These peccadilloes – which was the word he always used to himself about them – did not, he felt sure, affect his marriage. Even so, it was disconcerting to find that Evelyn's ability to understand him extended to them.

'Would you say you married me for my money, Court?' she asked one evening. That was ridiculous, he said, he hadn't had a penny from her family. 'Correction, I should have said in hope of making useful contacts, perhaps daddy getting you into some glamorous job, and finally inheriting a nice little packet when he died.'

'If you put it that way – well, not exactly, but some of those thoughts might have been in my mind.'

'Still, it hasn't worked out badly, has it?' He kissed her and said it had been marvellous. 'No, marvellous isn't the word, but it's been all right. You're doing well, we have a lot of friends, I'm good at running the house—' He interrupted her to say truthfully that she was a wonderful manager. 'Only trouble is, you don't like fat women. Don't interrupt, you know it's true. And I'm fat, can't be helped, something to do with metabolism, I've read it all up. You go on doing your duty, but I know it is a duty. Remember when you used to bring me flowers, give me scent? Not any more. And you're working off some of that surplus energy when you're away for the night. No need to worry about it. I just want you to know that I know, and don't mind, that's all.'

There was something uncomfortable about being so thoroughly understood, but he did not deny what she had said. Instead, he asked how she could put up with him. She said, with a sparkle in her eye, 'Because you're just about the handsomest man I ever saw, that's why.'

At this time Courtney Vance was certainly handsome. In youth he had looked immature and uncertain, but success, confidence, and the passing years had greatly improved his appearance. He looked, he thought himself, like a film star in the days when they dressed well, bathed and shaved often, had hair that was properly brushed and combed – Cary Grant perhaps, with a touch of David Niven. An old-fashioned look? Well, he didn't pretend or wish to be one of your long-haired teenagers in jeans. His thick dark hair was becomingly flecked with grey at the sides, his figure as slim now as it had been when he married, his profile as clear-cut. There was a suggestion of weakness in the wobbly, shapeless mouth, and of self-satisfaction in the way he smoothed his little moustache, but taken all round Courtney Vance was undoubtedly a handsome man, and for many women an attractive one.

A day or two after that conversation Courtney brought Evelyn flowers, and a week later a bottle of 'Magical Night', the tangy fragrance of which had enlivened their honeymoon. Evelyn smiled, thanked him, patted his cheek. He was pleased, but also a little resentful. Did one bring home a bottle of sexy perfume to be patted on the cheek like a child? But he enjoyed his job, admired his wife even though he did not love her passionately. If he had been asked whether he was a contented man he would have said *yes*.

Then, a year before the murder, he acquired a mistress.

Thelma was the American-born wife of a local building contractor named George Hartley, a great bull-necked man with a voice which seemed always to be issuing through a megaphone. Courtney had found himself sitting next to her at a Conservative Club dinner, and they had got on wonderfully well from the start. Not surprisingly perhaps, since almost her first words were: 'I've seen you at meetings often enough, and you know what I've always thought? One day I'm going to be sitting next to that man, and then I'll say it straight out to him.'

'Say what?'

'Tell him he's the most attractive man in the room. There, I've said it.' Dark eyes flashed at him. 'I know Evelyn already, we're on a couple of committees together, she's a honey. But you've got no time for that sort of stuff, I know. Evelyn says you're a busy man.'

He told her what he did, implying that it was only a matter of time before he was invited to join the DPN board. 'And your husband is—'

'Over on the next table. The man with the thickest neck in the room. And the thickest skin. He only thinks about one thing.' There was a pause before she said, 'Money. He's away a lot too.' She turned and faced him directly. She had a high colour, strong features, flaring nostrils. The side of her face that had been turned away from him was marred by a birthmark, going from cheekbone to temple, purplish and menacing. A smile touched her lips, then she turned away abruptly, spoke to her neighbour on the other side. What had she been hinting?

He asked Evelyn about her, casually, tactfully, and learned that Hartley had met her at some convention where she was handling public relations for the English end of an American firm. They had been married within a few months, both for the second time.

'Some of the Tory ladies don't like her. Think she married George Hartley for his money, and that might be true – she's years younger than he is. Then she offers to do this and that, and they think she's pushy. If you ask me they're just jealous, I like her. How old do you suppose she is, thirty?'

'I really hadn't thought.'

'She *is* very direct, says what she thinks. How did you get on?'

'Well enough. She's rather aggressive for my taste.'

'You like everything to run smoothly, no rows, I know that.' She smiled at him. It was true, but he slightly resented her knowing it, and saying so. Indeed he found himself more and more irritated by the way in which Evelyn seemed always to know what he thought in advance.

It has been said that Courtney Vance was a cautious man. He had no wish to do anything that might affect his marriage, his work, or what he thought of as his social position. All the peccadilloes had taken place well away from home, and although he thought about Thelma Hartley and the look she had given him, it was not until she came into the local pub where he was having lunch that he did anything about it. It would have been absurd not to eat their sandwiches and drink their beer together. He asked what she was doing there.

'When George is on a trip and I can't be bothered to cook for one, I often go to a pub. What about you? I thought you were always away.'

'Doing a round of local calls. I'm off on a little tour tomorrow, Surrey and Sussex. I'll be away two or three days.' She said he was lucky. He thought quickly. On the following day his calls would, or could, take him within a few miles of Warners Green. He asked if she would have dinner with him, naming a hotel near enough for her to drive to it, far enough away to make it unlikely that any Warners Green resident would be there.

She drained her beer and said, 'I thought you'd never ask.' The birthmark glowed a fiery red. In some curious way he found this flaw on her otherwise perfect skin attractive.

In the hotel on the following night they did not eat dinner, but went straight up to the room he had booked in the traditional name of Smith. Before the act and after it, Thelma talked. She said that she was bored with the bull, which was what she called her husband, bored with Warners Green, bored with the stuffiness and pettiness of local politics. Courtney said he was bored too, although that was not true.

She walked out naked to the bathroom, showered, came back. 'You've done this kind of thing before.'

'Not *this* kind of thing,' he said, and meant it. Her passion and eagerness was strange to him. Afterwards she had been dripping with sweat. He did not ask about her own experiences, afraid of what he might hear. What followed was not exactly a night of bliss, for Courtney was nervous of such raw excitement as she displayed, but it was certainly a night of a kind outside his knowledge, one he wanted to repeat.

At one moment she said, 'What about Evelyn? You going to tell her?'

He was shocked. 'Good heavens, no. Certainly not. You surely don't intend—'

'To tell the bull? No, he might fly off the handle, though let me tell you, he's no reason to complain. He's got a string of floozies, I've found letters in his pockets. If I wanted to I could take George for half the money he's got.' Her mouth shut like a trap, her natural colour was heightened, the birthmark glowed.

Over the next months there were a dozen occasions when she stayed at hotels with him. Sometimes Hartley was at home, and she had to say no. Courtney then felt deeply frustrated, but he did not seek out other girls in her absence. They had been peccadilloes, this was the real thing, a grand passion.

He was slightly embarrassed by the fact that Thelma and Evelyn became very friendly. Twice he came home from trips during which Thelma had spent a night with him to find her in the living-room.

'She's really interesting,' Evelyn said. 'Got quite a different slant on things. Perhaps it's because she's American.'

'I shouldn't see too much of her if I were you.' He added rather feebly and absurdly that she had a doubtful reputation. He never had a real row with Evelyn – as she had said, he did not care for raised voices – but some acrimonious words passed, and he brought her flowers on the following day. She accepted them with a smile, and patted his cheek.

One night, at a hotel in Brighton, Thelma told him that she and George Hartley had parted. She laughed at his look of shocked surprise.

'Don't look so amazed, these things happen. No need to look worried either, your name hasn't been mentioned. I told you I had the goods on George, it's separation by mutual consent, with what you might call a truly handsome settlement. He wants to marry one of the floozies after the divorce, which won't be yet awhile. Do you know you've got the finest body of any man I've ever seen? Come here and let me make a spot check.'

A little later he said, 'You'll be leaving Warners Green.'

'Right. I've got my eye on a flat in Kensington.'

'That means the end for us.'

'I don't see why.'

But he knew it did. In Kensington, meeting again her sophisticated London friends, public relations people and the like, she would soon forget him. He found the thought of life without her dismaying, and said so. Indeed, he used the word unbearable. She looked at him consideringly.

'We do seem to suit each other, don't we? Much better than most. Be a pity to lose it. But you'll come up to town and see me. And I'll still make little trips out to hotels, I quite enjoy the sordidness.'

They didn't have to lose it at all, he said wildly, they could live together.

'What about Evelyn? I couldn't do that to her, break up her life. She's my friend.'

'I could talk to her, make her understand. She wouldn't want to stand in my way.'

'You're talking rubbish and you know it, Courtney Vance. For me you're a playmate, for Evelyn you're a husband. I don't even know that I like you, I just like what we do. And you might find that this puts you off, when you saw it every day.' She took his hand and put it on the birthmark. He protested that he hardly noticed it. 'Mind you, you're such a pretty playmate that if Evelyn weren't there I might want to have you for keeps. But she is.'

He knew that what she said was true, and went home dejected. Evelyn said, 'It's Thelma, isn't it? I shall miss her too.'

'What do you mean?'

'I know about the two of you, of course I do. Oh, not from Thelma, she's said nothing. I knew what was going to happen when you asked those questions after the dinner.'

'But didn't you *mind*?'

'Oh yes, I minded.' Her placid moon face, a double chin now distinctly visible, smiled at him. 'But it seemed to make you happy in ways I couldn't, so I put up with it. A lot of marriage consists of that, putting up with things.'

When Courtney paid his quarterly visit to the laboratories outside Northampton, Thelma was still living in Warners Green. She had moved out of her husband's pretentious neo-Gothic house, but the Kensington flat was still the subject of argument about the lease. Evelyn had suggested that she should move into their spare bedroom, but the idea shocked Courtney, and he rejected it out of hand. So Thelma was staying with a niece of her husband's, but she saw Evelyn almost every day.

On the drive up to Northampton Courtney felt he was escaping from an awkward and slightly ridiculous situation. He had been altogether bowled over by Thelma, but could see no chance of a permanent relationship with her while Evelyn was there, and he quite accepted that Evelyn would always be there. The thought of Evelyn's death, and the possibility that he might cause it, never entered his mind. If he had ever considered such a thing he would have rejected the idea as far too dangerous. It might rather fancifully be said – and afterwards Courtney often and tediously said it – that Heinz Muller turned Courtney Vance into a murderer.

Heinz was an experimental research chemist, who was allowed to be a law unto himself within the firm. He was the chief of something called the Possibilities Ambit Laboratory, called Pal for short, where ideas derived from articles in scientific papers all over the world were tried out. Most of them never got beyond the testing stage, but every so often Heinz came up with a winner, something that could plausibly be called a variant on an existing product or technique, and was marketed successfully. He was unmarried, a Pickwickian little man with merry eyes behind gold-rimmed glasses, a hard drinker and inveterate womanizer. He and Courtney had got along well from the first time they met, and had done some peccadilloing together.

On this visit Courtney went as usual round the various labs, including Pal, talking to the scientists and technicians about what was in the pipeline. In Pal he was greeted warmly. Heinz showed him blends of this or that bubbling in retorts, rats and mice injected with various serums that made their behaviour depressed or manic, caused or were meant to cure skin infections and various deseases. At one end of the lab were little jars and bottles of possibilities promising enough for full-scale testing. Most would be found to have undesirable side effects, with luck one or two might be considered for marketing. Heinz talked about them all with enthusiasm, little eyes gleaming. Courtney knew enough to ask informed questions, and he was genuinely interested. Heinz picked up two bottles, one large containing a cloudy liquid, the other small with liquid of a clear yellow colour. He held up the large bottle, which was labelled *Noscan*.

'*Very* promising, *quite* revolutionary, amazing. You know pregnant women now all have the maternity scan to see where the baby is positioned, and so on? But it can have bad effects if repeated, so some doctors say. You take Noscan, and you can forget the scan. After a dose of it everything shows as clear as if it were an etching.'

'What's the snag?'

Heinz looked comically offended. 'I do not say there is any snag. There is perhaps a little local difficulty, a matter of adjustment.'

'How do you mean? What's in the other bottle?' The small bottle was labelled simply NX.

Heinz chuckled. 'Pure poison.' He might have been Mr Pickwick enjoying a Christmas game at Dingley Dell. 'I read an article by a German scientist about the properties of the juice of the beloa shrub which grows in the Brazilian rain forests. The Indians there use it mixed with mud to heal wounds and sores, and they think it is magical, a cure for everything under the sun. I don't tell you how I get it, but this is pure beloa juice. No colour, no taste, but pure poison. You handle it with kid gloves, as they say. Spread a little on your handkerchief and inhale it, let a few drops go on the skin, and – phut, you are dead. No pain, no symptoms, no traces, just dead.' He laughed heartily.

'Then it's surely no use.'

'Ah, that is the local difficulty, the adjustment needed. It is the beloa juice that makes the etching, you understand. We have to find out how to counteract its poisonous effects, yet it must remain effective. We cannot be like the Indians and mix it with mud, it has to be a liquid. So we tried different mixtures. This is Noscan 7, the seventh mixture. We tried the first six on mice, rabbits, guinea pigs.'

'With what effect?'

'They all died. That is our local difficulty. But enough of Noscan; shall we see each other this evening? Go out on the town? I have arranged a little something.'

Heinz came round to Courtney's hotel after dinner, they had drinks and talked. Then they met two of what Heinz called his professional amateurs, housewives ready to make a little extra money, but in the end Courtney declined the chance of a peccadillo, feeling a guilt about being unfaithful to Thelma which had never touched him in relation to Evelyn. Muller took one of the professional amateurs back to his apartment, but Courtney gave money to his and apologized for not being in the mood.

He spent a sleepless night. It was true he had accepted that Evelyn would always be there, but that was based on the belief that anything else was impossible. She had known about and tolerated the peccadilloes, known about and tolerated Thelma, what was it she had said? 'Marriage consists of putting up with things.' He saw years and years of toleration ahead, years in which she would get monstrously fat, plumping up like a giant cushion. And she would know always, as she seemed to, just what he was thinking and doing, and would put up with it. The prospect appalled him. And in the back of his mind there echoed those words of Thelma's: 'If Evelyn weren't there I might want to have you for keeps.' He changed it mentally to *I long to have you for keeps*.

All this – he had to be honest with himself and admit it – would never have come to the front of his mind but for Heinz's talk about Noscan and the little bottle of NX. He had asked one or two questions – casually, quite casually – while they waited for the professional amateurs, and Heinz had been delighted to expand on his discovery. The poison worked by inhalation, by drinking, by contact with the skin. It caused no pain (very important, Courtney thought, he would never have considered anything painful), and left no traces (equally important). Rabbits and guinea pigs just keeled over, suffering heart failure. (Evelyn was overweight.)

Courtney thought and thought about it. He was a cautious man, and if there have been the smallest possibility of detection he would never have considered the idea. But there was no such possibility. If Heinz had exaggerated and the whole thing failed, nobody would know.

The problem, then, was to get access to the bottle without being seen by Heinz. But there again, he told himself, if no opportunity arose he would take it as a sign that he should leave the whole thing alone, having nothing to do with it. Nonetheless he prepared himself by buying a tiny phial, a little pipette, a pair of rubber gloves.

In the end that particular problem was solved with absurd ease, as if by destiny. He always stayed three days at the laboratories, and on each day visited Pal to chat with Heinz. On the last day Heinz's assistant was on the next floor searching for some records in the library, and Heinz was called to the telephone so that he was alone in the laboratory. The little bottle was three-quarters full. He put on the rubber gloves, poured no more than half an inch of liquid into his phial, stoppered it. The operation took no more than a few seconds. He was pleased to see the total steadiness of his hand.

After that, the car of destiny bore him onwards. If he had any doubts about the need for action they were removed when, on his return, he found Thelma installed in the spare bedroom. The Kensington lease was still presenting problems, Thelma had had a row with the niece, Evelyn thought it only right that she should come and stay.

'After all, Thelma's almost one of the family,' Evelyn said in the placid unshockable way that succeeded in shocking, and even disgusting him. Thelma looked at him with sparkling dark eyes, and seemed amused by his reaction. The limit came when, a couple of nights after his return, Evelyn said, 'If you want to go in to Thelma tonight, I shall understand.'

He was horrified. 'Certainly not. Under our roof, how can you suggest such a thing?'

'What does it matter whose roof you're under?'

He could not explain. The essence of his affair with Thelma was its romantic, exciting quality. To fornicate with another woman, with his wife's knowledge and compliance, in their own home – the idea was unthinkable. The suggestion removed any lingering doubt about the need for action, sealed Evelyn's fate.

Evelyn had used up her 'Magical Night'. He bought another bottle, unscrewed it, and with the utmost care added the contents of his phial. When he gave it to her she thanked him, then said with her placid smile that they had had few magical nights lately.

He was going away on the following day, and said with what he felt was false heartiness that if she used it on the day he returned – or even before, if she felt inclined, in preparation as it were – they would see what they would see. He hoped that with this hint the affair, which was the word he preferred to use, would be over before his return. It seemed wise to be absent, and if Heinz should have been mistaken and the procedure was *not* painless, he feared that he might be unduly distressed.

He was therefore not greatly surprised when, on the third evening of his four-day tour, he was told that Inspector Jezzard was in the hotel lobby, and would like to see him. He was prepared to show shock and a touch of grief, the speech ready prepared. 'Good God, Inspector, I can hardly believe it. Evelyn seemed perfectly well when I left home, but of course, now that I think of it, she'd complained of what we both thought were indigestion pains.'

The speech, however, was never made. The Inspector, a sharp-eyed, sharp-nosed man accompanied by a Sergeant, said, 'Mr Courtney Vance? I have a warrant for your arrest on the charge of wilful murder of one Thelma Hartley – hold up, man.'

Courtney Vance had fainted clean away.

His bewilderment was total. How could it conceivably have happened? At first he tried to fence with the Inspector, discover how much he knew. How was Courtney accused of administering this co-called poison?

'No point in playing games, Mr Vance. You know very well it was contained in a bottle of scent called "Magical Night".'

'And you have been able to isolate the poison in the bottle?'

The Inspector smiled, not pleasantly. 'We know where it came from. We know you abstracted a certain amount of a highly toxic plant poison known as NX from your firm's laboratory, and added it to the bottle of scent.'

'I don't accept that for a moment, but I ask again, have you been able to isolate the poison you say is in that bottle?' There was no reply. Heinz had been right, it was undetectable. 'If not, how can you be sure it was present.'

'In the most practical way. Very small quantities from the bottle have been added to food given to rats and mice. They died within half an hour. Painlessly, I understand.'

This was a shock. Perhaps he should have been present at the time after all, to remove the bottle, pour away the contents. The Inspector continued. 'When we contacted your friend at the laboratory, Mr Muller, he confirmed that the effect was exactly that of this particular poison. He then checked the NX bottle and confirmed also that the level was lower than it should have been, although the fact had not previously been noticed.'

But why, why did you have any suspicion at all, he longed to ask? Instead he said, 'I admit I gave a bottle of "Magical Night" to Evelyn. I certainly didn't give one to Mrs Hartley.'

'It is not suggested that Mrs Hartley was the intended victim. That was your wife.'

'Then how—'

'Mrs Vance seems to have suspected some joke on your part, a cruel joke she said. According to her, you had an intimate relationship with Mrs Hartley. Do you wish to comment on that? It isn't important, since we have been able to check on some of the hotels where you stayed together. The bottle was meant for your wife. She gave it to Mrs Hartley, saying something to the effect that it had not secured any magical nights for her. Mrs Hartley laughed, opened the bottle, sniffed it, dabbed a little on her hand, then on her face. Within a few minutes she collapsed, in less than an hour she was dead.'

Had Evelyn suspected, had her uncanny understanding of him gone so far that she realized he meant to do her harm, and deliberately passed on the bottle? It was something he never knew.

'And then?'

'Your wife called a doctor. By the time he arrived Mrs Hartley was dead, apparently from heart failure. The death would have been accepted as natural, but for one remarkable thing. It was something your wife noticed. Once it had been pointed out, it was clear that something must be wrong, and that further investigation was needed. We were called in, and took it from there.'

'Yes,' he said. '*Yes?* What was it?'

The Inspector smiled again. 'I think Mr Muller told you not only how powerful NX was, but also of its remarkable properties?'

'He did, but what then? What was it Evelyn saw?'

'It was rather what she did not see. Mrs Hartley had a red birthmark on one side of her face. She had dabbed a few drops of scent near to it. What your wife noticed was that, within a minute or two of the liquid being applied, the birthmark had completely disappeared.'

DAVID WILLIAMS

The Other Woman

'THANKS Gary. You can kiss me if you want,' she said. And all I had to do was step closer. She did the rest: the first time, at least.

Well, she took me a bit by surprise: even me. It was only my second day in the job. We were in the master bedroom. I'd just driven her back from Guildford. She'd sat with me in the front of the Jag.

On the inward journey, her husband had been with us and they'd both been in the back. We'd dropped him at the station, then she'd gone shopping. She hadn't said much in the car; just watched me a lot, especially my hands. I'd taken the dress-shop bag upstairs as she'd ordered. It wasn't a heavy bag. I mean, she could have managed it herself: no strain. I'd wondered if she had anything else in mind. Then I'd thought, no such luck. I was wrong about that – if you'd call everything else that happened lucky.

'Not bad at all,' she said, taking her mouth off mine, as if I was something she'd just eaten. Except the words had sounded more like a challenge than a compliment; that she'd expect me to do better next time. She hadn't let go of me either. 'So when are you picking up Rick?'

'At five.' Up to then, I'd called her madam; now it didn't seem right, not with the way she was groping me.

'Five? So what you waiting for?' She swivelled in my arms. 'Undo my zip. Silly boy.'

She was a fantastic lover.

'You really a public-school drop-out?' she asked later, when we were just lying on the open bed: it was mid-June, and very hot. She was smoking a cigarette.

'I dropped out *after* school,' I told her. The public-school bit always created interest – because I was a chauffeur.

Not that I'd ever been near a public school, but the idea went with the posh accent. I'd worked a lot on the accent since leaving my comprehensive in Manchester.

'My husband was impressed with your Army service,' she said.

I'd guessed that much. And my service record was pretty accurate: it needed to be, because it was easy to check – not like the other stuff. Like a few of the references, for instance. People never check on references. If they checked mine they'd find most of the writers had gone abroad or died.

But the story of my five years in the REME was kosher. The Army taught me everything I'd ever need to know about car engines – enough to be an overworked fitter in a garage if I'd wanted. Only the part about refusing to go forward for a commission was invented.

'Why didn't you want to be an officer?'

I knew she'd be asking that. It works every time, especially with the birds. 'I didn't want the responsibility,' I said. 'I like my freedom. It's why I stopped soldiering in the end, too.'

The last part was mostly true. Fact is, I've never really been a drop-out. I'm just someone who uses his skills to work for the biggest return over the shortest period, and always with an eye to the main chance. But that's not the kind of thing you mention at a job interview.

Her husband was Colonel Rick Brota, mercenary extraordinary. He was retired, or else the call for hired assassins had dried up. That was what some locals in the village pub had said to me the night before. They didn't seem to like him.

I'd known already that Brota's speciality was masterminding military coups on islands where the government troops were underequipped or potentially disloyal, or both. He'd done a bit of the same in submergent Central Africa too. He hadn't always been successful. Except the word was, win or lose, he got paid in advance. The 'freedom fighters' he'd worked for were always well bankrolled.

You could tell Brota had done well, from the shapes of his house and his wife. Mark you, he was getting on – over sixty I reckoned, and writing his memoirs. With one eye and one arm lost along the way (he wore a black eye-patch but no artificial substitute for his right arm) he looked a bit of a crock, and he couldn't have been exactly a dashing military figure to begin with. He wasn't British for a start: Spanish or Portuguese I'd guessed, up to then. He was small, gaunt, wizened, and asthmatic. He hardly ever spoke.

Of course, if he'd been in better nick I wouldn't have risked taking instant liberties with his wife.

The house was stockbroker Tudor, air-conditioned throughout, with five acres of grounds, and a chauffeur's flat over the garage. It stood by itself, backing on to woods, on the outskirts of a village south-east of Guildford, about thirty miles from London. I was engaged for chauffeuring and general maintenance. There was a lot of plant and machinery. Beryl, a middle-aged biddy from the village, came in early every day to clean the place and prepare the food. She left at noon and came back at six to cook and serve the dinner. There was a regular gardener on Mondays, Wednesdays, and Fridays.

It was now 1 p.m. on a Tuesday.

'You've got a very sexy body,' she said, fingering bits of it.

'Not as sexy as yours.' I was reciprocating in all senses.

I'd figured she was around thirty-five, three or four years older than me. Her first name was Connie and she was an old-fashioned blonde bombshell. By which I mean she wasn't one of your flat-chested, underfed dollies, held together with eye shadow. She was more the Marilyn Monroe type, if you remember her in her prime – or maybe just a bit past it.

Connie was tallish and well built all over, not fat, but plenty for a man to get hold of. She had big brown eyes, pouty lips, and tousled gold hair that she probably paid a lot to keep looking untamed. You wouldn't call her a raving beauty – her nose was a bit large – but she had real magnetism. She carried herself like an athlete, or a dancer maybe – plenty of energy, with an urgent thrust in the upper leg movements. And she had a grip like steel.

Socially Connie wasn't top-drawer. The heavy Mayfair accent had touches of Bermondsey that the charm school, or whatever, hadn't been able to iron out. It takes one to spot one.

'I've waited a long time for you to come along,' she said later. We'd just finished another little orgy. She was sitting astride me at the time, massaging my chest. She seemed to like doing that.

'You mean you don't screw with all the new chauffeurs?'

Without any warning she slapped me hard across the face. Well I suppose I'd asked for that. Then she slid off me and started weeping, back towards me.

'I'm sorry,' I said. 'I didn't mean that. I was only joking.'

She didn't answer for a bit, just went on sobbing, fit to burst. Then she said: 'You wouldn't joke if you'd been stuck here for five years with a has-been. It's no life for me. We've no friends. He never takes me anywhere. All he wants every night is to listen to Wagner recordings. And that's *really* all.' She turned to look at me. 'And I thought you were different. I could see you were interested. When we were in the car.' She dabbed at those lovely eyes. 'I'm not promiscuous, just desperate for affection. I have so much to give to anyone who'll really care for me!' She'd ended sounding bitter.

'I've said I'm sorry.' I was, too, for nearly blowing everything. 'So why do you stick it? A gorgeous woman like you?' I kissed her on the forehead.

'Because I used to think the swine couldn't last for ever. There was never any love between us. It was a marriage of convenience. We met through an up-market dating bureau. My previous husband ran out on me. Left me with a load of debt. Rick needed British nationality. He got that through the marriage.'

By now she was recovering pretty fast.

'Why did he need the nationality?' I asked.

'In case they ever try to extradite him.'

'Who?'

'Take your pick. There are half a dozen governments-in-exile who hate his guts. The ones he got deposed. If any of them ever got back in power, they'd want him strung up. After a show trial. It's an obsession with him. But he's sure the British would protect him.'

'So what nationality was he?'

'Argentinian. Only they don't like him either. They'd have shopped him any time. To the first bidder. His first wife died years ago in Buenos Aires when he was away. The death certificate said heart attack. I've seen it. He thinks she was murdered.'

'And he married you to get a British passport? So what did you get out of it?' I knew the answer, but it was polite to ask.

'His money. He's very rich.' Well she was honest, at least. 'As his wife, I get everything. That was the deal. Except he can go back on it. I can't.'

'How can he go back on it?'

'By leaving me. Divorcing me. He's got what he wanted after all. They wouldn't cancel the nationality.'

'But why should he divorce you?'

'Because he's found another woman.'

'You're kidding?' He looked to me hardly capable of a good cough let alone . . .

'I wish I *was* kidding. I had him followed once. To where she lives in London. Afterwards I followed him myself. Twice last month. It's a block of service flats in Victoria. That's where he'll be today. Why he took the train. Otherwise you'd have been driving him. He's deadly secretive about her. Anyway, I've seen her. She's . . . she's older than me.'

That last bit seemed to hurt the most.

'Why not tell him you know?'

'I wouldn't dare. In case he walks out on me.'

'But if he did that, it's you who'd have the grounds for divorce.'

She shook her head. At first I thought she wasn't going to explain, then she said: 'He caught me with a man. It was two years ago. His name was Paul. He's an actor I'd known before.

When I was on the stage. We ran into each other again when he came to Guildford. To the theatre. It wasn't an affair, just a . . . a . . .'

'Renewing of an old acquaintance?' I helped her over the awkward bit.

'That's right. Rick didn't see it that way. He's insanely jealous. Possessive, even though he hardly ever wants me himself. I swore there was nothing lasting with Paul. But Rick made me promise in writing I'd never see him again. And I had to put that Paul and I'd been . . . been to bed together.'

'Pity you did that.'

'I'd no alternative. And now he's got that to hold over me.'

She'd forgiven or forgotten my mistake by this time, and was snuggling in my arms again.

'So what are you going to do?'

'Sometimes I think I'll kill myself. I would, too. Or else kill Rick.'

I didn't take the suicide bit seriously. It sounded too much as if she was playing for sympathy. And the idea of killing her husband was even less believable, at the time.

It seemed to me she was a highly sexed, unsatisfied wife urgently in need of regular relief. So who better than Gary Powell to provide the necessary? And there were long-term possibilities on the cards as well. The job was going to be even more perfect than I'd hoped. The wages were well over the odds, with short basic hours, and paid overtime to include all weekend work. Brota wasn't mean in that department. I had my own furnished flat, and the off-duty use of a four-year-old Honda 450 c.c. motorbike.

It was the sort of billet I'd been after for years. And while keeping madam happy would be no effort, I'd make sure I wasn't caught at it like Paul, her actor friend.

Meeting discreetly was easy – even on the days the gardener was around. There was no joy in the mornings because of the daily woman, but the afternoons were a cinch. Brota always slept a while then, if he was home. Later he'd go to his study and work on his memoirs. Connie would slip up to the flat, usually while he was sleeping. There was a door into the garage off the kitchen, and an inside stairs from the garage up to the flat, so no one ever saw her.

She still kept on about how miserable and trapped she was – and worried about Brota leaving her for this older bird. It was because I couldn't credit the other woman really existed that Connie finally got me to follow Brota and see for myself.

On the days I drove him to London – once or twice a week – I knew there was no chance he was seeing a woman. The routine was dead regular. In the morning I'd drop him at the British Library in Bloomsbury, pick him up and take him to his club in Pall Mall for lunch, then back to the library, and home from there at five. Sometimes it was other libraries or museums he worked in, but the routine was the same. I mean, this life story he was doing was serious work. Connie said he needed it to throw a whitewash over his gruesome past: she kept saying it.

Anyway, she was right about what he did in London when he went by train. On the day I mentioned, Connie drove him to Guildford station in her own car. She made the excuse that she'd sent me off early on an important errand on the Honda. That was nearly right, too. I was parked opposite the house in Victoria when Brota arrived there in a taxi.

He didn't stay long; about half an hour. But when he left, the woman was with him. Connie was right. Her rival might have been a bit older, but that was the only minus. She was quite a looker – very dark, good figure, and the face of a madonna. They got into a taxi. I followed closely on the Honda. With the crash helmet on, my own mother wouldn't have spotted me. We finished up in Bedford Row. They went into a lawyer's office there and stayed two hours.

That convinced me.

Meantime my affair with Connie was getting pretty torrid. I was crazy about her. She behaved in bed like no one else I'd ever known; don't get me wrong, but she had a real professional touch. The idea of losing her for any reason got to be unthinkable. You know how that can happen to a man with a very special woman?

'There's a way we could be together for always,' she said to me one afternoon, as if she was reading my thoughts.

'How, lover?'

We were in my bed in the flat: it wasn't as big as hers in the house, but it was cosier.

'You know what he did for a living?' Connie asked, instead of answering my question.

'He was a mercenary.'

'He murdered without cause or justification. For money.'

'Other soldiers.'

'Soldiers, civilians, women, and children.' She shuddered. 'He didn't discriminate. It's all in the filthy record. The one he's trying to cover up with this obscene biography. How can such a man live with himself?'

'I wonder that as well.'

I remember her pulling her body closer to mine as she said, 'If he committed suicide, no coroner would be surprised. With all that guilt weighing on him. I could say I'd seen it coming for years.'

'He'd never do himself in?'

'But we could make it *look* as if he had! It'd be easy. And think of what we could do after? All that money? Over three million. Plus the house. Just for the two of us?' She thrust her open mouth over mine before I could answer.

In the next ten minutes Connie gave me a fantastic, unforgettable demonstration of what daily life could include, alone with her. It made all our other times together seem tame and lacklustre. It even made the money look simply like the icing on the cake.

It was then that I agreed to murder Colonel Brota.

Connie had the whole thing worked out. She had a dental appointment in London on the following Thursday afternoon. She would arrange with her husband that I should drive her there and back in the Jaguar, in case the treatment was painful.

She knew he wouldn't want to go to town as well on Thursday because he had fixed to go up the day before.

On the day, Connie and I would set off at one fifteen. Close to London, I'd leave the car and switch to the Honda where I'd left it the night before. She would drive on, while I doubled back, stopping in the wood behind the house. I'd hide the bike there, and at two thirty – the time Brota took his nap – slip up to my flat, using the garden gate to the wood. I'd change out of the clothes I was wearing, then go through the kitchen and hide in the hallway until Brota went to his study. He worked at a desk facing the window with his back to the door. He always left the door wide open.

Once he was busy, I'd creep up on him and shoot him with one of his own revolvers through the left side of his head. After I'd made it look like suicide, I'd change clothes again, pick up the Honda, and meet Connie at six o'clock where I'd left her. Later, we'd both swear we'd been together off and on all afternoon; that I'd waited outside in Sloane Street while she was at the dentist, then behind Harrods where she'd have done some shopping.

We'd stop at the service station on the A3 near Esher. Connie would call the house from there. She'd speak to Beryl, the help, who'd be in the kitchen by then. Connie would explain we'd been held up by traffic, and tell Beryl to warn Brota in case he got worried.

It was tough on Beryl, but she was a solid citizen, well able to stand shocks. We both agreed it was definitely better that we didn't find the body ourselves.

Connie had thought of everything. She even had a ready-made suicide note. It was a card written in Brota's own hand that said: *Forgive me. Rick*. It wasn't perfect, and it wasn't new, but it looked convincing enough. It was a note he'd done to go with some flowers he'd brought her after a quarrel three years before. She'd saved it; afterwards, I wondered if she'd been planning her husband's 'suicide' all that time ago. I was to plant the note after I'd done the shooting.

The gun was no problem. There were four hand-guns in the

house – two service revolvers, and two small automatics. One of the automatics was in the bedroom, but the others were kept in a locked drawer in the study: Connie had a duplicate key. It was she who decided I should use one of the revolvers, a single-action Webley .45. If Brota really had shot himself, she said, he'd have used a heavy gun: he thought of automatics as weapons for women. This was all right with me: I knew how to handle an Army revolver; except I'd never shot anyone before.

Somehow Connie had me feeling that in wasting Brota I was doing a public service. I suppose it was easier to think I was avenging all those women and children he'd liquidated.

When it came to it, the first part of the plan went like clockwork.

At three I was standing in the hall closet, watching Brota go into his study for what was to be the last time. Five minutes later I crept in behind him. He was bent over his work. There were open books all over the desk. He wrote everything in pencil, with his head close to the paper. He didn't wear glasses for his working left eye. The carpet was thick. I had on rubber sneakers. I know I made no sound getting up behind him. I moved slightly to his left as I started to raise the gun. I was holding it with both gloved hands: it was already cocked.

It was then that he sensed I was there. I'm certain it was nothing he heard: it was his training or something – uncanny. With no warning, without looking round, he rammed his chair backwards into me, throwing his body forward and downwards, twisting around clockwise, to the right, scattering books and papers like confetti.

The next moment he was crouched in the knee-hole of the desk; then he was starting at me like a spring uncoiling – and there was a bloody great flick knife gleaming in his only hand. The chair had caught me in the groin, off-balance, and off-guard. I'd fallen back, nearly fallen over, but I didn't panic. It stayed in my mind that I had the best weapon, that I had to shoot him, that I had to shoot him close-to, and that nothing else would fit for a self-inflicted wound.

Although I was scared, I let him come at me. He'd used the

chair again, jumping on to it, levering off the seat as if a cat, so he ended aiming himself downwards at me, like he was flying. He didn't shout or speak: just made sharp groaning breaths that I'll never forget.

For a split second I didn't move; then I ducked and feinted to the left. As he passed me, I brought up the revolver again, double-handed, and squeezed the trigger. The gun went off with a roar. I thought the muzzle was pretty close to his head.

Brota hit the floor with the far side of his skull exploded by the exit wound. There was blood splattered all over him – none of it mine, though. It had been a good try for an older guy, but he hadn't touched me. I'd managed to stay out of knife range. He'd been leading with his left, it was all he had to lead with, poor sod. I'd dodged the other way.

I'd dodged to my left.

It only came home to me the second time. Even then I had to look again before it sunk in.

His skull was a mess all right, because of the heavy calibre of the weapon – except the clean bullet entry hole was on the right side of the head. I'd missed out on one thing when he'd turned on me.

I suppose I'd been so obsessed about getting the gun close, and so thrown at his resisting at all, I'd forgotten I had to shoot him on the left side. Not that I could have done much else anyway. If I'd feinted the other way, he'd probably have got me with his knife.

As I moved the chair behind the body, I was telling myself that a man with only a left arm just might decide to shoot himself through the right temple.

I kept telling myself that.

Otherwise things weren't a lot different from the way we'd planned.

I didn't try putting him into the chair. It would have to look as if he pushed it back, stood up and turned around before he'd shot himself. I left him exactly where he'd fallen, being careful not to step where there was any sign of blood. There was some blood on the sleeves of my shirt, but I'd allowed for that.

I took the flick knife from Brota's hand, and put the gun in its place. I wiped the knife, closed it, and put it on the desk, then buried it under books I picked up off the floor. It was where it must have been at the start.

I left the suicide note on the desk blotter – lying on the centre of a clean sheet of paper.

Going back to the flat, I took off the shirt and jeans and made a bundle of them. I put on my chauffeuring clothes again, under my bike gear, all except my suit jacket which was in the car.

I left the property the same way I'd come, without being seen by anyone: I was sure of it. Once on the road, I was just another motorcyclist buried under tin-lid and ton-up gear. I stuffed the clothes bundle into a half-full builder's skip outside a clearance job.

I was back at the meeting place ahead of Connie. We'd fixed it that way so she wouldn't be seen sitting in a big parked car, looking conspicuous on the edge of Wimbledon. It was safe enough to leave the bike there. She was over the moon that I'd done the job. She wasn't so pleased when I told her exactly where I'd shot him, not any more than I was. We'd both known the importance. After a bit, she agreed the police would accept that Brota had chosen to shoot himself in a cack-handed way – because what other explanation was there?

Connie made the phone call at the service station.

'OK?' I asked, when she got back in the car.

'It should be, in a minute,' she said. 'When Beryl gets to the study.'

'If she rings the police straight away, they ought to be there in ten minutes.' I was timing it so we'd be home in half an hour.

Connie didn't say anything for a bit.

'You all right?' I asked later. She was frowning.

'Look, in case anything goes wrong, that's for both of us, or just one of us, let's make a pact.'

'About what?'

'The money. Rick's money.' She paused. 'Half each.'

'But we'll be spending it together,' I was trying to be cheerful, but I knew what was in her mind, and why. It was I who'd cocked things up.

'I mean *if* things go wrong, if one of us has to skip, or anything. We should be prepared.'

'And by "anything", you mean me ending up in the nick?' I said, and I wasn't joking.

'That could happen to both of us. But if it does, or just to one of us, when it's over, still half each?'

'That's fair.' What she meant was if I got rumbled, and she didn't, my half would be waiting for me when I'd done time. 'But I still don't see—'

'And neither of us admits anything,' I remember her interrupting, her voice very firm. 'Whatever happens, we agree to stick to the story?'

'Sure.'

I think my optimism started draining from then.

When we got to the house there were two police cars, two ordinary cars, and an ambulance in the drive. Beryl had done her bit.

Connie acted as if she'd been born to the part. Surprise, shock, horror, hysterics, all came in the right order. In no time she was being helped to her bedroom, weighed down with inconsolable grief. It was left to me to explain where we'd been, except Beryl had done a good advance job over that too. I was just as bowled over as the loving wife, but in a manly, loyal way.

'Yes, the colonel had been depressed. For the last three days,' I answered the direct question. It seemed to satisfy them at the time. 'I couldn't say whether he had frequent fits of depression. I've only been employed here five weeks.' Then they wanted to know how I'd got the job, where I'd worked before, and before that. They seemed almost as impressed with the Army bit as Brota had been. I didn't bother with the up-market trimmings, though.

The questions appeared pretty routine, but they went on a bit: 'Yes, I knew the colonel had been a mercenary,' and, 'No, there hadn't been any visitors expected that afternoon,' and again, 'No, I hadn't seen any strangers hanging about the place.'

There were two of them doing the asking, both CID – a Detective Inspector Stewart and a Detective Sergeant Montgomery.

'It's pretty certainly suicide, Mr Powell,' the inspector said, like he was taking me into his confidence. 'But we have to check all possibilities, you understand?'

'Of course,' I said, relaxing a bit.

'Where's the motorbike, Mr Powell?' Montgomery asked suddenly.

I'd been ready for that one. I said I'd taken it to Wimbledon the night before, to a special dealer, because of a dodgy clutch I couldn't fix myself. But the dealer had been closed. So I'd left the bike and thumbed a lift back, not wanting to risk any more damage to the gearbox.

'You didn't use it this afternoon?' That was the sergeant again.

'No. How could I? I was driving Mrs Brota.'

'Of course,' Stewart chipped in. He nodded, and smiled before he changed the subject. 'The colonel and his wife, what sort of terms were they on?' he asked. 'Good terms, would you say?'

'Very good terms. Very loving. So far as I could see. But like I said, I haven't been here that long.' I didn't want to overdo it.

And that was nearly it. I had to give them a timetable of where we'd been in the afternoon, and they wanted to know exactly where the Honda was, as well as its licence number. More routine, the inspector said. They didn't mention exactly how Brota had shot himself. There was nothing said either about how the shot was fired, or about his only having one arm – the wrong one for aiming a gun at the right temple.

There were police about the place till nearly midnight. They left then. The body had been taken away earlier. It looked as if it was all over, except they locked and sealed the study – door and windows. Said it would have to stay that way till after the inquest: it was understandable, I thought.

Connie was left to herself, but not totally alone. The local doctor came, and gave her a sedative. He said she should have someone sleeping in the house for the night. Beryl volunteered, so we had no celebration that night – not that we'd have risked it in any case.

Stewart and Montgomery came back next morning at eight thirty. I was hosing the Jag when they arrived. They waved to me but didn't speak. It was a detective constable who came later who asked to see my crash helmet and the rest of my bike gear. His car was pulling a trailer: the Honda was on it.

The two senior coppers were in the house for over two hours. When Beryl brought me a cup of coffee at ten thirty – she always did that – she said they'd been alone with Connie since before nine.

When they came round to the garage I was doing a job on the work-bench. They asked to talk to me in the flat upstairs. They wanted to know again if I'd used the bike the previous afternoon. I answered the same as before. Then they said someone had been seen getting out of a blue Jaguar in Wimbledon, dressed in identical bike-gear to mine, at one fifty-eight, and then ridden off on a bike like mine. I said it couldn't have been me. Montgomery said Mrs Brota had just had to admit it was me. That I'd left her around two and met her again later.

Apart from sweating all over, wanting to be sick, and wishing the world would stop, I had to think like lightning. If Connie had said that much, she'd have to have been desperate.

I made the decision: 'OK. It's a fair cop,' I said, looking a bit ashamed. 'The colonel never gave me time off in the day. Mrs Brota's more understanding. When I drive her to London, she sometimes drops me off for the afternoon. There's a girl in Croydon I've been seeing if I've got the bike handy. She works nights. It's what happened yesterday. Except I found the girl's gone away.'

'Why didn't you tell us this before, Mr Powell?' Stewart asked.

'Because when we got back, with the suicide and everything, I thought I'd best stick to what we'd have told the colonel. That's if he'd asked.'

'"We" being you and Mrs Brota?'

'I didn't want to let her down, like.'

Montgomery stood up after his boss gave him the nod. 'Mr Powell,' he said, 'I have to tell you we have reason to believe that after you left Mrs Brota, you came back here, concealed the motorbike in the wood, shot Colonel Brota dead, and later rode back to Wimbledon.'

'That's a lie,' I said. 'A diabolic lie.'

But I was convicted of murder three months later.

I never talked to Connie again, but I stuck to our agreement. I never admitted anything: still haven't. I always reckoned it was police harassment that got her saying I'd left the car.

The rest of the evidence was all circumstantial. The shot had been made too far from the right temple for Brota to have fired it himself with his left hand. There were fine traces of his blood on the knife, even though it had been wiped, closed and deliberately hidden under papers on the desk. The house had been locked tight, as always, because of the cooling system, with no signs of a break-in. I was the only one with a key besides Beryl, who'd been at a Mother's Union meeting all afternoon. Two local women had seen a motorbike in the wood when they'd walked a dog there at three. They'd thought it was my bike, and it was gone when they came back later. The ink on the 'suicide note' showed it was more than two years old.

None of these things amounted to that much on its own. But when you put them all together they were enough for a jury – and an appeal court later.

My story is still that I'm the victim of a miscarriage of justice. That way there's always hope that if you keep on, some do-gooder will take up the case, shake somebody's testimony, and get you pardoned: it happens all the time, if you wait for the dust to settle and memories to dim. You have to stick to your testimony, though.

Connie never got implicated. There was a time at the start when I thought she would be for sure. That was when they tried to get me to involve her, saying that if I admitted she put me up to the murder, I'd get a lighter sentence. They said the same to my lawyer. But I couldn't see any real benefit in it, even if I'd been ready to shop her, which I wasn't. Whichever way you looked at it, I'd have had to admit I'd committed a crime in the first place. There was no point in both of us serving time if one could stay in the clear, looking after the money.

They suspected her all right, but no jury would have convicted Connie in her widowhood. The Director of Public Prosecutions must have seen that, even if the police didn't. In the end it was his decision not to charge her, or so my lawyer said. They figured a jury would say I hadn't been around long enough to have had anything going with the colonel's wife, on top of which her grief had everyone convinced. In court it bloody near convinced me. She came there as a prosecution witness against me: that must have been part of the deal with the DPP. Of course, she didn't shop me altogether – only said I'd been off alone for the afternoon. Well, she'd been made to admit that already: I've never found out how. Anyway, I didn't blame her. The foul-up was still down to me.

I think they lost interest in Connie when some*thing*, or some*one*, put them on to a motive for the murder that didn't involve her, and made it seem I'd used her without her knowing. At the end they'd definitely persuaded themselves I'd been put up to the job, as a contract killing, by one of Brota's old enemies, and everyone knew there were plenty of those to choose from. It was why they didn't expect me to grass. My being an ex-soldier fitted, too.

I thought even if I had to do eight years of the 'life' sentence before parole, I still had something to look forward to. I didn't include Connie as part of the something: that was being realistic, especially after her actor friend Paul got permission to see me following the appeal hearing. He was a good-looking bloke, officer class from birth: I could see that. Connie had sent him to tip me the wink that my share would be waiting as promised. At the same time he made it pretty clear I wasn't to expect a share of Connie as well.

So imagine the surprise when I saw this law report in the

paper. It said Mrs Eva Brota, second wife of Colonel Rick Brota, had been to court to claim the whole of her husband's estate. Fair enough I thought at first, wondering why she'd had to go to court, and why they'd got her first name wrong. But it went on to say it was Connie who'd *lost* the case. It was then I noticed there were pictures of two women. I recognized the dark one as well, from the time I followed her and Brota from Victoria to the lawyers.

This Eva had been his second wife all right, with an Argentine wedding licence to prove it. He'd married her, then later deserted her and two children, years ago. That was in some South American outback village, where he'd been hiding while the heat was on. She'd been no more than a peasant then – so she'd improved herself since. But she'd still thought he was dead until a few months before, the same as he must have hoped she was: to my knowledge he'd never mentioned her to Connie.

When Eva found out her husband was alive, and loaded, and living in England, she'd come over demanding maintenance. The report said they'd had 'several meetings alone and with their lawyers to work out a secret settlement'. The circumstances for Brota, it said, had been 'very delicate'.

Well, dying had settled every kind of delicate circumstance for him, but not for her: it also produced an outsize delicate circumstance for Connie.

Brota had been trying to keep Eva's existence quiet to protect his British nationality – because he'd known she was putting that on the line. Eva could prove his marriage to Connie was bigamous, and like all bigamous marriages, the paper said, this one was null and void, 'along with all benefits stemming to either party'. But even though one of those null-and-void benefits was Brota's new nationality, you wouldn't have guessed that could hurt anyone now. It did though. A bigamous wife has no rights.

The report said the judge expressed his sympathy to Connie.

But Eva got all the money.

MARGARET YORKE

Gifts from the Bridegroom

ONLY ten more days to go!

'Are you nervous?' Wendy asked, meeting him by chance in the lunch hour. He had gone into town to buy toothpaste; there never seemed to be time at weekends for such mundane shopping, for every moment had to be spent buying the things Hazel decreed essential to their future married life.

'Why should I be?' Alan answered. He'd known Hazel for over two years; they'd been to Torremolinos together, and had often made love in his bed-sitter. Once, when her parents were away, he'd even stayed overnight at the Elms, giggling with Hazel as they clung together in her narrow bed in the room where a row of stuffed teddy bears gazed down at their transports.

'It's going to be quite a do, isn't it?' Wendy said. 'How many bridesmaids are you having?'

'Three. Hazel's niece, and her friends Linda and Maeve.' He sighed. All three had to be given presents. He'd thought of gold bracelets, but it seemed Maeve wanted a pearl on a chain, and Linda favoured dangly earrings. This problem had yet to be resolved and the gifts purchased.

'Well, I'm sure it will be a great production,' said Wendy. 'Best of luck,' she added. 'I'll be thinking of you on the big day,' and she hurried off to her office.

Her words echoed in his head as he returned to his own, where a pile of papers waited for his attention. If he worked hard and was never made redundant, in forty-two years' time – nearly twice as long as he had lived already – he might be head of a department and retiring with his graduated pension.

Retiring to what?

Why, to Hazel of course.

Through Alan's mind ran images of Hazel as she was now: small, pert, and pretty, a bank clerk with the Midland. He saw also a mental picture of her mother, hair rinsed brassy gold, figure trimly girdled, neat ankles twinkly as, high-heeled on short legs, she stepped about her day, ordaining the lives of her family. Her husband was a civil servant employed by the local authority and they moved in ever-rising circles. Hazel's mother had planned the wedding to the last detail; she had vetted the guest list, not permitting him to include Wendy, with whom he had been at school, because her father ran a betting shop.

A production, Wendy had called the wedding, and it was: like some sort of pageant, Alan thought.

Would Hazel choose his future friends? Alan's mind ranged over the years ahead, past the freedom to make love at will and the honeymoon in Corfu. At first, due to a hold-up in arrangements over the small first-time buyer's home for which they were negotiating, they would be living in his bed-sitter, to Hazel's mother's great chagrin; but later there would be the house, then a bigger one when their finances improved. One day there would be children. He foresaw their regimented lives, their freshly laundered, spotless white socks and shirts, their well-scrubbed faces, their diligently completed homework, all firmly supervised by Hazel. He thought of the comforts he would enjoy: the well-cooked food, the tastefully furnished home for which even now he was committed to paying by instalments. The previous weekend they had chosen an expensive three-piece suite. The salesman at Fisher's Furnishings had said it had been made by one of the foremost firms in the world. Testing its suedette comfort, Alan had wondered; he had wondered, too, about the cooker Hazel had selected, split-level hob and all, which would take up so much space in their tiny kitchen. He thought of the money in his building society account, all pledged in advance for coping with the down payment on the house, and with an effort he turned his mind's eye to Hazel in her bikini, spread out on a Corfiot beach. As he stood, eyes closed, on the marble flooring of the town's new shopping arcade, he felt her soft, responsive body in his arms. All that would be wonderful, he knew; it already was when they had the chance.

But first there was the wedding, that performance which must be enacted to please Hazel and her mother. There would be Hazel's progress on her father's arm up the aisle of the local church, which Hazel herself had visited only once to hear the banns read, and her mother on the other two occasions to show willing to the vicar. There had been half an hour's talk in his study with the vicar himself, when Alan and Hazel were advised to show tolerance to one another throughout their lives, expect from each other not perfection, but simply kindness, and adjured not to give up at the first sign of trouble but to work through storms into harbour.

Standing there while the shoppers eddied about him, Alan knew panic. What had he done in his twenty-three years? Where had he been? What could he look forward to, except routine?

He'd gone straight from school into his first job with the firm which still employed him. He had been to Spain and Ibiza. He had spent a day in Boulogne.

There was a whole world beyond this town – a world beyond Spain and Corfu. There were Australia, Siam, and India. There was China, too, and he'd see none of them, for Hazel and their children would have to be fed and the rates must be paid.

As he went back to his office, Alan knew that Wendy's words had changed his life for ever.

Five days later – it took him that long to work out a plan – Mrs Doreen Groves, whose husband managed the bank where Hazel worked, was just washing up the breakfast things when the telephone rang.

'Mrs Groves?' asked a voice, male, and carefully articulating.

Mrs Groves owned to her identity.

'I'm afraid I have bad news for you,' said the caller, and went on to tell her that Mr Groves, driving to the bank earlier that morning, had had a serious accident and was on his way to hospital by ambulance. Because of the grave nature of his injuries he was being taken, not to the local hospital, but to the regional one twenty miles away where all facilities were to hand. There was no answer when she asked for more details.

For some seconds Mrs Groves was made immobile by shock. Then she attempted to dial the bank to find out if the assistant manager could give her more details, but the telephone was dead.

Alan had cut the line. In the nearby call-box, from which he had rung Mrs Groves, he had inserted enough coins to keep the connection for several minutes, and he left the receiver off the hook while he hurried round to the Groves' house. He slipped into the garden through the fence, and under cover of the shrubbery went up to the side of the building where, on an earlier reconnaissance, he had observed that the telephone line was attached, and snipped the cable neatly. He waited, hidden behind some laurels, while Mrs Groves reversed her Mini out of the garage and sped off. Then he returned to the telephone-box, replaced the receiver, and made a call to the bank.

He asked to speak to the manager. It was an urgent matter, he said, concerning Mrs Groves. To the girl answering the telephone he said he was a police officer, and gave his name as Sergeant Thomas from the local headquarters.

When Mr Groves came on the line, sounding worried as he asked what was wrong, Alan held a scarf to his mouth and spoke in a false voice. His heart beat fast with excitement as he told the manager, 'We've got your wife. Bring fifty thousand pounds in used notes, fives and tens, to Heathrow Airport by twelve noon. More instructions will wait for you at the information desk in Terminal Two.' Alan had intended to ask for twenty thousand; he was quite surprised to hear himself name the larger sum. 'And don't get in touch with the police or it will be the worse for your wife,' he remembered to add, in menacing tones.

He rang off before Mr Groves could reply. Would it work? He'd read somewhere that bank managers were instructed to pay up at such times – to risk no one's life – although certain alarm routines had to be followed. It was a pity he'd never asked Hazel more about security measures; he knew that she was not meant to disclose what precautions were operated and until now he hadn't been interested. He had tried to turn the conversation that way at the weekend, but she'd wanted to talk only about the wedding.

Alan had already telephoned his own firm to say he wouldn't be coming in, pleading a stomach upset. There were jokes and quips about first-night nerves.

After making the call, Alan got straight into his ramshackle old Fiat, which Hazel had long since condemned, and drove to Heathrow. He left the car in the short-stay park and crossed to Terminal Two, where he noticed a boy wandering around without apparent purpose. Alan said he was late for his flight and asked the lad to deliver a note to the information desk. He gave the boy a pound and, skulking among the shifting people, watched to see his commission executed. Inside an envelope addressed in capital letters to Mr Groves were instructions to place the bag beside the nearest newspaper stand. Alan intended to walk rapidly by, collecting it as he passed and vanishing into the crowd before he could be detected. He felt sure that by now the police would have been alerted in some manner. As soon as she reached the hospital, Mrs Groves would have discovered that her husband had not been admitted, but she was sure to be confused. She might telephone the bank, but by then Mr Groves would have left with the ransom if he were to reach the airport by noon. He would have had no problem in finding the actual cash; now Alan wondered with misgiving whether there might not be some bugging device attached to its container. If Mrs Groves was known to be safe, the police might be close behind her husband, waiting to pounce when Alan claimed the ransom.

He began to feel uneasy. What had seemed a perfect plan now revealed flaws.

Mr Groves was, in fact, almost at Heathrow before his wife learned that the call to her had been a hoax. She spent some time telephoning other hospitals before she rang the bank, and in the interval Mr Groves had parked his car in the short-stay park near a small, shabby Fiat which looked very like one he had seen outside his own house that morning.

Awaiting his prey, but with waning confidence, Alan tapped

his pocket. The previous day, he had withdrawn all the money that stood to his credit with the building society. It was not fifty thousand pounds, but it was enough to keep him for some time and it was all rightfully his own. He had his passport, and a small case in which he had planned to transport his booty out of the country.

As suddenly as Wendy's words had earlier opened his eyes to the future, Alan saw that if he went ahead with his plan he would never be free from fear of detection. Here was another moment of decision, and there was no need for any theft; he could simply walk away from the rendezvous and disappear. No one would connect him with a dumped case of bank notes.

Alan went to the Air France desk, where he bought a ticket to Paris. His original plan had been to drive to Dover, sell his car there for whatever it would fetch, and catch the ferry to Calais. He had been afraid, if he flew, that the security inspection at the airport would reveal the wads of money in the case, but now he had nothing to dread.

He'd spend a few days in Paris, then hitch south, maybe to Rome. Perhaps he could pick up some work as he went along. He'd stay away at least while his money lasted, possibly for good, depending on what opportunities arose.

At the airport post office Alan mailed, second-class, a package to Hazel. It contained the tickets for the honeymoon in Corfu; she could still use them, taking Linda or Maeve with her. He attempted no explanation beyond a note saying he was sorry to upset her but he wasn't ready to settle down just yet and it was better to find that out now rather than when it was too late. Luckily, he hadn't bought the bridesmaids' presents.

Alan sat in the plane waiting for take-off. To the other passengers he was just a young man on a business trip with the minimal luggage of a small bag and his raincoat; only he knew that at last he was starting to live. He could always come back one day; even if the hoax telephone calls were attributed to him, such a minor offence wouldn't merit much of a punishment. At the moment he felt that a journey to freedom now was worth a few months in jail later on.

In another area of the same plane sat an older man on his way to adventure.

Mr Groves was six months short of retiring. He did not look forward to spending more time with his wife, who was one of life's cosseters and would fuss over him much too tenderly, making him old before his time. She had turned down his suggestion that they should go on a trip to Australia; even a cruise did not appeal to her. A stay-at-home girl was Doreen, and their holidays, apart from a weekend in Venice, had been spent in either Scotland or Cornwall. She'd made him into her child, perhaps because they had none of their own.

If they had, he couldn't have done what he was doing now. On the way to Heathrow he had called in at his home. The cleaning woman did not come today, and it had been odd to find the breakfast dishes still in the sink. There were, however, no signs of struggle.

Poor Doreen! How terrified she must have been, he had thought, and, on impulse, collected his passport from his desk; who knew where the trail might lead?

On the way to the information desk in the main concourse at Terminal Two, another impulse had turned Mr Groves towards a telephone, from which he had called the bank. They might as well know he had arrived. The police might have some instructions for him – if they were shadowing him, they could not come forward now, just as he was about to 'make the drop', wasn't it called?

Mr Groves had been told that his wife had telephoned and, though distressed, was unharmed. She had been to look for him at the hospital as the result of a hoax telephone call; the whole thing was some prank.

Mr Groves had replaced the receiver, relieved beyond measure to know that Doreen was safe. Then he had realized that here he was, as the result of someone's idea of a joke, with fifty thousand pounds of the bank's money.

What a chance! But the police would be watching him and he mustn't waste time.

He had collected the envelope left for him at the desk – there had been one; the hoaxer had clearly meant business – opened it and read the message. Then he had turned and gone, as if instructed, to the Air France counter where he had bought a ticket to Paris. The police would reason that, having discovered his wife was safe, he intended to lead them to the perpetrator of the hoax kidnap. It would be some time before they would suspect him of having fled himself. Interpol might have to be invoked, and by then he would be on his way to Australia. If he were to be traced, he could be extradited from there but there might be time, before he was apprehended, to move on to Spain, where barons of crime still lived in safety, although he thought plans were afoot to end that.

Mr Groves mingled confidently with the other travellers at Charles de Gaulle Airport. He noticed a pretty woman, perhaps thirty-five years old, walking ahead towards Passport Control. The world was full of pretty young women with broader views than those of his wife. Hitherto a strictly moral man, Mr Groves' thoughts dwelt happily on the delights that might lie ahead.

Thus enjoying his future, he saw a young man who seemed vaguely familiar going through customs. He carried only a case and a raincoat, and he looked eagerly confident, the world at his feet. Ah youth, reflected Mr Groves, and his mind turned to Doreen. She would be very upset and she would never forgive him. No matter what happened now, he could not go home because he had stolen the bank's money. Well, at his age it was easy to resolve that he would not be caught alive. He would seek present pleasure, and if capture threatened he would take the final escape.

Hazel wept when the holiday tickets arrived. How dreadful of Alan to behave like this! She could not understand what had got into him; it was all so humiliating.

Her mother was furious, but it seemed that Hazel had, in the nick of time, been saved from wrecking her life. To think that that quiet young man could be so deceitful!

She drew comfort from the troubles of others, however, when she learned that Mr Groves at the bank had apparently set up a fake kidnap to lure his wife from home, then pretended to receive a ransom demand so that he could obtain a large sum of money and flee the country. The police had found his car at Heathrow. Oddly enough, Alan's car was found there too, in the very next bay. It was almost as though the two had conspired.

ACKNOWLEDGEMENTS

Collection and introduction © Maxim Jakubowski, 1992.

'The Party of the Second Part' by Ted Allbeury. © 1984 by Ted Allbeury. First appeared in *Winter's Crimes 16*.

'The Blood Bargain' by Eric Ambler. © 1970 by Eric Ambler. First appeared in *Winter's Crimes 2*.

'Little Terror' by Robert Barnard. © 1986 by Robert Barnard. First appeared in *Winter's Crimes 18*.

'Double Glazing' by Simon Brett. © 1979 by Simon Brett. First appeared in *Winter's Crimes 11*. Reprinted by permission of Victor Gollancz Ltd.

'A Case of Mis-identity' by Colin Dexter. © 1989 by Colin Dexter. First appeared in *Winter's Crimes 21*.

'The Gift' by Dick Francis. © 1973 by Dick Francis. First appeared in *Winter's Crimes 5*.

'The Julian Mondays' by Jonathan Gash. © 1986 by Jonathan Gash. First appeared in *Winter's Crimes 18*.

'The Jackal and the Tiger' by Michael Gilbert. © 1988 by Michael Gilbert. First appeared in *Winter's Crimes 20*.

'Killer' by Paula Gosling. © 1989 by Paula Gosling. First appeared in *Winter's Crimes 21*.

'Those Awful Dawns' by Patricia Highsmith. © 1977 by Patricia Highsmith. First appeared in *Winter's Crimes 9*.

'A Very Desirable Residence' by P. D. James. © 1976 by P. D. James. First appeared in *Winter's Crimes 8*.

'The Evidence I Shall Give' by H. R. F. Keating. © 1989 by H. R. F. Keating. First appeared in *Winter's Crimes 21*.

'Family Business' by Michael Z. Lewin. © 1988 by Michael Z. Lewin. First appeared in *Winter's Crimes 20*.

'A Case of Butterflies' by Peter Lovesey. © 1989 by Peter Lovesey. First appeared in *Winter's Crimes 21*.

'Scandal at Sandkop' by James McClure. © 1975 by James McClure. First appeared in *Winter's Crimes 7*.

'A Fine Art' by Jill McGown. © 1988 by Jill McGown. First appeared in *Winter's Crimes 20*.

'Dinah, Reading' by John Malcolm. © 1990 by John Malcolm. First appeared in *Winter's Crimes 22*.

'The Trinity Cat' by Ellis Peters. © 1976 by Ellis Peters. First appeared in *Winter's Crimes 8*.

'The Berzin Lecture' by Anthony Price. © 1983 by Anthony Price. First appeared in *Winter's Crimes 15*.

'Playback' by Ian Rankin. © 1990 by Ian Rankin. First appeared in *Winter's Crimes 22*.

'A Drop Too Much' by Ruth Rendell. © 1975 by Ruth Rendell. First appeared in *Winter's Crimes 7*.

'The Birthmark' by Julian Symons. © 1985 by Julian Symons. First appeared in *Winter's Crimes 17*.

'The Other Woman' by David Williams. © 1988 by David Williams. First appeared in *Winter's Crimes 20*.

'Gifts from the Bridegroom' by Margaret Yorke. © 1986 by Margaret Yorke. First appeared in *Winter's Crimes 18*.